By Wendy Corsi Staub

SHADOWKILLER
SLEEPWALKER
NIGHTWATCHER
HELL TO PAY
SCARED TO DEATH
LIVE TO TELL

Coming Soon
THE GOOD SISTER

WENDY CORSI STAUB

SHADOWKILLER

HARPER

An Imprint of HarperCollinsPublishers

This is a work of fiction. Names, characters, places, and incidents are products of the author's imagination or are used fictitiously and are not to be construed as real. Any resemblance to actual events, locales, organizations, or persons, living or dead, is entirely coincidental.

HARPER

An Imprint of HarperCollins*Publishers*
10 East 53rd Street
New York, New York 10022-5299

First Harper mass market printing: February 2013

HarperCollins ® and Harper ® are registered trademarks of Harper-Collins Publishers.

Printed in the United States of America

Visit Harper paperbacks on the World Wide Web at
www.harpercollins.com

10 9 8 7 6 5 4 3 2 1

For Jane,
sushi pal, walking partner, shopping buddy—
thank you for taking me away
from it all in the afternoons!

And for my three favorite guys—
Brody, Morgan, and Mark.

Acknowledgments

Special thanks to Barb Mayes Boustead, Margaret Malloy, Kathy Piede, and David Staub; to my agent, Laura Blake Peterson, and the gang at Curtis Brown; to my editor, Lucia Macro, and the gang at Avon Books/HarperCollins; and finally, to Mark Staub, loving husband, competent editor, and talented writer, whose own books I will be reading someday soon.

Please note: This is a work of fiction. While certain names, places, and events are real and/or based on historical fact, the plot and narrative action depicted within are strictly products of the author's imagination.

PART I

The past lies like a nightmare upon the present.
Karl Marx

I believe that one can never leave home. I believe that one carries the shadows, the dreams, the fears and the dragons of home under one's skin, at the extreme corners of one's eyes and possibly in the gristle of the earlobe.

Maya Angelou, *Letter to My Daughter*

Chapter One

Saint Antony Island, the Caribbean
May 10, 2012

It's been a while since Carrie's spotted someone with enough potential, but . . . here she is.

The woman in the orange and pink paisley sundress is about Carrie's age—forty, give or take—and has the right features, the right build. She's a few inches taller than Carrie; her hair is much darker, and she's wearing glasses. But really, those things don't matter. Those things can be easily faked: a wig, some heels . . .

What matters far more is that the woman is alone. Not just alone in this particular moment, but alone as in socially isolated, giving off an indefinable vibe that any opportunistic predator would easily recognize.

Carrie's natural instincts tell her that this is it; this woman is her ticket off this Caribbean island at last.

Always listen to your gut, Daddy used to tell her. *If you tune in to your intuition, you'll find that you know much more than you think you do.*

A part of her wanted to mock that advice later, when he'd failed her.

The words didn't even make sense. How can you *know* more than you *think* you do? Whatever you *think* is what you *know.* Knowing . . . thinking . . . it was all the same thing.

Anyway, if she really *did* know more than she thought, she wouldn't have been so shocked by his betrayal.

That was what she told herself afterward. Even then, though, she heard his voice inside her head, chiding her, telling her that she'd ignored the signs; ignored her gut.

Well, she'd done her best never to make that mistake again.

Right now, her gut is telling her that this woman, unaware that she's being watched closely from behind the bar, is the one.

She's been sitting on a stool at the far corner for almost an hour now, nursing a rum runner and looking as though she'd like some company.

Male company, judging by the wistful glances she's darted at other patrons. But that's obviously not going to happen.

It isn't that the woman is unattractive; she's somewhat pretty in an overweight, unsophisticated, patchy-pink-sunburn kind of way.

There's someone for everyone, right? Some men are drawn to this type.

Not *these* men, though.

Not here at the Jimmy's Big Iguana, an open-air beach bar filled with tanned and toned scantily clad twenty-somethings. Island rum is flowing; the sporadic whirring of bar blenders and raucous bursts of laughter punctuate the reggae beat of Bob Marley's "One Love" playing in the background. Lazy overhead paddle fans do little to stir heavy salt air scented with coconut sunscreen, deep-fried seafood, and stale beer.

Beyond the open-air perimeter of the bar, against a backdrop of palm trees and turquoise sea, tourists browse at vendors' tables set up on the sand. Fresh from shore excursions, those with local currency to burn are pawing through T-shirts and island-made trinkets, snatching up cheap souvenirs before their ships set sail for the next port of call.

The woman at the bar darts a look at her watch as she slurps the last inch of her rum runner, and Carrie realizes it's now or never.

"Ready for your second drink?" She reaches across the bar to remove the empty glass, with its gummy pink film coating the inside.

"Oh, that's okay. I don't want another—"

"It's a freebie. Two-for-one happy hour for cruise ship passengers."

"Really?"

No, not really.

Carrie nods, already reaching for the bottle of Tortuga Rum. "All you have to do is show me your ship ID. What's your name?"

"Molly."

Carrie nods, smiles, points to her own plastic name tag. "I'm Jane."

As in Doe.

Well, not quite. Jane Doe had translated, in her clever mind, to Jane Deere—*doe, a deer*—and that's the name she's been using for years now. Jane Deere. Before that, she was Carrie Robinson MacKenna, and before that . . .

Before that doesn't matter.

"Nice to meet you." Molly's face glistens with island humidity, and moist strands of her dark hair are plastered to her forehead. She glances again at the Timex strapped around her thick wrist.

"Don't worry. You have time."

"How do you know that?"

"I've been working here a long time. I know the sailing schedules." That is most definitely *not* a lie.

Such is life in this harbor town: the same-but-different routine every day, set to the rhythm of the cruise lines' itineraries.

Carrie has always appreciated the precision with which she can see the gargantuan vessels begin to appear every morning out on the turquoise sea, an hour or two after sunrise. From the window of her rented apartment above the bar, she watches the same ships glide in and out of Saint Antony harbor at the same time on the same days of the week, spitting thousands of passengers onto the wide pier.

The same passengers, it sometimes seems: waddling Americans in shorts and fanny packs; hand-holding honeymooners; chain-smoking Europeans in open-collar suits and dresses with high heels; multigenerational families of harried parents, tantrum-throwing toddlers, sullen teens, silver-haired, scooter-riding grannies . . .

Carrie serves them all; knows them all. Not on a first-name basis, but by type and, often, by ship. Sure, some crowds of passengers are interchangeable—on, say, Tuesday, when megaships from Carnival, Royal Caribbean, and Princess are simultaneously in port. They all cater to middle-class Americans—families, retirees, and honeymooners alike.

But today is Thursday. Three different cruise lines; three distinctly different crowds.

"Which ship are you on," Carrie asks, "the Carousel?"

Molly raises an eyebrow. "How'd you know?"

Easy. It's a singles cruise out of Miami. There are two others in port for the day, but one is a Disney ship favored almost exclusively by families with young children; the other, a small luxury line popular with wealthy South American couples.

This woman is definitely single, U.S. born and bred . . . and U.S. bound, or so Molly thinks. Little does she suspect that if all goes according to Carrie's plan, the Carousel will be setting sail in a little over an hour, at five o'clock sharp, without her.

"How'd I know? Lucky guess." Carrie shrugs. "Like I said, I've been working here long enough. "

"It must be hard to be inside on the job when it's always so beautiful out there."

"Sometimes." Much easier to agree than to explain that she prefers it this way.

Carrie's never been an outdoorsy girl—not by choice, anyway. After all those childhood summers working the fields in the glaring, burning sun of the Great Plains, she welcomed the architecture-shaded canyons of Manhattan. And yes, she had regretted having to leave New York behind so soon. Given proper time to plan her exit strategy a decade ago, she'd have opted for a fog-shrouded city like London or San Francisco, or perhaps rainy Seattle or Portland . . .

But at the time, her objective was to get out quickly—in the immediate aftermath of September 11, no less, when public transportation was at an inconvenient standstill. Had she been trying to enter the U.S., she'd have been out of luck, given the sudden, intense border scrutiny on incoming travelers.

But she only wanted to leave—and hitchhiking was the way to go, from truck stop to truck stop, down the East Coast. Riding high in the cabs of eighteen-wheelers along an endless gray ribbon of interstate brought back a lot of memories. Good ones, mostly.

As she made her way to Florida, she perfected her cover story: she was supposed to meet her terminally ill fiancé in the Caribbean to marry him that Saturday.

People were in a shell-shocked, help-your-fellow-American mode. Every time she mentioned that she'd escaped the burning towers in New York, strangers bent over backward to help, giving her rides, food, money.

Eventually she encountered a perpetually stoned, sympathetic trucker who was more than happy to connect her with a man willing to help her complete her so-called wedding journey. For a steep price—one she could easily afford, thanks to years of stockpiling cash—she was quite literally able to sail away on a little boat regularly used for smuggling illegal substances *into* the country, as opposed to smuggling people *out* of it.

She'd chosen Saint Antony for its relatively close proximity to the United States and for its unofficial look-the-other-way policies when it comes to just about everything. She figured she'd stay awhile—six months, a year, maybe two—and then move on. Once she was here, however, complicated post-9/11 security measures made it a challenge to return to the States.

She could have gone elsewhere—Europe, maybe, or the South Pacific—but she wasn't really interested in doing that. America was home, and someday, she might want to go back.

As always, she'd done her homework and figured out how she would eventually be able to get around the new security obstacles. She came up with the perfect plan, but she wasn't in any hurry to put it into action. Maybe she'd stay here forever. Maybe not. It was just good to know she could escape if she wanted—or needed—to.

She didn't, until the morning six months ago when she turned on her television and was blindsided by her own face staring back at her. There she was, in an old photograph that accompanied a news report from suburban New York.

"So do you like bartending?" the woman at the bar, Molly, asks her. "I bet you meet a lot of interesting people."

"Sure do," Carrie agrees, but of course that's another lie.

These people don't interest her. At times, they bore or frustrate her, but mostly, they merely remind her that there's a world beyond this island. A world Carrie is ready to rejoin at last.

A generous shot of rum splashes into the blender, and then another for good measure, along with ice, mixer—and the powdered contents of a packet Carrie surreptitiously pulls from her pocket, where it's been waiting for months now. Waiting for just the right opportunity . . .

This is it.

Carrie reaches for the blender switch. It's sticky; everything here in the bar—and everyone, for that matter—is sticky, and damp.

Oh, it's going to feel so good to escape the looming Caribbean summer, with its oppressive humidity, daily rainstorms, and hurricanes lining up out in the Atlantic like steel balls in a pinball shoot. Disembarking in the States tomorrow morning—yes, even Miami—will be a literal breath of fresh air.

Her stomach fluttering with excitement at the thought of it, Carrie flips the gummy switch. The contents of the blender erupt, sucking the white powder into a frothy vortex. Carrie lets it whirl for at least thirty seconds before filling the waiting glass with frozen slush the color of the Caribbean sky at dusk—her favorite time of day.

I'm probably going to miss those sunsets, if nothing else, she acknowledges. *But I've seen enough to last a lifetime.*

She's spent more than ten years in this barefoot, rum- and ganja-laced, easy-living part of the world, where no one bats an eye or asks too many questions of a newcomer. Ironic, Carrie has always thought, that countless people come to the sunny Caribbean to slip into the shadows. Here, they can escape their past; maybe—if they're lucky—erase it altogether.

But last November, when Carrie saw her own face in that news report about her ex-husband and his new wife, she was swept by a fierce, unexpected wave of emotion. Resentment swirled up from the murky depths of her memory, churning renewed frustration and rage.

It's been six months since that day. Six months of planning and plotting. Six months of growing obsession, just like before—years ago, when she was little more than a girl and developed the fixation that would consume her life.

I couldn't help it then, and I can't help it now.

It's time to go home, confront the past, battle the demons she'd left behind. Time to make things right at last, the way she couldn't the first time she'd tried, because something got in the way: an unexpected yearning for a so-called normal life, a glimmer of hope that she might somehow achieve it.

I should have known better.

Ah, but she *did* know better.

Maybe you were right after all, Daddy. Maybe I knew much more than I thought. But she'd gotten sidetracked, caught up in desire. She'd been foolish. *Human.*

And now?

What am I now, all these years later?

Inhuman?

Adding a straw and the obligatory paper umbrella to the doctored rum runner, Carrie smiles, certain that her plan is going to work.

I thought the same thing the last couple of times, and I was wrong.

The first candidate she'd found, about two months ago, hadn't been alone after all. That was a close call. Before the female tourist Carrie had selected could lift her doctored daiquiri to her lips, a pair of friends—the woman's roommates on the Carousel, it turned out—burst into the bar to join her, toting bags from a souvenir shop down the street.

Carrie managed to accidentally-on-purpose knock over the glass, spilling the drug-laced slush all over the bar. She made the woman a fresh drink on the house, along with two more for her friends, and when the Carousel set sail, the tipsy threesome were all aboard.

A few weeks later, she saw her chance again.

Another solo woman at the bar, one who bore enough of a resemblance to Carrie that it just might be possible. Her name was Beth and she was the chatty type. She had just survived an ugly divorce, she said, with no children, and was on her cruise to celebrate leaving behind her old life in rural Maine to start fresh in New Orleans, where she didn't know a soul.

Perfect, Carrie thought. But this time, before she could reach into her pocket to add the powder to the frozen piña colada she was mixing, Jimmy Bolt, the Big Iguana's owner, materialized.

"Hey, Jane," he said, "I need you to stay on till closing tonight, okay?"

Of course she said yes. You don't mess with Jimmy. Ever. About anything.

She learned that years ago, not long after she came to work for him and foolishly—fleetingly—got caught up in his charismatic web.

Theirs wasn't a full-blown affair, by any means. It lasted only a couple of months. She told him nothing about herself; asked nothing about him in return. She knew he was married, one of the most powerful men on the island, and had his share of shady connections, not to mention plenty of enemies—a fact Carrie is actually counting on now.

On the day Beth from rural Maine crossed Carrie's path, Jimmy stuck around just long enough for her to change her mind about the second piña colada.

"I think I'm going to go hit the casino back on the ship," she told Carrie as she left. "I'm feeling lucky today."

You have no idea how lucky you are, Carrie thought, and that night, instead of sailing away in Beth's cabin, Carrie was mopping someone's vomit from the bar floor at closing.

Really, that was okay. Patience is a virtue—one that was uncharacteristically in short supply when she was living in New York as Carrie Robinson MacKenna a decade ago. But that was due, in part, to the hormonal injections when she and Mack were trying to conceive.

Thank goodness she's long since gotten back to her methodical old self.

"Here you go." She slides the drink across the bar to Molly. "I just need to see your ship ID."

"Oh. Right." Molly reaches into her large straw tote and pulls out a plastic card dangling from a lanyard patterned in the Carousel's signature purple and gold colors.

Carrie takes the card from her and glances at it as Molly sips from the straw.

Along with the name of the ship and the embedded code that will be scanned for reboarding, the card bears the passenger's name, Molly Temple, her disembark date— tomorrow—and her lifeboat assembly station.

"Great, I just need your cabin number," Carrie tells her easily, then holds her breath, praying the generous rum in the first drink—and the first couple of sips Molly's taken from this one—impaired her better judgment.

Yep:

"It's 10533," Molly tells her, thus confirming—as Carrie had already suspected—that she's staying in one of the ship's new studio rooms—tiny inside cabins that accommodate just one passenger. No frills. No roommates.

No problem, mon, as they like to say here in the islands that are soon to become mere specks on the horizon in the Carousel's wake.

"Oooh, I love your bracelet." Molly has caught sight of the unusual silver and blue bangle on Carrie's wrist, a constant source of compliments. "Is that topaz?"

"Larimar. It's a Caribbean gemstone."

"It's beautiful. I don't think I've ever seen it before. Where did you get it?"

"Punta Cana."

She'd visited only once, recklessly daring to leave this island on a clandestine private yacht trip with Jimmy at the height of their affair. The vendor who sold her the bracelet had assured her that it was real larimar, not the plastic imitations that are rampant in tourist traps. He used a lighter to prove it, holding a flame to the stone to show her how durable it was.

"The real thing won't melt," he told Carrie, "or burn. The real thing, you can't destroy."

She liked that.

She bought it.

She wears it every day.

If Jimmy ever noticed, he probably thinks that's because it's a treasured memento of their time together. It isn't. For Carrie, it's a reminder that some things in this ever-precarious world can't be destroyed.

"I'd love to bring a bracelet like that back for my mom," Molly tells Carrie. "She just lost my dad a few months ago, and I've been looking for a souvenir for her. Where is Punta Cana? Is that one of the shops down the road?"

The woman's stupidity makes it even easier for Carrie to silently rationalize what's going to happen to her as she says aloud, "No, it's a different island. It's a city in the Dominican Republic. That's the only place you can find larimar in the whole world."

"I've never been there."

"I'm sure you'll go someday." The lies spill so easily off Carrie's tongue. They always have.

"I hope so," Molly tells her. "Oh well. Maybe I can find something for my mom in the jewelry store on the Carousel. Anyway, thanks for the drink."

"You're welcome. Enjoy." Smiling, Carrie hands back the ship ID card—for now.

Glenhaven Park, New York

Five o'clock on a Thursday, and Allison MacKenna finally—*finally!*—finds the opportunity to sit down on the couch with the novel she was supposed to have finished reading for her May book club meeting tonight.

She started it over a week ago and has been trying to get back to it since Monday morning when her daughters left for school and her youngest went down for his nap. But one interruption after another derailed her plans for that day, and the three subsequent days.

That's okay. They were just ordinary household events—a forgotten lunch box, a broken dishwasher, unexpected drop-in company, a high-maintenance playdate . . .

Allison can handle those kinds of disruptions. She actually welcomes anything that reminds her that life is back to normal; that nothing earth-shattering or life-threatening is going to pop up and rob her of the things she treasures most in this world: her husband and children, a quiet suburban life as a stay-at-home mom.

In this moment, Hudson and Madison are happily occupied with a "top secret" project involving felt and glue sticks at the kitchen table. J.J. is industriously stacking blocks in his ExerSaucer across the room. And Allison has just three hours until the book discussion at her friend Sheila's house.

She's loved to read since she was a little girl, and ordinarily, she likes to savor the pages, not rush through them. But this dense book just isn't her cup of tea, and it's not the sort of thing you can casually put down and pick up right where you left off.

Those would be more my speed these days, she thinks, eyeing a stack of the girls' library books on the coffee table. *My brain is mush. Maybe I can suggest Shel Silverstein or Dr. Seuss when it's my turn to pick the next book.*

Wondering how many pages she has left to go, she flips to the back of the novel—a trade paperback with a matte cover whose illustrations are heavy on the nature imagery and conspicuously missing human beings, as all the book club selections seem to be.

The epilogue—all these books have epilogues, too—concludes on page 283.

She sighs and starts reading. Rather, *tries* to start reading.

In the kitchen, the girls' voices have gone from pleasant chatter to bickering.

"Maddy, please keep your eyes on your own work," Allison hears Hudson telling her younger sister in her best imitation of her kindergarten teacher's voice.

"I just wanted to see where I'm s'posed to glue the flower."

"You can glue it anywhere! Be creative!"

"I *am* being creative!"

A moment later: "Noooo! Don't copy me! That's exactly where I have mine!"

"It's on top of the stem, Huddy! That's where flowers go!"

Listening to them, Allison sighs. Even if all hell doesn't break loose around here in the next fifteen minutes—and she wouldn't bet against that—she'll be lucky if she manages to get through a couple of chapters, let alone almost two hundred pages.

Oh well. She can always fake it, or show up late. The group usually spends the first half hour on the book, but meetings generally stray after that into a pinot grigio–fueled bus-stop-gossip free-for-all.

Having been the topic of said gossip herself last Novem-

ber, Allison had been tempted to drop her membership in
the book club altogether. Oh hell, she'd been tempted to pick
up and move the whole family out of suburban Westchester
County, make a fresh start.

"Where do you propose we go?" her husband asked the
first time she mentioned it, on the morning they were heading back home after their ordeal. "Back to the city?"

"No! Not the city. Not with all this . . . stuff." No way
would they ever be able to fit the contents of their thirty-
five-hundred-square-foot house and garage into a Manhattan apartment.

Besides, now isn't the time to sell the house, even though
it's fully paid for, thanks to the life insurance policy and
9/11 victim relief funds Mack collected after Carrie's death.
They bought the house for just over a million dollars at the
peak of real estate prices, and it'll be a while before the
market bounces back.

Anyway, she doesn't want to live in the city anymore. Not
with kids. Nor does she want to return to her Midwestern
hometown, as her husband assumed when she first tried to
explain her yearning for an easier life, something less intense.

"Where were you thinking we should go? Centerfield?"
Mack asked. "Because I have to say, Nebraska to midtown
would be a hell of a commute for me."

"Mack, you know how I feel about Nebraska. I moved
away from there the second I was old enough, for good
reasons—and they haven't changed."

"Then where?"

"I don't know. Someplace else. Where nobody knows us,
and nobody knows what happened."

"We can't just drop out of sight, Allie. That's not fair to
the kids. We owe it to them to go home and live our lives,
get back to normal. We didn't do anything wrong. We're not
going to slink around acting like we did."

He was right, of course. And right again when he added, "After all, no one knows better than we do how to pick up the pieces and get on with life."

Ten years earlier, on September 11, Mack—who was Allison's across-the-hall neighbor at the time—had lost his first wife. Carrie was working on the 104th floor when a plane struck the north tower at the World Trade Center in Manhattan. In the days that followed the attacks, he and Allison regularly crossed paths with each other—and with the Nightwatcher, an opportunistic serial killer who murdered a fellow tenant in their building, along with three other New Yorkers.

Traumatized by the terror attack and confused by the murders, mentally impaired handyman Jerry Thompson confessed to the crimes. It was Allison's testimony that sent him to prison, where he'd finally taken his own life last September.

Or had he?

NYPD detectives on the case believed that another inmate might have been behind Jerry's so-called suicide. The truth about his death will probably never be known.

On the heels of his suicide, what appeared to be a copycat killer resurfaced on a vengeful mission to frame Mack in a new rash of murders, hell-bent on destroying Allison's family to settle the score. When the ordeal was finally over, the killer lay dead—courtesy of an illegal gun Mack had borrowed from a friend.

But he'd acted in self-defense, and in the end, wasn't charged.

Thank God. *Thank God.*

Allison can't imagine what her life would be like now had her children not been rescued and her husband not been exonerated.

She *won't* imagine it.

Even with the nightmare behind them, it wasn't easy for

the MacKennas to return to this house where their privacy had been so chillingly violated: the family's every move captured by a twisted voyeur's hidden cameras and microphones.

Gradually, though, they've been able to rebuild their lives. To keep the press at bay they changed their home phone number to an unlisted one, canceled their cell phone accounts and got new ones, and planted thicker hedges to protect their house from prying eyes on the street. They threw themselves back into work and school routines, nurturing friendships that have proven surprisingly, blessedly resilient.

Not that life is perfect now, by any means.

But then, it never really was. That was an illusion, one to which Allison fiercely clung, wanting her children to experience the childhood she never had; the mother she never had.

In the end, she learned the hard way that it doesn't really matter whether you do everything right, the way she attempted to, or everything wrong, the way her own mother had. No matter how hard you try to insulate your family—and yourself—the big, bad world has a way of intruding. Fate, as her father used to say, is the great equalizer.

Or is it *time* that's the great equalizer?

Speaking of time . . .

I have three hours to finish this book, so why am I sitting here staring at the page without reading it, thinking about the past?

Allison pushes the troubling memories from her mind and forces herself to read.

One page, another page . . .

God, I hate this book.

"Maddy! Don't glue that sunshine *there*!"

"You said to be creative! You said not to copy you!"

"But the sun has to be in the sky, not on the grass! You can't give Mommy a card that has the sun in the grass!"

Allison can't help but smile. So the girls are making cards for her—no wonder they kicked her out of the kitchen.

Mother's Day is coming up on Sunday. It wasn't one of Allison's favorite holidays back when she was a daughter, and it isn't now that she's a mother—though of course, she's grateful to be blessed with three beautiful, healthy children.

But the problem with Mother's Day, as with most holidays, is that it brings back memories. Memories of her difficult childhood, raised by a forlorn woman whose own conservative parents had turned their backs on her when she got pregnant and whose husband—Allison's father—did the same thing years later, but for other reasons. God only knew what they were.

And God only knows who he really was. I'll never know, and I shouldn't care.

"Memories are good for nothin'," Mom used to say, and no wonder. "It's better to just forget about all the things you can't change."

Allison was nine when her father took off. Her mother, Brenda, hung in there until she was seventeen, when the final overdose in an ominous string of them put her out of her misery at last.

Hell, yes, it would be better to forget those things—forget a lot of things that can't be changed—but that doesn't mean it's always possible.

All you can do is try. And of course, you just keep going forward, making the best of every day. You weather the inevitable storms, and you take the sunshine wherever you can get it—even if it's lying in the grass.

Across the room, J.J. topples a two-block tower and explodes in gleeful babble.

Watching him, Allison realizes that while he hasn't grown disinterested in the activity just yet, he's probably about to.

That's okay. Playing with a toddler is right up her alley at this point. The book is a lost cause. She sets it aside and goes over to the ExerSaucer.

"What's up, little man?"

"Mom-mom-mom-mom . . ."

Ah, music to her ears.

Her son had been a difficult baby—and an even more difficult toddler. But now that he's past eighteen months, he seems to have gotten a bit more manageable. Either that, or she's simply used to his energy. After two docile little girls, it wasn't easy to adapt to a demanding little boy, especially with all the drama that unfolded here last fall.

She scoops him up and hugs him close, breathing the powdery-diaper and baby shampoo scent of him.

"Mom-mom-mom-mom . . ."

"Are you talking to me? Hmm?" Relishing his drool-spilling, three-toothed grin, Allison sighs contentedly.

Yes. Life is good.

Again.

And this time, it's going to stay that way.

When at last Carrie exits the small apartment above Jimmy's Big Iguana, for the first time ever, she leaves the door behind her unlocked.

The island is relatively safe, and it's not as though she's ever had possessions that are worth stealing.

Even you *don't want them*, she reminds herself as she heads down the fourteen steep, rickety steps leading into an overgrown little yard. But she's always kept her secrets locked away in that apartment: the only tangible evidence of who she once was and where she came from.

Now, they're in the straw bag over her shoulder—Molly's straw bag. The few things worth bringing along into the next phase of her life: her laptop, cash, a couple more packets of the powder that had come in so handy at the bar, and an envelope filled with old photos and documents, including her original birth certificate, and the key to a safe deposit box back in the States.

Oh, and of course, she also has her ticket home, in the form of Molly's ship ID, passport, and wallet.

That she would eventually find her way back to America via cruise ship, posing as a lookalike passenger, was never in question. After all, it's not as though she can just hop a plane back to the U.S. using her own passport—the real one, not the Carrie Robinson MacKenna identity she was using when she disappeared on that September morning over ten years ago.

No, and she can't use Carrie Robinson MacKenna's passport, either. Carrie is dead, after all. Or so the whole world believes. She herself saw the name on list after published list of World Trade Center victims; she read a touching tribute to her life in the *New York Times*.

There was no obituary. She'd watched for one, wondering how Mack might handle it, given what he knew—which was next to nothing—about where she'd been born, and to whom. Even the memorial in the *Times* was sketchy, based upon what her husband knew about her life in New York.

Funny—faking her own death had never been part of her agenda. It had occurred to her, of course, but she'd thought it would be impossible to pull off.

On the day that fate proved her wrong, she'd already realized their marriage was a big mistake; had already been planning to walk out of Mack's life without a backward glance.

Mack unwittingly gave the plan a premature jump-start when he told her, the morning of September 11, that he wanted a divorce. She feigned tears, as if all her dreams had just been shattered when the reality was that the marriage, for her, had ultimately been little more than a smokescreen.

She hadn't intended it to be that way. When she met Mack,

she had, admittedly, gotten lost in the promise of something more than she'd bargained for, the promise of a family. A real family. She almost dared to believe that it was possible to have that; to actually become the person she was pretending to be.

But of course, she came to her senses and grasped that it wasn't meant to happen.

She hardened her heart long before he told her it was over. On the morning that he did, she dried her fake tears, got dressed for work and left the apartment on Hudson Street. She hopped on the subway and arrived at the office just before seven-thirty, same as always. She'd been working at Cantor Fitzgerald for almost two years by then, making great money.

All good things must come to an end, she clearly remembers thinking on that last day, as she made her way to her desk in front of a north-facing window with an incredible view of the uptown skyline against a cloudless blue sky.

Had she been looking out that window a little over an hour later, she'd have seen American Airlines Flight 11 gunning straight for her. By then, though, she was long gone.

Instead of grabbing a cup of coffee and getting down to business as usual before the bond market opened for the day, she had unlocked her desk drawer and removed the packet that had been waiting for months. How many times, before that morning, had she congratulated herself on cleverly hiding the incriminating evidence of her past at the office, where she could get to it on short notice—but where Mack would never stumble across it? How many times, after that morning, had she marveled at the close call she'd had because of her final detour to her desk in the World Trade Center?

But she couldn't leave without the packet, which contained the very items she's carrying with her now: cash, the key to the safe deposit box that held even more cash, photos, her birth certificate . . .

Relics of her old life.

Her *real* life, the one she'd had long before she commemorated the start of the new millennium by moving to New York City and becoming Carrie Robinson.

On that last morning, she tucked the bulky envelope into her briefcase and greeted several of her coworkers on her way back to the elevator, silently telling them good-bye. She knew she'd never see them again.

What she couldn't know in that moment was that *no one* ever would see them again.

Less than thirty minutes after she rode the elevator down to the ground floor of the north tower and calmly tossed her gold wedding band into a trash can on the street, the Boeing 767 struck the building a few floors below her office.

Not a single Cantor Fitzgerald employee who was at his or her desk that day made it out alive. They were trapped there, helpless, all of them.

The terrorist attack was a divine gift—one Carrie accepted as a sign that she was following the right path.

Now there was no need to take elaborate steps to cover her trail and her true identity. Mack wasn't going to look for her. The woman he knew as Carrie Robinson MacKenna had died on that bright Tuesday morning.

Just as the woman known here on Saint Antony as Jane Deere will die on this increasingly overcast Thursday afternoon.

Well, evening, technically. It's almost five o'clock.

With the straw bag over her shoulder and a box in her hands, Carrie picks her way through the grass and weeds in the heeled sandals she chose to make herself appear several inches taller, keeping an eye out for snakes. That's one thing she definitely won't miss about the tropics. Snakes, or those big, hairy spiders that are everywhere. She shudders just thinking about them. She hates spiders; has hated them ever since . . .

No. Don't think about that.
The past is the past.
Hell, the *present* is about to become the past.
And the future . . .
Ah, the future.
The future has finally arrived.

Chapter Two

The phone rings as Allison is spreading frozen chicken nuggets onto a stoneware baking sheet—the healthy kind of chicken nuggets, if there is such a thing. Free range, no antibiotics, organic whole-grain breading . . .

She bought the chicken at Greenstone's Natural Market on Glenhaven Avenue, where groceries cost at least twice as much as they do at the A&P. But of course, the MacKennas can afford to buy all that pricey health food—thanks, ironically, to Mack's high-pressure ad sales job, which is far more capable of shaving years off his life than the preservatives in cheap supermarket chicken nuggets.

Allison checks the caller ID on the phone. Seeing the 308 area code, she knows exactly who's calling.

Brett Downing, her half brother and only sibling, still lives in rural Nebraska with his wife and their two teenagers. Until November, their number rarely popped up on Allison's phone, and she rarely dialed it. Now, she knows it by heart.

After her family's run-in with the notorious Nightwatcher

made the national news, Brett and Cindy-Lou started calling. A lot.

At first, Allison suspected that their sudden urge to reconnect had less to do with genuine familial concern than it did with ghoulish fascination with the media spotlight that had been cast on the MacKennas.

But as time went on and the glaring press attention began to fade, Brett and Cindy-Lou continued to call. They sent Christmas gifts to the kids, and they've been talking about wanting to get together over summer vacation. In Nebraska.

"Why don't you come on out and visit us?" Cindy-Lou suggested the last time she and Allison chatted. "I bet your little ones ain't never seen a real cattle farm."

"They haven't. But it's so hard for Mack to get away . . ."

They've always spent their precious week of summer vacation with his sister, Lynn, and her family at their beach house down the Jersey Shore. But that's where they went to escape a cold-blooded killer last November. The girls were stolen from their beds in Lynn's beach house; nearly drowned, along with J.J., off the very beach where they frolicked every July with their Boogie Boards.

How, Allison has wondered countless times since, *are we ever going to go back there as if none of that ever happened?*

Still . . . it's not as if she has warm, fuzzy memories of Nebraska, either.

"That was so long ago, Allison," Mack said when she brought it up. "It's not like your parents are still there."

"For all I know, my father might be."

"Well, what are the chances that you're going to run into him on the street in the town where your brother lives?"

"Mack, there *are* no streets—or towns—where my brother lives."

"Good. It sounds nice and relaxing. And I'd like to meet

your family. That's probably not going to happen unless we go out there."

He's right about that. Brett and Cindy-Lou have no desire, or money, to travel to New York with their teenagers—even if they could manage to leave behind the farm they'd inherited from Cindy-Lou's late parents.

Nebraska it is.

"Maybe it wouldn't be a bad idea to stop in Centerville," Mack suggested.

"Center*field*. And no, thank you."

"But maybe it would help you feel better about things if you could—"

"It wouldn't. And there's no one there I'd ever want to see again."

"Was it really all bad, Allie? You said you did have a few friends there."

"And every single one of them turned her back on me right after my father left."

Well, that wasn't entirely true, she thought, remembering her next-door neighbor Tammy Connolly. She'd cried on Tammy's scrawny shoulder quite a few times after her life fell apart. But then Tammy and her mother wound up moving away almost as suddenly as Allison's father had left. She said she'd write and call, and Allison really believed that she would—but Allison never heard from her again.

"Believe me," she told Mack, "there's no reason to go back to Centerfield. I just want to see my brother."

"Then that's what we'll do."

Now, Allison picks up the ringing phone. "Cindy?" She can never quite bring herself to say Cindy-Lou, though it's what her sister-in-law prefers. Back in the old days, Allison used to call her Cindy Lou-Who—but only behind her back, of course.

I never gave her a chance. Back then, I just hated her for taking my brother away from us.

"Hi, Allison!" Ever cheerful, Cindy's voice bubbles across the miles. "How the heck do you do that?"

"I told you—we have caller ID." You'd think basic technology hadn't made it to the Midwest, the way Cindy-Lou had reacted the first time Allison explained it.

"No, I mean, how did you know it was me and not Brett?"

"I guessed."

She'd based it on the time, knowing that Cindy-Lou likes to call while she's "washing up the supper dishes," as she says, while Brett naps in his "Barcalounger." Indeed, Allison can hear running water and clattering pans in the background.

"And here I thought we had a psychic in the family."

Allison is as warmed by her sister-in-law's easy laughter as she is by the word "family."

"I hope I'm not interrupting your supper, Allison. I know you're an hour ahead and you all eat later than we do here."

Yes, but it's still early for an evening meal—and of course, even earlier in Nebraska, where it's barely past four. By the time Mack gets off the commuter train at around eight o'clock in this time zone, Brett and Cindy-Lou will be thinking about bedtime in theirs. The next morning, they'll be up to tend to their cows and fry up a big, unhealthy, non-organic country breakfast long before the sun appears on the horizon there—or here, for that matter.

How, Allison wonders, not for the first time, *are we ever going to spend an entire week together without driving each other crazy? We have such different lifestyles. Ours is beyond hectic, and theirs is . . .*

Well . . . *low-key* is a nice way to put it. And these days, as far as Allison's concerned, low-key has a certain appeal.

Even *dull* has a certain appeal, in the wake of all they've been through.

After assuring Cindy-Lou that she isn't interrupting a meal, Allison asks how the kids are, how Brett is, how the farm is.

And this time, when her sister-in-law tells her how much her own children would love it—a real live farm!—Allison not only agrees, sincerely, but asks when would be a good time to visit.

"Oh, gosh, anytime!" Cindy-Lou sounds so thrilled that Allison feels as though she's just been heartily hugged. "Are you really going to come out?"

"We'd like to," Allison tells her, and she means it.

Mack was right. It's time to get together with the only family she has left.

"You're always telling the girls to be good to each other and J.J., and that siblings are best friends," he pointed out when they were discussing it. "Don't you want them to at least see you and your brother in the same room? In this lifetime?"

Of course she does.

Not only that . . .

And not that she'd ever admit it to Mack . . .

But all last fall, when she was feeling overwhelmed by the fast-paced world in which she'd chosen to raise her children, she found herself fantasizing about the one she'd left behind—the last thing she'd ever imagined doing.

No, she doesn't really want to live in her small Nebraska hometown again. But at least now she grasps that it couldn't have been all bad. She just had so many unpleasant memories associated with her deadbeat father and her suicidal mother.

Then there was Brett, born to an unwed, teenage Brenda a decade before Allison came along. He grew up fast, married young, and moved away. She can't really remember a time when he was truly a part of her life.

But that doesn't mean he can't be, going forward. She wants to see him again, and Cindy-Lou, too, and get to know the niece and nephew she's met only once before.

"When can you come, Allison?"

"Well, the kids finish school at the end of June"—she

thrusts the tray of chicken nuggets into the preheated oven—
"and Mack has always taken off work the week of the Fourth
of July, so—"

"That's great! I'll mark the calendar!"

"Wait! I have to check with Mack first," Allison cautions.
"Last year, he didn't even get a vacation because he'd just
been promoted."

"What? That's terrible!" says Cindy-Lou, who's probably
never gotten a vacation—a true one—in her entire adult life.
Or perhaps even her childhood, considering that she was
raised on the farm, and her parents were just as saddled to it
as she and Brett are.

Growing up, Allison couldn't imagine choosing to spend
every day from birth to death with the same roof over your
head, the same view out your windows, the same people
coming and going, day in and day out . . .

That's part of the reason she left.

And it was the right decision, she reminds herself, closing
the oven door. Of course it was.

"If you can stay here until the middle of July," Cindy-
Lou says, "we can celebrate your birthday together. It's the
twelfth, isn't it?"

Allison is touched that she remembers, and even more
touched when she promises to bake a big chocolate birthday
cake. "And we can all go to the county fair that week, too.
Your kids would love it."

"I'm sure they would." Allison thinks of the carnival rides
and games on the boardwalk at the Jersey Shore, bleak and
deserted in November, on that awful day when the children
were . . .

*No, don't. Don't do that to yourself. Don't think about
that.*

"Do they like deep-fried Twinkies?" Cindy-Lou is asking.
"Best deep-fried Twinkies in the world are right here."

"They've never had them, but I'm sure they'd love them."

To think she was feeling guilty, just minutes ago, about the frozen chicken nuggets and the little bowls of Goldfish crackers she'd given the kids to eat as they watched television because they were all too hungry to go without a snack before dinner, which won't be ready for . . .

She checks the directions on the box and sets the stove timer for twenty-seven minutes.

That means the kids will be fed by six, bathed by seven, and trying to keep their eyes open long enough to spend five minutes with Mack when he gets home after eight.

Then she and Mack will eat—sushi delivery, she decides—and tell each other how exhausting the day was before Allison heads up to bed, leaving Mack to deal with the work-related e-mails and the spreadsheets he inevitably has to have finished by morning.

She won't hear him when he slips into bed beside her, and most of the time, he won't hear her when she slips out of it a few hours later, summoned by J.J. the human rooster.

The insomnia that's plagued Mack all his life still strikes now and then, but some recently prescribed medication has been helping. It's not as effective as the Dormipram he was taking last fall, but thankfully he isn't experiencing the frightening side effects he'd suffered with that medication.

Maybe he'll sleep better when they get to Nebraska. All that fresh air, early-to-bed, early-to-rise . . .

"I can't wait to tell Brett you're really coming," Cindy-Lou tells her. "It's going to be great for the two of you to see each other after all these years."

I hope so, Allison thinks. *I really do.*

Glancing around to make sure no one is in the vicinity, Carrie picks her way through the overgrown yard to the back door that leads to a small storage room just off the Big Iguana's kitchen. It's ajar, as always.

She swiftly reaches inside and sets the box on the scarred plywood floor there, against the wall alongside a couple of spare propane tanks used to power the deep fryer.

Even if someone happens to spot the carton, it won't draw suspicion. It's identical to stacks of others in the storage room, stamped with the name of a liquor distributor; the kind of box that is delivered nearly every day.

Only this one isn't filled with bottles of rum.

Satisfied, Carrie crosses the yard again. The humid air is hot and terribly still; a thunderstorm is brewing. The sky, barely visible beyond a canopy of tangled vines and fronds, still retains a high patch of blue, assuring her that by the time the bad weather hits, she'll be settled in the air-conditioned comfort of a cabin at sea. That will be . . . *bliss.*

Her scalp is already beginning to sweat beneath the long, dark wig, also left over from her old life. She's accumulated quite a few wigs; all of them now abandoned, along with her tropical wardrobe, in dresser drawers in the apartment upstairs. Having gone gray fairly young, she started dying her hair a dirty blond shade a few years ago. She did it less out of vanity than practicality: she got better tips as a blonde, most of it in American dollars. More cash to stockpile, waiting for the day she would make her escape . . .

Waiting for today.

But I have to stay calm. Take it step by step . . .

She's wearing Molly's orange floral print sundress now— not Carrie's style, by any means, but all that matters is that it will get her onto the Carousel. Between the wig, the sundress, the bag, the heels, and Molly's glasses perched on her nose, she's willing to bet no one will give her a second glance when she arrives at the ship in ten minutes. Even if the crew scanning ID cards noticed Molly coming and going over the past couple of days, chances are they don't know her well enough—and will be too busy getting thousands of passengers back on board—to suspect anything is amiss. After all, Carrie looks like Molly, she's wearing Molly's clothes, offering Molly's ID . . .

As for Molly herself . . .

Carrie has never been prone to backward glances. Even on September 11, she didn't spend more than a couple of moments watching the north tower burn from her vantage point across the river in Jersey before she went on her way.

Now, though, she shoots a quick last look at the upstairs windows above the bar, just making sure that Molly Temple hasn't suddenly appeared in one.

The windows are empty. Molly is much too far gone to bat an eye, let alone get to her feet and scramble to save herself.

The sedative had hit her so hard that Carrie was lucky to get her out of the bar at all. Seeing her start to slump on her stool, she'd reached Molly's side just in the nick of time, escorting her outside "for some fresh air" before she keeled over. From there, she managed to walk/drag the woman up the steps to the apartment, where she now lies on Carrie's bed, wearing Carrie's clothes, with Carrie's keys and ID in her pocket and the distinctive larimar bracelet on her wrist.

Molly will be burned beyond recognition, but the blue gemstone bracelet will remain intact. Anyone in this tiny harbor town who's ever met "Jane" will remember seeing it glinting on her wrist at one time or another as she mixed drinks behind the bar.

Smiling to herself, Carrie slips down a side alley that leads to the sparkling white ships in the harbor. Emerging in the glare of late day sun on the pier, she feels dangerously exposed and fights the urge to turn back to the sheltering shadows. Hundreds of passengers are streaming back to the Carousel, where two gangways are set up to admit them to the lowest deck adjacent to the dock. She allows the crowd to swallow her and sweep her toward the ship.

As planned, she chooses the fore gangway, which is closer and thus busier, with a long line of overweight American tourists too lazy to walk in this heat to the aft gangway, where there is no line at all.

Carrie isn't lazy, by any means. But she's watched this reboarding process many times from afar, and is well aware that it suits her purpose to get lost in the crowd that's being hustled along by the nautical-white-uniformed human assembly line crew.

When it's her turn, she hands Molly's ID card to the waiting officer and holds her breath. He takes a cursory glance at the photo, then at her, swipes it through the slot on the reentry kiosk, and nods her through. Suppressing a sigh of relief, she puts the straw bag onto the conveyor belt to be X-rayed and dutifully holds up her hands for the mandatory squirt of antibacterial spray.

After rubbing her palms together to ward off germs that could sicken an entire ship full of passengers, she retrieves her bag from the X-ray machine and can't help but marvel that the Carousel's security force has thought of everything.

Almost everything.

I'm the one who's thought of everything.

Calliope music plays merrily on the speakers as Carrie makes a left toward the midship elevator banks and stairwell, having memorized the deck plans that are conveniently mapped out on the cruise line's Web site. No one would ever guess she hasn't been navigating the ship's passageways and levels every day of this weeklong cruise.

She waits a few minutes for the elevator, but ducks her head and opts for the stairs the moment she's joined by a boisterous crowd of fellow passengers who reek of coconut oil and booze. For all she knows, she mixed drinks for them this afternoon.

She climbs six flights and emerges, winded, in an empty but brightly lit corridor on Deck 10. She makes a left; oops;

backtracks, makes a right. Moments later, she's unlocking the door marked 10533. Before crossing the threshold, she hangs the "Do Not Disturb" sign on the knob.

The inside cabin is tiny, as she had expected it to be, and she leaves the light off, taking refuge in the darkness at last. Without a porthole, she won't have a cabin view of the island home she's leaving behind forever, but that's okay. Maybe she'll venture out to one of the decks as they set sail. Not for sentimental reasons, but because the timer inside the box she left in the storage room is set for five-fifteen. She'll be able to watch Jimmy's Big Iguana—and everyone in it—go up in an explosion of flames and smoke.

Flames and smoke . . . just like the scene she left behind on another island over ten years ago, where the landscape was concrete and steel, not fronds and foliage.

There shouldn't be too many casualties here, relatively speaking. With the exception of a few stragglers, the passengers should all be back on board by the time the bomb goes off at the Big Iguana. The Disney ship is always the last to leave, at five-thirty, but that isn't a bar crowd anyway.

Of course the investigation will reveal the explosive device planted in the bar's storage room. But with all Jimmy's enemies, it won't be a stretch, by any means, for the authorities to conclude that someone might have reason to blow up the place. Certainly someone other than one of the victims, who will include a handful of locals, a couple of employees, and of course, poor Jane the bartender, who will have been killed in her apartment upstairs.

As for Molly Temple: Carrie wonders who's waiting back at home for her in . . . where, Ohio? Yes, according to the driver's license in her wallet, and last Friday's paycheck stub for an accounting firm in Cleveland. Also among her things: a room reservation for three nights at the Miami Marriott, and a plane ticket to fly home on Monday morning.

Well, whoever is waiting for her back in Ohio will just

have to wonder why she never caught her flight. The ship's records will show that she disembarked on Friday morning, checked into her hotel—and then vanished into thin air.

As for Carrie . . .

All she has to do, once she's back in the States, is rent a car and drive away.

She can be in New York before the weekend is over . . . if that's what she wants.

Or she can take it slowly, savor the journey.

That's the beauty of it. She has all the time in the world to catch up with her past. At least this time, she knows right where to find Allison.

That wasn't such an easy task twelve years ago. All she knew back then, when she arrived in New York City, was that Allison Taylor was somewhere in Manhattan, the proverbial needle in a haystack in those days before it was possible to locate just about anyone in a matter of seconds via the Internet.

I found her, though, eventually.

Found her, and moved in right across the hall from her. She never suspected a thing . . .

Nor did Mack.

He honestly thought they were moving to Hudson Street because Carrie's commute to the World Trade Center would be shorter if they lived downtown. He also believed the apartment's previous tenant, an elderly woman named Mrs. Ogden, had died in an accidental fall—as did Mrs. Ogden's family, and the landlord who listed her newly vacated apartment as available for rent on June first.

And when Carrie and Mack introduced themselves to their pretty blond neighbor across the hall, it never occurred to Mack—or, apparently, to Allison—that Carrie wasn't meeting her for the first time.

That was how it went, throughout that long, hot city summer when they lived across the hall from each other.

Whenever Carrie ran into Allison in the hallway or down by the mailboxes, they'd exchange polite greetings and go on their way.

Every time that happened, Carrie was left shaken. She'd gone to such great lengths to engineer the whole thing—now what?

What was she supposed to do next? What did she want out of all that? She thought she knew . . . until she found herself face-to-face with Allison. It infuriated her that there wasn't a flicker of recognition in those blue eyes, but . . .

But by then, you were too distracted by Mack to let it bother you as much as it might have. By then, you were foolishly thinking you could escape the hand you'd been dealt, and live a normal life.

Now, though, that time has dulled those foolish hopes and dreams—and the sting of having been forgotten by Allison—it's all more amusing than anything. To think that she'd been right under Allison's nose all that time . . .

To think that, after Carrie's "death," Allison—*of all people, of all people!*—went and married the grieving widower . . .

Unbelievable. Daddy used to tell me that I could be a writer when I grew up because I was so good at making up stories, but I couldn't come up with this stuff if I tried.

That final twist—Allison marrying Mack—was, like September 11, just another cosmic coincidence; a sign that the stars have aligned so that she—

Her thought curtailed by a sudden blast of noise, Carrie thinks, for a moment, that it's the bomb going off back at the Big Iguana.

But it can't be. A glance at Molly's glow-in-the-dark Timex, now strapped around her own wrist, tells her that it's not time yet. It's only five o'clock—on the dot.

The noise, she realizes, was one she's heard nightly, repeatedly, from shore; a noise that sounds drastically different when it's coming from somewhere overhead: it's the ship's giant horn blasting the news that they're setting sail.

Carrie smiles.

It worked. It really worked.

She's going home.

PART II

Night-dreams trace on Memory's wall,
Shadows of the thoughts of day;
And thy fortunes as they fall,
the bias of the will betray.
Ralph Waldo Emerson

Chapter Three

Kingsbury County, South Dakota
July 11, 1977

"**H**igher, Daddy! Push me higher!"

"Any higher, and you're going to go right up to the moon!"

"I want to! I want to go *over* the moon, like the cow in the nursery rhyme!"

"You're getting too old for nursery rhymes," he told her.

"I am not!"

"Sure you are. No more 'Hey, Diddle-Diddle' for you!"

"Yes! I like 'Hey, Diddle-Diddle'! And I like 'Jack Be Nimble,' and I like 'Little Boy Blue,' and—oh! I know! I want to go over the moon so that I can see the man inside it, like in the song."

"Which song?"

"Your favorite song, about Little Boy Blue and the kitty cat and the daddy!"

"What? Oh—you mean 'Cat's in the Cradle'?" He laughed. She couldn't see him, but she could hear him, and she could picture that broad grin on his handsome face, flashing teeth beneath his mustache, and the way he'd throw his dark head back, laughing as though he didn't have a care in the world.

"Hey, there, Diddle-Diddle." He caught the back of the swing in his hands when she came sailing back toward him. "Guess what? You can't go over the moon."

She giggled. "My name isn't Diddle-Diddle!"

"No? I thought it was!" He wrapped his arms around her from behind and tickled her, making her giggle harder.

Then he stopped. Still holding her fast against him, so that she could feel his mustache against her cheek and feel his heart beating against her back, he said firmly into her ear, "It's time to go home. It's late. Mom's going to wonder where you are, and I have to get on the road, remember?"

"Not tonight, Daddy. Please. Can't you stay tonight?"

"Not tonight."

"*Da-addy!*" she whined.

"*Diddle-Di-iddle!*" he whined right back. "I told you that before. Don't you remember?"

Remember . . . what was she supposed to remember?

There was something . . . a memory swooped close enough to touch and then swung up and away, and she couldn't catch it. She couldn't . . .

Or maybe you don't want to.

"Come on. If we go now, I can tuck you in and read you a quick story before I go. But no Mother Goose."

That was fine with her. All the nursery rhymes in that book were much too short.

"How about *Tikki Tikki Tembo*?" she asked.

"Nope—that's not a quick story!"

That was the point. But it was just as well he didn't want to read it to her again. The last time he read it, the book had given her nightmares about falling down a well—the one on their own property, which Daddy had once proudly told her had been hand-dug a hundred years ago by an early settler somewhere back in his family tree.

There were tens of thousands of those old wells dotting the prairie, dug by homesteaders on their claims a hundred years ago, he told her.

Theirs was covered by a heavy wooden lid. One day, as Daddy was taking a break from working outside to roll her around in the wheelbarrow, she asked him if they could look inside the well.

"Why?"

"I want to see what it looks like."

"There's not much to see. I filled in most of it years ago," he told her. "It's the law. But it's still pretty deep, so you stay away from it."

"How deep?"

"Six, maybe eight feet. See?" He held a flashlight and she leaned forward in the wheelbarrow and peered over the edge, breathing the dank smell of earth. There were worms, she remembered, and then a big shiny black spider crawled toward the opening, and she screamed and made him close it back up again.

"That was a black widow," he told her. "They're poisonous. You don't want to get bit by one of those."

"What would happen? Would I die?"

"You might. At the very least, you'd have terrible pain, starting about a half hour after the bite, and your muscles would begin cramping as the venom enters the bloodstream and attacks the nervous system. After a few hours, if you didn't get help, your blood pressure would go up and you'd have trouble breathing, probably convulsions—"

"Daddy, stop! I don't want to hear any more!" Why did he always have to give her such complicated responses to basic questions?

"Why not? I'm teaching you about black widows. They're fascinating."

"I'm afraid of them."

"Well, you don't have to worry about them at all if you don't go near the well. They're nocturnal creatures. They like it down there in the damp dark hollow. Make sure you stay away."

"Don't worry. I will."

In the nightmare, she was walking along on a summer afternoon through the high grass in the open field way out behind the house. The cover must have been left off the well, and she was swallowed up and trapped there, alone in the dark with the big spider, lots of spiders . . .

Her mother must have told her father that she'd been waking up screaming in the night, because the next time she saw him, he had a present for her.

"What is it?" she asked, trying to mask her disappointment. She'd been hinting that she wanted a new set of furniture for her Barbie house, and instead she got . . .

Some kind of contraption made out of sticks, feathers, and a network of strings that looked like a spider's web?

"It's a dream catcher," Daddy told her. "I bought it at the reservation."

The reservation, she knew, was where the Native Americans lived. Sometimes, Daddy stopped there on the way home from a trip to get gas and cigarettes, and once in a while he'd bring her something from the store there. Usually, he just liked to give her books as presents, because he wanted her to be smart, but when he went to the reservation he came back with other things. A leather coin purse. A beaded bracelet. A dark-braided little doll in a pouch, whose name, she mistakenly thought he said, was Papoose. She thought it was nice that Daddy had bothered to give the doll a name.

Later, she found out that "papoose" was a Native American word for "child." By that time, the name had stuck. She carried Papoose with her everywhere for a long time, until one day, she disappeared, along with lots of other toys.

She searched frantically, and when Daddy came back from his trip she asked him if he'd seen Papoose. His response was simply that she was too old for dolls.

That was untrue.

"I'll never be too old for dolls," she told him. "Never."

"Yes, you will. Someday, you'll be all grown up. And grown-ups don't play with dolls."

"Then I'm not going to grow up. I'm going to stay this way forever."

"That's a stupid thing for a smart girl to say," Daddy said, and she cringed. She hated it when he said that.

"What do I do with this?" she asked, trying not to show her disappointment when he gave her the dream catcher.

"Come on, I'll show you."

Daddy climbed up on a chair and hung it in the window of her purple and white bedroom. "There. Only good dreams can get through that web. Nothing scary."

"Really?"

"Really."

He'd been right about that. Every night before she fell asleep, she looked at it hanging there in the glow of her nightlight, and she told it to catch all the nightmares about falling down a dark well.

So far, it had.

But that didn't mean she was ready to leave the swing set and go home to bed—with or without reading *Tikki Tikki Tembo*. She wasn't ready to say good-bye to Daddy again just yet.

She flailed her legs, pumping futilely in the air. "I want to swing a little longer. Just a couple more pushes? Please?"

Sometimes, he gave in when she begged for something.

Not usually, though.

She had a feeling he wouldn't tonight. He was in a hurry to get going. She could sense his impatience; had noticed him looking at his watch during dinner: hamburgers, fries, and milk shakes served by a carhop at Eddie's, their favorite drive-in restaurant out on the highway. People kept saying the old place was going to close any day now, but she hoped it wouldn't. She liked to go to Eddie's because it was where Daddy used to take her mother on dates when they were boyfriend and girlfriend.

That was a long time ago, in the sixties, long before she was ever born.

Sometimes, when she went to Eddie's with Daddy, she saw teenagers there together—boys and girls, kissing in the car while they waited for their food to be brought to the window. She imagined her parents doing that when they were young, and it made her happy inside, and sad, too. Because now that they were husband and wife, they didn't ever kiss each other. Sometimes, they didn't even talk to each other—and when they did, it wasn't in a nice way. She couldn't even remember a time when her parents didn't fight a lot.

Remember . . . what is it? What am I supposed to remember?

After dinner tonight, Daddy used the pay phone outside Eddie's. Then he said he had to get going right away, but she convinced him to stop here at the playground behind a school down the road from Eddie's. She showed him how she could get all the way across the monkey bars. Well, she tried, and fell, twice.

"I can do it!" she told him. "Really! I can! I did it while you were gone this week. Watch me! One more try . . ." She fell.

"Don't give up. You have to keep working at it. It's all about the rhythm. Get into the rhythm of it."

She tried again. Fell again.

"You have to try harder. I told you, if you put in the effort, you'll be able to do it. You can do anything. Hard work makes things happen. If you would just—"

"Come on, Daddy!" she cut in, sensing he was about to embark on one of his lectures. "Race you to the slide!"

They both went down the slide a few times, and then he made her try the monkey bars again. And again. And again.

Fighting back tears of frustration, she turned to the swing set. "Push me, Daddy! Push me!"

Up, up, up she sailed, over and over again. Up toward the silvery pale crescent moon in the purple-blue night sky, clearly visible above the tall silo across the road from the school.

Up, up, up . . .

Down, down, down . . .

Now, she was stuck, legs dangling helplessly.

Behind her, holding her close in his warm embrace, Daddy said, "Come on. I mean it. We have to go."

She kicked her legs furiously. "Not yet!"

"Stop that. I said five minutes, and it's been ten. You promised to listen when I said it was time to go, remember?"

Remember . . .

What am I supposed to remember? There's something . . .

"Let's go. Now."

"Why?"

"Because I have to work. You know that."

"I don't care!"

"Stop that. Stop acting like a two-year-old. You know better."

She did, of course. She was seven. Old enough to know that Daddy had to leave tonight, and that he'd be away for a long time. Weeks, probably.

"No!" she shouted. She couldn't help it. "I want to swing!"

"You've had enough swinging."

"But I want to swing up over the moon! I want the dish to run away with the spoon!"

She waited for a response from him. He liked rhymes. They always made him laugh.

But he was silent. Suddenly, his hands felt ice cold. And she could no longer feel his heart beating.

She turned her head, slowly, to look at him.

"Daddy? Daddy . . . ?"

A scream erupted from her throat.

He was grinning at her, his rotting teeth protruding from the withered mouth of a hideous corpse with vacant eye sockets.

And that was when she finally remembered.

"Nooooo!" Carrie screamed, sitting up in bed. "Noooo!"

She pressed a hand against her wildly racing heart, looking around.

Her bedroom was dark. Too dark. Where was the dream catcher?

She could barely make out the slats of the blinds across the window—but they were up and down, vertical slats, not horizontal. And a strange light filtered through the cracks. Far too bright for prairie starlight . . .

It's city light, she realized, even as she heard the sirens outside, on a street too far below her window, and remembered the rest.

Her name was Carrie now. She wasn't in her purple and white bedroom. She was all grown up, in New York City.

That was just a dream. The same old nightmare, back to haunt her.

Tears rolled down her face, and she hugged herself, rocking back and forth, back and forth, comforting the lost little girl who still lived somewhere deep inside of her—the little girl whose daddy had died so long ago.

Chapter Four

New York City
March 7, 2000

On an ordinary Tuesday evening, Carrie wouldn't set foot outdoors until the tail end of her commute to the opposite tip of Manhattan.

There was a subway station located directly beneath the World Trade Center concourse, and it had come in handy during the wintry weather these past few months. She could leave her desk at Cantor Fitzgerald on the 104th floor of the north tower and, without being exposed to the elements, emerge from the subway right around the corner from her Washington Heights apartment building.

That commute had become so choreographed that she could probably do it blindfolded. Every night, faced with a row of concourse escalators, all of them descending toward the bowels of the building, she chose to ride the second to the right. At the bottom, entering the subway, she always put her token into the same turnstile—the one on the far left—and positioned herself in front of the same pillar on the platform, precisely where the doors to the fourth car on the next uptown train would open. That would allow her, when she reached her stop, to exit the train directly at the foot of the stairs to the street.

Elevator, escalator, subway, stairs.

Elevator, escalator, subway, stairs.

It's all about the rhythm. Get into the rhythm of it . . .

Elevator, escalator, subway, stairs.

She liked knowing exactly where to go and what to do. There was a certain comfort to order; to *ordinary*—most of the time.

Tonight, she was feeling uncharacteristically restless; tired of knowing exactly what was going to happen next. Tired of the commute, of the job itself, of going home alone to that drab little apartment.

Little? That was an understatement. Every night and every morning, she had to crawl in and out of her double bed across the foot, because the edges of the mattress on either side were right up against the walls. Usually, that didn't bother her. She could afford the rent, and she was exactly where she wanted to be: in Manhattan.

Tonight, though, she was in no hurry to get back home. And so, after riding the elevator down to the lobby, she faltered.

What the heck are you doing? she wondered as, instead of taking the escalators on down to the concourse and the C train, she impulsively exited to the street.

I'm listening to my gut. That's what I'm doing.

Was it a case of spring fever? If so, she must have caught it from her coworkers, in much the same way that being surrounded by an office full of coughing, sneezing people would inevitably lead to a tickle in your own nose and throat by the end of the day.

Today's workplace chatter had been all about the unseasonably warm weather. According to the calendar, springtime was still a couple of weeks away. But the city had been bathed in warm sunshine all afternoon, and while at this time of year the concrete didn't hold the heat, the evening chill was nowhere near as biting as it should be.

Carrie found the open space between the two towers alive with twilight activity. Despite the pleasant weather, no one lingered on the low benches surrounding the spherical bronze sculpture at the plaza's center. Businessmen and women in suits and trench coats scurried past, following their own well-worn paths of least resistance from office to train, bus, or ferry. At the end of a long day, all anyone wanted in this city—at least here in the financial district—was to get home, the sooner, the better.

Not me. Not tonight.

Carrie knew she couldn't walk all the way up to Washington Heights—not wearing pumps, pantyhose, and a skirt—but she was going to stroll for as long as she felt like it.

After being confined to a skyscraper's artificial ventilation for nine hours straight, she found the fresh night air almost intoxicating. The few blocks she'd expected to walk turned into miles.

As she moved north, Broadway, all business at the lower end of Manhattan, transformed into a neighborhood where people lived and dined and shopped. She passed storefront pizzerias, trendy boutiques, and—when she reached the Village—NYU's massive academic buildings.

Backpack-toting college students milled about smoking cigarettes between swigs from Starbucks cups; fancy women window-shopped; hand-holding lovers strolled and mooned; nannies pushed their charges in baby carriages; office workers scurried around all of them.

Sometime in the past twenty-four hours, enterprising downtown restaurateurs must have hastily dragged chairs and tables from winter storage to transform sidewalks along the network of side streets into outdoor cafés that ordinarily wouldn't materialize for another couple of months. People lingered at small, votive-lit tables drinking wine, gazing at the pedestrian parade.

Although Carrie had never walked up this stretch of Broadway before—all the way from the financial district through Tribeca and SoHo—the terrain felt familiar. That was because she'd prudently learned the lay of the land long before she even moved to Manhattan four months ago, having been taught, as a child, to take a methodical approach to new ventures.

"If you do your homework in advance of any situation," Daddy told her, "you'll always be able to fit in, no matter where you go or what you do. No one will ever guess that it's your first time for anything."

Like everything else he'd ever said, those words resonated—particularly years later, when she was able to grasp their bitter irony.

And so, she'd spent a good portion of last autumn in Midwestern libraries, poring over street maps, tour guides, photo collections. She learned New York City's key landmarks and thoroughfares, and how they all fit together. She practiced the mathematical formula one could use to figure out the nearest numbered cross street for any address on any avenue in the city. Brilliant.

As Daddy so aptly, and frequently, said, "Order is a great person's need and their true well-being."

Only later, much later, did she realize that he was quoting the Swiss writer Henri-Frédéric Amiel—and that Daddy wasn't exactly prone to giving credit where credit was due.

That wasn't his worst fault, though. Far from it.

"Excuse me, ma'am?" Someone tapped her shoulder as she stood waiting for the light to change at Third Street in the heart of Greenwich Village.

She turned to see a middle-aged couple. Tourists—she could tell by the pastel jackets—and undoubtedly from the Midwest: the flat A that drew "ma'am" into two syllables was unmistakable.

"Can you please tell us where Houston Street is?" The woman pronounced it like the city in Texas.

"You mean Houston?" Carrie couldn't help asking, emphasis on the proper pronunciation: *How*—rhymes with "now"—*ston*. Not *H-you*—rhymes with "new"—*ston*.

"Houston, How-ston—whatever you call it. Do you know where it is?"

Carrie resisted the urge to inform this impudent stranger that one shouldn't just go around calling things whatever one felt like calling them. Some people simply had no sense of right vs. wrong, of order vs. chaos.

Suppressing a sigh, she pointed back over her shoulder, to the south. "It's down there. Go past Bond Street—you'll see it on the left but you don't have to cross it if you stay on this side of the street, because it only runs east of Broadway—and then go across Bleecker, and it's the next intersection after that."

"After Bleecker?" the man asked. "Are you sure?"

Carrie just looked at him. Granted, he didn't know her; didn't know how her mind worked, or that she never made mistakes when it came to directions—or anything else. *Never.* But still . . .

"I'm sure," she said crisply, and turned away.

Behind her, the woman called, "Thank you." "Thank" was also two syllables. *Thay-ank.*

The light changed and Carrie resumed walking north, inexplicably unsettled at having heard that familiar accent again. It made her think of what she'd left behind, and of the reason she was here instead of there.

But it wasn't healthy to look back, especially with a past as dysfunctional as hers. She tried, instead, to focus on being flattered that those tourists had recognized her as a local, despite the fact that she'd been here only a few months herself.

She had Daddy to thank for that. She'd certainly done her New York City homework. Long before she ever actually set foot on Fifth Avenue, for example, she could recite not just the cross street, but the address of every notable skyscraper and flagship store that lined it, from Trump Tower at 725 to the Flatiron Building at 175; Saks at 611 to Lord & Taylor at 424 . . .

Oh, how she admired the way the glorious boulevard neatly bisected the city! Oh, how brilliant that numbered addresses on perpendicular streets increased accordingly east and west, with a mathematical formula available for locating those addresses as well . . .

She appreciated, too, that the venerable avenue disappeared altogether below Fourteenth Street, as if, after having been swallowed into the bohemian wilds of Washington Square Park, it couldn't bear to reemerge in the meandering chaos of the Village.

Of course, Carrie—being Carrie—couldn't blame it. She herself much preferred the symmetry north of Fourteenth Street to the randomly intersecting streets below.

Up on Forty-second Street, for instance, the main branch of the public library, with its stone lions standing sentry, was marvelously centered at the intersection with Fifth Avenue, bookended by Times Square two blocks to the west and Grand Central Terminal two blocks to the east.

Down here in the Village, by contrast, there were anomalies galore. Not only did West Fourth Street defy the simple rule that traffic on one-way even-numbed streets ran east—so simple to remember because of the E: even, east— but West Fourth Street somehow made its way *north of itself* to intersect with Eleventh Street, Twelfth, Thirteenth . . .

Madness. Sheer madness. Numbered streets were meant to keep a parallel distance from each other. They might intersect with numbered avenues, of course—but not other numbered streets.

Oh, and it wasn't just downtown that all bets were off. There was senseless chaos underground as well.

Carrie had spent a full week studying the subway map, determined to learn every stop along the confusing network of color-coded lines that branched to distant boroughs— something she'd since discovered even native New Yorkers didn't bother to do.

When she arrived in the city, she found that no one even referred to the three subway lines by their official names— the IRT, IND, BMT. And that half the time, the express train ran local. Or vice versa. Or there was station construction, a disabled train, flooded track, congestion ahead—any number of reasons that she couldn't use the damned subway to get where she needed to go, even though she knew exactly how to do it.

But of course, she didn't regret having spent so much time learning the system; learning everything she could about her new hometown. All that information was bound to come in handy sooner or later, and even if it didn't . . .

It's much better to be ambitious enough to learn things you might never use than to be too lazy to learn things you might need.

That wasn't something Daddy had ever told her; nor was it a quote from a famous writer. It was all hers.

At least *something* was all hers.

At the next corner, she made a left and headed down the block that would lead her directly to Washington Square Park.

"Planning a trip?" a smiling librarian asked her one day back in Omaha, shelving travel books near the table where Carrie was sitting.

She nodded, forcing a smile.

"We have a new computer for our patrons to use. I'd be

happy to show you how to use the World Wide Web for your research. There are all sorts of things you can look up if you—"

"No, thank you," Carrie cut in curtly, and turned away from the librarian's expression of surprised dismay.

She never returned to that branch. She didn't need anyone looking over her shoulder, asking questions about where she was going, or why.

All that research, conducted the old-fashioned way, paid off. She rarely got lost once she got to Manhattan, and hands-on experience quickly provided some additional navigational skills. For example, whenever she emerged from a subway station onto an unfamiliar midtown street, all she had to do was find the twin towers on the skyline. They acted as a reverse-compass point: if she was facing the towers, she was facing south.

She liked looking at them—from far away, from close up, from inside out. She liked their symmetry, their unbroken lines and perfect right angles, their no-frills construction and gridlike facades. They didn't seem to belong downtown. They should have been midtown buildings.

Should have been . . .

So damned many should-have-beens.

But you'd drive yourself crazy dwelling on them. Carrie preferred to think about the many things that had gone right.

Like the fact that just a few weeks after her arrival, she found herself working as a secretarial temp in one of the twin towers, having landed a short-term assignment at the global financial firm Cantor Fitzgerald. The assignment was extended by a week, and then another, and she'd been offered a permanent position in February.

Now she, Carrie Robinson, was actually employed in one of the most famous buildings in the entire world. She *belonged* there. Heady stuff: almost—but not quite—heady enough to eclipse the real reason she was in New York.

Lots of other positive things had happened since she got the job, leading up to the extraordinary weather tonight, which—she didn't even realize at the time—was about to send even better things her way.

The last time she ventured into Washington Square Park, she found it a frozen wasteland; tonight, it was a churning sea of pedestrians, skateboarders, Rollerbladers, joggers, musicians. Kids frolicked on the playground; dogs romped on the dog run; chin-stroking chess players pondered moves at the chess tables; withered elderly people in wheelchairs reminisced together as their nursemaids chatted with each other.

Carrie hadn't yet experienced a New York City spring, but she was, of course, familiar with the seasonal climate statistics. As she strolled along the paths inhaling the warm evening air, she reminded herself that it could very well snow again soon, and for another whole month, maybe even two. Yet it seemed jarring, in this warm weather, to see that the grass was dull and patchy and that the tree branches, like the flowerbeds, were bare, not even a hint yet of buds.

Around the big fountain, she spotted hordes of chanting protesters and remembered that today was Super Tuesday—the presidential primary election. Here in New York, Gore was expected to capture the Democratic vote, and on the Republican front, McCain might give Bush a run for his money. But Carrie didn't care much about politics. There were plenty of other things to worry about.

Like Allison Taylor.

Carrie had learned, last summer, that Allison had graduated from the Art Institute of Pittsburgh and moved to New York, presumably to find a job in the fashion industry.

Where are you now, Allison?

Casting her eyes up at the midtown west skyline, Carrie listened for her instincts.

Was it her gut telling her that Allison was probably out

there—up there—somewhere? Or was it just common sense? Most of the showrooms were in the West Thirties, in the garment district.

Carrie had spent hours wandering that neighborhood when she first got into town, scanning the face of every attractive young female who passed. She'd never spotted Allison, though so many of those women seemed to look like her: tall, blond, pretty. But because they all wore large sunglasses, even on stormy days in the dead of winter, Carrie might have missed her.

Meanwhile, she was working her way through the city's massive telephone directories, going through the residential listings for every borough. There were pages upon pages of Taylors. None had the first name Allison—though there *was* an Alison, one L. Carrie called it, and the line had been disconnected. She wasn't really disappointed. She doubted that a young woman in this day and age would be naïve enough to put her first name in the phone book, which would undoubtedly invite a host of calls from anonymous heavy breathers.

Most females would know enough to use just a first initial, and so Carrie methodically called every "Taylor, A" in the book. When that didn't pan out, she called designers' showrooms or offices and asked for Allison Taylor, only to be informed that no one by that name worked there.

She wasn't sure what she'd have done if a receptionist had said, "I'll put you through."

Would she hang up?

No—she needed to actually hear her voice. Then, after Allison picked up, she would simply claim that she'd dialed a wrong number, or, if she wasn't ready yet to sever the connection, she could just make up some reason she was calling, something that would keep the voice talking . . .

Not, of course, about anything meaningful. There would be time enough for that down the road.

What if Allison recognized her voice, though?

It wasn't likely, but—

Caught up in her reverie, she walked squarely into someone.

"Oh! Sorry!" a male voice exclaimed.

She looked up to see a businessman standing there looking apologetic, as though it had been his fault. It hadn't—Carrie wasn't watching where she was going—but if he wanted to take the blame, why stop him?

She took a step back and studied him more closely. He was tall, with nice green eyes and dark, barber-buzzed hair. He carried a leather briefcase-like bag over his shoulder and a trench coat over his arm, and wore a charcoal pinstripe, well-cut suit with a white shirt and green tie that matched his eyes.

Yes, she noticed his eyes. Noticed that they were deep green with flecks of bluish-black. Noticed his dark lashes and the manly straight slashes of brow, with a furrow of concern between.

There was something about him that captured her interest in a way that no one had in a very long time. The men she'd met at work were mostly brokers: brash and busy, men who worked hard and played harder, married or not. She wasn't interested in anyone like that.

She wasn't interested in anyone, period.

Well, anyone other than Allison Taylor.

"That was a major head-on collision," the guy said. "Are you okay?"

She noticed that both his hands were on her upper arms—and that she liked it.

That was unusual, because she wasn't big on being touched. Especially by strangers.

He was just trying to steady her, but it was almost as if he were holding her. It had been a long time since anyone had done that.

"I'm okay," she said, but it wasn't true. She didn't like

liking the sensation of being held by him. And she didn't like *not* liking it when he took his hands off her arms.

There was something about him—about the way he'd held her steady—that made her feel safe, for the first time since . . .

Well, in years.

Daddy.

"Here," he said, sort of pulling her over to a vacant bench just a few feet away, "sit down for a second. Are you sure you're okay?"

"I am. I'm okay." She sat and was disappointed when he let go of her again and took a step back.

"So what's so fascinating?" he asked, and she was confused—and embarrassed, wondering if he somehow knew what she'd been thinking.

Then he pointed at the midtown skyline beyond the network of winter branches. "You were staring up there. Like you were looking at something interesting."

"I was just . . . um, noticing how pretty the buildings are at night, when the sun goes down and the lights go on."

"You're visiting, then? From out of town?"

"What makes you say that?" She was disappointed. Irked, even. Was it the accent? She'd worked so hard to lose it before she ever left the Midwest.

"If you lived here," the guy said, "you wouldn't be taking the time to notice how the buildings look at night, or any other time. Most people just rush along looking down, not up, or around."

"Actually, I *do* live here."

"Really?" He looked almost—pleased? Pleased to have been wrong?

She tried to remember whether *she'd* ever been pleased about being wrong.

Nope. Especially when the things she'd been wrong about in her life were often people she'd trusted. Like Daddy.

Being wrong about him was the worst thing that ever happened to her.

But she didn't want to think about that right now. She wanted to think about the fact that this stranger was still standing here talking to her instead of pushing past her; that he was actually glad—for some reason—that she lived here after all.

And *she* was glad that she was wearing her nicest suit, a slimming black one, and that she'd taken the time to brush her hair and put on lipstick before leaving the office, which she rarely bothered to do.

Spring fever? Was that really what was wrong with her?

You'd better get over it, fast. You can't afford to forget why you're here: to find Allison, and . . .

And figure out what to say—what to do—when you've found her.

"Are you coming from work?" the guy was asking. "On your way home?"

"Yes. How about you?"

"Coming from work, but I live in New Jersey and right now, I'm headed downtown. I'm meeting some buddies for drinks at McSorley's."

"That's nice," she murmured, wondering if her end of the conversation sounded as stiff as it felt on her tongue. She'd never been good at small talk with strangers. With anyone.

"Eh," he said, and shrugged.

"You don't like McSorley's? Or your friends?"

"I like them both, but not tonight."

She noticed something else about his eyes: there was a note of sadness in them. She wondered what was wrong. The question seemed much too forward, so instead, she asked, "Then why are you going?"

"Good question. I really don't want to."

"Why do something you don't want to do?"

"Don't you ever do anything you don't want to do?"

"No. Not if I can help it. Can you help it?"

"Yeah—I guess I can."

Carrie shrugged. "Then don't go."

"It's not that simple."

"It *is* that simple."

He just looked at her for a minute. Then he sat beside her and reached into his pocket.

She watched as he took out a pack of cigarettes, placed one between his lips, and offered the pack to her.

Daddy had been a smoker. Personally, she could take or leave it.

Tonight, she took it.

After lighting her cigarette and then his own, he took a drag, exhaled, and said, "You're right. I just changed my mind."

She inhaled smoke deeply into her lungs, exhaled, waited.

"You know what I'm going to do instead of meeting my friends?"

"What?"

Could there possibly be . . .

Was there any way he was going to ask her to go have a drink with him or something?

Are you kidding? There's no way in hell. You know that.

But once the crazy thought flashed into her head, she couldn't help but hold her tobacco-saturated breath until he answered.

"I'm going to go home and see my mother. That's what I'm going to do."

She exhaled, secretly disappointed—but not surprised at having been right, as usual.

"Do you live with her?"

"No. But near enough. My parents are in Hoboken. I'm in Jersey City."

She nodded and stood up. Now she was anxious to get going, away from him and this unsettling connection that had come out of nowhere on a night when nothing was as it should have been.

He stood, too, and pointed at the skyline to the north. "How far uptown are you walking?"

She wasn't sure yet. Maybe she'd just jump on the subway at Union Square. Maybe she'd had enough warm fresh air. Enough . . .

She looked down at the cigarette in her hand, tempted to toss it down and grind it out with her heel.

"Because I'm heading back up to the Port Authority," he continued, checking his watch, "to catch a bus home to Jersey. It's a quarter to six. I can make the six-thirty bus, no problem. So maybe I'll walk with you, as far as you're going."

And maybe she hadn't had enough warm fresh air after all. Or smoke.

She bit back a smile, took another slow drag. "That's fine. I'm catching the subway at Times Square, so I thought I'd walk all the way up Fifth and then go across Forty-second Street."

"Works for me."

Together, they started walking north, toward the solid old stone arch, an homage to Paris's Arc de Triomphe and the gateway to Fifth Avenue and the part of the city she loved best, where everything fell neatly into place and made sense.

As they walked, puffing companionably, he asked what her name was. For a fleeting, wild moment, she was tempted to give him her real name.

But of course, she couldn't.

"Carrie Robinson," she said.

"Carrie. Nice to meet you." He stuck out his hand, and shook hers as they walked. His brief clasp was warm, as she'd known it would be. Safe.

"I'm James," he said, "but everyone calls me Mack."

She almost gasped. Surely she'd heard him wrong. "Did you say Matt?"

"No, Mack. It's short for my last name, MacKenna."

Mack.

His name was Mack.

It was a sign, Carrie thought. A sign that he was meant to be a part of her life.

"**D**id you go vote yet, babycakes?"

Allison Taylor looked up to see her friend Luis standing in the doorway—if you could call it a doorway—of her cubicle.

He was a production editor at *7th Avenue* magazine, where she'd been working for about six months now, having been hired away from her postcollege internship at Condé Nast.

The glamour factor was higher there, but here, she was actually getting paid. Her duties were pretty much the same: basic entry-level stuff—though sometimes, not even. Her supervisor, Loriana, kept her hopping with ridiculous nonsense, such as fetching cups full of tepid water—Loriana's preferred afternoon "snack," ever since she read somewhere that tepid water burns more calories than hot or cold water.

Having adapted a your-wish-is-my-command corporate philosophy, Allison figured she could put up with just about anything for the promise of working her way up the ladder and one day—hopefully soon—seeing her own name on the magazine's masthead.

"Why are you calling me babycakes?" she asked Luis.

"Because you asked me to stop calling you toots."

"Okay, well, stop calling me babycakes, too, okay?"

"Only if you promise me you've voted. Or that you're going to vote."

"I can't. I'm not registered here yet."

She hadn't been registered back in Pittsburgh, either—or

in Centerfield, for that matter, though she'd celebrated her eighteenth birthday shortly before she moved away.

If you could call packing your bags and paying one last visit to your mother's lonely grave "celebrating."

Anyway, she'd known all along that both Centerfield and Pittsburgh were temporary; that she was destined to settle here in New York City.

"What? You're not registered to *vote*?!" Luis feigned horror, slapping his hands to his cheeks and staring at her with his mouth agape.

"I just haven't gotten around to it. I will."

"You'd better. We can't take any chances on another four years with Dubb'ya."

"What makes you think I wouldn't vote Republican?"

His eyebrows shot even higher. "*Would* you?"

"If I liked what the candidate had to say," she told him, mostly to get a rise out of him. "I have strong Republican roots, you know."

Her maternal grandfather, Thurston Downing, had been a staunch conservative who'd held some kind of high-profile public office in Nebraska long before she'd been born. She didn't know the details; nor had she ever bothered to look them up—though now, sometimes, she thought about using the World Wide Web to see if she could find out more about her mother's parents.

She'd never met them, had no idea whether they were alive or dead, or if they even knew she existed. Probably not.

Whenever her curiosity got the better of her and she thought seriously about searching for them—or her father— she stopped herself.

If her grandparents hadn't disowned their only child, Mom might still be here.

And if her father had never walked out on his wife and child, Mom might still be here.

So, no. She wasn't interested in finding anyone, even if it

was just a matter of hitting a few keys on the computer. No, thank you.

"You're a Republican?" Luis was asking.

She forced away thoughts of the past and laughed at the look on his face. "What?"

"You said—"

"I was just busting your chops. And don't worry . . . *babycakes*. I'll register between now and November."

"I'll hold you to it. So are you ready to go?"

They were taking an accessory design class together on Tuesday evenings, down at the Parsons School of Design.

Allison looked at her watch. It was ten of six. "We don't have to leave for at least another half hour."

"I know, but since it's so nice out, I was thinking we could walk down to class tonight instead of taking the subway."

"Walk? From Thirty-seventh Street to Thirteenth Street? In these?" She lifted her foot to show him the four-inch Louboutins she was wearing.

"Definitely not in those. What size are you?"

"Nine." She cleared her throat. "And a half."

He eyed her foot and raised a dubious eyebrow.

"All right," she conceded. "More like a ten. Why?"

"Be right back." He disappeared for less than a minute and reemerged wearing a smug expression and holding a pair of black flats. "Try these."

She took them, looked them over, read the label. "Really?"

"What do you want, Chanel? They're free."

"Do you *have* Chanel?"

"In a ten? And a flat?" He rolled his eyes. "Sorry, Sasquatch. Wedge those giant dogs of yours into these shoes and let's go."

She grinned, already unbuckling the ankle straps on her Louboutins.

Five minutes later, they were strolling south on Fifth Avenue.

Carrie was so caught up in what Mack was saying that, for the first time since she'd arrived in New York City, she'd forgotten all about Allison Taylor.

Mack.

His name was *Mack*.

She still couldn't believe it. If only she could tell him what the name meant to her. But of course, she couldn't. So she focused on listening to him talk, wondering what it would be like to connect—really connect—with him.

Granted, her experience in that area was pretty limited. She was almost thirty and reasonably attractive; she'd gone on a handful of dates over the past decade or so.

Never anything serious, of course, because she'd learned the hard way that you can't trust even the person you love more than anything in this world; the person who claims to love you in just the same way. She would never, ever let anyone get close to her. Never again.

Not even if someone ever came along who seemed to *want* to get close to her.

This guy—Mack, with the easy smile and quick laugh that belied the hint of sadness in his eyes—hadn't indicated that he was interested in anything more than company for his walk up Fifth Avenue. If he were, she didn't know *what* she'd do. A date with someone to whom she was this physically attracted might be dangerous.

But for the moment, it was nice to have someone to talk to about something other than the weather and the stock market.

The protesters in the park had spurred a conversation about politics that then meandered to travel, and on to food, and movies. The discussion turned to books when they reached the famous stone lions in front of the public library. As they made a left onto Forty-second Street, Mack asked Carrie what she was reading now.

"*Harry Potter*," she said after a moment's hesitation, selecting a title she'd seen open on countless strangers' laps on the subway lately.

"Isn't that a kids' book?"

Was it?

She had no idea. She shrugged, said, "I like it," and prayed he wouldn't ask her anything specific about the story.

What he asked, though, was even harder: "Do you have kids?"

"No," she said, so sharply that he glanced over at her.

"Not big on kids, huh?"

"What? Why do you say that?"

"Just . . . never mind. It was stupid."

Yes. It was stupid, she thought, enraged.

It wasn't that she didn't like kids, it was . . .

But *that* was none of his business.

Even which books she liked to read was none of his business, which was why she'd lied. She wasn't about to tell him about the stack of titles on her nightstand. Definitely not after the way he'd reacted to *Harry Potter*.

"What are *you* reading?" she asked Mack, as much to defuse her own anger as to break the awkward silence.

"If I said *Harry Potter*, would you believe me?"

"No."

"You'd be right."

Yes. I'm always right.

He reached into his briefcase and held out a book.

She slowed her pace to see the title, reading it aloud. "*Final Gifts: Understanding the Special Awareness, Needs, and Communications of the Dying.*"

"Just a little light reading." He tucked it back into his bag.

She didn't know what to say. Whatever she'd been expecting—this wasn't it. Now she understood the sadness in his eyes, although not entirely.

Who was dying? Someone close to him?

Was *he* dying?

That would be horribly unfair.

The thought was immediate, and struck her as bizarre.

Unfair to whom? To him?

Yes, of course.

But maybe also . . . to me? Because I actually like him?

"I'm actually not reading it yet," he told her. "I just bought it at lunchtime. It was recommended to me by the hospice nurse who's going to be taking care of my mom."

His mom. Not him.

She was relieved—for his sake, she told herself, and not for hers, because after two more blocks, she was never going to see him again anyway.

"I'm sorry," she said. "That must be hard."

"Yeah. We just found out. The doctors say that nothing more can be done for her—they've run out of treatments, and so . . . she gets hospice. And I get to read this book to try to make it a little easier—at least, on me. I don't see how anyone's going to make it any easier on her. She's in a lot of pain, and nobody seems to be able to help with that."

"I'm so sorry. Really."

"Thanks. Me too. Really."

No wonder his eyes were so sad. No wonder he wasn't in the mood to go out for drinks with his friends. No wonder he'd decided to go home, instead, to Jersey—to see his mom.

"Have you ever lost anyone?"

His question might have caught her off guard, but her answer was instantaneous:

"Yes."

Maybe not in the way he meant, but loss was loss. Loss was devastating, no matter how it happened. Whether it struck out of nowhere like a sucker punch or crept in slowly and loomed with the inevitability of a funnel cloud on the prairie horizon, it was devastating. Anyone in its wake would be left raw and angry and alone, forever changed, forever fearful, forever haunted by nightmares . . .

Dream catcher, or not.

"You know what's funny? Not funny ha-ha, but funny strange?"

"No, what?" she asked.

"When I was a kid, I used to watch all these old reruns on TV—*My Three Sons*, *Courtship of Eddie's Father*, *Bonanza*—did you watch any of those shows?"

"Yes." Growing up, she'd loved to escape into television. Even those ancient reruns. Especially those, actually, with their wholesome families and happy siblings.

The Patty Duke Show was her favorite, about identical cousins. She knew the theme song by heart, with its lyrics about a pair of matching bookends being different as night and day.

"Those shows were all about mothers who'd died and left their boys behind to be raised by their fathers. And I'd worry—nothing against my father, but I'd worry that something would happen to my mother, and I'd pray to God that she'd stick around long enough for me to grow up," he said, maybe more to himself than to Carrie.

Praying that someone would stick around . . . ha. She knew firsthand that didn't work.

"And she did stick around, and now I'm grown up, so I guess—" He broke off, cleared his throat. "But the thing is, I'm not ready to lose her. Are you ever? I mean, when you think about it, who can ever be ready for the worst to happen?"

She wanted to tell him that the worst could happen and even after it had, you'd still be left with the sense, forever after, that it could somehow happen again even though, of course, that was impossible.

When someone you loved was wrenched from your life, you'd lost them. You couldn't lose them again.

But you can lose someone else, Carrie reminded herself, *if you let yourself care about someone else.*

"I'm sorry," he said. "I don't know why I'm unloading all this on you."

"You need someone to talk to."

He tilted his head, then nodded. "You're right. I guess it is that simple. And you're a good listener. Women—they tend to be chatty, and interrupt, and fill all the space they possibly can. At least, most women I know. Like my sister, and . . . and a friend of mine. Ex-friend," he added, and she got the sense that he might have just escaped a relationship with the kind of female he'd just described.

"But *you*," he went on, "you wait until someone is finished speaking, and you don't jump right in to blurt out the first thing on your mind, either. You absorb it before you comment."

As she weighed his words, he pointed at her, grinning. "See? You're doing it now. It's nice to talk to someone who doesn't just want to hear her own voice. Although . . ."

"What?" she asked, when he'd trailed into silence, wearing a wry expression.

"I guess that's kind of ironic for me to say, since I've been talking your ear off for miles. You probably can't wait to get rid of me, right?"

"Right," she said, like she was teasing, but she half meant it. The sooner they went in opposite directions, the sooner things would be back to normal for Carrie. No more sparks of longing for things she couldn't have.

Yet there was that other part of her that didn't mean it at all; the wistful, foolish, lonely part that was reluctant to "get rid of him," as he put it.

"I don't blame you," he said. "I'm getting on my own nerves tonight, too. Good thing I changed my mind about going to McSorley's. My friends wouldn't have been up for listening to all this—that's for sure."

"Maybe you need some new friends."

"Nah, I've known these guys for years. It's just me. It's just . . . tonight . . ."

She nodded. She got it.

Tonight was different for him.

It was different for her, too.

What she didn't realize then was that things weren't ever going to go back to the way they were. Things had changed. For the better, she would soon come to believe.

Allison shivered—again—and Luis interrupted his lament about the latest snakeskin trend to say, "If you're that cold, put on your coat! Who cares if it's ugly?"

Ugly?

She sighed inwardly. Leave it to Luis.

"I'm not cold—"

"Then why are you shivering?"

"—and this coat"—she gestured with the fake-fur-collared Escada slung over the crook of her arm—"is not ugly!"

"It's hideous."

"It is not!"

"The poor dear is delusional," he murmured to an imaginary companion. To Allison, he said, unconvincingly, "All right. It's not hideous."

"It's not!"

"That's what I said."

"But you didn't mean it."

"Calm down, Sass." He'd been calling her that—an abbreviated version of Sasquatch—since they left the building.

Affectionately, of course. Everything Luis did was offered with utmost affection. Even trashing the gorgeous designer coat she'd gotten for a song at a Saks end-of-season sale.

But right now, she wasn't in the mood.

"Stop calling me Sass."

"Sorry." He put an arm around her shoulder. "Apology accepted?"

Why did she always find it impossible to stay peeved at Luis? "Apology accepted."

"And if you're cold, put on that . . . um . . . *attractive* . . . coat of yours."

"I'm not cold. I told you."

"Then why are you shivering?"

"I have no idea. I just feel funny."

"Are you getting sick?"

"Maybe."

The malaise had swept over her about fifteen minutes ago with the grim, all-consuming persistence of a physical illness that takes hold in an instant, accompanied by that familiar sinking feeling of grim inevitability. With a stomach bug, it was the realization that you were about to spend the better part of the next twenty-four hours on your knees.

With this chill, there was a similar feeling of foreboding; that same sensation that something unpleasant was about to happen to her.

But of course, it wasn't true.

Unless this was some kind of weird premonition, and she was about to be hit by a crosstown bus.

She hugged herself, shivering again.

"Maybe you shouldn't be going to class if you're sick."

Luis, she noticed, had removed his arm from her shoulders, considerably widening the berth between them as they walked on down Fifth Avenue toward the next intersection.

"Don't worry. I'm not sick."

"Then what are you? Scared?"

She hesitated. "Maybe. I don't know."

Luis shot her a rare, serious glance as they stopped at the crosswalk to wait for the light at Thirty-fourth Street. "What's wrong, Allison?"

"I just feel like something bad is going to happen."

She expected a return quip from him, but after taking a good look at her expression, he said only, "I hope you're wrong."

So do I, she thought, and tilted her head back, closing her eyes briefly.

When she opened them again, she saw the twin towers of the World Trade Center, twinkling in the distance, and found herself thinking of her father.

He'd always told her to pay attention to her instincts.

Yeah, well, what did he know?

Ha. Everything about everything, if you asked him.

"He just likes to hear himself talk," Mom used to say, rolling her eyes whenever he launched into one of his long-winded, advice-laden monologues.

And yet, ironically, when his words might have mattered the most—the day he picked up and left—he opted for silence. Not a word of explanation; no indication where he was going, or why, or how they were supposed to pay the bills and keep their heads above water without him. Not a spoken word at all, though he wrote seven of them on the scrap of paper Allison and her mother found on the kitchen table on that final morning: *Can't do this anymore. I'm sorry. Good-bye.*

Mom held her lighter to the paper, recklessly tossed it into the sink, and left the room. Seeing a lick of flame edging toward the curtains above the faucet, Allison had turned on the tap. Later, she'd wonder why she'd even bothered. She might as well have just let it burn—take the whole damned house with it—rather than wait for foreclosure to claim the roof over their heads, the one thing Mom had hoped to salvage from the marriage.

"Why did he do it?" she asked her mother, and herself, and—of course—Winona, the imaginary sister who came to live in Allison's head the day her father left.

It was ironic that Allison had woken up that morning

from a happy dream about having a sister, and had taken it to mean that her parents were going to have another baby. In fact, she was headed into the kitchen to tell her mother about it when she found the note saying that her father was gone.

Why? Why? Why did he do it?

Even Winona couldn't tell her why a man would just turn his back on his wife and child one day out of the blue, leaving them destitute. Even Winona didn't know how he could have transformed overnight from father of the year to heartless monster.

Okay—he'd been neither of those things in reality. But Allison had spent the first decade of her life loving him and the second decade hating him; in her mind, the paradox was, for too many years, the primary source of her pain. How did someone go from loving you one day to leaving you the next? How did you guarantee that it wouldn't happen again, with the next person you allowed yourself to love, and trust?

What about her father? Did he have regrets? Was he out there somewhere even now, wondering what had ever happened to them after he left? Or didn't he care?

Of course he didn't care, Allison reminded herself. *And I don't care, either. Not anymore. Not in a long time. Not about him.*

Yet even now, on a weirdly warm March evening in New York City, hundreds of miles—as far as she knew—and a lifetime away from her father, Allison couldn't help but think of him anyway.

Was that why she was feeling chilled to the bone?

Once in a while, she'd catch a flicker of something—the smell of a certain aftershave, or a few notes of an old song—that stirred a long-buried memory. Sometimes, she knew right away what it was, other times, she'd find herself feeling ill at ease before she even put her finger on the cause.

Channel surfing on a recent stormy Saturday, she came across the movie *Toy Story*. Something about it made her vaguely uneasy, but she didn't understand why until she realized that the Woody character was voiced by Tom Hanks—the actor who'd starred years earlier in *Big*, a movie she'd watched with her father on that last day, before he took off.

Tonight, she had the same inexplicably unsettled feeling, though it was tinged with foreboding. What had triggered it? An overheard snippet of conversation, a passing face that reminded her of his?

Or what if—

No. The possibility was too outlandish to even consider.

There were eight million people in this city. Even if her father happened to be here on vacation or on business or something, what were the odds that she'd run into him on the street?

Actually . . .

If you ruled out the boroughs and all the areas where tourists and visiting businessmen weren't likely to go, you'd come down to a couple of relatively condensed Manhattan neighborhoods.

This was one of them.

Allison had to at least wonder whether, if she were anywhere in the vicinity of her own flesh and blood, some deep-seated, primal awareness might take hold.

And so, as she and Luis walked on down Fifth Avenue, she found herself scanning the faces in the crowd, looking for him in the faces of strangers. After he left, her mother had burned every photo of him, relegating his image to an increasingly dim corner of Allison's memory.

He'd be older now—perhaps gray or balding. Would she even recognize him? If he was here somewhere, she didn't see him, and at last, the feeling of dread began to subside.

In this part of town, the blocks just west of Fifth Avenue were wider than the crosstown blocks east of the avenue. To

Carrie, it always seemed to take forever to walk along Forty-second Street to reach the intersection with Sixth. Tonight, though, covering that same distance with Mack, she felt as though they'd covered that stretch in no time.

When the "Don't Walk" turned to "Walk" just as they reached it, meaning they didn't have to stop, she felt a pang of regret—which was ironic, because ordinarily when that happened, she'd welcome the efficiency of not having to stop and wait.

She hated to wait. For anything.

She'd grown up waiting. For *him*.

For all the things she had been promised; things that never came to pass.

"You know I'm trying to spend more time with you," Daddy had said. "I'm doing my best. Bear with me. Be patient . . ."

You're full of shit, Daddy, she wanted to tell him—but not, of course, at first. Back then, she listened to him, believed him, and tried to do what he asked her to do.

Be patient . . .

I was patient! And you—you were full of shit!

Can I say it now, finally? I've been waiting a long time to tell you.

Of course, it was too late for that.

But not for everything.

Tonight, at long last, she had patience. Tonight, she wouldn't have minded lingering at the crosswalk for a minute, prolonging the completion of her journey to the subway station at Times Square, where she would part ways with Mack.

"So I guess," he said as they crossed the wide avenue, "it's pointless of me to ask for your phone number then?"

Carrie's heart skipped a beat. Unable to think of a light, flirtatious response, she said, "You can have my number if you want it."

"Do you have a business card?"

When she shook her head, he reached into his bag again. He pulled out a pen and, after a bit of hunting, a manila folder to write on. It was full of papers, and it struck her that she didn't even know what he did for a living.

Yet she knew that his mother was dying.

She also knew, crazy as it seemed, that there was something about this stranger that had made her feel safe even before she found out his name.

She knew, too, that she wanted to see him again—the first time she'd ever met anyone and cared whether he was just passing through her life, or might possibly make a repeat entrance.

That was more than enough reason to give him her real phone number. Well, just her work number.

Despite her connection with him, she felt protective of her cell number, and of her home number, too. The walls she'd built around herself were designed to keep people out; to keep herself hidden away from those who might pry. They weren't going to come down easily—if ever.

Mack wasn't prying, though.

He was too caught up in his own problems to pry. Maybe that was part of the appeal. Maybe that was why she found herself fervently willing him to call her when he jotted down her number and said that he would.

"Do *you* have a card?" she asked, and he reached into his pocket and handed one to her.

She saw that he worked in midtown, in television advertising sales.

For some reason, that made her think of Allison.

Remembering why she was here in New York, she put his card into her pocket and picked up her pace, seeing the Times Square subway station up ahead.

Mack, too, seemed to have fallen back into his own reality, silent as they covered the final block.

"Well . . . it was nice bumping into you," he said lightly.

"You too."

"Thanks for listening."

What was she supposed to say to that?

You're welcome?

Thanks for talking?

Better to not say anything at all.

Except, of course, good night.

Which she did.

As she descended the subway stairs, she forced herself not to look back over her shoulder. She had a feeling he'd already moved on, but she suspected she was meant to see him again.

See that? Daddy's voice seemed to say, triumphantly. *If you hadn't listened to my advice—and your own instincts— you never would have met him.*

Yes. Now if those same instincts could just lead her to Allison, she could set things straight—whatever that entailed—and get on with her life.

Rather, actually *have* a life. Build a life of her own . . .

Or, perhaps, with someone else.

A smile played at her lips as she fed her subway token into the closest turnstile.

Chapter Five

Ordinarily, McSorley's wasn't Mack's idea of an appropriate restaurant for a first date. La Grenouille was much more fitting, or Daniel; maybe even Le Cirque.

Not that he was particularly fond of French food. His taste ran more to burgers and onion rings.

But most women, he'd discovered, enjoyed being extravagantly wined and dined. He had dated plenty of women, been infatuated with many, though not in love. Now, on the heels of his latest failed relationship, a disillusioned Mack had finally reached the conclusion that when it came to dating, it was a big mistake to go all-out from the very beginning. He was only setting up those women—and himself—for disappointment down the road, when his finances, not to mention his energy and his emotions, would inevitably be depleted.

He'd met Chelsea Kamm back in December, when he was Christmas shopping at Saks on his lunch hour. She was browsing the silk scarves as an attractive salesgirl helped

Mack pick one out for his sister. When she stepped away momentarily, Chelsea leaned in and said, "That's not really for your sister, is it?"

Startled by the question, he looked up and found himself looking at one of the most beautiful women he'd ever seen.

"I thought you were an angel, standing there," he later told her. Bathed in the glow of thousands of white twinkle lights, everything about her—from her white blond hair to her porcelain skin to her ivory cashmere coat—seemed ethereal.

"Sure it's for my sister," he told her. "Why?"

"I thought you were just saying that because you were trying to hook up with the salesgirl and you didn't want her to know you were shopping for a girlfriend. Or your wife."

"If you knew me, you'd know that I would never do that," he said. "I'm a lousy liar."

"So you really do have a sister?"

"Yup."

"What about a wife?"

"Nope. Not even a girlfriend."

"Kids?"

"Not unless you count Marcus." He explained about the eighteen-year-old he'd met a few years ago through his volunteer work with the Big Brother organization. Marcus had graduated from high school in June, enlisted in the army, and just sent a Christmas card saying he'd finished basic training in Kentucky and was about to head overseas.

"I'm not counting Marcus," Chelsea said.

He got her phone number on the spot, and they went out for almost three months—"out" being the operative word. Fancy restaurants, exclusive nightclubs on New Year's Eve and Valentine's Day, a couple of ski weekends in Vermont . . . his idea, all of it. Really, he only had himself to blame.

The whirlwind got the better of him when a cold snap set in just as the stress level at the office heated up. All Mack wanted to do on February weekends was curl up on the couch with a movie and takeout; Chelsea didn't see why they couldn't fly off to the Caribbean.

"No better R&R than that," she crooned, resting her red-manicured fingertips on the sleeve of his suit coat.

"I'm exhausted, Chelsea, and I'm broke."

"I'm exhausted, too, and I'm more broke than you are. I really need you to take me away for a few days. Come on." Her fingers tightened on his arm, and he cringed as if they were bloody talons, finally acknowledging that his first impression of her had been wrong. She was no angel.

Whatever he said next—later, he didn't even recall what it was—launched the fight that resulted in her ceremoniously deleting every trace of him from her Palm Pilot and cell phone, thus ending the relationship.

Looking back and dissecting it, he knew he probably should have realized at the very beginning—when he bought his sister a silk scarf and Chelsea treated herself to a couple of them, same pattern, different shades of blue—that she had expensive taste and a petulant, self-indulgent streak. Those were her fatal flaws.

His own was that he'd always been a sucker for glamorous, statuesque blondes.

"What guy isn't?" his friend Ben asked, when the relationship was on the verge of crashing and burning a few weeks ago.

"Randi"—she was Ben's wife—"isn't a glamorous, statuesque blonde."

"I didn't say you should marry them. Just that I get why you want to date them. Don't beat yourself up, Mack. You're only human."

"I'm a walking cliché—and I'm dating one."

"So what are you going to do about that? Dump her and only go out with mousy, unassuming brunettes from now on?"

"Maybe."

He couldn't think of a better description for Carrie—or a reason not to give her a chance.

Of course, it wasn't just that he was open to a new type of woman when he met her last Tuesday night. Having learned hours earlier that his mother was dying, he was spiraling; she unwittingly wandered into his path, broke his emotional freefall.

In the days since, he'd found himself forcing his thoughts to go to her when they wanted to wander someplace darker. Forcing himself, too, as the weekend approached, to take out her number and dial it—to make a date, because that was what he usually did on Friday or Saturday nights, and he wanted some semblance of normalcy in the face of tragedy.

Or maybe he really was just lonely and isolated in his grief, wanting someone to talk to, selfish as that might be. Someone who would listen.

For the first time in his life, he was at a loss as to where else he might turn to find that human connection.

Not Ben, close as they were. It was one thing to confide in him about women, or work. But Ben had recently been promoted: he was no longer just Mack's friend and colleague; he was also his manager.

You don't cry on your boss's shoulder.

Mack would have to tell Ben about his mother eventually—he would need time off to be with her. But not just yet, when his emotions were so raw that he wasn't sure he could get through a conversation about his looming tragedy without breaking down.

There were other friends, too, of course—friends who were always happy to share a couple of beers or watch a ball game. But guys—at least, these guys—didn't summon each other to pour out their personal problems.

Nor could he turn to his father or his sister or brother-in-law, or even the dozens of aunts, uncles, and cousins back in Jersey. Some were closer to him than others, but they were all facing the same loss and seeking the same solace. He didn't want to commiserate. He wanted to make sense of what was happening, or forget that it was happening, or maybe he just wanted to purge.

Sometimes, when you needed someone, only a perfect stranger would do. Rather, a decidedly imperfect stranger.

Carrie had nice brown hair, pleasant features, and a decent figure that, when you added them all up, fell far short of beautiful, and even somewhat short of pretty.

But something about her appealed to him. She had struck him, Tuesday night, as—maybe not lonely. More like . . . alone. Isolated. Maybe not by choice. She was new here, probably didn't have a lot of friends. Even if nothing came of it . . . he decided to see her again.

"Hi," he'd said when he called on Friday afternoon, "it's Mack. From the park. And the walk. The other night."

Another woman—a woman for whom flirting was second nature—might have quipped, in return, "Hi, Mack from the park and the walk the other night."

Not Carrie. She just said, "Hi."

That was fine with him. He wasn't feeling flirty himself, and not in the mood to make small talk, so he got right to the point. "Do you want to get together tomorrow night? Are you busy?"

"No. I'm . . . not busy."

Her stilted response made him wonder if he was making a mistake, but he forged on. "So do you want to?"

"That would be nice," she said. "Where do you want me to meet you?"

That she didn't assume he was going to come to her doorstep to escort her, hand on elbow, was so refreshing—and such a relief—that it didn't strike him as unusual at the time.

Only now, when he walked into McSorley's and looked around for her, did it occur to him that she might have wanted to give herself an out. Or that she might not have wanted him to see where she lived, for whatever reason. Maybe she was destitute, or super-wealthy, or married . . .

Not immediately spotting her, his mind raced through the possibilities.

He was right on time. Was she on her way, maybe running a little late?

Had she stood him up?

Taken one look around this place and fled?

With Saint Patrick's Day looming, the legendary Irish pub was raucous and even more crowded than usual. Nearly all the patrons were male; most of them guzzling dark or light ale from glass mugs, shouting at each other and the bartenders above the music and the other patrons who were shouting at each other and the bartenders. Those who weren't shouting or sipping were feasting on the bar's signature dish: wedges of orange cheese and raw onion served with saltines and hot mustard.

Adding a visual note of chaos to the cacophony, a hodgepodge of paraphernalia—mugs, caps, framed vintage photographs and clippings—cluttered the walls all the way up to the high dark plank ceiling.

What the hell are you doing, Mack, inviting a girl here on a first date?

Trying to prove a point—to himself, and to her.

The point being: *Don't get your hopes up. This is as good as it gets, so take it or leave it.*

Who'd blame her if she'd already left?

But she hadn't. Suddenly, he spotted her, sitting alone at a table in the back. No, it was more that he *recognized* her. He'd seen her and glanced right past her at first, not realizing it was she, because she looked . . . again, not beautiful. She wasn't beautiful. But now he saw that she was actually pretty.

Her hair was loose and she was wearing makeup, and a navy blue sweater with jeans—not tight, but her clothes hugged her figure in a flattering way. But she wasn't trying too hard. No, she was as unpretentious as the place he'd so deliberately chosen for their first date, and for him, tonight, it worked.

Gazing at the chalkboard menu, she didn't seem to see him as he made his way across the sawdust floor, enveloped in the familiar scent of beer and the lively chatter, and the familiar opening strains of one of his favorite U2 songs playing in the background.

He made his way past a group of drunken former frat boys, swaying arm-in-arm. On another night, Mack might have been right there with the likes of them, sing-chanting the familiar lyrics. *But I still . . . haven't found . . . what I'm looking for.*

Not tonight, though.

Tonight—he had a feeling he might have found it.

Another Saturday night and I ain't got nobody . . .

The lyrics of the old Cat Stevens cover ran through Allison's head as she climbed the steps of her Hudson Street apartment building, holding an open umbrella in one hand and in the other, carrying a paper-in-plastic bag of Chinese takeout and a rented Blockbuster video.

The movies had been pretty picked over at this hour on a Saturday night—to get the new releases, you really had to show up before the start of the weekend. But she'd gone out with friends from work last night, and she was supposed to have a date tonight—a blind date with a biologist named Justin, who was a cousin of a friend of a friend.

He'd called to cancel last night, saying something had come up and he'd get back to her.

He hadn't yet, but she was hoping he would. He'd sounded nice and casual and normal on the phone, as promised by his cousin and her friend's friend. In general, she wasn't entirely comfortable with blind dates, but they seemed to be a necessary evil when you worked long hours in an industry that suffered a perpetual shortage of straight, eligible men.

So here she was, spending yet another rainy March weekend alone, trying to get the old song out of her head because it reminded her of her father, who'd constantly played that ancient *Cat Stevens Greatest Hits* cassette on the tape deck in his car.

" 'Another Saturday Night' was Stevens's remake of an oldie by Sam Cooke. It was released in 1974, the year I met your mother," he would tell her. "That was a great year for music. Here, listen to another one from that year."

Then he'd play Harry Chapin's "Cat's in the Cradle," and they'd sing all the lyrics together.

And the cat's in the cradle and the silver spoon . . .

She loved that song.

Then, anyway.

After he was gone, she couldn't bear to hear it.

When you comin' home, Dad? I don't know when . . .

Yeah. She'd hated that song for years now.

At the top of the stoop, Allison shifted the umbrella to feel in her pocket for her keys, and raindrops spilled down her cheeks like tears.

Another Saturday night and I ain't got nobody . . .

But on a raw, blustery night like this, she'd just as soon stay home. She'd been hoping to rent a good scary movie like *The Sixth Sense*, but it wasn't out yet on video, and she'd already seen *Stir of Echoes*, the only other recent thriller they had in stock. So she'd settled on a romantic comedy, deciding she might as well live vicariously through Julia Roberts. It wouldn't be the first time.

And she wouldn't be the only one, according to Luis, who was a huge Julia fan.

"What woman wouldn't want to be Julia? I would if I were a woman."

"You mean, you'd want to be the characters she plays," Allison told him. "Although—that's probably the same thing."

"Not at all. Julia is an amazing actress, Allison. She's going to win an Oscar one of these days. You mark my words."

"Yeah, sure, Luis. I wouldn't hold my breath for that if I were you."

Finding her keys, Allison quickly unlocked the door. As she stepped into the vestibule of her building, she heard someone call her name from the street behind her.

"Hold the door!" Her upstairs neighbor, Kristina Haines, came hurrying along the shiny wet sidewalk, *sans* umbrella. Her dark, wet curls were wind-blown and her cheeks were bright red from the chill. Her coat was open, as usual, and she was wearing her waitressing uniform: white blouse, black slacks, and black sneakers.

"Thanks!" Kristina took the steps two at a time as Allison stood waiting for her. "I forgot my key!"

It wasn't the first time for that, either. "Is Ray home?"

"He's supposed to be—when I left for work he said he was staying in all night—but I've been calling and no one's picking up."

That didn't surprise Allison. Kristina's live-in boyfriend didn't strike her as the most trustworthy guy in the world—not that she'd offer that opinion to Kristina. They were friends, but not the kind that shared deep, dark secrets. Allison had never really had—or wanted—a friend like that. Luis was becoming one, but she even held him at arm's length most of the time.

"What are you doing home from work already?"

"Slow night," Kristina told her, huffing a little as she reached the top step, "and Maury—he's the manager—asked if anyone wanted to leave. I volunteered because I figured Ray was home, but who the hell knows where he went? He's not picking up his cell, either."

"You can come hang out with me until he gets back, if you want," Allison told her. "I've got lo mein and a movie."

"Sounds fascinating. Which movie?"

Allison held up the video in its blue and white Blockbuster box.

"*Runaway Bride*?" Kristina read off the label. "It was okay. Not great. I saw it in the theater last summer on my first date with Ray. I knew that night he was The One."

Yeah, well, you might want to rethink that, Allison wanted to tell her. Hopefully, Kristina would figure that out for herself.

"But I'll watch it again," she went on, "because it beats sitting here on the steps for God knows how long, waiting for Ray to come home and let me into the apartment."

"Maybe you should give me a spare set of keys," Allison suggested. "In case this happens again."

"That's probably a good idea. And you can give me your keys, too, in case it happens to you."

"Sure," Allison agreed, though she knew it wouldn't happen to her. Growing up, she'd learned to be responsible at an early age. Her mother was the one who frequently forgot her keys—although there was one night when she was so high that Allison had actually deliberately locked her out.

That was early on, after her father left, when she still thought that anything she said or did could make a difference in her mother's behavior. Eventually, she realized that there was no reasoning with an addict, and, ultimately, resigned herself to the fact that her mother wasn't long for this world.

Things would have been different if her father hadn't left. Mom wasn't straight, by any means, before that—in fact, Allison assumed her drug use was the reason her father had walked away.

What about me, Daddy? I didn't do anything wrong. How could you just leave me?

Because he was obviously a coldhearted SOB. She'd just somehow never grasped that while he was around. Which, even when he lived with them, wasn't much. He worked as a long-haul trucker and was gone for weeks at a time. Sometimes when he came back, he'd bring little gifts for Allison and her mother: salt water taffy from the East Coast, tiny vials of gold flakes from a river out West . . .

Allison was torn between longing to see him and dreading his homecomings, because when her parents were together, they often fought. About what, she couldn't even remember. Everything, probably. Shouting, tears, slaps, slammed doors. A couple of times, one or the other would take off in the car, tires squealing, then come crawling back in the morning to beg forgiveness. Not from Allison—from each other. Nobody ever apologized to her.

Once her father was gone for good, her mother's habit spiraled out of control, devouring every shred of normalcy in their lives. Allison was angry at her some of the time— how could she not be?—but mostly, she just felt sorry for her. For both of them, her mother and herself; they were victims.

It was her father who infuriated her, more and more as time went on. She'd channeled her anger toward him, while every ounce of compassion she possessed went to her mom.

For her brother, Brett, she had only indifference.

He was so much older than Allison. Far too old to be a playmate, but not old enough to become, or perhaps just not interested in becoming, a father figure to his little sister. By the time she was in high school, he was married with children of his own, living on his in-laws' farm way out in Hayes Township. When Mom died, he'd offered to have Allison come live with him and his wife, Cindy-Lou, but she had no interest in doing that. She only wanted to finish high school in Centerfield, then leave Nebraska behind and never look back.

That was exactly what she did. It meant leaving her brother behind as well, but even now, she didn't miss him. She just missed the idea of having a family somewhere.

Luis—who came from a large, close-knit family here in New York—was convinced that one day, when she married and had children of her own, she'd want to reconnect with her brother. "You know, for old times' sake."

When Allison explained that there were no shared fond memories to speak of, he said, "For your future children's sake, then. Just so they'll know that you came from somewhere. You know what I mean?"

"Yes, but . . . I'm not proud of where I come from."

"Nebraska? Come on, it couldn't have been *that* bad."

"It's not about *where* I grew up. It's about *how*."

"We all have skeletons in our closets."

Maybe. But it was much easier to just try to forget.

"You'll change your mind someday," Luis predicted. "You'll see."

Maybe. But in the here and now, it was hard enough to fathom ever wanting to go back there—let alone to even imagine being married, with children.

If that ever does happen, Allison thought, *if I ever am lucky enough to have a family of my own, I'll never make the mistakes my parents made. I'll never take my husband and children for granted. I'll be there for them, and I'll hold on tight, no matter what, because nothing in this world is more precious than family.*

Back home alone at her apartment, Carrie paced well into the wee hours.

Not because her date with Mack hadn't gone well. It had gone very well, actually, from the moment he'd complimented her on her appearance to the moment he'd kissed her good night as she got into a cab.

In between, he'd done most of the talking over a couple of beers—well, maybe more than a couple for him, but just one for her, and a shared platter of fries. He talked about his big, close-knit Irish family, mostly. But about his last girlfriend as well. The one who, Carrie gathered, hadn't been a very good listener.

Chelsea. Chelsea Kamm. That was her name.

She was blond, he mentioned—and attractive, Carrie imagined, though he didn't come right out and say it. Oh, and she worked in the fashion industry.

He revealed that detail, like the others, in passing.

Carrie's heart skipped a beat. "What does she do?" she asked, trying to sound casual. "In fashion?"

"She's a merchandise assistant for a showroom."

"Really? Which one?"

He had to think about it, and though she didn't press him, it was all she could do not to give away just how important it was to her that he remember. When he did come up with the information, the designer's name was slightly off—though close enough for Carrie to figure out which one he was talking about. It was one of the showrooms she'd called looking for Allison.

Allison, who was also blond and attractive and worked in the fashion industry.

Carrie couldn't help but be struck by the coincidence. They weren't talking about Allison, but somehow, as the conversation went on, the two women began to mesh in her head: Mack's pushy, selfish ex-girlfriend, and Allison, who, she became certain, possessed the same unpleasant characteristics.

Now, as she paced the length of her living room—which took all of four steps—and back again, she clenched her hands and her jaw, resenting the woman. Both women.

Allison. Chelsea. She muttered their names to herself, between counting steps: across—"One, two, three, four . . ."—

and back—"one, two, three, four. Allison . . . Chelsea . . .
Chelsea . . . Allison . . ."

"Do you miss her?" she had asked Mack.

"Chelsea?"

Chelsea . . . ? Yes. Of course, Chelsea. That was whom
they were talking about. Chelsea, not Allison.

"Not anymore," Mack said. "It was one of those things
where we had nothing in common at all, no mutual friends.
I have no problem with the fact that I'm never going to see
her again."

"What if you run into her?"

"I won't," Mack said with a firm nod.

No, Carrie thought now, her eyes narrowed. *Probably not.
But I might . . .*

Chapter Six

"So I had this date Saturday night," Mack told Ben, as he used his chopsticks to scoop up a dab of green wasabi paste and deposited it into his rectangular little bowl of soy sauce.

Ben looked up from his own sushi with interest. "You had this date with . . . ?"

"That woman I met last week, in the park."

"*What* woman you met last week in the park?"

"The one I told you about. She wasn't my type . . ."

"Right. The mousy brunette. So you asked her out?"

"I told you. This is my new MO. I want someone who likes me for me."

"Oh, yeah, that's right. You want a mousy brunette. So was she?"

"Not all that mousy." Mack stirred the wasabi into the soy sauce. "She was kind of cute."

"And did she?"

"What?"

"Like you for you?"

"She seemed to."

"So you're seeing her again, then?" Ben asked, and popped a piece of maki into his mouth.

"I called her yesterday and invited her to the Knicks-Lakers game with us."

He and Ben had scored four courtside tickets, courtesy of a grateful client. Ben's wife, Randi, was coming, and Mack figured Carrie would be happy to join them.

Wrong.

"That's cool," Ben said. "Randi will like having another girl around."

"She said no."

"What? Is she nuts? Did she not get the part about the seats being courtside?"

"I guess she doesn't like basketball."

"Tell her Randi doesn't, either. She just likes to hire a sitter and get out of the house."

Ben and Randi had a toddler daughter, Lexi, who was quite a handful now that she'd reached the Terrible Twos.

"I don't know . . . I really don't think Carrie wants to come." Mack hesitated, wondering if he should confess to Ben that she'd seemed somewhat interested until he mentioned that his friend and his wife would be there, too.

"Maybe we can just go out to dinner instead," Carrie had suggested.

"The four of us?" he asked dubiously, knowing there was no way Ben would give up the chance to see the Knicks-Lakers courtside. It would have to be a different night.

"No—the two of us. I mean . . . I don't know your friends, so . . ."

And she didn't want to know them. He could hear it in her voice.

Maybe it was just too soon to double date. But at least she did want to see him again.

It would still have to be a different night. Mack—who also wasn't willing to give up the courtside opportunity—

arranged to see Carrie on Friday instead. She seemed okay with that.

But was Mack okay with it? After he hung up, he wasn't so sure.

Ben wasn't, either, when Mack explained the situation. "She doesn't want to meet me and Randi? What's up with that?"

"Maybe she's heard about you guys," Mack cracked half-heartedly.

Ben didn't smile.

"Maybe she just wants me all to herself. What woman wouldn't?"

Still not playing into the quip, Ben said, "Just watch yourself, Mack. Don't go latching on to some girl just because . . . well, you know. You're vulnerable right now." Mack had told Ben about his mother just now, as they walked from a sales call to the restaurant. He couldn't avoid it: his sister, Lynn, had called his cell phone, upset because of something one of the hospice nurses had said about getting Mom's affairs in order.

Lynn was in denial.

Maybe Mack was, too, on some level.

"You're going through a rough time," Ben went on, chopsticks poised above his sushi. "Maybe you shouldn't get involved with anyone right now. Maybe you should take a break from dating, you know, until . . ."

He knew his friend was just worried about him, but Mack found himself bristling at the implication that he wasn't fully in control.

"You and your breaks," he told Ben, who was always giving up something or other. Last year, he'd taken an entire week off from eating Italian food, and just the other day he'd announced that he was giving up reading newspapers for at least a month because the headlines only depressed him.

"Sometimes taking a break from something is a good idea, Mack."

He moodily dunked a hunk of raw yellowtail, sending soy sauce splashing over the edge of the bowl.

"Mack."

"Yeah." He didn't look at Ben.

"You okay?"

"I'm fine."

It was the same thing his mother had said yesterday afternoon, when he'd caught her just before she fell while trying to get from the couch to the bathroom.

"Just tripped on that old rug again. I'm fine," she said with a grin.

She hadn't meant it any more than he did now, but in his family, that was what you did. You showed your brave face to the rest of the world, and you carried on, no matter what. Even in the face of death, you had to live and laugh and love.

Love.

Someone to love, someone who loved you—a spouse, children . . .

In the end, that was what everyone wanted, wasn't it? That was what mattered most in life.

No, now was not the time for Mack to put his love life on hold. Quite the opposite, in fact.

Yes, he was going out with Carrie again. The sooner, the better.

Chelsea Kamm wasn't particularly superstitious, but today had been a lousy day—the worst she'd had in a long time. It started when she got out of bed with a raging migraine, and things went downhill from there, right through the end of the workday, when she got an ink smudge on her white silk blouse while changing the toner on the copy machine.

"It's no coincidence," she told her friend Tiffany, the showroom's receptionist, as they waited for the elevator to carry them down two floors to the lobby, "that it's the thirteenth."

"But it's not Friday."

"It's Monday. That's worse. I hate Mondays."

Let's face it, she thought, impatiently punching the lit down button again, *I'm not a big fan of* any *weekday.*

Weekdays, unfortunately, meant work. And work was no fun at all. She had no interest in a career of any sort, not even in fashion. But at least this job came with perks—the samples were divine—and besides, a girl had to support herself until the right guy came along and whisked her off to enjoy the good life.

Which reminded her . . .

"I was wondering," she said to Tiffany, "if I could borrow your new green Dior on Friday for a date."

They were the same size—two—and build, although Tiffany, at five-seven, was a couple of inches shorter and her blond hair was a brighter, brassier shade. Chelsea often wondered why she didn't ask her colorist to tone it down, but of course, Chelsea wasn't about to suggest it. She and Tiffany often went out on the town together, and Chelsea obviously had the edge as the more attractive of the two.

"You want to *borrow* my *Dior*?" Tiffany shook her brassy blond head. "You're kidding, right?"

"Please?"

"I've only worn it once!"

"But Andrew is taking me out and I want to wear something special—and it's Saint Patrick's Day, and the dress is green, and it would be perfect. Please?"

"Who's Andrew? Wait—is he the guy from the other night who asked us if we were sisters?"

"Yeah." Of course, lots of guys asked them that. Sometimes—if they thought it would get them free drinks or entry to the VIP room—they said yes. But only if they were sure they never wanted to see the guy again.

Saturday night, Chelsea had quickly said no, she and Tiffany weren't sisters. Andrew was a class act, and she knew from the moment she heard his last name—one she'd encountered before, carved into granite high above the entrance of a century-old building—that she definitely wanted to see him again.

Now she had a date with him, and she really wanted to wear that green Dior. It would look better on her than it did on Tiffany, anyway, because it was so short, and she had longer legs.

But Tiffany shook her head vehemently. "I don't think so."

Before Chelsea could protest, a dinging bell signaled the elevator's arrival. They curtailed the conversation, wedging themselves into the tiny space filled with office workers from the three floors above.

The elevator resumed its halting descent. Too jammed up against the door and the person next to her to even bend her head to look down, Chelsea felt around in her purse for her pack of Salems.

Craving nicotine had contributed to her lousy day—and to every lousy day ever since smoking had been forbidden in the office. She wondered what it would be like to make all the rules, like you would if you owned the building—well, if your husband's family owned it. Not this dingy, damp old place in the garment district, either, but a sweeping, historic skyscraper on Park Avenue—or was it Fifth? She couldn't remember. She only knew that she'd walked past the building that bore Andrew's last name plenty of times, and that it meant his family had the big bucks and Manhattan pedigree she sought in a man. Marrying him would mean happily-ever-after, for sure.

To think she'd wasted any time on someone like James MacKenna. The guy misled her from the start, letting her think that he had money to burn. She should have known better. She knew his suits were off the rack, not custom, from the first time she saw him that day in Saks. But he was cute, and funny, and nice to her—and by the time she figured out that he was just some Irish guy from New Jersey, she'd fallen for him.

To be fair, she was from Jersey, too—not that she went around admitting it to anyone. As she told Mack, she'd sooner jump off the George Washington Bridge than she would cross it to get home. The same went for the Brooklyn and Queensboro bridges, and all the rest. She'd never live in a borough, either. She'd never live anyplace other than Manhattan. But never with a guy who'd grown up in Jersey.

She was glad she'd never mentioned to anyone—not even Tiffany—that she was seeing Mack. It was that much easier—and oh, so satisfying—to delete him completely from her life. She did it right in front of him—erasing every trace of him from her Palm Pilot, and telling him never to call her again.

He hadn't. Good riddance.

The elevator doors opened and she stepped out into the small lobby and headed toward the door to the street.

"Night, ladies," called the young security guard, Ralph, predictably. He was always checking out Chelsea and Tiffany, acting all friendly, as if they'd ever give him the time of day. He looked like he'd stepped off the set of a seventies porn movie, with that thick dark mustache and sideburns and a pair of slightly tinted aviator glasses.

Ignoring Ralph as usual, Chelsea said, "Tiff, please, if you lend me the dress, I'll—"

"No way," Tiffany said. "I'm wearing it to my cousin's wedding."

"When is that?"

"May."

"May? I'll give it back to you Sunday."

"It would have to be cleaned, and—"

"So I'll have it cleaned. It'll be back next week. Plenty of time for May."

"No. Stop asking."

They stepped through the revolving doors, and Chelsea pulled a cigarette from her pack. Tiffany, who'd quit smoking when the building outlawed it, kept on walking.

Bitch, Chelsea thought, giving up on the dress conversation. For now.

As she lit her cigarette, she noticed that a woman on the sidewalk had stopped Tiffany to ask her something. Her friend shook her head, turned, and pointed in Chelsea's direction. Then she gave a quick wave at Chelsea and walked on.

Chelsea didn't wave back, still pissed about the Dior.

The woman approached as Chelsea tucked her lighter back into her bag. "Excuse me . . ."

She was frumpy-looking, in a sensible winter coat that could have used a dry cleaning, tan pantyhose, and pumps. Her long brown hair was pulled back into a dime store clip and she wasn't wearing a hint of makeup.

"Are you Chelsea?"

"Why?"

"I heard you worked in this building, and I work right across the street, and I just wanted to say hi."

"Do I know you?" Chelsea coolly regarded the stranger through a satisfying, menthol-flavored fog.

"A long time ago. We went to school together."

"Really? What's your name?" she asked, not really caring. School had been a long time ago, and on the wrong side of the Hudson River, and was not something she liked to look back on. She remembered very few people from that era— and not many were females.

"Sue."

There had been a lot of girls named Sue. Chelsea didn't

know which one this was, and she wasn't interested in asking.

"Well," she said, and glanced west, down the block, toward the subway, "it was good to see you again."

"You too."

"I've got to run."

"Where are you living these days?" Sue asked, and something in her tone made Chelsea suddenly wary. She looked more closely at the woman and noted that she seemed oddly edgy—and then it hit her.

This woman was supposedly from her school days—yet she was calling her *Chelsea*?

She hadn't started using the name Chelsea Kamm until after graduation, when she moved out on her own. Before that, she was Janice Kaminsky. Granted, she'd never officially changed her name, but if someone from the old days somehow recognized her, they wouldn't call her Chelsea. Just as no one from her new life would know she'd once been Janice.

"Sue . . . which Sue did you say you were?" she asked, eyes narrowed.

"Sue Calvert." The name that rolled readily off her tongue didn't ring a bell. No surprise there.

Was Sue one of the girls Chelsea had made fun of back in the day? Had she somehow tracked her down, figured out who she was now? Or . . . was she just making that up about school?

Was she someone's jealous ex-wife? Or . . . *wife*?

Chelsea was pretty sure Mack hadn't been married, but there were plenty of other men in her recent past—including Andrew—whom she wasn't so sure about.

Unpleasantly unnerved, Chelsea said, "I have to get going," and without another word, turned on her heel and walked off down the block.

Good riddance, Sue . . . or whoever you are.

But she had the distinct feeling that she was being followed. Just before she reached the corner, she looked back.

She didn't see Sue. That was a good sign. She breathed easier, all the way to the subway.

But as she wedged herself into a jam-packed train minutes later, she could have sworn she glimpsed Sue's face in the crowd on the platform as they made their way into the next car. And again, in the Fourteenth Street station when she changed trains.

Maybe she was just paranoid.

Maybe not.

Whatever. Even if, by chance, she was someone Chelsea had wronged in the past—perhaps by sleeping with her husband . . .

So what? What's she going to do about it? Kill me?

"It's called Google," Luis told Allison, standing behind her as she sat at her desk with her fingers poised on the computer keyboard.

"Google?" she echoed. "That sounds like a kid's toy."

"Well, it's not. It's a search engine, and it'll come back with information on anything you type in. Go ahead. Go to www.google.com . . ."

She did, and as they sat waiting for the screen to load, she said, "I'm telling you, you're wrong. This is crazy."

"And I'm telling you *you're* wrong. But I guess we'll find out now, won't we."

She rolled her eyes and looked pointedly at her watch. "I really have to get going home. It's getting late."

"You can go, as soon as we resolve this."

This, of course, being yet another friendly little squabble with Luis. It had all started when she heard him singing, falsetto, along with the radio in his cubicle. He always turned it up at the end of the workday, after the bosses were gone.

The search engine screen popped up, and Luis commanded, "Type in the song title."

She did.

"Wait . . . before you hit enter, type in the word 'lyrics.'"

"'Every Breath You Take' . . . lyrics," she read aloud. "Now what?"

"Hit enter." He leaned closer, resting his chin on his shoulder, to see the results as they came up.

Allison raised an eyebrow when she saw all the hits, and clicked on the top one. Moments later, she was saying triumphantly, "See? Sting is saying, 'My poor heart aches,' not 'I'm a pool hall ace'! I told you so!"

"Well, he should learn to enunciate if he's going to be a singer," Luis grumbled. "It sounds exactly like 'pool hall ace.'"

"But that doesn't make sense."

"This is the guy who wrote 'De Do Do Do, De Da Da Da,' Allison." Luis shook his head. "I've got to get going. I'm late for a date."

"Where? At a pool hall, Ace?"

"Funny. You're funny."

Alone again in her cubicle, Allison reached for the mouse to shut down the computer.

Luis was right about one thing: this Google search engine was pretty good. It worked fast, and it was accurate.

"You can use it to find anything," he'd told her.

Anything . . . and anyone?

Allison used the mouse to click back to the search box, then hesitated, staring at the blinking cursor.

After a moment, she typed in her father's name.

Hit enter.

Somehow, she couldn't seem to make her fingers move to the key.

Go ahead. Just to see what will come up.

What if nothing did?

What if something did?

What, exactly, did she want to know about him? That he was living happily ever after without her? That he wasn't living at all?

After her mother died, her brother, Brett, said he was going to try to find their father. Allison told him that if he did, she didn't want to know about it. She never wanted to hear his name again.

She stared at it on the screen for another long moment. Then she reached for the mouse and, with a single, decisive click, closed out of the search engine.

After all these weeks—months—of fruitless searching, Carrie savored the sweet taste of triumph at last.

Standing in the shadow outside the glow of a streetlamp on a narrow side street off West Broadway, she gazed up at the four-story brick building. Five minutes ago, *she* had unlocked the door and disappeared inside.

Now I know where she works and *lives.*

Finding out had been almost too easy. After calling in sick to Cantor Fitzgerald this morning, Carrie had disguised herself in a long, dark wig, put on the old winter coat she hadn't gotten around to donating to charity, and taken the subway down to West Thirty-sixth Street. She'd been hoping to waltz right into the building that housed the designer's showroom, but a security guard was posted in the tiny lobby.

Ralph. That was his name. Friendly guy, though in a leering kind of way. Under other circumstances, that might have made Carrie feel uncomfortable—not just because his dark mustache, sideburns, and retro glasses reminded her of her father—but she used his smarmy interest to her advantage.

Ralph was happy to help her, for a price.

Fifty bucks richer, he agreed to signal Carrie when Chelsea appeared in the lobby at the end of the day.

That, he did. But clumsily.

From her perch on the sidewalk outside the building, she saw him motioning at two blond women. But which of them was Chelsea Kamm?

For a moment, she was so enraged at Ralph that she almost allowed the women to slip past her. But she could deal with him later, she realized, and forced herself to focus on identifying Chelsea.

As luck would have it, Carrie approached the wrong woman first, which left her feeling rattled when she approached the right woman—even more so when Chelsea's standoffishness hindered the conversation's flow.

She's a bitch, Carrie decided, when Chelsea turned and walked away. *I hate her. She didn't deserve Mack—and she deserved . . .*

Well, time would tell what she deserved.

At least now, Carrie knew where she lived. Not because Chelsea had played nice and told her, but because Carrie had followed her downtown on the subway. Once, she thought Chelsea might have spotted her, and she quickly ducked behind a conveniently located, grossly overweight man until the coast was clear again.

Now, as she stood gazing up at the building, knowing she was in there someplace, Carrie couldn't help but smile.

You did it!

You found her!

She closed her eyes, picturing the look of surprised recognition—and horror—she would see on the blonde's face if they met again, under decidedly less pleasant circumstances . . .

No.

Wait a minute.

Carrie's eyes snapped open again.

This is Chelsea, she told herself. *Remember? Chelsea lives here. Not Allison.*

You found Chelsea.

It was still a victory. Yes, a temporary one—but somehow, it made it easier to swallow that she had yet to find Allison.

I will, though. I'll savor the thrill of the chase, but sooner or later I'll find her.

In the meantime, Chelsea would be good practice.

So, she thought as she reached into her pocket, pulling out a slip of paper, *will you.*

On it were the words "Call me," followed by a phone number and a name: *Ralph.*

Chapter Seven

There weren't many perks to being a lobby security guard in a commercial building in the garment district.

Ralph didn't get hefty Christmas tips from well-heeled tenants, like his friend Carlos, who was a doorman at a fancy co-op building on the Upper East Side. And, unlike Carlos, he didn't get to see movie stars coming and going at all hours of the day—and night, with people who *weren't* their equally famous spouses, yet another opportunity for Carlos to pocket a nice tip: hush money, he called it.

"If you want," Carlos had offered not long ago, "I'll see if I can get you a job in one of the buildings up here."

"That's okay. I'm happy where I am."

"How is that possible?"

Ralph just shrugged. He didn't like change of any kind. That was why, at thirty-one, he still lived with his widowed mother; that was why he hadn't yet proposed to Juliana, his girlfriend of five years. Well, mostly why.

Ralph couldn't wait to tell Carlos his latest news: that he had finally gotten a nice little chunk of change a few days ago, for two seconds' worth of work. And now, it looked like he was about to receive an unexpected added bonus.

"Yeah, sure," he told the woman who'd just called his cell phone out of the blue. "I remember you. Sue, right?"

"That's right. You said to call, so . . . I'm calling."

He'd been surprised, yesterday, when she asked for his number after he agreed to help her out. She hadn't struck him as the type of woman who might do that.

It just went to show that you never know.

Maybe he was going to get laid this week after all. With Juliana visiting family down in Puerto Rico through the nineteenth, he hadn't been counting on that.

"I thought maybe we could meet for a drink or something," Sue said.

"Sure. Name the time and place."

She did—so readily that he couldn't help but smile.

Sorry, honey, he told Juliana silently. *But I told you not to leave for so long. When the cat's away, the mouse will play.*

"**A**llison? Ready to go?"

She jumped and turned to see Luis standing behind her in his Armani overcoat, his black leather messenger bag— which she liked to call his man purse—slung over his shoulder.

"What? What time is it?"

"Time to go." Taking in her blank expression, he added, "It's Tuesday night. Parsons. Accessory class. *Helloo-oo?* You're a million miles away, aren't you?"

More like fifteen hundred.

Nebraska.

Was it time to plug it into the new search engine Luis had shown her yesterday, along with her father's name?

All day, she'd been tempted—but too busy to do anything about it. Finally, as her colleagues had begun to power down their computers, turn off their cubicle desk lights, and trickle toward the elevator banks, she had opened Google.

For the last fifteen minutes she'd been sitting here, staring at the blinking cursor.

"I just have to finish one last thing for Loriana," she told Luis. "Give me five minutes, okay?"

He sighed. "You have two. I don't want to be late. I'll be in the lobby flirting with Henry," he added, referring to the amiable Rastafarian who manned the security desk.

Left alone once again with the search engine, Allison told herself it was now or never.

Not never . . . *there's always tomorrow.*

That was what she'd told herself yesterday. And after a largely sleepless night, tomorrow became today, and she promised herself she'd get it over with.

Now she had two minutes to find out whether her father was dead or alive.

She began typing.

Allen . . . Taylor . . . Centerfield, Nebraska.

After a long moment, she hit enter and waited.

Mack stubbed out his cigarette with his heel on the sidewalk outside his childhood home. He'd never smoked in front of his parents, and he wasn't about to start now.

Opening the front door, he heard barking dogs and the familiar theme music from his mother's favorite television game show. Was it that late already? He checked his watch and saw that it was past seven. He'd been planning to leave the office early enough to get to Hoboken for dinner, but it was too late for that; his parents always finished eating before *Jeopardy!* started.

"Who's that? Lynn?" his mother called as he stepped into the front hall.

"It's me, Mom." Mack locked the door behind him and

pocketed his keys, then stooped to greet Champ and Bruiser, former strays he'd rescued when he was a soft-hearted teenager and they were puppies. Wagging their tails and offering their heads to be patted, both mutts were aging and somewhat frail—par for the household, Mack thought grimly.

"Mack?" Mom sounded pleasantly surprised. "What are you doing here?"

"I thought I'd stop in on my way home to say hi." As he tossed his overcoat over the newel post at the foot of the stairs, he saw that the lower steps were cluttered with household items: a ShopRite bag that contained toilet paper rolls and tissue boxes, a stack of folded sheets, another of towels, a third of books and magazines.

"What's all that stuff on the stairs?" he asked, crossing through the archway into the living room, with its comfortable furniture and his mother's prized Irish lace curtains.

"It all needs to go up," his mother said, curled up beneath a quilt on the far end of the couch. Ordinarily, she'd already have been on her feet, hurrying over to hug her only son. And ordinarily, anything that had to go upstairs would have been brought upstairs immediately. Maggie MacKenna was a real hustler-bustler—as her husband liked to call her—when it came to housekeeping. When it came to everything.

But those days were over. Beneath the turban-style scarf wrapped around her bald head, her pale face was etched in exhaustion. And wedged into a corner of the room, where Mom kept her treadmill at an angle facing the TV—primed for her daily hour of exercise and *Oprah*—was a hospital bed.

The hospice team had delivered it early on, perhaps underestimating their patient's stamina—or perhaps just wanting to spare the family the difficult task of ordering it on the day it became apparent that Maggie could no longer get up and around the house.

None of the MacKennas had verbally acknowledged this

grim harbinger of what lay ahead. The bed was just there, all made up and ready.

Ready . . .

Mack couldn't even look at it. He wasn't ready. He would never be ready for this.

"I came downstairs for dinner and almost tripped and killed myself," his father reported from his recliner, turning down the volume on *Jeopardy!* as Champ and Bruiser settled themselves again on the rug.

"I can't run up and down the stairs all day, Brian."

"Nobody wants you to, Maggie. I told you to let me know whenever something needs to go up and I'll carry it. Whenever you need help with anything. That's what I'm here for."

Mack's mother rolled her lashless eyes and said to the ceiling, "I'm going to make him come running every five minutes? I don't think so."

"She doesn't like to ask for help," Mack's father told him. "That's her problem."

"And you do?" Mom was indignant. "He lost his wallet for two days last week and do you think he'd tell me so that I could find it for him?"

"You don't need to be running around the house looking, Maggie."

"I would have just told you to look in the glove compartment. That's where it's been the last three times you lost it. And that's where it was this time."

Mack sighed inwardly. The glove compartment—that reminded him that his father shouldn't be driving anymore. He and Lynn had agreed they'd have to do something about that.

Just last week, Lynn noticed his car's fender was dented and streaked with bright yellow paint and called Mack saying, "I think Dad might have hit a school bus, but he says he doesn't remember hitting anything at all."

A few days later, running errands for his parents, Mack figured out that it had probably been a yellow concrete post in the parking lot of the neighborhood CVS—but it *could* have been a school bus. Or a schoolchild.

He and Lynn needed to tell him he wasn't capable of driving anymore—their big, strong capable father. Brian MacKenna still looked the part—a sturdy-postured, broad-shouldered six-foot-one with a pile of dark hair on his head—but Alzheimer's was ravaging his brain the way cancer was ravaging Maggie's body.

Tonight, Brian was lucid. But last time Mack was here, his father thought he was one of the hospice workers. It wasn't until an hour into the visit that the light dawned in his blue eyes and he made it a point to work his son's name into every sentence, just to show that he wasn't clueless . . . until, eventually, he forgot again.

"I'll carry the stuff upstairs," Mack told his parents. "And I'll take out the garbage, too, before I go."

Brian shook his head. "You can't let it sit out at the curb for two days. The animals will tear it apart."

"Dad, this is Tuesday night. Tomorrow's Wednesday. Garbage day."

"See, Brian? I keep telling you that." Mom sighed, and told Mack, "He's all confused."

"I know, Mom. It's okay. Where are you going, Dad?" he asked, seeing that his father was getting up.

"I can take out my own garbage."

"But Mack is here. And *Jeopardy!* is on."

"So what? I don't know any of the answers anyway." His father tossed the television remote at Mack on his way out of the room.

Moments later, the back door slammed shut.

Mack looked at his mother, who shrugged, refusing to say what was on both their minds.

Instead, she asked him about work, and about the

weather—she hadn't been outside in days now—and she showed him the picture frame his little niece had made for her out of Popsicle sticks and yarn.

"Do you know Lynn made the same exact frame for me when she was that age?" his mother marveled. "I still have it."

"Of course you do." Mack often teased his mother that it was time to get rid of the proudly displayed art projects, crayon drawings, shellacked macaroni Christmas wreaths, and other handmade gifts he and his sister had given her over the years.

"You can't keep that stuff around for the rest of your life," he would tell her.

"Sure I can," she'd say.

Now the rest of her life had been reduced to a matter of months, and he couldn't bring himself to tease her about anything, so he admired the Popsicle stick frame and the torn page from a coloring book that his nephew had meticulously filled in and signed, "I love you, Grammy."

"They're growing up so fast," his mother said wistfully, wearing an expression that tugged at Mack's heart. Then she shook her head a little, as if she'd snapped out of it, and asked him what time he'd be over on Friday.

"Friday?" he echoed. "What do you mean?"

"What do you mean, what do I mean? Saint Patrick's Day."

"Oh!"

"Did you forget?"

"No, I . . ." Mack shook his head, then—because there was no putting anything past sharp-eyed Maggie—admitted, "Yeah. I forgot."

"You have other plans—a date," she guessed. "You don't have to come."

"Are you kidding? I wouldn't miss it," he said, hoping she couldn't hear the emotion clogging his throat or the unspoken words that seemed to hang in the air between them: *Especially since it's the last one.*

Saint Patrick's Day festivities were second only to Christmas in the MacKenna household. Corned beef and cabbage, cases of Irish ale, a houseful of relatives including his eccentric Aunt Nita and her equally eccentric mother, Great-Aunt Fiona.

Aunt Nita went around pinning green carnations on everyone in attendance—even tucking them into Champ's and Bruiser's collars. And Aunt Fi, despite being an octogenarian, would show up in her traditional step dancing outfit and—after a couple of Jameson's on the rocks—order the men to move the furniture and roll up the area rug so that she could perform on the hardwoods. Eventually, the entire crowd would be dancing jig after jig, well into the wee hours.

"Bring her."

"What?"

His mother shrugged. "Your date. Bring her. The more, the merrier."

He pictured his great-uncle Paddy, an aging but harmless flirt—all liquored up and grabbing Carrie to spin her around the dining room in time to fiddle music. "I don't know . . . it might be a little much for her."

Spotting the familiar glint of wariness in his mother's pastel green eyes, he knew he should have kept his misgivings to himself. Who knew? Maybe Carrie would fit in here. Maybe she had a fun-loving side he hadn't yet glimpsed. After all, they'd been on only one date.

He made up his mind to invite her to celebrate Saint Patrick's Day with him here in New Jersey. If she was game to meet his family—the whole rowdy MacKenna clan—then great. And if she wasn't interested, then . . .

That would be that. He'd say good-bye and move on.

Back home on Hudson Street at last after her Parsons class, Allison had to look up her brother Brett's phone number.

He'd had the same one for years—she'd been a child when he married Cindy-Lou, and he'd lived in his in-laws' farmhouse ever since—but Allison could probably count on her hands the number of times she'd dialed it over the past decade.

Usually he was the one who called her, though several months would go by between calls, sometimes several seasons. Then the phone would ring and she'd hear Brett's voice jokingly asking whether she was still alive.

"I'm sure someone would let you know if I wasn't," she always said in response—though, truth be told, she really wasn't so sure about that. Technically, her brother was her next of kin, but it wasn't as though she'd bothered to write a will, or even had friends who'd know Brett's last name or where in Nebraska to find him.

Then again, she supposed that these days, you could find just about anyone, even if you had no idea where to look. You just had to know *how*.

That was why she'd decided to call her brother tonight, after her Google search at the office turned up nothing at all.

Allen Taylor, Centerfield, Nebraska, came back with a couple of hits on her own name: Allison Taylor, Centerfield, Nebraska. Both were archived articles in the *Centerfield Register*. One was a listing of Centerfield High School graduates in 1995; the other was a mention in her mother's obituary from the *Centerfield Register*—which, of course, didn't list her father at all, not as a survivor or as a predeceased husband.

She'd waffled on the decision ever since she left the office, and almost mentioned it to Luis, who definitely noticed her preoccupation.

But she didn't feel like discussing it with him.

She didn't feel like discussing it with her brother, either, but she was in this deep—she might as well get it over with. She couldn't afford to lose another night's sleep, didn't want this weighing on her mind for days. It wasn't worth it. *He*—her father—wasn't worth it.

She just wanted to know, that was all. And then she could push him back into the shadowy past where he belonged.

As the phone rang, she perched nervously on the ugly orange futon she'd inherited from the previous tenant. She was saving to buy several pieces pictured on bent-cornered pages in last fall's Pottery Barn catalog. Real furniture wouldn't change the fact that she was alone here—alone in the world, really—but she felt that it would go a long way toward making this small one-bedroom apartment feel like a real home.

"Hello?"

"Brett—it's me."

"Jody?"

"Allison. Your sister."

"Oh! I thought you were Cin's friend, Jody. She's supposed to—never mind. How are you doing, Allison? How's life in the Big Apple? Are you biting it or is it biting you?"

He laughed hard at his own cleverness.

Ordinarily, Allison would force a chuckle as if she were hearing his little quip for the first time. But it was how he kicked off every conversation, and she wasn't in the mood for niceties, so she got right down to business.

"Remember when you said you were going to look for Daddy?"

There was a long silence on the other end of the line. She could hear Brett's television in the background: Alex Trebek posing the Final Jeopardy question.

Alex . . . she'd tried that name, too. Just in case.

Alex Taylor, Centerfield, Nebraska.

And, just in case it made a difference, Alexander.

Along with Alec, Allan, Allen, Alvin, Albert, even Allesandro, and Alejandro . . .

"Do you mean, after Mom died?" Brett asked at last.

She realized that the sound of his television had faded away, as though he'd muted the volume or left the room.

"Yes. Did you find him?"

"You said you didn't want to know if I did. You said you never wanted to hear his name again."

"I know what I said. But now I need to know. Did you find him?"

Another long pause.

Then: "No. I didn't find him."

Unsure whether to believe that, she asked, "Did you try?"

"Not very hard. Not as hard as I tried to find out who my own father was."

"*What?* I never knew you did that. When was that?"

"After my own kids were born. I figured he might want to know he had a son out there somewhere, because if I were him, I'd want to know. And I was pretty sure Mom never told him."

"*Told* him? I thought she didn't even know who he was."

"That's probably true. But you never know. Mom might have lied about it."

"Why would she?"

"Why do people lie, Allison?" Without waiting for a reply, he went on, "She did it to protect me, probably. Or him. Or herself. We'll never know if she did, or why."

"But you tried to find your father, and you couldn't?"

"Right. He's listed as Unknown in the official birth records in Omaha, and when I tracked down a few of Mom's so-called friends from that time, I realized that if he was anything like them, I'd probably be better off not finding him. So that was that."

"I'm sorry, Brett."

"Me too. But why are you asking about *your* father now?"

"I just wanted to know . . . what was his name?"

"You're kidding, right?"

"No."

"Why would you want to go dredging all that up again after all these years? Why can't you leave well enough alone?"

"What was his name, Brett?"

After a very long pause, her brother said, "You know his name: Allen Taylor. You were going to be named after him if you were a boy, but—"

"I know that," she cut in impatiently, all too familiar with the story of her birth, which her brother—never her mother—had shared with her, years ago. Many times.

He'd delighted in telling her that her father went around telling everyone he met that Mom had better be carrying a boy, because he'd always wanted a son of his own. That in itself was insensitive, considering that Allen Taylor was the only father Brett had ever known, though he'd never formally adopted him. But he wanted an Al Junior, the story went; instead, he got a daughter. She became his namesake, in a way: *Al's son* became *Allison*. That was how Brett explained it.

"Well, you were named after Mom," Allison once told him when she was a little girl, feeling sorrier for her big brother than she did for herself.

"So what? She changed hers to Taylor when she got married. Now I'm the only Downing in the house."

"No, I mean her first name. She's Brenda, and you're Brett. It's almost the same thing."

"No, it isn't," Brett said darkly. "It's not the same thing at all."

Of course, he was right. It wasn't the same thing. Allison had two parents. Brett just had one.

But then, after her own father left, so did she.

And then there were none.

Tonight, there was no pushing the ugly truth to the back of her mind as she usually did whenever it popped up. Tonight, she wanted to get to the bottom of it, once and for all.

"Mom called him Al," she told her brother, "and I always thought it was short for Allen, but—"

"It was."

"Spelled A-L-L-E-N? Or A-N? One L or two? One A or two?" Not that it mattered. She'd plugged every combination into the search engine, to no avail.

"Two Ls, one A," Brett said tersely. "Why?"

"Because I tried to find him."

"Why? You actually want to see him again, after the way he left?"

I don't know. I don't know what I want.

Aloud, she said, "No. I don't want to *see* him. I was just curious about what ever happened to him. And I thought maybe Al could have been short for something else. I tried it spelled different ways, and I tried Alex, and Alvin, and—"

"It wasn't. It was Allen," he says in his flat Midwestern accent that makes it into *Ay-al-an.*

"Are you sure?"

"Look, Allison, I don't get why you're trying to find him after all these years. I mean, did he ever try to find you?"

"I don't know. Maybe."

"You really believe that?"

"Maybe," she said again. Something about talking to her brother made her feel like a stubborn child all over again, believing in . . .

What? Her daddy? Fairy-tale endings?

"Did you find any documents lying around when we moved out after Mom died, Brett?" she persisted. "Like their marriage license, or his birth certificate? Anything like that?"

"You really think Mom would have kept them?"

Remembering how her mother had nearly burned down the house destroying every last photo of her father, she said, "I guess not. But it's like he vanished without a trace."

"Exactly. That was the way he wanted it. That's the way you should leave it."

"You didn't want to leave it that way. After Mom died, you said you were going to look for him."

"I thought it was the responsible thing to do. You were a minor. He was your only living parent."

He still is, she thought. *If he's alive.*

"And you never came up with anything at all?"

"Dead end."

Right. Just like now.

Realizing that she couldn't find him even if she wanted to, Allison leaned back against the futon cushion and closed her eyes, exhausted, frustrated, and angry.

But not at her father. Not this time.

Angry at herself.

This is your own fault. After all these years of leaving well enough alone, you had to go and look. And when you did, admit it—you weren't just thinking you'd find out what happened to him and leave it at that.

You were thinking you'd actually find *him. Reconnect with him. Welcome him back into your life.*

But that was never going to happen.

Not just because her father had made damned good and sure he'd covered his trail so that he'd be impossible to find, but because even if she *did* somehow manage to track him down, he wasn't going to be her long-lost daddy, grateful to have his little girl back.

"Face it, Allison. You're better off this way, just like I am. I mean, even more than I am. Chances are my own father didn't even know I existed. Yours did—and he left you. You're never going to see him again, but after what he did, I can't believe you even thought you wanted to."

"I don't," she told Brett, and this time, she meant it.

It hadn't been much of a date, Ralph thought, as he and Sue stopped to wait for the light at Central Park West and West Sixty-sixth Street. After a couple of drinks at a bar near Lincoln Center—which was completely dead on Tuesday evening—she'd abruptly announced that she had to get going.

It was probably just as well. She wasn't bad-looking. Not great-looking, either, though he wouldn't kick her out of bed.

But now that they were alone together, he realized he might have had the wrong idea about what tonight might hold. Occasionally, he glimpsed a fleeting spark in something she said or in her expression that did make him wonder if she was holding back. But he really didn't get the sense that she was playing hard to get—more that she wasn't connecting to him on any level. Or maybe she just didn't have much personality to begin with.

Whatever—it was time to put an end to the night.

"So are you going to walk me all the way home?" she asked, as the light changed and they started across the street.

Surprised by her sexy tone, he glanced over at her, and noticed a gleam in her eye. His pulse picked up again. Was it possible that he'd been right after all?

Wow. Never again would he complain about Juliana's monthly mood swings. Forget PMS, this Sue woman ran hot and cold like a two-handled faucet.

"Where do you live?"

"East Sixty-third."

"Let's grab a cab," he suggested, thinking she was probably going to invite him inside for a nightcap. So to speak.

"It's a nice night. I'd rather walk."

"East Sixty-third's a hike from here, though."

"We can cut through the park," she said. "It's faster."

It was also more dangerous. His mother had taught him never to set foot into the park after dark. But Ralph didn't want to appear less than manly, so he kept his fears to himself.

Into the park they went, surrounded by shadowy clumps of trees. There was traffic, of course—including a couple of cabs that went zipping past, dome lights indicating that they were available.

"Are you sure you want to walk?"

"Positive."

Now he couldn't see her eyes, but her tone wasn't exactly sexy. It was almost brusque.

They walked deeper into the park. She was silent, striding along with her heavy-looking tote bag over her shoulder and both hands buried in the pockets of her coat. It was a long, bulky down parka, the kind you wore to keep warm, not to look good—or even halfway decent.

Juliana wouldn't be caught dead in a coat like that, even on the coldest day of the year. Or in the rubber rain boots Sue was wearing—though it wasn't really even raining.

Ralph tried to think of something to say. Something other than *Forget this, I'm going back*.

Finally, just as those very words were about to spill off his tongue, Sue reached out and grabbed his arm. "I'm getting tired. Aren't you?"

Tired? No.

Pissed off? Hell, yes.

"We should stop and rest." Her tone hinted that she didn't mean just *rest*.

Perking up immediately, he looked around, seeing only trees and shrubs and a couple of garbage cans. "There aren't any benches, so how about if we go back and grab a cab to—"

"Who needs a bench? There's a nice, secluded spot back in there where we can stretch out and . . . you know . . . *relax*."

"You mean . . . on the ground?" His heart raced as he looked at the wooded spot where she was pointing.

"Sure, why not?"

Grinning, he allowed her to lead him off the path. Wait till he told Carlos about *this*.

So Sue was a hot number after all; in a matter of minutes, he was going to get to see her naked and in the throes of ecstasy.

A few yards off the path, ducking and weaving amid clumps of bushes and low limbs, she paused and turned back to him.

She's going to change her mind, he thought. *Figures.*

"Would you mind going first, Ralph?" she asked in a small voice. "It's kind of dark . . ."

"What? No! Not at all. Here, get behind me." He stepped around her and kept going, gallantly holding back branches so that they wouldn't snap back in front of her. All they needed was a small clearing, but he couldn't tell how far in they'd have to go before they found one. It was dark back here, just enough moonlight to keep him from smacking into a tree.

Carlos was always bragging about the crazy places he'd gotten lucky, but as far as Ralph knew, he'd never—

The pain was sudden, stinging. He clutched his shoulder, thinking he'd been jabbed somehow by a jagged stick. His jacket, at the spot, was wet. Sap? What the . . . ?

Blood, he realized, dazed, wondering how the stick could have sliced through the fabric, how it could have been sharp enough to hurt this badly.

He saw metal glinting in the moonlight as he turned, and then he felt the cold blade against his bare neck, slicing *into* his neck . . .

We're being mugged, he realized as he fell, eyes squeezed shut in agony. His mother had been right. The park was dangerous after dark, and now he and Sue had been attacked by . . .

He hit the ground hard, on his back, and his eyes snapped

open. In shocked horror, he saw Sue standing over him, a long knife clutched in both her gloved hands, poised high over her head. The hood on her parka was up now, tied tightly around her face, but enough of it was visible that he noticed her expression. It was pure ecstasy, just as he'd fantasized about her moments before, but this wasn't—this was—dear God, she was about to strike again.

Ralph tried to scream, but managed only a bloody gurgle as he braced himself, closing his eyes for the last time.

He registered just one word she hurtled at him, and it made no more sense than anything else.

"Daddy," he heard, in a guttural voice, and then the world went silent.

The phone started ringing seconds after Carrie walked into her apartment, before she even had time to turn on a light or pull the door closed behind her. Her pulse—which had finally slowed to a bearable rate as she covered the last ten blocks on foot—picked right up again.

She stood there in the dark, listening to it ring.

What if it was the police?

You idiot! The police don't dial your phone number if they think you've killed someone. They show up at your door and arrest you.

Carrie quickly reached back to close the door and lock it.

She'd better not answer the phone.

No, wait . . . she'd better answer it.

That way, if anyone asked questions later, she'd have an alibi—whoever was calling would be able to confirm that she'd been here tonight, in the apartment. When the body was found, the investigators wouldn't be able to pinpoint the exact time of death—just a window, right? And within that window, she'd have answered her own phone, right here at home.

Not stopping to turn on a light, she lurched toward it and snatched up the cordless receiver.

"Hello?"

"Carrie?"

"Yes?" She tried not to sound breathless.

"This is Mack."

"Mack. Hi. Sorry it took me a few minutes to answer, I was just getting out of the tub."

"Oh, that's . . . I thought for a second it might be too late, and I didn't want to wake you up."

"What time is it?" she asked, wanting him to make note of it, so that he'd remember.

"Ten twenty-eight. Listen, I won't keep you . . ."

No, don't keep me. I need to get off the phone and get into the tub. I need to wash away every trace of blood.

The parka had gotten most of it, just as she'd planned.

She'd dashed over to Loehmann's on her lunch hour this afternoon to buy it, along with the rain boots and gloves, using cash. When they had served their purpose, she'd quickly stripped them off and traded them for her good coat, leather pumps, and leather gloves, all of which had been stashed in the tote bag, along with the knife. She'd thought of everything—even had a big black Hefty bag ready for the last—and perhaps most brilliant—part of the plan.

Yes. She'd done her homework, as always, allowing her to execute the execution, as it were.

Daddy would have appreciated that. He'd always loved a good play on words.

No plan was without risk, however. Carrie's biggest one came when she emerged back onto the path from the thicket where she'd left the body. At that point, she looked like a Wall Street businesswoman again; no one would expect to see someone like her, dressed as she was, coming out of the bushes this deep in Central Park late at night.

But luck was with her again; there wasn't a soul around.

Minutes later, as she made her way back toward the West Side, she passed a jogger and then a couple walking a dog. No one gave her a second glance.

Just before she reached the end of the path and was about to emerge onto Central Park West, she saw exactly what she was looking for. A homeless person lay sleeping on a bench, beside a wire cart loaded with his—or her—worldly possessions, all of it stashed in black garbage bags.

It was a common sight around the city—less common, she knew from her homework, now that Mayor Giuliani had succeeded in his famous campaign to clean up the streets, but there were still homeless people, and they could be counted on to have shopping carts filled with black bags they shuttled from place to place and guarded with their lives—when they weren't passed out cold.

Again making sure there was no one in the vicinity, Carrie quickly unfolded the garbage bag she'd brought and stashed the entire tote inside, with its bloody cargo: coat, boots, and gloves—plus Ralph's wallet, to make identifying the body that much more difficult when he was found.

She gingerly lifted the top garbage bag from the bum's cart, stashed her own garbage bag beneath it, and was on her way.

Only the knife stayed with her, wrapped in a plastic deli bag from her lunch, but not for long. At Seventy-second Street, she descended to the subway and boarded a southbound B train, going in the opposite direction from where she lived. She got off at Times Square—arguably the busiest station in the city—and took an elaborate detour past a garbage can on a far-flung, yet predictably crowded, platform, where she didn't even break her stride as she dropped the deli bag inside.

If the police happened to find it there—and that was a big *if*—they'd assume that the killer, having made the southbound trip from the park, lived or worked or had business in this neighborhood, or had transferred here to go farther downtown, or across town, or to one of the boroughs.

Instead, Carrie had cleverly made her way to an uptown platform, boarding a northbound express train to her apartment here in Washington Heights at the very top of Manhattan.

The whole thing had taken half an hour, maybe forty minutes. And now she was home, and Mack was on the phone, and if—by some wild chance—she should ever need someone to vouch for her whereabouts tonight, he would be able to.

Some wild chance . . .

Yeah. Right.

No one—*no one*—was ever going to connect an executive assistant to the murdered corpse of that loser in the park.

Just as no one would have ever connected her to—

No. Don't think about that. Not now.

You'll get upset, and it'll show up in your voice, and you need to sound as normal as possible. He likes you because you don't talk. You listen. So listen.

"I just wanted to ask you a quick question."

"Sure," she said. "What is it?"

She reached out and flipped the light switch beside the door. The room flooded with light, and she felt exposed. Instinctively, she flipped it off again.

Better. Much better.

Strange—after all those early childhood years of feeling afraid of the dark, now she preferred it. The shadows seemed to wrap protective arms around her, hiding her, keeping her safe.

"You know how we have a date for Friday night?"

"Yes."

"Well, I said I'd take you out to a nice dinner—you know, to make up for McSorley's, and—"

"I liked McSorley's."

You cut him off! What are you doing? You're not acting like yourself. He's going to notice!

Dammit. She really needed him to stop beating around the bush and ask his question so that she could answer it and get off the phone. The longer they talked, the more room there was for error, and if she slipped and gave anything away, she'd have to—

No. I could never just get rid of Mack the way I got rid of Ralph.

That had been different. She'd known that once she made the first cut, there would be no going back. She wanted to get it over with quickly, but at the same time . . . she wanted to do it. All night. She looked at him across the table and she couldn't wait. Couldn't *wait*.

Finally, when it was time, she aimed for his neck, but he was a moving target and she wound up hitting his shoulder. The second quick cut found its mark and took him down. It was then, seeing the satisfying look of terror in his eyes, and realizing that his life—what was left of it—was in her hands, that euphoria swept over her. She didn't remember the third time she stabbed him, or the fourth, or much of anything, really, until she found herself stripping off her bloody outerwear.

But disposing of Mack wouldn't be as easy, or as pleasurable. Not like that. Not by any means.

"When we made our plans for Friday," he was saying, "I completely forgot that it was Saint Patrick's Day."

She waited for him to go on, willed him to go on. *Hurry up, Mack. Get off the phone, and don't make me talk to you, because . . . because I don't want any regrets when it comes to you.*

"That's a big deal in my family," he said, "and I need to be out in Jersey that night, so—"

"We can get together a different time. It's okay."

There was a pause. "Would you rather just . . . forget it?"

"No," she said quickly, hoping she hadn't made him suspicious. "I want to see you, but if that night isn't good, we can do it a different night."

"No, I want to stick with seeing you that night. Would you like to come with me?"

"To New Jersey?"

"Yeah."

"Sure."

"Really?"

"Yes. That would be fine."

"You know my parents will be there, and my sister, and—"

"Great." She cut in again, despite her resolve to let him do the talking. Anything to avoid prolonging this conversation. Anything to keep Mack from figuring out that she hadn't been home all night, that she hadn't just gotten out of the bathtub, that she had just killed a man in cold blood.

"I'm really glad you're coming, Carrie. It'll be fun, I promise. Maybe a little crazy, but fun."

"Sounds good. Thank you."

"You're welcome. I know it's late, so I'll let you go."

Yes. Let me go, Mack . . . and then I'll be able to let you go.

She hung up the phone and in the dark, made her way into the bathroom. There, she turned on the tub faucet, and then the light. Blinking in its glare, she caught sight of herself in the mirror above the sink and was surprised to see that she looked the same as she always did.

Leaning closer, she searched for a stray speck of blood on her face; anything that might have given her away to the people she'd encountered during her journey home from the park, had anyone given her more than a passing glance.

There was nothing at all. Her face, bare of makeup, was perhaps more pale than usual; certainly much plainer. She knew how to enhance her features with eyeliner, mascara, lipstick . . . with them, and without this drab wig she was wearing, she looked like a different woman.

She'd sat facing the wall while she and Ralph were having drinks, but even if someone had spotted them together, no one would recognize her—the real her.

Whoever that even was.

Steam was rising from the bathtub behind her. She reached up and yanked the wig off her head, tossing it into the garbage can. Then, thinking better of it, she retrieved it. She still had Chelsea to contend with.

She stripped off her clothes and turned off the faucet, then the light. Sinking into the hot water, enveloped in darkness, she smiled, remembering what it had felt like to kill him again, after all these years.

But later, when she had dried herself off and slipped into bed, she missed him again. She wanted him there beside her; wanted him to tell her that the dream catcher would keep the nightmares away; wanted his voice to soothe her off to sleep the way it did when she was young and silly enough to believe that he'd always be there.

"Read me a story, Daddy," she whispered. "Please?"

All she heard was the traffic flying up the West Side Highway, and distant sirens—always sirens, here in the city. Always noise.

But after a few moments, she heard instead the wind stirring prairie grasses, and the cicadas whirring their night song, and her father's voice.

I'll do something even better for you. I'll teach you how to read. That way, when I'm not here with you, you can read your own bedtime stories. How about that?

No. I want you to be here instead. I want you to read to me every night forever and ever. Even when I'm a grown-up lady. I don't want to learn to read.

That's a stupid thing for a smart girl to say. Now go ahead, pick out a story . . .

Carrie sat up, reached over, and turned on the bedside lamp. She was surprised, momentarily, to see that she wasn't in her girlhood bedroom. But when she saw the stack of books on the nightstand, their familiar titles stamped on well-creased bindings, she nodded.

Hurry up. Pick out a good one.

They're all too hard.

Not if you can read, and I'm going to teach you how. Then no matter what happens, on nights when I'm not here with you, you'll read yourself to sleep.

Carrie perused the stack. *Charlotte's Web . . .*

No! Not spiders! Nothing about spiders!

Tikki Tikki Tembo . . .

No! Not that one, either! It was about a well!

Wells and spiders reminded her . . .

She shuddered and grabbed the book off the top of the pile, Mercer Mayer's *I Was So Mad.*

She had been thirteen when the book was published—too old for a picture book, really. That was why she was so surprised when she found it in a Barnes & Noble shopping bag pushed way back under the passenger's seat in his car.

"What is this, Daddy?"

"That? Oh . . . that—that's for you. I forgot to give it to you. I bought it a long time ago."

Thinking maybe he meant years ago, she pulled the receipt from the bottom of the bag and saw that it had been purchased just a few weeks earlier, in Omaha. Why would he buy a children's book for a teenager?

"You have a terrible temper," he told her, not for the first time—and not without reason. Everyone said that: her mother, her teachers, her friends, even Arthur, the kindly old farmhand who looked after the place while her father was away.

Arthur looked after Carrie, too. He wasn't as smart as Daddy—not book smart, anyway—but he taught her things, too. Like how to fish and how to shoot and even how to drive, even though that was something she'd always expected her father to do. By the time she was old enough, Daddy was gone more and more often, for longer stretches of time.

When he was around, he was more critical than ever.

"You fly off the handle much too easily," Daddy said the day she found the Mercer Mayer book, "and that's what this story is about. Learning to control your anger. Wouldn't it be nice if you could do that?"

She agreed that it would be nice. A lot of things would be nice. That didn't mean they were going to happen. But she didn't say that to her father, because what would be the use?

Now, Carrie opened the book with hands that had been scrubbed clean of blood. Sure enough, as she began to read aloud, she felt the last bit of anger melt away.

"See? I told you. I was right, wasn't I?"

"Yes, Daddy. You were right."

Chapter Eight

Friday, March 17, 2000

When Justin the biologist had called her midweek to re-schedule their blind date for tonight, Allison said yes, hoping an evening out would take her mind off things.

Well, one thing in particular: her father.

All these years, she'd thought that if she really wanted to find him, she'd be able to. Now that she knew she couldn't, she felt as though she'd lost him all over again. Grief—not, this time, for what had been, but for what could never be—snaked its way into her days and nights, even into her dreams. Whenever she finally managed to drift to sleep, she saw her father's face. But it wasn't as she remembered it. There were wrinkles around his eyes now, and his dark hair had gone gray.

"I'm so sorry," he said in every dream, holding his arms

out to hug her. "I never meant to hurt you. Please, Allison, please . . ."

But she refused to accept his apology. She saw her dream self backing away from him, heard herself shouting, "No! I'll never forgive you for what you did!"

Then she'd wake up, shaken, with tears streaming down her face. Depending on what time it was, she'd either lie there making a futile effort to get back to sleep for another hour or two, or she'd drag herself out of bed and numbly go through the motions of another exhausting day.

Now, at last, the workweek was over. If she'd had her way tonight, she'd have taken the subway home, crawled into bed, and slept until Monday morning's alarm clock. In fact, first thing this morning, she'd promised herself she'd do exactly that.

But she hadn't gotten around to canceling on Justin, and she couldn't just stand him up. So here she was, sitting across from him at a small Mexican restaurant in the Village. Between them was a big bowl of guacamole—half price, the waitress had told them, and the margaritas they were sipping were two for one. Everything green was on special tonight, in honor of Saint Patrick's Day.

"I forgot that was today," Justin said as they perused their menus. "I guess I could have taken you to an Irish restaurant. I'm sure there must be some in New York."

"There are definitely plenty of Irish pubs."

"You don't take a girl to a pub on a first date."

She smiled. "I wouldn't have minded. Especially on Saint Patrick's Day. *Especially* if you're Irish."

"But I'm not. Are you?"

"No."

"Really? A blue-eyed blond—you look like you could be."

She wasn't about to tell him that her blond hair wasn't natural—or that for all she knew, she might very well have some Irish blood somewhere in her lineage. Her mother had always referred to herself as a WASP, but her father—well, who knew? By the time she was old enough to wonder, he was gone. And his branch of the family tree wasn't something her mother would have been willing to discuss.

Right now, on a blind date, she wasn't interested in getting into any of it: her cultural background, her parents, her past.

She changed the subject, asking, "What do you think? Are you going with the chicken and salsa verde or the stuffed jalapeños? A big salad? Or perhaps just some broccoli?"

"I know it seems like I'm not in the spirit of the holiday—maybe if they were playing something from Riverdance instead of mariachi music—but I was thinking I might order something that isn't even green."

"Party pooper."

"I don't know if my cousin told you, but I'm a lab scientist, and I'm kind of shy, and for fun, I like to read. I'm not usually the life of the party."

She returned his grin across the table, noticing that he was actually more handsome than she'd initially thought. Catching sight of him waiting by the hostess stand when she walked in, her first impression had been that he looked like a nerdy scientist: ears that stuck out a little, glasses, earnest expression, tall and a little gawky.

But he had a cute smile, his brown eyes were kind, and he was wearing a distressed leather jacket that she could see, close up, was vintage, with an impressive designer label. When she complimented him on it, he said, "I knew you worked in fashion, so I didn't want to show up dressed like some schlub."

"Is that what you'd usually do on a date?" she asked, and he grinned.

"Probably."

"You're not supposed to admit that, you know."

"Really? Then forget I said it. I'm always a snazzy dresser. Ask anyone. Except my cousin. Or her friend who set us up."

"It was actually a friend of your cousin's friend."

"Don't ask her, either," he said without missing a beat, she laughed, and the ice was broken.

Now, as she asked him about his work, she realized she was actually glad she'd come. Maybe he wouldn't turn out to be the love of her life, but at least she wasn't sitting at home, staring into space, thinking about her father.

Besides, who knew? Maybe Justin *would* turn out to be the love of her life. Maybe they'd fall head over heels and get married and have babies and live happily ever after.

That's all that really matters in this world, isn't it? she thought, sipping her second margarita, feeling as though the first one had already gone to her head. *A husband, children. Loving, and being loved. Knowing where you belong—and to whom.*

As for the career—sure, she still wanted that, too. A nicely furnished apartment and a closet full of gorgeous clothes wouldn't hurt, either. But tonight, thanks to tequila and the emotionally grueling week she'd just endured, those things didn't seem to matter as much as they usually would.

Tonight, she was convinced that if she just had someone to count on, a family of her own, she'd be perfectly content. She'd never again look back, wishing things had been different, longing for something—someone—she'd never had, and never would.

This was a big mistake.

Mack had known it from the moment he met Carrie in the PATH station after work. He saw her before she caught sight of him. She was standing stiffly at the entrance to the Hoboken track, wearing a dark wool coat and sensible pumps, looking preoccupied. He wondered if, by chance, she might have on a green skirt and sweater beneath her coat, but somehow, he doubted it.

He found out when they reached his parents' house that he was right about that; she had on a businesslike brown suit. He was pretty sure, by that time, that she wouldn't be tossing the jacket aside, hiking up the skirt, kicking off her shoes, and dancing a jig with his aunt Fiona, either.

When she spotted him at the station, she'd pasted a smile on her face, greeted him with a hug, and told him she'd been looking forward to tonight. But then she asked, as they boarded the train, "How long do you think we'll be there?"

That was not a good sign.

"It goes pretty late," he told her. "Are you sure you want to go?"

"Of course," she said, not very convincingly. "I want to meet your parents. And your sister will be there, too, you said?"

"Everyone will be there. Remember? I told you the other night on the phone—it gets kind of crazy."

She frowned, as though she were hearing that for the first time. "Crazy in what way?"

"Don't worry—just in a party kind of way. You know—drinking, singing, dancing . . . that sort of thing."

"Dancing?" she echoed, as if that were the worst kind of crazy imaginable.

" 'Fraid so," he said with a wry smile, and gave her another out. "Look, if you want to skip it, I'll completely understand."

"I thought you said you were obligated to go."

"I am—but *you're* not."

"Oh. So you would still go, alone . . . ?"

"I have to. My mom—well, you know. It's a big deal, like I said the other night. If you'd rather not come with me, we can get together another time."

But that wasn't really an option. He knew, and he could see by her expression that she knew, too, that if she backed out now, they wouldn't be seeing each other again.

"No, I'll come. I'm sure it'll be fun." The resolute set of her jaw conveyed that she thought exactly the opposite.

So they took the PATH train to Hoboken and walked the few blocks to his parents' house. A felt leprechaun banner he'd made in Cub Scouts twenty-odd years ago hung on the front door; beyond it, the foyer was so jammed with friends and relatives that they could barely get past the threshold. Seeing Carrie shrink back, wide-eyed, Mack grabbed her hand and began shouldering his way through, pulling her into the fray with Champ and Bruiser barking underfoot.

The overheated air was heavily scented with beer and cigarette smoke, corned beef and cabbage, and Aunt Fiona's Jean Naté perfume. His cousin Mary Beth was futilely trying to shush raucous conversations so that everyone could hear her seven-year-old banging out a halting, discordant version of "Danny Boy" on the old upright piano, which only made people raise their voices; all of that competed with a vintage vinyl version of the Chieftains' "The Rocky Road to Dublin" blasting from the stereo.

Mack's father had crossed paths with the band back in the sixties, when they were up and coming and he was a record industry executive. Once in a while, hearing familiar music seemed to jar Brian MacKenna from his twilight world. Mack fervently hoped that would be the case tonight.

"Hey, Mack's here!" someone shouted, and somehow, he lost his grip on Carrie's hand as he was swept into one warm embrace after another. Everyone, particularly his aunts and older female cousins, seemed eager to give him a loving squeeze, as if to reassure him that everything was going to be okay somehow, despite his mother's illness. But they weren't fooling him or themselves.

They were all so somber, he noticed. Gone were the usual teasing questions and quips; gone, even, was the innate black humor that had seen this clan through some pretty tough times from nineteenth-century Galway to twenty-first-century New Jersey.

He was grateful when his brother-in-law, Dan—married, albeit shakily at the moment, to Mack's sister, Lynn—put a beer into his hand and asked about the upcoming Knicks-Lakers game.

"I heard you have courtside seats. How'd you score those?"

"Client."

"I'm in the wrong business or on the wrong side of the Hudson River," said Dan, a dentist down in Middletown.

"You mean your patients don't reward you with courtside seats?"

"I'm lucky if they pay their bills. You're a lucky SOB, Mack."

"Want to come?"

"Oh, yeah, sure, I'd love to come."

"I'm serious, Dan. I've got an extra ticket."

"And you want to waste it on your sister's husband? Don't you have some hot babe to impress?"

Uh-oh. Suddenly remembering Carrie, he looked around and realized he'd not only lost his grip on her, he'd lost sight of her, too.

Rather than explain to Dan that she wasn't exactly a hot babe, nor was she impressed by courtside Knicks-Lakers seats, he said hurriedly, "Listen, the extra ticket is yours if you want it, and I actually am seeing someone and she's here with me, and I'd better find her before Uncle Paddy does."

"Good idea. Count me in for the game, Mack."

He nodded and turned away, looking around for Carrie but instead finding his aunt Nita making a beeline for him with a red-lipstick-stained coffee mug in one hand and a bouquet of green carnations in the other.

"How are you, honey?" she asked, giving him another one of those long, hard hugs and sad, searching looks. "Hanging in there?"

"I am, but I have to go find—"

"Wait, wait, your corsage." Aunt Nita set down her cup, pulled a pair of nail scissors from her pocket, snipped the stem off one of her carnations, and deftly pinned the flower to his lapel.

Back when he was a perpetually mortified adolescent, Mack would have protested that boys didn't wear corsages— even though his mother told him they did, but they were called boutonnières—then discarded it the first chance he got.

But he had long since learned to deal with Aunt Nita— with his entire crazy family, in fact. So he just thanked her and smiled when she admired the way it matched his shamrock-printed tie *and* his eyes—"And your sister's, too," she added before stepping away to add another shot of whiskey to her coffee. "You got them from our side of the family, you know."

Aunt Nita was a fair-haired, green-eyed O'Hara, like Mack's mother, in sharp contrast to the blue-eyed MacKennas—some of whom were heavily freckled redheads, while the rest were "Black Irish" like Mack.

"What was that about me?"

He turned to see that Lynn had come up beside him.

"You have green eyes."

"Oh. I thought maybe you were badmouthing me or something."

"Me? Never."

"That's why I love you." She clinked her own beer bottle against his. "Hey, I thought you were bringing your new girlfriend."

"I did, but she's . . . she's not . . ."

Never one to wait patiently for a reply, Lynn tossed out her next question. "Have you seen Mom yet?"

"No, I just got here. Why?"

Lynn shrugged and said nothing, which was rare for her. Not a good sign.

"Where is she?"

"Upstairs."

"Upstairs?" Mack's heart sank. "What is she doing upstairs?"

"Lying down. She said she wasn't feeling up to a big party. Go see her."

"I will." Mack turned away abruptly and started pushing his way toward the stairs, then remembered again—Carrie.

He looked around, afraid he was going to find her cornered by his uncle Paddy, but it was worse than that. Still wearing her coat, now with a green carnation pinned to it, she was utterly disengaged from the festivities—not an easy accomplishment in this boisterous, welcoming crowd. She stood completely alone by the front door, looking as though she was preparing to open it and slip out into the night.

He made his way over to her. "Carrie. I'm so sorry. I didn't mean to leave you. I sort of got dragged away."

"It's okay."

He set down his beer and took her arm. "Let's go someplace quiet, away from all this. I know it's probably a little overwhelming."

At that moment, Mack's cousin Colin stuck his curly red head through the kitchen doorway and bellowed, "Who wants Jell-O shots?"

"A *little* overwhelming?" Carrie said to Mack with a faint smile.

He gestured at the carnation pinned to her coat. "I see you met Aunt Nita. Thanks for being a good sport. Come on."

He led her upstairs, past a gallery of framed family pictures that Maggie had hung, one by one, throughout his lifetime: baby portraits and school photos of him and Lynn, First Communion and cap-and-gown shots, a family portrait done at his parents' twenty-fifth anniversary party, then Lynn's wedding, his niece and nephews as babies, and now their school portraits . . .

Mack had walked up and down these stairs thousands of times without paying much attention to the photographs. Now it hit him: his own wedding picture would never hang on this wall, nor would pictures of his babies. His mother wouldn't be alive to meet his wife and children, and even if his father was around for that, he'd most likely have to be reintroduced every time he saw them.

Engulfed by a ferocious wave of sorrow, Mack halted at the top of the steps, still gripping the railing with one hand and Carrie's arm with the other.

This is the end of an era. I'm losing both my parents, and it's happening too soon, too fast . . .

"Are you okay?" Carrie asked.

He tried to blink tears from his eyes and succeeded only in allowing them to roll down his cheeks.

"Yeah," he said, surreptitiously wiping his eyes on his sleeve. "I'm good. Come on—I'll take you in to meet my mother."

"Meet your mother?" she echoed.

"She's lying down in there." He gestured at the closed door to the master bedroom.

"I'm sure she doesn't feel like meeting a total stranger."

Carrie was the one who didn't feel like meeting a total stranger, Mack realized—then, to be fair, reminded himself that she'd just been bombarded with dozens of total strangers downstairs. Could he really blame her for not taking all of that—and now a terminally ill mother—in stride?

"Never mind. Come on," he said, leading her down the hall to his boyhood room. He opened the door and stuck his head in to make sure the room was vacant and presentable.

His twin bed was still covered in the denim quilt his mother had bought on sale at Caldor years ago, to replace the "little boy" one printed with fire trucks. Matching denim curtains hung at the lone window, and dangling from the rod was another old Cub Scout project: the Native American dream catcher he'd made from a twig, twine, beads, and feathers. Somehow—no doubt courtesy of too-sentimental-to-throw-it-away Maggie—it had recently found its way back to his room, along with a couple of other crafts he'd made back in his school days.

The bookcase was lined with childhood favorites: the Hardy Boys and Narnia sharing space with Tom Wolfe and V.C. Andrews's entire Flowers in the Attic series, which he'd borrowed from his sister, Lynn, and later wished he'd hidden away so his friends wouldn't see it.

The shelf beneath his old stereo—complete with a cassette deck—was crammed with stacks of tapes that revealed an equally eclectic taste in music: Foreigner, Warren Zevon, Culture Club. His father used to bring albums home from work, saying, "Here, Mack, give this a listen and tell me what you think."

How could he possibly reconcile the memory of that sharp-eyed, sharp-eared businessman with the fog-shrouded senior citizen his father had become?

Mack cleared his throat and told Carrie to wait for him in the bedroom. "I won't be long," he said. "I just want to go see her."

"Take your time." Carrie unpinned the carnation from her coat as she sat on the bed, but she didn't unbutton it.

"Do you want to take off your coat? It's a little warm in here."

He waited for her to say, "A *little* warm?" The house, which had always been drafty, was uncomfortably toasty tonight, between all those bodies downstairs and the thermostat being raised for his mother, who was always cold now.

But Carrie just tucked the carnation into her bag and said, in her quiet way, "No, I'll be fine. Wait—do you have a cigarette?"

"I do, but . . . you really can't smoke here."

She just looked at him, probably waiting for an explanation, given the fact that at least half the people downstairs were puffing away.

"It's just . . . my parents don't really know that I smoke."

"*How* old did you say you were?" The words themselves might have been meant in a teasing way, but her expression and tone weren't the least bit lighthearted. "Everyone is smoking down there."

"Well, it's not allowed up here. My rule. Not theirs." Jaw set, he headed for the master bedroom.

He knocked, heard his mother's voice, and opened the door. "Mom?"

"Hi, Mack."

The room was dim, and it smelled funny. Stale, medicinal.

He closed the door, shutting out the sounds of laughter and music from below, and crossed over to the bed.

"You can turn on a lamp," his mother said, and he did. She winced and blinked her lashless eyes.

"Sorry—do you want me to turn it off again?"

"It's okay, I'll be fine."

No. Unlike Carrie, his mother wouldn't be fine.

She was dying.

It still seemed surreal. Emotion clogged Mack's throat again, and he tried to think of something to say, wondering if he could even push words past the lump of grief.

It was so hard to look at her, lying there wearing one of her cancer turbans. She had wigs, but she said they scratched her scalp and anyway, they looked stiff and fake. The turbans were soft and kept her head warm, and this one was green, Mack noticed with a pang, wondering if he should compliment her on it.

"Did you eat?" she asked.

"Not yet. I just got here."

"Go eat. I made corned beef in the Crock-Pot. Daddy helped."

"You're kidding, right?" His father didn't cook.

"No, I wanted to teach him how to make it, because . . . because."

Because she wasn't going to be around next Saint Patrick's Day.

Mack forced a smile. "How'd he do?"

"You know your father. It took him forever to chop the cabbage and he wanted all the pieces to be exactly the same size. Like it matters." His mother tried to laugh, but it morphed into a coughing fit.

He reached for a glass of water on the bedside table, offering it to her.

"No, thanks," she sputtered.

"Mom, please . . . it'll help."

Reluctantly, she accepted the glass.

"I would have helped you with the cooking," he said as she sipped. "Maybe I could have left work early."

"Don't be silly. We were fine."

Yeah, sure, and I'll be fine and you'll be fine and everyone and everything will be fine . . .

Except it won't.

"I thought you were bringing a date tonight, Mack."

"I did. She knows you weren't feeling well and she didn't want to bother you, so she's in the other room."

His mother would have raised an eyebrow if she still had them. "Which other room?"

"Down the hall. My old room."

"It's dusty in there. I haven't gotten to it in weeks. Why isn't she downstairs with everyone else?"

He thought about saying that she was just shy, but opted instead to deflect the question. "I was just going to ask you the same thing."

"I was too tired to deal with a crowd tonight."

Too physically tired? he wondered. Or too tired of seeing

the fear and sympathy in the eyes of everyone who loved her—including her own son?

Stoical Maggie MacKenna certainly didn't need Mack tip-toeing in here and treating her differently, too. She needed someone to treat her as though she still inhabited the land of the living. She needed to laugh, or at least smile.

"By the way, I like your festive beanie," he said, sitting on the edge of the bed and giving her turban a gentle pat.

"Oh, sure you do." She shook her head, but she was grinning. "But it's not as festive as your corsage."

"This," he said, looking down at the green-tinted carnation Aunt Nita had given him, "is a very manly boutonnière."

"Sure it is."

Ah, there was the old Maggie, busting his chops.

"Hey, I'm on a date here, remember? I can't afford to go around wearing a corsage." Mack unpinned the carnation from his lapel and leaned toward his mother, carefully fastening it to her turban. "There. That makes your beanie even more festive."

"It smells like church on Easter morning when I was a little girl." She inhaled deeply and smiled, eyes closed. "It seemed like Easter always fell on a miserable rainy day. Sometimes we even had snow. But every father in the neighborhood would get corsages for their wives and daughters to wear to Mass—just like Daddy always did for me and Lynn when you were little. And when you stepped into church and breathed in the scent of all those flowers, it was as if springtime had come after all."

She fell silent, lost in her memory.

"When *is* Easter this year?" Mack fervently hoped there would be warm sunshine.

Her eyes popped open. "Late. Not until April twenty-third."

"That's good. The weather should be better by then."

Seeing the shadow that crossed his mother's face, he remembered. *She* wouldn't be better by then—she might be much worse. She might even be—

No. Not that soon. When pressed, privately, by Lynn, the oncologist had guessed six months, so . . .

September.

That's always been one of Mack's favorite months of the year, even when it meant going back to school. Summers here were hot and sticky, while Labor Day literally brought a breath of fresh air.

Now he would dread it.

"Don't leave your friend waiting," his mother said. "It isn't nice. Take her downstairs and have something to eat."

"I will." He stood up again.

"Be sure you tell your father he did a nice job with the cabbage."

"I will. I just hope he doesn't ask me what cabbage is," he added, his own black humor still intact.

Maggie only sighed and shook her head. "He might. Poor Daddy."

Mack sighed too, and bent to kiss her pale cheek. She was right, he thought, catching a whiff of the carnation. It did smell like church on Easter. He fervently hoped they would all be together on April 23, just as they had been every Easter of his life.

Just one more holiday. That's all I want. Please, God. One more Easter.

But that *wasn't* all he wanted. It wouldn't be enough. He wanted one more Mother's Day, one more Thanksgiving, and Christmas, and New Year's . . . one more year. One more lifetime . . .

"What's her name?"

"What?"

"What do you mean, what?" Ah, sassy old Maggie was back. "Your new girlfriend. What's her name?"

Again, he hesitated, and opted not to inform his mother that she wasn't exactly a girlfriend. *Yet*, anyway. "It's Carrie. Carrie Robinson."

"Carrie." His mother nodded, and settled into her pillows. "I'll meet her next time. She's very nice, I'm sure."

"She is." *I'm sure.*

Pretty sure.

"Good." She started to close her eyes and then opened them again. "Mack?"

"Yeah?"

"Make sure you tell Dad you like the food."

"I will," he told her again. She wasn't the kind of mother to nag and repeat herself.

"And can you make sure he remembers to eat?"

"Mom, the house is full of food. Every surface down there is covered in plates and bowls. Eating is one thing I'm sure even Dad can't forget."

"Not just tonight. I mean . . ."

He knew what she meant.

His instinct was to pretend that he didn't—denial was a seductive balm.

Again, he thought about all the people downstairs who loved and pitied his mother, talking to her face about how prayer or modern medicine could work wonders, then weeping and grieving behind her back . . .

She had always been a straight shooter who appreciated the same in return.

"I'll take care of Dad," he promised hoarsely. "And so will Lynn. We'll look out for him, make sure he eats, make sure he takes his medicine, make sure he doesn't drive . . ."

"That's not going to be easy."

None of this was easy.

He shrugged. "I've got it covered, Mom. You don't need to worry about Dad right now."

"Thank you, Mack. Go."

"I'm going."

He closed the bedroom door behind him and leaned against it with his eyes closed, thinking about what lay ahead.

"Mack?"

Startled, he opened his eyes and saw Carrie in the hall.

"You look upset," she said.

Upset. Devastated.

"Do you want to talk about it?" she asked. "Someone recently told me that I'm a good listener."

He couldn't help but smile at that. "It must have been a very wise man who said that."

"It was."

Mack was surprised to realize that he did want to talk to her about it. She'd told him, that first night they met, that she knew what it was like to lose someone.

"We can go someplace quiet," he decided.

"There?" She pointed at his room down the hall.

"No. Someplace quieter. I can't do this tonight."

Visibly relieved, she nodded and held out her hand. She didn't say she was glad to get out of here, and she didn't say that everything was going to be okay.

She didn't say anything at all, and for that, he was grateful.

Allison was smiling when she walked into her apartment just after midnight.

Who'd have thought Justin the biologist would turn out to be such an accomplished kisser?

Or that this blind date would lead to plans for Sunday?

He'd actually asked her out for tomorrow night, but she told him she was busy, which was the truth. She didn't elaborate, though. No reason to tell him that her plans involved seeing the new Julia Roberts movie, *Erin Brockovich*, with her best friend. Why not let him think he might have some dating competition?

"How about the next day, then? Brunch?"

"Sure," she said, and after one last kiss, she sailed into her building.

As she turned on a light and kicked off her shoes, she noticed that the answering machine was blinking across the room. She made her way over to the phone, shrugging out of her coat and draping it over a chair as she went.

"You . . . have . . . three . . . new . . . messages," the machine's electronic voice informed her.

She guessed that at least one would be from Luis, and she was right.

"Allison, I cannot *wait* until tomorrow night! My friend Thomas just saw the movie and he said Julia *is a-may-zing*! I swear she's going to win an Oscar for this one! Call me if you don't get home too late!"

This wasn't too late by Luis's standards, she knew, but after her pleasantly surprising romantic evening, she wasn't in the mood to listen to him gush over his movie idol. She erased the message and listened to the next one.

"Allison, it's Brett."

Her brother? Why was he calling?

All he said was "Give me a call when you can."

She erased that message, too, and moved on to the last.

"Allison, it's Brett again. It's past ten o'clock. Are you there? . . . Allison? . . . No? Okay, I left you a message a couple of hours ago and I thought maybe you didn't get it. Call me back."

It was definitely too late on Brett's end, even though his time zone was an hour behind. He'd be getting up in a couple of hours to milk the cows, and would probably be eating lunch by the time she rolled out of bed.

She toyed with the idea of returning the call now regardless of the hour, curious about what he might want to say.

Then again, no one welcomed a wee-hour phone call.

And he probably just wanted to rehash their conversation

Tuesday about her trying to find her father. But what else could he possibly want to say about that? He'd advised her to forget about the search, and she'd agreed.

A return call, she decided, would just have to wait until tomorrow. Why dredge it up now and ruin what was left of her afterglow?

The all-night diner was just down the block from the PATH station, and crowded at this hour on a Friday night. There were groups of teenagers, couples, cops and senior citizens. Several limo drivers sat at the counter, chatting with the waitresses and each other—obviously regulars who came here to kill time while they were waiting for their customers to call for a pickup, or on their way to Newark airport and back.

At a table in the very back of the restaurant sat a group of men. Most wore dark shirts under their suit coats, and some had on pinky rings or gold chains. They could have stepped off the set of *The Sopranos*, that new HBO series about Jersey mobsters.

Sitting in a booth nearby with Mack, Carrie was still trying to absorb all that had happened this evening.

She didn't know which had caught her more off guard: Mack's willingness to walk out of his parents' house with her in the midst of the festivities, or her own reaction to what had happened there; not her utter dismay at the party pandemonium, but the fact that she liked this guy enough that she hadn't bolted the moment that crazy lady pinned a green flower to her coat—or sooner.

It had been bad enough when Mack was swallowed up by the crowd right after they arrived, leaving Carrie alone in a sea of strangers. But when that woman popped up shouting, "Happy Saint Patrick's Day! I'm Aunt Nita!" and stuck a corsage on her without asking . . .

At first Carrie had merely been stunned. By the time she found the presence of mind to protest, Aunt Nita had moved on to assault someone else.

What on earth am I doing here? Carrie wondered as she stood alone by the door, desperately scanning the crowd for Mack. She didn't belong here in this house, with these people . . .

And that meant she didn't belong with him.

Or did she?

So many possible scenarios had crossed her mind when she thought about what might happen to her in New York, but this—falling for Mr. Nice Guy who had a nine-to-five job and a big circle of friends and a close-knit family—this was not one of them.

She wasn't used to that kind of life, by any means. Growing up in the middle of nowhere, miles from the closest town, she'd gladly kept to herself. So, for the most part, had her mother. As for her father . . .

What her father had done, or hadn't done, didn't matter.

The point was, Carrie wasn't comfortable in crowds. Not at parties, anyway. She was fine on the subway or on the city street, where people minded their own business and largely ignored each other. But when you were supposed to mingle with strangers who asked nosy questions that could lead to trouble . . .

"Are you here with Mack?" a freckle-faced, ginger-haired woman about her own age had asked, right after he left her side.

"Yes."

"From the city?"

She nodded.

"Did you grow up there? Or are you from someplace else?"

It was none of her business where Carrie had grown up, and she almost said it. Instead, she just ignored the question and turned her back on the redhead.

She knew she should get out of there, and fast—but she also knew that if she did, she'd never see Mack again.

She should want that—should want to put as much distance as possible between them as possible, because this was dangerous territory. But she didn't want it. She didn't want to leave.

Always listen to your gut.

Her gut was telling her to stay, so she stood in the spot where he'd left her, avoiding eye contact with everyone else, waiting for him to find her again. Just when she'd all but given up hope—there he was. He took her arm, and suddenly, everything was okay again.

Until he told her he wanted her to meet his mother.

To his credit, he didn't push her. Still, she immediately regretted going upstairs with him, too far from the escape hatch for comfort. Especially when he told her she wasn't allowed to have a cigarette, which might have taken the edge off her nerves.

A grown man who hid his smoking habit from his parents didn't sit well with her. She'd taken it as a good sign that he didn't live under his parents' roof, but he might as well.

Waiting there on the bed in his boyhood room as the minutes ticked by, she had grown increasingly uncomfortable. She reminded herself that she could still be out of the house—even down the block and back on the PATH train—in a matter of minutes.

She was about to flee when suddenly, she spotted it.

A dream catcher, just like the one her father had hung in her window when she was a little girl.

"Only good dreams can get through that web," Daddy had told her, and somehow, as she sat there on Mack's bed staring at it, that was exactly what happened.

A dream—just a daydream, a pipe dream, but it was definitely good—drifted into Carrie's head. She saw herself with Mack. He had his arms wrapped around her from behind, holding her against him. It was so real she thought she could feel his heart beating against her back and feel his chin resting on her shoulder; so real she dared to think that it could actually come true.

But of course, it couldn't. He could never love someone like her.

Why not? He asked you out, not once, but twice. He likes you. Like can turn to love. That's how it's supposed to happen, isn't it?

For ordinary people, maybe. People who didn't have terrible secrets buried in their distant—and not so distant—past.

Carrie would never be free of what had happened to her. What her father had done. What *she* had done.

She stood up, walked to the door, stepped into the hall—and there, she saw Mack.

The way he was standing, with his head tilted back against his mother's bedroom door and his eyes closed, caused something to shift deep within Carrie.

He seemed utterly alone, radiating emotional isolation. That might have been off-putting to some, but to Carrie, it was a beacon. She had assumed Mack was vitally connected to all those other people, those insufferable, nosy people.

But perhaps his life wasn't irrevocably intertwined with the others'. His mother wouldn't be around for much longer, and he'd mentioned that his father, too, was ailing . . .

Maybe there was hope after all, she thought. If he wasn't a package deal . . .

Once again she was ensnared in the happy dream-catcher vision of her future.

She *might* be able to handle a relationship. Just with Mack—as opposed to the many new ties she'd have had to make—or fake, or fend off—with his friends and family members.

Yes. It could work, if it was just the two of them.

Dipping his last French fry into ketchup, he said, "I've done all the talking here. I'm sorry."

"It's okay. You have a lot going on." He'd told her about his mother's illness, and his father's, and feeling as though his life was on the verge of changing forever.

She had listened intently and made sympathetic comments here and there, but inside, she rejoiced. He was clearly coming to a crossroads.

Just like I did, before I came to New York.

Mack was going to have to build a whole new life for himself, whether he wanted to or not.

Just like I did.

But what about her new life?

What about finding Allison and making things right?

Somehow, that had mattered less to her these last few days. Why?

Because she'd met Mack?

Or because she'd met Ralph?

Ah, Ralph. Maybe taking care of him had allowed her to get it out of her system—maybe for the long run, now that she'd found Mack and dared to dream of a future with him.

Ralph's body had been found, though it wasn't yet identified. There had been a small article in yesterday's *New York Post*, easy to miss if you weren't looking for it.

Carrie had been looking.

She wasn't worried. She had gone over every scenario—every possible way anyone could ever connect her to that crime—and come up with absolutely nothing. She'd covered her tracks well. Much better than the last time.

But that was years ago. She was older now, much wiser. She'd done her homework.

Thanks to you, Daddy.

Wasn't *that* ironic.

The waitress appeared to clear away the remains of Carrie's sandwich and the empty plate that had held Mack's burger and fries.

"Would you like coffee and dessert menus?" she asked.

"I'll have coffee," Carrie said. "No dessert."

"Want to share a piece of pie?" Mack asked.

Imagine that. Imagine sharing a piece of pie with him, like boyfriend and girlfriend. The vision that popped into her head was so cozy that it unnerved her, and she stammered, "No—no, thanks."

Mack ordered a piece of apple pie and told the waitress to bring two forks anyway, "Just in case."

"Coffee for you, too?"

"At this hour? No, thanks."

"Does it keep you up?" Carrie asked him when the waitress had stepped away again.

"It doesn't help. I haven't found anything that does. I've had insomnia most of my life. Especially lately. I can't remember the last time I slept through the night."

"That's understandable, with all that's been going on."

"Yeah, well . . ." He sighed. "I don't want to talk about that stuff anymore. It's your turn now. Tell me about you."

Just like that, she was uncomfortable again, filled with misgiving.

Why am I here?

What am I supposed to say to him?

She cleared her throat. "There's not much to tell, really."

"Don't be shy. You're not the only good listener at this table."

"I just . . . I don't know what you want to know." She'd already told him, on their first date, that she'd lost both her parents years ago. He didn't press her for details. Maybe he sensed that it was a painful subject. Or maybe, facing that loss himself, he just didn't want to know.

Now he said, "Start with the easy part. Where are you from?"

Easy? Ha. None of it was easy.

If she told him the truth, even just the name of the rural South Dakota county where she'd been born, she'd be opening the door to more questions. If she didn't answer them, he'd be suspicious. And if she did, and they continued to see each other, and he ever decided to go poking around in her past . . .

No, she couldn't tell him the truth.

"Carrie?"

"It's a long story."

"Where you're from is a long story?"

"Yes."

"I've got all night." He rested his chin on his hand.

"My parents and I . . . we moved around a lot. So I'm not really from any one place."

"Was your father in the military or something?"

"No, not that . . ."

He was watching her, waiting for her to go on. She looked away and her gaze fell on the group of men at the next table, the ones with the dark shirts and pinky rings.

Her head was spinning. How could she make Mack stop asking questions she couldn't answer?

"Carrie . . . ?"

"I've never told anyone this." She shifted her eyes back to Mack. "I mean, maybe it's okay, after all these years, but maybe . . . maybe I still shouldn't be talking about it."

She half expected him to tell her that it was okay, she didn't have to. But she could see the curiosity in his eyes, and she knew he wasn't going to let her off the hook that easily.

So she took a deep breath, and, feeling as though she were inching out on a tightrope that was as sturdy as thread, she said it.

"Witness protection program."

"What about it?"

"I was in it. Growing up."

Mack's eyes widened. "You're kidding."

"Why would I kid about something like that?"

"You wouldn't," he said quickly. "I'm sorry. I was just sur-prised. What happened?"

"When I was really young," she said, "I lived with my parents in a city, and something happened—it involved my father. He got into some kind of trouble, and his life—our lives—were in danger. So we . . . you know . . . disap-peared."

"What did—"

"I was too young to remember. All I know was that one day, we were living a normal life, and after that, we weren't. Even after we were settled into our new life, we had to pick up and move again, without any warning."

"Where did it all start?"

"I have no idea. Like I said, it was a city—I don't know which one, though, or even which part of the country. I don't even know what my name was when I was born."

"So Carrie Robinson isn't your real name?"

"It's real enough. It's who I am."

"But who *were* you?"

"Does it matter?"

"No, but . . . aren't you curious? Didn't your parents ever fill you in?" Mack asked. "Later, I mean."

"No."

"You mean they refused to tell you?"

"I mean I never asked. What did it matter? All I knew was that I'd had a normal life, and then one day, suddenly, I didn't."

The waitress showed up with a pot of coffee, and Mack and Carrie waited silently as she turned over one of the two cups on the table and filled it. She set down a metal creamer and a little dish of sugar packets and artificial sweeteners, and left.

"What happened, exactly, with your father? I mean, was he involved in criminal activity himself? Or was he just in the wrong place at the wrong time? Did he see something he shouldn't have seen?"

"I have no idea," she said for the second time in as many minutes. "I just don't know what happened."

"Really?"

Again, she bristled. "*Really.*"

They shouldn't be talking about this. *She* shouldn't be talking about this. It was dangerous.

She reached for the creamer and dumped some into her coffee. Feeling Mack's eyes on her, she opened a sugar packet and poured it in, and then another, even though she didn't ordinarily take her coffee sweetened.

"I'm just trying to understand," Mack said. "So you didn't ever ask him for the details?"

She picked up a spoon and stirred vigorously. "No. It didn't matter to me."

"Why not?"

Irked that he wouldn't just drop it, she suddenly wished she'd fled his parents' house earlier and not looked back. This was much harder than she'd expected.

Already, she was in over her head.

He was waiting.

She forced herself to look up and meet his gaze head on. "This is really hard for me. I told you, I never talked about it before with anyone. I don't . . . it's not something I'm comfortable doing."

He reached across the table and took her hand in both of his. His grasp was big and warm.

"It's okay, Carrie. I'm glad you told me. I'm honored. I figured you weren't the type who let your guard down very easily, but I had no idea that the reason was this intense."

Oh, Mack, if you only knew . . .

She was unaccustomed to the depth of the emotions that coursed through her as she sat looking into his kind green eyes. What had begun with casual interest and mere attraction had given way to fierce longing. She wanted this man— this deliciously ordinary man. Wanted him in every way; wanted him to want her, to need her, to love her.

She had never imagined that such a thing was possible, and now that she'd glimpsed what might be . . .

This was it for her. There was no turning back now.

"Here we are . . . apple pie, two forks." The waitress was back, setting a plate on the table between them. "Enjoy, guys."

Mack nodded, but didn't break his eye contact with Carrie. When they were alone again, he gave her hands another squeeze. "Are you okay?"

"I am."

"I have one last question for you."

Uh-oh.

The tightrope wobbled again.

"What is it?"

"Why me?" he asked.

"Why . . . you?"

"You said you never told anyone your story. After all these years of keeping people at arm's length . . . why did you finally choose to let someone in? Why tonight? Why me?"

Relieved by the question, she dared to answer it with utter honesty. "I guess it was just . . . there was something about you that made me want to let you in. That made me want to know you."

He smiled. "My sparkling wit? My dashing good looks? What was it?"

She shrugged, shook her head, thinking about how snug her hand was with his wrapped around it. "You just felt safe."

"I'm glad."

He nodded, as if that was all settled then, and let go of her hand. He picked up the forks and offered one to her. "You have to have pie."

"No, thank you."

"You sure? It's really good here."

She took a fork and tasted it, because he wanted to share it.

"Do you like it?"

She nodded.

"I knew you would. I've been coming here for years. The food is a lot better than you'd think. But next time, I promise, I'll take you out to a great dinner in Manhattan."

Next time. Finally, she managed a smile.

"I mean, two strikes so far . . . I can't afford a third."

"Two strikes?"

"I took you to a pub on our first date. And now a diner. Some women wouldn't like it."

She narrowed her eyes. "Are you talking about Chelsea?"

He looked startled. "Chelsea? How did you know about her?"

"You told me. Remember?"

"Nope." He shook his head. "I guess I've had so much on my mind lately I can't remember what I told you."

She's had a lot on her mind, too—but she knows damned well she's not going to forget a single detail about what she told him tonight.

"You told me about Chelsea," she says.

"I guess it must have been pretty memorable, considering that you actually remember her name. Did I say she was an evil bitch or something?"

"Not . . . you didn't say *that*, exactly."

"I didn't? Are you sure?" He laughed.

"*Was* she?"

"You could say that. Or *I* could say it. Hell, I could say a lot of things—but I don't want to waste my breath on Chelsea. She's not worth it."

No. She certainly isn't, Carrie thought, watching him stab his fork into the pie. *She's not worth your breath, and she's not worth the air she breathes. Guess I'll just have to do something about that.*

Chapter Nine

Lower Manhattan's skyline, topped off by the twin towers of the World Trade Center, was tinted with the first pinkish streaks of dawn as the yellow cab turned onto Chelsea's street just off West Broadway.

She'd been expecting Andrew to send her home with his personal chauffeur, but maybe he didn't have one. She'd almost asked about it, but decided not to. She didn't want him to think she was a gold digger.

It was enough, for now, to have been wined and dined at the Pierre, bedded in a lovely suite upstairs.

When he'd suggested a private nightcap, she'd expected him to take her back to his place, but he said he was having renovations done.

Maybe that was true.

Or maybe he had a live-in girlfriend, or even a wife. Who knew? Who cared? Just potential small obstacles, as far as Chelsea was concerned. She had her sights set on Andrew, and she was going to get him.

He was just as handsome as she remembered from the first

night, and impeccably dressed. She wished he knew his way around a woman's anatomy as well as he did a wine list, but was willing to chalk up his rather perfunctory performance to first-time jitters and, yes, all that pinot noir he'd had.

They'd really hit it off in every other possible way.

Well, other than the fact that he abhorred cigarettes. When she asked if he minded if she lit up, he said that he did, then launched into an antismoking tirade she tried to tune out as much as possible. It was okay. Maybe she'd quit for him. Or maybe she'd just sneak them when he was around.

At least the conversation never once lagged—though if it had, she was armed with a mental list of questions to ask him. He answered most of them without being asked, telling her almost everything she wanted to know about him, plus a lot of extra information that was—well, not boring, exactly, but . . .

All right. It *was* boring. It could have just been that she was tired after a long workweek, or simply wasn't in the right mood to hear about his starring role in boarding school rugby matches, or his recent business trip to Saskatchewan. She was sure he was full of fascinating stories about other things, and that he'd get around to asking her about herself on their next date.

Of course, there would be one, because when they parted ways on the street in front of the hotel, he'd said, "I'll call you."

Maybe there would already be a message waiting on her home answering machine, she thought, and eagerly reached for the car door handle as the taxi pulled to a stop outside her building.

"Hey, lady!" the cabbie said as she started to climb out. "The fare?"

"My fiancé took care of it," she reminded him. *Fiancé*. She liked the sound of that. "Remember? He told you to keep the change?"

"Your *fiancé*—" his tone made it clear he didn't buy that for one second—"gave me ten bucks. The fare is twelve-seventy-five."

Ten bucks?

Chelsea had figured Andrew was giving him a twenty, or even a fifty. In fact . . . how did she know he hadn't?

"I suggest that you look again," she said haughtily. "Why would he give you a ten?" Even if he had, it must have been a mistake. He probably thought it was a twenty. Or a fifty.

"Sure, I'll look again. Oh yeah, you're right, he didn't give me a ten . . ."

Aha.

"He gave me two fives." He waved them at her.

"What proof do I have that you're not lying?"

"Call your *fiancé* and ask him . . . *if* you have his phone number."

She was too incensed to think of a snappy comeback.

"Look, just pay the rest of your fare, lady, and I'll get out of your hair, okay?"

Chelsea fumbled in the white silk bag that exactly matched the dress she was wearing, came up with three singles, and tossed them into the front seat. "Here. Keep the change, *okay*?"

She heard the obscenity he threw at her just before she slammed the door, and she returned it under her breath.

Storming toward her building as fast as she could on the pair of barely-broken-in five-inch strappy silver stilettos she'd bought yesterday, she heard the taxi pull away and screech around the corner.

She repeated the obscenity, this time louder, just before she noticed the homeless person huddled on the sidewalk a few feet away from the entrance to her building. He appeared to be asleep. If he wasn't, he might think she'd been directing the profane phrase at him. Well, so be it. Vagrants weren't welcome on this block. Chelsea made a mental note to inform the landlord that the neighborhood was going downhill and she deserved a rent reduction.

Then again, maybe she shouldn't bother, she thought, as she stood in front of the door feeling around inside her bag for her keys and the pack of Salems she hadn't touched in hours.

Maybe she'd soon be moving in with Andrew uptown, once his renovations were completed or his girlfriend had been kicked to the curb or whatever—

The thought was curtailed by a rush of movement behind her . . .

Much too close behind her.

Now what? Had she pissed off that bum? Was he going to do something about it? Was she going to be attacked or mugged right here on her doorstep?

No way. Absolutely no freaking way, she thought, and started to turn.

"Don't move," a voice whispered harshly, and something jabbed into her ribs.

She went still.

"Unlock the door. Don't make a sound. Hurry up."

Chelsea's hand shook as she felt around in her bag. A lipstick, a comb, a compact—she couldn't use any of those things to fight back, dammit. At last she found the key, and it took her several tries to insert it into the lock.

"Hurry up!" the voice whispered again, and she was prodded once more from behind with what could only be a gun.

Chelsea unlocked the door and pushed it open, knowing he was going to rape her, sickened at the thought of it.

"Go ahead, get inside. Walk to your apartment. And I know which one it is, so don't try anything. Make a sound, and you're dead."

It's not a man, she realized. *It's a woman.*

Thank God. Thank God rape wasn't going to happen. She could handle anything but that.

"I'll give you whatever you want," she said softly, forcing her wobbling shoes to carry her to the stairway. "I have money upstairs, and some jewelry."

Money—maybe twenty bucks that would be in her wallet, which was still tucked inside the purse she'd carried to work today, along with some subway tokens.

And jewelry? She owned plenty of costume pieces, even a few that could pass for the real thing—but there was no way she'd give this creep the diamond tennis bracelet she'd inherited from her stepmother, or her emerald earrings, which she'd have been wearing right now if Tiffany had loaned her the green Dior to wear tonight.

I'm glad you were so selfish, she silently told her friend. *Thanks to you, those earrings are safe and sound and hidden away where this thieving bitch will never find them.*

The building's public hallways and stairway were deserted at this hour. If Chelsea screamed, someone would come to help her—but by then, she'd be shot dead. Unless it wasn't a real gun in her ribs—not that she was willing to take any chances and find out.

Up one flight they went, and down the hall to apartment 2C.

"Unlock the door."

"I *am*," Chelsea bit out, trying to get the key into the lock, and was rewarded with another sharp nudge in the back.

"Be quiet."

"I *am*." This time, she whispered.

She opened the door and started to step into the apartment, but was shoved roughly from behind. She cried out as she stumbled forward and caught herself on the back of a chair. Her thoughts spun as she clung to it, trying to regroup, wondering if she could possibly grab a lamp or something to use as a weapon.

No. She'd have had to act in the two seconds it took her assailant to close and lock the door behind them; it was already too late for that.

"Stand up straight," the voice commanded. "Turn around."

Chelsea did as she was told and came face-to-face with her attacker at last.

The woman wore baggy clothes that included a hooded jacket pulled tight around her head, leaving only a small circle of face visible. It was dark in here; Chelsea could barely see a tuft of dark hair, a protruding white nose, and eyes that were narrowed into slits of fury.

"You don't even know why I'm here, do you?"

About to answer, Chelsea spotted the small flashlight she was holding. Was that what had been prodding into her back?

Before she could react, the woman revealed a big knife in her other hand. "Don't try anything. Believe me, I'll use this."

And that, Chelsea realized, would be a different kind of attack than the one she had envisioned.

With a gun, you took aim and pulled the trigger. With a knife, you had to get close enough to use it.

If I don't give her an opportunity to do that, she thought wildly, *I can get away.*

She'd still be taking a chance—a huge one. After a long evening in these shoes, she could barely walk, let alone run.

But, fixated on that sharp blade, she now realized this wasn't just a random mugging. Muggers carried guns, or switchblades, maybe. Not chef knives with long, tapered blades.

If she tried to escape, she might die. If she didn't try, she most certainly would.

"*Do* you, Chelsea?"

"Do I what?"

"Do you even know why I'm here!" The woman was no longer whispering, and there was something familiar about her voice.

"No, I don't." Chelsea looked more closely at the circle of face, trying to see if it was recognizable.

"Because of him."

"Because of who? Andrew?" And then it dawned on her.

That day, maybe a few weeks ago . . . or was it this week? It must have been this past week, because she'd just met Andrew last weekend. Yes, she was leaving her office building with Tiffany, and a stranger had come up to her, claiming to be an old school friend.

This was that woman.

"Who's Andrew? What are you talking about?"

"What are *you* talking about?" Chelsea shot back, momentarily as furious with herself as she was with the woman, remembering something wasn't quite right that day. And then later, on the subway, she'd felt like she was being followed, even though she'd glimpsed the woman's face.

"I'm talking about what you did to Mack!"

Mack . . .

Mack . . . ? The guy she'd dated recently?

This was about *him*?

"I didn't do anything to Mack. I don't—"

"Shut up!"

Clamping her mouth shut, Chelsea took a step back.

"I'm his girl! Do you understand? *Me!* Not you!"

"That's fine. Seriously. I'm not—"

"Just because he lives with *you* instead of with me now doesn't mean—"

"Wait, what?" It was Chelsea's turn to interrupt—maybe not the best idea, but she couldn't help herself; this lunatic had it all wrong. "Mack doesn't live with me! I live alone!"

"Don't you dare lie to me! Do you think I'm stupid? Do you think I don't know what's been going on?"

"It's not a lie! It's the truth! Go ahead, look around. None of his things are here. He doesn't live here. I haven't even seen him in weeks!"

"You're lying! How do you think I found out you even

exist? I followed him here, and I saw you with him. I saw you, and you had Papoose! Papoose was mine!"

What was she talking about? Chelsea felt panic beginning to take hold; felt her body beginning to quake and a cold, clammy sweat oozing from her skin.

"You didn't even know about me until now, did you? He didn't even bother to tell you, did he? Did he?"

She was screaming now. Praying someone would overhear and call the police, Chelsea took another step backward.

The woman moved closer and her eyes were no longer angry little slits; they were wide and wild and full of accusation that made no sense at all.

She's crazy, Chelsea realized. *She's truly crazy, and she has a knife, and . . .*

And she's not here to rob me. She's here to kill me.

Summoning every ounce of calm her body would allow, she said, "Look, you can have him. I mean it. He's all yours."

"He is not! He's all *yours*. I hate you, Allison!"

Allison?

Dear God, no wonder there's no logic to what she's saying. She doesn't even know who I am.

Wait a minute. She *did* know. She'd called Chelsea by her own name just a minute ago. Now she was calling her Allison, as if something had snapped inside her and she'd lost her grip on reality.

"Listen to me, you obviously have me mixed up with someone else!" Chelsea was desperate to get through to her, to bring her back from the brink of violence. "My name isn't—"

"Shut your mouth!"

Chelsea tried again to back away, but her heel hit the wall behind her. She was literally cornered, and if she didn't convince this delusional stranger that her name wasn't Allison and she wasn't living with Mack . . .

The edge of the knife settled against Chelsea's throat.

If I don't convince her, then I'm going to die. Right now.

"All those times he told me he was working, he was really with *you*. All the times I needed him and he couldn't be there for me, it was because of *you*."

Chelsea turned her head and felt the blade press into her straining neck, felt her skin splitting, felt blood running over her collarbone.

Her first thought was that she was never going to get the stains out of her white silk dress.

Her next, as she fell to the floor amid her attacker's rants and vicious knife thrusts, was that this terrible fury was meant for someone else.

For Allison, whoever . . . wherever . . . she was.

The ringing phone should have jarred her from a sound sleep at this hour, but Allison was already—rather, *still*—wide awake, watching the first gray light inch across her bedroom walls.

She reached for the phone, knowing whose voice she would hear when she answered it.

"Allison? It's Brett. I'm sorry to call so early."

"What time is it?"

"A little after five here, but it's already six where you are, so I figured you might be up."

On a Saturday morning? He truly did inhabit an entirely different world.

Then again, she *was* awake, if not technically *up*.

She'd been lying here for hours now thinking about the past, and about her future.

Last night, giddy with margaritas and first date fantasizing, she'd imagined falling in love with Justin. She'd thought that getting married and starting a family of her own was all she really wanted out of life, all she needed.

But when she got into bed, darkness swallowed the afterglow, and the familiar empty feeling took hold again. How could she have thought that loving someone else, even being loved by someone else, could erase the damage that had been done when first one parent, then the other, abandoned her?

Anxious for her brother to get to the point so that she could hang up and attempt to move on, she asked, "What's going on, Brett?"

"It's about your father."

Not "Dad," or "*our* father." Nope, clearly, as far as Brett was concerned, Allen Taylor was all Allison's, and probably had been for over twenty-three years now, ever since he'd been so insensitively vocal about wishing for a son of his own.

"What about him?" she asked, swinging her legs over the side of the bed and thrusting her feet into her slippers before she realized what she'd done.

It was as if her subconscious mind were preparing her to flee.

But you can't run away from a conversation, Allison.

"You caught me off guard when you called me the other night, and I . . . I guess I wasn't as truthful when I answered your questions as I could have been."

And you can't run away from the truth.

"So you *did* find him?" she asked Brett flatly.

"No! You know I wouldn't lie about something like that."

"Well, you said you weren't truthful, so that means you lied about something."

"No, it just means I didn't tell you the whole truth, and that was only because I didn't want to hurt you any more than he already did."

"You mean Allen Taylor?" She couldn't even bring herself to call him her father.

"That's the thing, Allison. He's *not* Allen Taylor."

"What do you mean?" She clenched the phone hard against her ear, her hand trembling.

"I mean that couldn't have been his real name. When I searched for him, I went looking for records that should have been available if he was telling the truth, and they weren't there. He always said he was born on Pearl Harbor day, remember?"

A faint memory made its way back to her: *A day that would live in infamy, Allison—that was my birthday. All the doctors and nurses at the hospital were so worked up about the attack in Hawaii that they were barely paying attention to my poor mama.*

"I remember," she told her brother. "Pearl Harbor day. That's right."

In her head, she could still hear her father's voice. *My mama—your grandma, may she rest in peace—said that if I'd been a girl, I'd have been named Pearl. But I was a boy, so she named me Al, after the Allies.*

Your name was Allies, Daddy?

No, it was Allen, sweetie pie.

But it wasn't.

In the grand scheme of what her father had done, perhaps the fact that he'd lied about his name shouldn't have been surprising. Yet she felt as though she'd had the wind knocked out of her.

"He said he was born in Council Bluffs," Brett went on. "Remember?"

Yes. That was directly across the Missouri River from Omaha, where her mother had grown up. She remembered him teasing Mom about how he hadn't just been born on the wrong side of the tracks, he'd been born on the wrong side of the river *and* the state line.

You coulda wound up with one of those fancy insurance fellows in Omaha, Brenda. Instead, you got stuck with an Iowa farmer.

But of course, he wasn't really a farmer. His parents had

been, but it wasn't a life he wanted for himself. "I'm not one for putting down roots," he'd say. "I like to get up and go."

Yeah. No kidding.

"When I went to look for him after Mom died," Brett said, "the first thing I did was check birth records. There was no documentation of an Allen Taylor having been born on December 7, 1941, in Council Bluffs or in any of the surrounding towns."

"Did you check Omaha, too?"

"I checked *everywhere*."

"Maybe it wasn't really Allen. Maybe it was Alan, with two As and one L, or—"

"I tried that, Allison. Just like you did. Remember what you said about looking for an Alex, or Alvin . . . ? I did the same exact thing. Not with the Internet, because there was no Internet back when I was looking, but I searched everyplace I could think of for anything that might even come close. There was nothing."

"So what does that mean?" she asked, though of course she knew. But she needed him to say it.

"It means he didn't want us to know his real name, or where he was born, or when."

"Or all of the above," she said slowly as the news worked its way into her brain like a sliver painfully jabbing the tender skin beneath a fingernail.

"Do you think Mom knew?" she asked Brett.

"Maybe. Maybe not."

Something else dawned on her. "Do you think—were they even married?"

"Who knows?"

"But you were around then. You must remember."

"I do, a little bit. I remember Mom telling me that Al was going to be my new dad, and I remember her getting all dressed up in a white dress—not a wedding gown, just a dress. They left me with Mrs. Franklin, the fat old lady who lived next door to us on Third Street, while they went off to get married."

"When was that?"

"It must have been in the early seventies because I was about four or five years old. And it was winter, or early spring, because I remember that it was snowing. I overheard Mrs. Franklin talking to a friend of hers on the phone about the weather, how the roads were getting bad and she was worried about them making it home in one piece. I remember picturing them *not* in one piece—you know how kids' minds work. And I was afraid they'd never come back and I'd have to live with Mrs. Franklin. But they finally showed up, and they were—you know. Newlyweds. Laughing, happy. They smelled like booze. Al picked me up and swung me around the room and told me to call him Dad."

Brett fell silent.

Allison digested the cozy little family tableau he'd just painted. "So they *were* married."

"That's what they told me and Mrs. Franklin."

"But you think—"

"I don't know what to think. Look, if they really went and got legally married that day, then it couldn't have been more than a hundred miles or so from Centerfield. They left me off with Mrs. Franklin after lunch—I remember, because I didn't want to eat lunch there, because she was always cooking something that stunk to high heaven. Fish, Brussels sprouts, cabbage . . ."

He paused, and she could picture him wrinkling his nose the way he did when they were kids—well, when she was a kid and he was almost grown up. He never did like vegetables, and that was fine with Mom, because she didn't, either. Back when everything was still relatively normal—when Brett was still living at home, before Allison's father left, before the drug habit took hold—Mom would occasionally attempt to cook dinner. Pasta with jar sauce, hamburgers, and frozen French fries. That was the extent of her "home cooking," but she was proud of it.

Allison was not. She still had friends back then. A few, anyway. They would tell her how lucky she was to have a mother who didn't force string beans or beets on her.

Lucky. Sure.

The only other girl who "got it"—aside from Winona, Allison's imaginary friend—was Tammy Connolly, who seemed like a godsend when she moved to town, renting the house next door to Allison.

Tammy didn't have a picture-perfect family, either. Her father wasn't around. Allison couldn't remember whether he'd died or there'd been a divorce. But she clearly remembered Tammy's brassy mother, a waitress at the local Cracker Barrel by day and God-only-knew-what by night. She was the kind of woman the church ladies called a tramp behind her back, while bringing casseroles to her front door to welcome her to town.

The church ladies' daughters didn't believe in that behind-your-back stuff. They ridiculed Allison to her face when her life fell apart.

Tammy just felt sorry for her. Allison didn't want the pity, either. She was torn between regret and relief when Tammy's family moved away abruptly not long after Allison's father took off. If only she, too, could have left Centerfield behind.

"We'll keep in touch," Tammy promised on that last day, when she showed up at the door to tell Allison she was leaving. "You can come visit."

For Allison, those words beckoned like an inflatable escape route on a burning plane.

Of course it never happened. She never saw or heard from Tammy again.

But I did leave Centerfield as soon as I got the chance, and I promised myself that just like Tammy, I'd never look back, and what the hell am I doing now?

"Anyhow," Brett said, "when they came back to Mrs. Franklin's that night, the ten o'clock news had just started—I definitely remember that, because I was watching it and worrying that there might be a report about a car accident. So it took them—what, about eight or nine hours?—to drive out on icy roads to wherever they were going, get married, have champagne and dinner at a decent restaurant—I remember Mom told me she ate lobster tail."

"You're kidding."

"What?"

"*Lobster?*"

"We have fancy seafood here in Nebraska, Miss Big Apple."

"I didn't mean—" *Yes, you did.* "Never mind."

"I'm glad Mom got to have it on her wedding night," Brett said.

"Me too." She ached at the thought of their mother, eating lobster in a pretty white dress on her wintry wedding night, toasting a bright, shiny future, believing the worst was over, hard times behind her at last . . .

Oh Mom. You were fooling yourself.

Or was he fooling you?

Did Brenda see her new husband as her knight in shining armor?

How could she not? She was a high school dropout, disowned by her family, a single mother on welfare . . .

She must have wondered what Allen Taylor—whoever he was—could possibly see in her.

What *did* he see in her?

"I used to be beautiful, you know," Allison's mother liked to tell her. "All the boys said so. You look just like me. You're beautiful, too, you know."

Allison would nod as if she agreed, but her mother had the haggard, emaciated facial characteristics of a junkie, and she couldn't see a resemblance. *Wouldn't* see it.

Not back then. Maybe now, given the perspective of adulthood—but of course, she could glimpse her mother only in her mind's eye. There were no snapshots of a happy, healthy, youthful Brenda. Mom had presumably left the photographic remnants of her childhood behind at her own parents' home, and if there had been photos later in her life, she'd destroyed them along with everything else.

Maybe it was better that way. Better not to see what once was—and fantasize about what could have been . . .

"The way I've always figured, they probably went about two hundred miles round-trip in that time frame in that weather," Brett said, and she forced her attention back to the conversation. "There's no record of an Allen and Brenda Taylor getting married anywhere in a hundred-mile radius of Centerfield at that time of year in the early seventies. That doesn't mean it didn't happen, but . . ."

"But there's no proof that it did."

"Exactly."

"And there's no proof that Allen was who he claimed to be."

"I'd say that's proof that he wasn't."

"Why would he lie to us? To her?"

"Why do people lie, Allison?"

There it was again. He'd asked her the same question the other night, and it had been running through her mind ever since.

Why do people lie?

"To protect themselves," she said slowly, "or someone else. And . . ."

"And what?"

"And because they have something to hide. Something dark, or damaging, or ugly. You were right, Brett. I never should have tried to find him. I don't want a man like him in my life, so like you said—what's the point?"

"Well, I'm just looking out for you, you know? Someone has to. And I'm the only family you've got."

That was true.

Yet the reverse was not the case. *She* wasn't the only family *he* had. Her brother had built a new life for himself, with a wife, children, in-laws, friends. He'd gone about it when he was so very young, and somehow he'd defied the odds. As far as she could tell, his life was fulfilling.

"Brett?"

"Yeah?"

"How'd you manage to leave it all behind and move on the way you did?"

"What do you mean?"

"The hurt. The memories. The shame of what he did to us, and what Mom did . . ."

"It's simple." She pictured him shrugging, tilting his sandy head to one side as he said earnestly, "You just don't ever let yourself look back. Just keep looking straight ahead."

Simple was right. When it came to advice from her big brother, she knew that was about as profound as it was going to get.

"That's all you need to do, Allison. Stop looking back."

"That's what I've always tried to do. I guess I lapsed for a couple of days there, but it's not going to happen again."

"Good." Brett cleared his throat. "I guess I'd better get going. I've got a lot of chores to do."

"One last thing, Brett, before you hang up? Can you please do me a favor and don't mention any of this to anyone?"

"Like who?"

"Just . . . anyone." It was private family business, as far as she was concerned.

"Allison, I live clear across the state from Centerfield. I don't talk to folks from back there, or anyone who might know you. Don't worry."

"What about Cindy, and her parents?"

"What about them?"

"Are you going to tell them?"

When he hesitated, she said, "You already did, didn't you?"

"Cin's known all along—about Allen, I mean. About the fake name, and all the other lies he told us."

"She knew—but I didn't?"

"I don't keep secrets from Cindy-Lou. She's my wife."

"I'm your *sister*. He was my *father*. Didn't you think I deserved to know, too?"

"You told me not to tell you if I found him, Allison. You said you never wanted to hear his name again. Now you're mad because I did what you asked me to do?"

Yes. She was. Maybe it wasn't fair to him, but she couldn't help it. Brett should have told her something as serious as this.

"I was just a kid, Brett."

"Yeah, well, so was I."

After a moment of tension-laced silence, she said, "Forget it."

"I will."

"Good. Go do your chores."

"Allison, wait—if you want to come visit us . . . you haven't seen the kids since they were tiny, and you've never been out here to the farm . . . Cindy-Lou was just saying last night, maybe you're feeling homesick for Nebraska. Maybe a visit would do you good. You're welcome to come."

Homesick?

For *Nebraska*?

"Thanks," she said quickly, "but . . ."

"But no thanks?"

Pretty much.

"That's what Cindy-Lou said you'd say."

"I'm just really busy, and really broke," she told him, and it was the truth—just not the whole truth. He ought to understand that, she thought, still smarting over the fact that he'd held out on her—not just for days, but for years.

"Thanks for the invitation. Really."

"Yeah. You're welcome."

Dammit. She didn't want to hurt his feelings, and of course she eventually hoped to get to know her niece, Samantha, and nephew, Jeff. She just didn't want to go back to Nebraska, even for a visit, and couldn't imagine that the day would ever come when she might change her mind about that.

"Why don't you come here instead?" she suggested. "I'd love to see you, and I have plenty of room . . ." Ah, a lie. Two of them, actually.

Guess it runs in the family.

She was relieved when Brett told her that he, too, was too busy and too broke for a visit. It wasn't that she never wanted to see him again—but a reunion with her brother wouldn't be conducive to putting the past behind her once and for all.

"Good-bye, Allison."

"Good-bye, Brett."

She hung up the phone, kicked off her slippers, and crawled back into bed, exhausted.

Mack was no stranger to sleepless nights, but it was unusual for him to not make it to bed at all.

His usual pattern was to climb under the covers at around midnight, then read or watch television for another hour, hoping to get sleepy. Sometimes he thought he was, but as soon as he turned off the television or set the book aside, he'd find himself wide awake, staring at the ceiling. Most nights, he tossed and turned till two or three, even four. If he was lucky, he'd finally drift off for a few hours until the alarm went off.

But tonight—rather, this morning—had been a total loss. It was eight A.M. and he'd just walked in the door.

After seeing Carrie onto a Manhattan-bound PATH train,

he'd doubled back to his parents' house, feeling guilty at the way he'd left the party without telling anyone. When he got there, things were in full swing. Aunt Fiona had succeeded in having the furniture pushed back, the rugs rolled up, and the living room had become a dance floor. Mack noticed that the hospice bed, back in the corner, was covered in coats—there were never enough hangers in the closet.

His sister told him that their mother was sound asleep upstairs despite the commotion. "But Daddy's been having a grand old time," she added, and Mack could see that for himself. Brian MacKenna was dancing a lively jig with his brothers, laughing his head off for the first time in months.

"Dan took the kids home," Lynn went on, "but I told him I'd better stay and keep the party going and clean up afterward. No way Mom and Dad can do it."

"Good idea. I'll help."

"Where's your friend?"

"She went home. She was exhausted."

"You didn't even introduce me."

"Next time."

"Belinda said she met her."

Belinda MacKenna was one of their cousins, a friendly, easygoing redhead. Mack could tell by his sister's expression that Belinda hadn't been particularly impressed with Carrie, so he quickly changed the subject.

The dancing lasted well into the wee hours. By four-thirty A.M., they were serving the traditional sausage and eggs with strong Irish breakfast tea; by six, the sun was coming up, the stragglers had left, Dad had gone to bed, and Mack and Lynn were wearily cleaning up the mess.

She drove him home on her way back to Middletown, and their parting conversation wasn't about Carrie. It was about their parents, a somber note upon which to end the night— rather, begin the day.

Just before Mack got out of the car, Lynn touched his arm. "Mack? Wait. I have to tell you something. It's, um, not good news."

He turned back to her. "Really? What a surprise. Because all I've had lately is good news, so I thought I was on a roll."

She smiled faintly. "Black Irish looks, Black Irish humor. That's what Grandma used to say."

He nodded, steeling himself for whatever was coming.

"Dan and I are separating. We haven't told the kids yet. Or Mom and Dad. I don't think anyone will be surprised, but . . . I don't think anyone really wants to deal with hearing it right now."

"Except for me."

"Yeah. Lucky you," she said, and tried to laugh, but wound up crying. He opened his arms and hugged her.

"It's going to be okay."

"Yeah . . ." She wiped her tears. "Tell me something I don't already know. The odds were against us from the start. When you get married that young, and you choose someone just like you . . . that's our problem, you know? Dan and I are just way too much alike to have any kind of balance. You know how Grandma used to say that Mom and Dad are like night and day? That's why it works. Me and Dan—we're like . . ."

"Day and day," Mack said, and his sister nodded.

"Exactly. We have the same strengths, the same weaknesses. It doesn't work. Opposites attract for a reason, I guess."

Those last words stayed with him after she drove away. Inside his apartment, Mack changed into sweats, brewed a pot of coffee, poured a cup, lit a cigarette, and sank onto the couch, alone with his thoughts at last.

Opposites attract . . .

What Carrie had told him about her past had caught him off guard, to say the least. No wonder she'd come across as so aloof, almost skittish, at the party. After all she'd been through in her life, she must dread meeting new people, with their inevitable questions about her past.

Mack couldn't help but feel honored that she'd chosen to tell him the truth—and he couldn't help but feel more drawn to her now that he knew. He'd always had a soft spot for vulnerable souls who'd been bounced around out in the cold, cruel world.

True, Carrie Robinson wasn't a stray or a defenseless child who needed to be taken under someone's nurturing wing. She was a grown woman.

A woman he'd asked on a third date, and kissed good night with a passion that seemed to have caught her off guard— and maybe Mack as well.

Was he trying to feel alive again after the pall his mother's condition had cast over his evening? Or was he trying to show Carrie that her past didn't matter to him? Whatever the case, he'd kissed her soundly, and when he looked into her eyes before they said good night, he sensed that something had flared up inside her. There was a sense of purpose in her expression that he hadn't seen earlier.

"I'll call you over the weekend," he told her.

"The weekend—oh, I might be busy," she said vaguely, surprising him. "But we'll connect on Monday."

Playing hard to get, was she?

Well, good for her. And good for him.

He'd have plenty of time to plan dinner out next week at a nice restaurant, though just about anything would be a step up from the diner and McSorley's. Meanwhile, he had a Knicks game.

Opposites attract . . .

Mack couldn't help but think that Carrie Robinson was night to his day.

He stubbed out the cigarette in an ashtray and reached for the remote control, needing something to take his mind off his troubles for a little while. He turned on the television and flipped past news, news, and more news—all of it ugly. Presidential politics, the global economy, war in Chechnya, mass murder in Uganda, natural disasters . . .

Disgusted, he turned off the TV.

The world beyond his doorstep was harsher than ever.

Maybe Ben had the right idea, taking a break from the news for a while.

Mack decided he was going to do the same thing. God knew he had enough problems of his own right now.

This wasn't the worst crime scene Detective Rocco Manzillo had stumbled across in two-plus decades as an NYPD detective, but it sure as hell wasn't the prettiest, either.

He guessed the victim might have been—pretty, that was—before someone hacked her face beyond recognition. Not in the sense that you wouldn't recognize her if you knew her, but in the sense that you wouldn't recognize that the red mass of pulp was even a face, if it weren't still attached—though just barely—to a slender neck and covered in long, blood-matted blond hair.

The case looked pretty open and shut, as far as Rocky and his partner, T.J. Murphy, were concerned.

The woman, Janice Kaminsky, had apparently come home from a date at around dawn and was followed into the building by a homeless guy. The whole thing was caught on the building's surveillance tapes, which had been furnished by the super. He'd called the police after the downstairs neighbor, a night shift nurse, walked into her own apartment to find blood dripping through her ceiling.

Now all Rocky and Murph had to do was catch the perp, who'd ransacked the place and, with any luck, left fingerprints behind.

A flash bulb went off as the CSU team snapped another photograph of the corpse.

Murph winced at the glare and sank into a chair, pressing a hand to his forehead. "Hey, Rock, you got any Advil on you?"

"You took three in the car. That stuff'll burn a hole in your stomach."

"Maybe, but it didn't even put a dent in this headache. I'm a hurtin' pup this morning."

Murph had taken last night off to celebrate Saint Patrick's Day, and wasn't thrilled when Rocky called this morning to tell him they had a DOA.

Yes, the Irish had celebrated their big March holiday yesterday, but Rocky's Italian family would have theirs tomorrow, Saint Joseph's Day. His wife, Ange, had been cooking since Wednesday and all three of their sons had flown in for the weekend.

If this case went like clockwork, Rocky would be home in plenty of time to enjoy the food and his family. If not . . .

Well, it wouldn't be the first time he'd missed a holiday to work a homicide.

And it wouldn't kill him to miss a meal, that was for sure. He'd moved his belt buckle another notch since Christmas, and his potbelly was making it hard to bend over to tie his shoes.

"This is all your fault, you know," he'd told Ange this morning on his way out the door.

She was standing at the counter dipping cardoon in egg batter, ready to be fried up for tomorrow's meatless meal.

"How is it my fault?"

"You're too good a cook. You even know how to make vegetables taste great." He pointed at a platter of battered, deep-fried broccoli and cauliflower.

"You should be eating your vegetables raw, Rocco, and you should be having salad for lunch, and—"

"I keep telling you, Ange, I don't want that rabbit food."

"Well then you'd better start hopping around like one instead."

"What are you talking about?"

"The weather's getting nicer. You need to get out and exercise."

"The weather's crappy. And I get plenty of exercise on the job."

Ange eyed his belly and said dryly, "I don't think plenty is enough. Hey!" She swatted his hand as he snagged one of the cannoli she'd just filled with sweetened ricotta cream.

"What, now you're hitting me? You gonna turn me into a battered husband?"

"*Battered* is your problem, Rocco. Battered and deep-fried and extra cheese and à la mode . . ."

"Yeah, yeah, yeah," he said around a mouthful of cannoli. "You love me just the way I am."

"You don't take care of yourself. You're no spring chicken, you know. You'd better—"

"Come on, Ange, I'm not even fifty yet."

"You will be next year."

"Talk to me then."

He grabbed another pastry on his way out the door and was still chewing—and smiling—when he got into his car and headed south from the Bronx toward Manhattan. Of course, the smile faded pretty fast when he called the station house and heard the details of the case.

That was how it was when you worked homicide. You had to compartmentalize everything, or you wouldn't make it through the day.

"Detective Manzillo?" Jorge Perez, one of the CSU guys, called from over by the apartment door. "Come take a look at this."

"Be right there." He stepped away from the body, reached into his pocket, and pulled a little plastic tube from his pocket. "Hey, Murph," he said. "Catch."

"What is it?" Murph caught it. "Advil? I thought you didn't have any."

"I brought it special just for you, Danny Boy. Figured you might need it."

"Thanks, Rock."

"No problem. But just take one." Before stepping out into the hall, he tossed over his shoulder, "You know, Murph, Saint Paddy's Day might be over, but you still look green. Don't you go puking on my crime scene."

He found Jorge Perez on his hands and knees by the door, shining a flashlight on something that lay on the floor beneath a table.

"What'cha got there, Perez? The perp drop something?"

"Maybe—if he was a leprechaun. Check this out."

Rocky leaned in to see what looked like a crumpled tissue. "What is it?"

"A green carnation with a pin through the stem. You know, like a corsage. Barely even wilted, so it couldn't have been here longer than a few hours. Think Janice Kaminsky was wearing it and it got torn off and tossed in the struggle?"

"A cheap carnation to go with those nine-hundred-dollar shoes of hers?" Rocky shook his head. "No way."

"Since when are you such an expert on flowers and women's fashion?"

"Everyone knows carnations are cheap—everyone who's married to my wife, anyway." Ange loved roses and lilies. "And Janice Kaminsky just bought those fancy shoes yesterday. Receipt's in her wallet. She must have had a hot date last night."

"Well, if she wasn't wearing the carnation, then who was? The perp? Is it a boutonnière?"

"Even if it was . . . Didn't you see the surveillance camera footage? He was no fancy gentleman."

The killer, clad in a hooded sweatshirt, sneakers, and baggy jeans, had been careful to keep his head down, shielding what might have been visible of his face from the cameras. He looked like your run-of-the-mill street vagrant—perhaps a junkie looking for some quick cash—but that might not be the case.

Especially, Rocky thought, considering the violent hack job he'd done on the victim's face. And now there was the green carnation that could very well have been deliberately left at the scene as part of the killer's signature.

Although, if that were the case, you'd expect the carnation to have been prominently placed, perhaps on or near the body.

This appeared to have been dropped, perhaps accidentally kicked into the corner.

"Can we lift any prints from this thing?" Rocky asked Perez, hoping the green carnation wasn't some twisted calling card that was going to pop up somewhere else in the near future.

"Sure can," was the answer. "Now all you have to do is hope you get a match when you enter it into the database."

Never again, Carrie told herself, walking briskly down Broadway—just walking, as though she had someplace to go.

She didn't. But she couldn't stand being cooped up in her apartment, feeling as though any second, she'd hear a knock on the door.

Police, they would say. *Open up.*

And then . . . what?

Would she try to escape?

Open the door and surrender?

There was no way of knowing how she might react until it actually happened, and of course, it wasn't going to happen. They hadn't connected her with Ralph, and they wouldn't connect her with Chelsea.

Never again.

Never, ever again would she lose control the way she had with Chelsea, and before that, with Ralph.

She had too much to lose now . . .

Now that she'd found Mack.

You can't screw this up. It's your one chance to have a normal life . . . and that's one chance more than you ever thought you'd have.

Even finding Allison had taken on less urgency.

She wouldn't give up trying to find her—but it was no longer her only purpose here. And if she ever did find her . . .

I'll be a lot more careful. I won't let myself get carried away. I'll never do anything like this.

Never. Never again . . .

PART III

The Present

We all live on the past,
and through the past are destroyed.
Johann Wolfgang von Goethe

Chapter Ten

"**W**ait a minute . . . Allison, did you just say you guys are *driving* to Nebraska?" Randi Weber's eyebrows disappear beneath the new bangs she had her hairstylist cut to hide the wrinkles on her forehead—a necessity now that her husband made her lay off the Botox just in time for her thirty-year high school reunion last weekend.

Ben, she told Allison, didn't like the preternatural Barbie that resulted from the injections. "I guess he wants me to look like an old lady."

"You? Never!" Allison told the petite, striking brunette, who has a big ego and a bigger heart.

"Look at me, Allie. I'm almost fifty."

"You are not! Not for another couple of years. And when you do turn fifty, you'll probably look exactly the same as you do right now—which is exactly the same as when I met you."

"This is why I've always loved you, Allison. You tell me just what I need to hear," was Randi's response.

As the wife of Mack's best friend, she had embraced Allison from the moment they first met ten years ago, and not just because Allison complimented her on what she was wearing.

"I was worried you were going to be like *her*," she'd said—*her*, meaning Carrie, Mack's late wife.

Randi had made no secret of the fact that she couldn't stand her, and neither could Ben.

"*You*, we love," she told Allison early on, and the feeling was mutual.

The Webers were the reason Allison and Mack moved from the city to Glenhaven Park, where they shared a neighborhood until Ben's promotion elevated the Webers to the estate side of town. They don't see each other as much as they did when they could walk from house to house with the kids in strollers, but it's not for lack of trying.

That's why this rare Saturday night dinner out at a new local bistro is such a treat—and also why Randi had no idea until now that Allison and Mack had decided to drive to Nebraska in two weeks instead of fly.

"You're driving five thousand miles with three small children? Are you people *crazy*?" Randi sets her glass of pinot grigio on the polished bar and turns to her husband.

Ben and Mack have been leaning against the bar talking sports and business as Randi told her about the high school reunion on Long Island last weekend.

"Some of these friends, I haven't seen since I was eighteen," she told Allison, "but it's crazy—it's like we picked up right where we left off. Even this guy I dated senior year, Mike Travers—I remembered him as being a complete jerk, but he isn't. He's a sweetheart. I guess that's what happens after you break up, right? You hate the person so much your memory is clouded."

The only person Allison ever broke up with was Justin, a biologist with whom she'd fallen madly in love when she was in her early twenties and new in the city. The relationship lasted a year, and the end was so bitter that even now, looking back, she thinks of Justin as a jerk.

But she has no interest in finding out whether that's really the case. It's complicated enough to deal with the rest of her baggage.

"You have no idea how good it felt to reconnect with all those people," Randi told her, "and laugh about old times."

"You're right. I don't."

Familiar with Allison's past, Randi said gently, "It might be good for you to look up some old friends when you go back to Nebraska. You might be surprised at how they've changed—or you might find out that they feel bad about how they treated you. You never know, Allison. It might be a healing experience."

"I can't imagine how it could be. Anyway, we're not going back to my hometown. By the time we get to Nebraska we'll have been driving for three straight days."

"*What?*"

Now, Randi clutches her husband's arm. "Ben, did you *hear* this?"

"Hear what?"

"That we're crazy," Allison tells him with a grin.

"You and Randi? Crazy? Well, that's half true."

"Hey!" His wife swats him. "I was talking about the two of them."

"Yes, but again—she's only half right." Allison playfully links her arm through her husband's. "Go ahead, babe. Tell them it was all *your* idea to drive five thousand miles with three small children."

"Actually, it's less than two thousand."

"Who's even counting after the first few hours?" Randi shakes her head at Mack. "You'll be delirious by the time you get to the Cross-Westchester Expressway. Last weekend was wall-to-wall traffic on the LIE when we went to my reunion, and that was just me and Ben. If the kids had been with us, it would have been a nightmare." Her shiny red fingernails flash through the air as she gestures to emphasize the last word, which in her Long Island accent comes out *night-may-uh*.

"Well, we're planning on leaving really early on Saturday morning to avoid the traffic, and hopefully the kids will sleep for a while in the car."

"All three of them at once? Don't bet on it," Randi tells Allison. "We only have two and I keep hoping my great-aunt Rhoda will hang in there for a few more months—not because I ever liked the old battle-axe, but because I dread the thought of driving a hundred and fifty miles round-trip to Massapequa with the kids for her funeral."

"How blessed is she to have a loving niece like you?" Mack asks dryly. "Here's to Great-Aunt Rhoda—may she live forever."

He lifts his bourbon, and they all clink glasses.

"And here's to your big road trip. I hope you survive it."

"Come on, Randi, don't knock adventure."

"Is that what you're calling it, Mack? Allison? Are you on board with this *adventure*?"

"Why not? He's had worse ideas."

"Name one," Mack says. "Wait—never mind."

She grins, enjoying the banter and welcoming the chance to take a lighthearted approach to the upcoming road trip. Ever since she agreed to the idea a month ago, she's been trying to wrap her head around it in a positive way.

Only now, over a glass of wine with close friends, does the thought of seeing her brother and his family again seem a little less daunting.

After all, even if she and Brett—and their spouses and children—don't hit it off after all these years, it's not the end of the world. Lots of people have people from the past whom they prefer to keep at arm's length. Particularly relatives. Randi's class reunion with old friends might have been a smash success, but look at her relationship with Great-Aunt Rhoda.

"It definitely sounds like an adventure," Ben says, "but I have to ask—why not fly?"

"You of all people should understand that," Mack tells Ben, who also works in the high-pressure advertising industry. "Last July I had to cut short our vacation down the shore because of a last-minute client crisis, remember? All we need is to buy almost three thousand dollars' worth of plane tickets and have the same thing happen."

"Three grand to fly to Nebraska?" Ben shakes his head. "No way."

"Not per person. Total. And not quite that much. A few hundred less."

"Still."

"What can I say?" Mack shrugs. "It's a hot ticket."

"You could fly to Rome for that. How could it be that much?" Randi's Five Towns accent is thicker than ever, as it always is when she drinks wine.

"Believe me, I've been looking all over the Internet for cheaper fares or at least nonstops to Omaha to make it less torturous," Allison says. "But they're all sold out, and there are five of us, so it adds up."

"You could always do four seats and hold the baby."

"J.J.? You're kidding, right?"

Randi, all too familiar with their perpetually squirmy toddler's antics, grins and shakes her head. "You're right. What was I thinking? Not holding J.J. for four hours is worth at least three grand. I just still can't believe fares are that expensive."

"Maybe they weren't a few months ago, but this is kind of a last-minute trip—we're leaving two weeks from today."

"How long will you be gone?"

"Through the fifteenth."

"That's forever! It's half of July! You're going to miss your birthday."

"I'm not going to miss it. You are." Allison smiles. "I'll be celebrating it in Nebraska."

"Well, you're going to miss our Friday the Thirteenth party." Randi loves to entertain, and she's always looking for an excuse to invite a crowd over. Years ago, she and Ben started throwing TGIF–13 parties, a tradition that continues every time one pops up on the calendar.

"Didn't you already have a Friday the Thirteenth party this year?" Mack asks.

"We've had two. One in January, one in April. But there's a third one coming up in July—I think that's a record—and after that, there won't be another one for over a year. I can't believe you're going to miss it."

"Don't worry," Allison says, "if it doesn't work out with my brother, we'll turn around and be back home in time."

Randi, who knows most of the details concerning Allison's past, squeezes her arm. "I'm sure it'll be a happy reunion. Look at what it was like for me last weekend—and those were just classmates. This is your own *brother*."

"Exactly. My own brother and I haven't seen each other since I was a kid. Talk about pressure."

"Listen, you'll deal. It's only two weeks."

"Didn't you just say that was forever?" Allison asks wryly.

"It all depends on how you look at it. You have to keep a positive attitude."

"All right, Miss Friday the Thirteenth," Allison says, and her brother's voice suddenly echoes in her head.

All right, Miss Big Apple.

Miss Big Apple . . .

Brett called her that for a while. Not as kids, though. They'd barely spoken as kids.

Well of course not as kids, she reminds herself. He only would have called her Miss Big Apple after she moved to New York.

But then, until very recently, they'd barely spoken as adults, either. A couple of cursory phone calls a year—that was the extent of it.

Her recollections of interacting with her brother are incredibly vague—deliberately so. She's spent so many years trying to forget anything and anyone associated with her childhood—how is she going to switch gears now? Does she really want to trigger all those memories? Any of them?

Suddenly, she's glad they're not flying to Nebraska. She needs as much time as possible to prepare for coming face-to-face with her brother again. And if they're on the road, it will be that much easier to back out if at some point she realizes she can't go through with it after all. They can make a U-turn and head back home, or to the beach . . .

Why aren't we just going back down to the shore in the first place? she finds herself wondering, just for a split second, conveniently forgetting what happened last fall at the beach house.

No. That's out of the question. She herself can't bear the thought of going back to Salt Breeze Pointe this year—how can she even consider changing gears and putting the girls through that?

J.J. is too young to remember what happened there, but Hudson and Madison have been seeing a child psychiatrist weekly since December. Dr. Rogel told Allison during the last parent consult session, in April, that they've been coping remarkably well.

"Your daughters are survivors, Mrs. MacKenna. They're blessed with extraordinary strength—as is their mother." His hands were steepled beneath his white beard and he looked intently at her as though he were seeing straight into her own traumatic past.

He knew, of course, that her father had abandoned the family and that her mother had killed herself. She hadn't relished sharing the information during the initial consult—without the girls present, of course—but it wasn't something that should be withheld from a psychiatrist who would be treating your children for emotional trauma.

She wasn't there to talk about herself, though. Not in the beginning, and not at any point in her contact with Dr. Rogel. It was strictly about her daughters.

Uncomfortable with his probing gaze that day, she shifted gears. "The girls have been asking about our summer vacation. We've always gone to the beach house, but . . ."

"I think a change of scenery is a good idea this year," he said, explaining that it was probably too soon to take the girls back to the shore. "Not yet. Someday, further along in the healing process, they might ask again to go back. Down the road, if that happens, we can revisit the idea, because it might help them to resolve some things. Some people need to return to the scene of the crime in order to move on."

Is that what I'm doing now? Allison wonders, absently sipping her wine and listening as Mack, Randi, and Ben chatter on. *Is it any healthier for me to drag my kids along to the scene of the crime in my own past?*

But of course, that isn't really the case. There *was* no crime. Nothing like what happened to her own children last November.

Abandonment by a Deadbeat Dad, Suicidal Junkie Mom . . .

Yes, it had all been very dramatic and traumatic at the time, but she, too, is a survivor. Extraordinary strength . . .

Anyway, they're only going to visit her brother. Returning to Centerfield isn't part of the plan.

Allison has assured Mack that she isn't interested in that,

and said the same to Cindy-Lou when she asked. It surprised her that even Brett seemed to think she might like to visit their old hometown.

"I'll go with you if you want," her brother offered, not very enthusiastically, and was audibly relieved when she vetoed that idea.

The plan is for Allison, Mack, and the kids to bypass Centerfield on their way to the dairy farm, which is almost two hundred miles west. They're going to spend the whole vacation getting to know Brett, Cindy-Lou, Samantha, and Jeff. Period.

Building family ties is a positive step in everyone's healing process. The girls will love the farm, and the county fair, and all that fresh air and space . . .

"Mr. Weber?" The host appears to touch Ben on the shoulder. Your table is ready. Please follow me."

As they head for the main dining room, Mack takes Allison's hand and gives it a squeeze. "Stop worrying. It's going to be great."

"Dinner?"

"You know what I mean. Nebraska."

Going back there after seventeen years isn't going to be anywhere near *great*. She'll settle for tolerable.

"Glenhaven Park is next," the Metro-North conductor announces, walking through the car. "All doors will open at Glenhaven Park."

From Saint Antony to Florida to New York to Glenhaven Park.

It's about damned time.

Carrie rises with the small duffel she's been holding on her lap since she boarded the train an hour ago at Grand Central Terminal. She wouldn't dare let it out of her grasp, let alone her sight. The bag contains her laptop, the all-important manila envelope, the key to her safe deposit box at a busy midtown bank—and the tens of thousands of dollars in cash and the small pistol she retrieved from the box when she opened it yesterday.

She places the duffel strap securely over her shoulder before reaching for a couple of large paper shopping bags she placed on the rack above her seat. The clothes they contain are her own, purchased weeks ago at a Super Wal-Mart somewhere in Georgia. But she's counting on the shopping bags' familiar Bloomingdale's insignia to provide mute testimony to just what a lone middle-aged woman might have been doing in the city on a Saturday afternoon, should anyone glance her way and wonder.

No one does as she makes her way along the aisle to the exit. She's glad she opted to wear basic black, noticing several similarly dressed female passengers, also with shopping bags stashed above their seats.

"Station stop is Glenhaven Park," the conductor announces again from the other end of the car as the train begins to slow.

Leaning against a pole near the double doors, Carrie watches the scenery beyond the window, seeing low, rambling stone walls shaded by towering trees with arching branches—a far cry from the Caribbean jungle.

She bites her lower lip to suppress a triumphant smile. At long last, the journey she began on board the Carousel last month is drawing to a close. She only hopes this part—the most dangerous since she disembarked the ship in Miami—goes as smoothly as the rest of it has.

After the ship dropped anchor on that gray morning five weeks ago, Carrie had held her breath all the way from the cabin to the taxi that finally shuttled her away from the pier.

What if word had already gotten out that Molly Temple had gone missing?

What if the American authorities were waiting to arrest her?

What if they knew who she really was, and what she had done all those years ago—not just in New York, but long before that?

Of course that didn't happen. As always, she'd planned carefully and covered her tracks with exquisite attention to detail.

Not a single official she encountered through the disembarkation process batted an eye when she handed over Molly's passport and her ship ID. She even remembered to thank the appropriate members of the staff and to tip them just well enough, but not so well that they'd take notice.

Besides, she needed to conserve as much of her cash— and Molly's—as possible, preparing for whatever lay ahead. There was no telling, at that point, exactly how she was going to get from Point B—Miami—to Point C—New York—and beyond.

She instructed the cab to take her to the hotel Molly had already so thoughtfully reserved, a large, busy Marriott overlooking Biscayne Bay. Again, she remembered to thank and tip the cabdriver and the doorman, firmly refusing his offer to get a bellman to help her with Molly's luggage.

He seemed surprised, but then smiled when she said, "I just got off a cruise ship. I need all the exercise I can get!"

The female desk clerk, an attractive blonde in her fifties, didn't bat an eye when she used Molly's ID and credit card to check in. Again, Carrie was asked if she needed help with her bags. Again, she said no, offering her quip about the exercise.

"Which ship were you on?" the girl had asked with a smile.

"The Carnival."

"Is that the one that goes to Barbados?"

Wondering if it was a trick question, Carrie shook her

head and rattled off the ports of call she'd memorized so
long ago.

"Oh, how did you like Saint Martin? Did you do the day
trip to Anguilla?"

"No," Carrie told her, wondering again if it was a trick
and disturbed by her own negligence. Why hadn't she bothered to memorize every shore excursion in the ship's ports of
call? Was there really one to Anguilla? Was the clerk stall-
ing until the authorities could get here?

"Anguilla's supposed to be one of the most beautiful
places in the world." The clerk, whose name tag revealed
that her name was Pamela, pushed her honey blond hair over
her shoulders as she tucked an electronic key card into a
paper folder. "I've had it on my bucket list for a while now."

"Your what?"

"My bucket list—you know, things I want to do before I
die."

That was a new phrase for Carrie, who forced a smile and
a nod, hoping that she wouldn't find it necessary to see that
this woman's bucket list remained unfulfilled.

It would be a shame to start eliminating problems like
these before she even left Miami, mostly because things
could get messy rather quickly. But of course, she'd do whatever she had to do.

I might even enjoy it, she thought, eyeing Pamela's slender, tanned neck and resenting her next question even more
than the previous ones.

"Are you traveling alone, Ms. Temple?"

"Why?" Carrie asked far more sharply than she'd
intended—so sharply that the clerk seemed taken aback.

"I was just wondering if one key is enough, or do you need
two?"

"One is fine." She took the paper folder, thanked the clerk,
and scurried away with her bags.

Safely inside an elevator, glad there were no other passengers, she leaned back and exhaled. It wasn't going to be easy being back in the States, particularly here in the South, where people's friendliness bordered on nosiness, something Carrie couldn't afford.

Not only that, she reminded herself, but this was a far different America than the one she'd left behind just after September 11. Acutely aware that Big Brother was most likely watching her every move from the moment she set foot on the pier, she'd kept her head carefully bent away from likely spots where security cameras might be concealed, and wore her hat and large sunglasses despite the overcast day outside.

She was tempted to spend her first hour back on American soil dining on room service pizza and surfing the Internet, but she didn't dare do either. Instead, she deposited the luggage in the room, took everything she was going to need from that point forward, and left the hotel.

She walked to a nearby mall, paid for a new outfit using cash, and changed into it in a ladies' room near the food court. She kept the dark wig on, but put Molly Temple's clothes and hat into the bag, which she deposited into the nearest trash can.

Now it was time to find a new candidate who might fit the bill. As she walked and browsed, she kept her eye on fellow female shoppers. She found several who bore enough resemblance to herself and Molly, but they were all too careful with their possessions.

Finally, after a couple of hours, just outside the dressing room of a crowded store, she found a woman who would do. She was so busy scolding her teenage daughter about the short skirt she'd just tried on that she wasn't paying attention to the large purse she was carrying. In an instant, Carrie had removed her wallet and was on the escalator, heading for the mall's exit.

She walked to the nearest hotel, got a cab to the airport, and used the stolen license and credit card to pick up a car at a busy rental counter. She got on the road immediately, heading north.

In Fort Lauderdale, she ditched the car and the Miami woman's wallet.

She stole another one in a crowded movie theater, from a woman who was too busy munching popcorn and engrossed in a thriller to notice that Carrie was reaching into the purse she'd left resting on the vacant chair between them.

She bought a bus ticket with cash from Fort Lauderdale airport to Orlando. There were plenty of budget motels in that touristy town, and the one she chose was locally owned. The night clerk didn't ask for an ID or register surprise when she paid for the room in cash.

She checked out the next day—and right into another motel down the road. Orlando was so pleasantly crowded with tourists that no one gave her a second glance. That was why she'd chosen it when she knew, even before leaving Saint Antony, that she'd need a place to stop for a while. She stayed for over a week, finally allowing herself to breathe more easily and get ready for the next phase.

Her first objective was to change her appearance as drastically as possible, as quickly as possible.

She visited a salon and had her hair cut short and stripped of dye, telling the young stylist that she thought it was time to go natural again.

"Gray hair will look right nice on you," the girl drawled politely.

It didn't. That was fine with Carrie, who had already lost herself in decadent American fast food that made short work of packing on pounds.

On motel televisions and public computers, she followed the unfolding search for Molly Temple, whose family back in Ohio had finally reported her missing. By all accounts, though, the authorities believed she'd met with foul play after she'd checked into her Miami hotel.

Her aging mother appeared at a news conference. "I just want my Molly back," Nancy Temple sobbed. "Please, whoever took her—don't harm her."

Too late for that, Mama, Carrie thought.

She had read, online in a Caribbean newspaper, about the explosion at the Blue Iguana. Jane Deere was, as she expected, listed among the casualties. So was the name of the bar's owner. Apparently, Jimmy Bolt had had the misfortune of paying one of his unannounced visits at precisely the wrong moment. All the better, as far as Carrie was concerned. The notoriously laid-back island detectives—who so often looked the other way when it came to Jimmy's dealings—would undoubtedly have assumed that one of his many enemies had gotten to him at last. Case closed.

The most important research Carrie conducted in Orlando was in preparation for her return to New York. High-speed wifi was a marvelous thing, she discovered—and readily capable of being "borrowed" from unsuspecting network owners with the help of some off-the-shelf software Carrie installed on her own laptop.

The Internet was chock full of personal information in this day and age. That made it much easier than she'd anticipated to find out everything she needed to know about modern life in the city she'd left behind—and about Mack and Allison and their children.

Newly aware that passenger scrutiny was more intense than ever at public transportation agencies in post-9/11 America, and that hitchhiking had becoming increasingly rare and might garner her unwanted attention, Carrie opted to work her way north using the bus system. She did so painstakingly, using cash to buy tickets on local bus routes, zigzagging her way up the East Coast. At the end of every day, she'd stop and stay put for a night or two, preparing for the next leg.

Rushing the travel would have been reckless, and she

couldn't afford that. It took weeks, but that was okay. She used her downtime in motels to research the best way to obtain the permanent new identity she was going to need when she got to New York. Homeland security might have come a long way since she'd become Carrie Robinson, but so had the underworld. It wouldn't be all that difficult or time-consuming to become someone new. Just a lot more expensive. That was okay, though. She had plenty of money.

A few days ago, she finally reached New Jersey, within commuting distance to New York. From there, it was easy to buy a PATH ticket from a machine—no ID required—and get lost in the crowd headed to Manhattan.

Her only regret was that she came into the city via an underground tunnel, without a view of the skyline she hadn't seen since it was smoke-shrouded on that fateful last day. That shouldn't have mattered, but for some reason, it did. The media evidence she'd followed so avidly from afar suddenly wasn't enough. Now that she was back she felt compelled to witness the new reality with her own eyes, longed to see for herself that the towers were really gone.

But the PATH she caught on Thursday morning took her to Penn Station, and it was raining. There was no view, from midtown, of lower Manhattan. The sight would have to wait.

She spent that rainy night and the next in a seedy hotel off Queens Boulevard, going through the final stages of her homework and covering her tracks one last time. She had to shed every bit of incriminating evidence she'd accumulated and prepare herself for this last leg of the journey, which couldn't begin until today, a Saturday.

On a weeknight, she knew, an early evening train to the northern suburbs would be crowded with commuters. Even if she had boarded early to ensure that there would be room for her, let alone the bag she didn't dare let out of her possession, there was still a much bigger risk that a fellow passenger would notice her.

She wasn't necessarily afraid of being recognized by someone she'd once known. When she'd lived in New York over a decade ago, her acquaintances were largely limited to her coworkers in the north tower, a few of whom did live in Northern Westchester at the time. But of course they're not living at all now.

Anyway, anyone who'd known her then—including Mack himself—would scarcely recognize her. She's older, yes, but more importantly, she's deliberately plainer, grayer, heavier. Even when she looks at her own reflection—something she so rarely bothered to do when she was living on Saint Antony—she's caught off guard by the frumpy stranger in the mirror.

Now, searching for evidence of the woman she once was, she imagines that she might find her if she could take a chisel and chip away at the fleshy, weathered face staring back at her. Only in her blue eyes can she clearly spot her old self—but she avoids looking into them, because whenever she does, she sees her father as well as herself.

Today her eyes are hidden behind sunglasses, to mask herself not from fellow passengers who might recognize her, but from those who might glance in her direction now and be able to identify her later.

That was the main reason she waited until Saturday to take the train. Relying not just on her research, but on her memory, she knows that for commuters, the weekdays are all about routine. Even those who ride the crowded PATH or subway lines follow certain patterns, and often see the same faces every day, but there are countless new ones, making it easy for Carrie to lose herself in the crowd.

Metro-North railroad to the wealthy northern suburbs is far more intimate, though. The same commuters ride the same trains every day, often in the same cars, the same seats, even—with the same people.

On a weekday, a fellow passenger glancing up from

her newspaper or opening his eyes from a nap might idly take notice of a newcomer carrying anything more than a briefcase. On weekends, these trains are not only far less crowded, but chances are higher that riders are largely strangers to one another and the conductors, far less in tune with patterns and aberrations.

Carrie's meticulous planning paid off, as always. She boarded early and got a double seat all to herself, pleased when no one filled the three-seater opposite her or even the row behind. The sun has yet to set, and even the suburbanites who spent the day in the city seem to have chosen to linger there. The car, just half full when they left Grand Central, has systematically emptied, discharging a passenger or two at each northbound stop until only a handful are now left.

There's a mechanical ding as the train pulls into the station, and a robotic voice announces, "Glenhaven Park."

Carrie is the only one to disembark here.

This is it, she thinks as the doors close. *I made it.*

The train rattles off to the north, leaving her alone on the platform. Giddy with anticipation, she carries her bags to the stairs that lead to the overpass that crosses the tracks. It, too, is empty, as is the stairwell that takes her back down the other side to Glenhaven Avenue, the main thoroughfare in this bucolic bedroom community Mack and Allison now call home.

Having studied the town's layout on Google Earth, Carrie memorized not just the names of streets, but the way they're laid out. Here in the business district, she knows, they run perpendicular to each other. Always one to appreciate an orderly grid system, she knows that turning left on Glenhaven Avenue will take her to Church Street, where she'll turn right, walk a few more blocks, and go left on Elm, right on Abernathy. In about twenty minutes, she'll find herself on Orchard Terrace, where the MacKennas now live. If she walks slowly, it should be suitably dark by the time she gets there.

But she finds herself instinctively picking up her pace just minutes into her trip. Lined with charming nineteenth-century storefronts that house boutiques and upscale restaurants, Glenhaven Avenue is surprisingly busy as dusk slowly falls on this, the longest Saturday of the year.

Nearly every one of the diagonal parking spots is occupied—most, it seems, by Mercedes and Lexus SUVs. Clean-cut teenagers in two-hundred-dollar sneakers loiter in the old-fashioned gazebo just beyond the train station. A sidewalk café is crowded with patrons, and more waiting for tables on benches near the door. Families congregate with ice cream cones on the steps and low wall beside a shop called the Sweet Tooth, exchanging greetings with one another and with passersby.

This is a small town, yes, but far more transient than the Midwestern ones she once knew. Here, newcomers are greeted with indifference at best. For all these people know, Carrie just moved with her family into one of the gabled houses on the residential streets branching out from the train station.

Still, there are far too many people out and about for comfort. Carrie's heart beats quickly as she makes her way past them, doing her best to appear as though she's on a leisurely stroll back from the train, having walked this route many times in the past.

At last, she rounds the corner onto Orchard, a quiet, leafy block lined with two- and three-story homes. The MacKennas' center hall Colonial, white with dark green shutters, lies about halfway down. Carrie recognizes it instantly, thanks to the real estate listing she'd found still available online though it's been six or seven years since Mack and Allison moved in.

The ad included exterior shots of the house, with its tall

shrub border and mature trees whose trunks are entwined with English ivy that also covers the trellis arching over the brick front walk and the black wrought-iron lamppost.

As an added bonus, there were interior shots as well, depicting formal living and dining rooms, a glass sunroom, half bath, large expanded kitchen, and an entrance hall with a stairway leading up to the second floor, where there are three bedrooms, a small study, another bath, and a master suite.

Only the floor plan was missing, but it was fairly easy to figure out using the photographs.

As much as she longs to stop and stare, Carrie forces herself to keep walking past the house. With its large homes set well apart from each other and back from the street, screened by lush shrubs and old trees, the neighborhood feels deserted—but she reminds herself that it most definitely is not.

People are most definitely lurking nearby. Mingling with the chatter of crickets and the whisper of lawn sprinklers, she can hear a basketball thumping on a driveway and children splashing in a pool in a nearby yard. The air is thick with barbecue smoke—the unmistakable aroma of grilling steaks makes her mouth water—and lights shine brightly, indoor and out, at every house, including the MacKennas'.

Wait—not *every* house.

As the large brick Colonial next door to the MacKennas' comes into view beyond the dense border of shrubbery, Carrie sees that it's completely dark.

This, she knows, is the house where a woman named Phyllis Lewis was murdered on Halloween night by a serial killer known as the Nightwatcher. It was the widespread media attention to that case—and Mack and Allison's connection to it—that placed them squarely on Carrie's radar again last fall.

The Lewis house isn't just dark, she realizes now, seeing the red and black "For Rent" sign posted near the door.

It's vacant.

Well, what do you know.

Carrie can't help but smile again. Yes, things are falling into place very nicely indeed.

Chapter Eleven

Miami, Florida

After fifteen years with the Miami-Dade Police Department's Domestic Crimes Bureau and five more on her own as a private investigator, LaJuanda Estrada has been working with the families of missing persons long enough to anticipate the likely reaction to certain stages in the investigation.

That's why she made sure there was a box of tissues on her desk before she started playing the surveillance tape footage for Nancy Temple, whose daughter Molly went missing after getting off a cruise ship here in Miami last month.

The woman had found her way to this rented office on West Flagler Street the same way many people do; she'd gotten fed up with the way the police detectives were handling her case.

"I feel like they're not trying hard enough to find Molly," she told LaJuanda earlier this week, when they first met.

It wasn't for LaJuanda to decide whether that was the case. Her job was to find out what had happened to Molly Temple, a Cleveland accountant who'd vanished back in May.

That was when LaJuanda had first heard about her, as the media was actively publicizing her disappearance. She'd even seen footage of a tearful Nancy at a press conference, pleading for her daughter's safe return.

Same old sad story, LaJuanda thought when she saw it, and wondered how long it would be before a body turned up somewhere, fitting the missing woman's description. But she didn't give the case more than a passing thought until it landed in her lap.

"I called you because your ad said that you leave no stone unturned," Molly's mother told her. "Promise me you'll do everything you can to find her."

LaJuanda promised, and true to her word, she's left no stone unturned.

She knew the MDPD detectives would have examined the surveillance video showing Molly's movements in the week before she disappeared. She also knew that they were perpetually overburdened and only human; in other words, they might have missed something.

It wasn't easy for her to get her hands on the tapes, but when you're acquainted with the right people and you know your way around the city—and the system—you can make things happen.

It had taken a couple of days, but this morning, she was finally able to download the video into her laptop.

Now, moments after it begins playing, Nancy Temple gasps. But instead of bursting into tears at the sight of her lost daughter, she covers her mouth with her hands and gapes at the screen.

Caught off guard, LaJuanda sees that her gray eyes behind her wire-rimmed bifocals are not—as anticipated—flooded with tears. They're wide with shock.

"What is it, Nancy? What's wrong?"

"That isn't Molly!"

"What?"

"That woman—it's not her!"

"As I said, this is the tape from the Marriott where—"

"I know what you said, but it's not her." She shakes her gray head rapidly. "I know my own daughter. That isn't her."

Folding her arms across her ample bosom, LaJuanda shifts her gaze from Nancy Temple back to the computer screen, where a female figure is making its way through the crowded lobby of the Marriott.

She herself has watched this footage from the hotel security cameras countless times in the last twenty-four hours, searching for signs of impending foul play as Molly Temple arrived at the hotel shortly before her disappearance. Now—unlike her police counterparts—she's asked Molly's mother to take a look, just in case something jumps out at her.

Something has.

But Nancy Temple—whose husband died of a heart attack on Easter Sunday, just over a month before their firstborn fell off the face of the earth—is obviously still reeling from the double blow. How can she possibly be thinking clearly?

LaJuanda herself is happily married with two teenagers. She can't imagine that she'd be in her right mind if anything ever happened to her own loved ones.

Not only that, but children—even adult children—are often different people when they escape their parents' watchful gazes. Particularly daughters of mothers who are as primly conservative as Nancy has proven to be.

So, while she won't come right out and dismiss Nancy's bizarre claim, LaJuanda is inclined to tread carefully around it.

"What makes you say it's not Molly, Mrs. Temple?"

"What makes me say that? It isn't her! That's what makes me say it!"

The retort is so out of character for the Ohio librarian, who has been reserved and unfailingly polite from the moment they met, that LaJuanda raises a dark eyebrow.

"I understand that, Mrs. Temple, but what is it about her? Because to me, that looks like Molly. But I've never met her in person. I don't know her the way you do. Tell me what you're seeing."

"It's . . . it's the way she's walking. That's not Molly's walk." Her voice quavers. "She doesn't move that fast."

She might if she were on her way to a secret rendezvous.

Aloud, LaJuanda says only, "I'll back this up so that you can take another look."

"I don't need another look. I'm positive. That's not Molly; it's someone who's wearing her clothes and pretending to be her."

LaJuanda allows those powerful words to sink in for a moment, her thoughts spinning off in an ominous new direction.

Keeping her tone and expression carefully neutral, she says, "Okay, let's go back a bit for a minute. Those are Molly's clothes?"

"Yes. Oh my God . . ."

"You're sure of it?"

"Positive!" The word is a wail.

LaJuanda's gold bracelets jangle as she reaches out to lay her tanned, manicured hand over Nancy's frail, trembling white one.

The contact seems to steady her, and she takes a deep breath before she goes on talking. "I was with Molly when she bought that top at Sears right before the cruise. She didn't want to get it, but I talked her into it. I told her the bright color was perfect for the tropics. I was the one who talked her into going on the cruise, too."

"She didn't want to go?" LaJuanda has heard this story before, but in light of what Nancy just said about the woman on tape being an impostor, every detail has taken on possible new meaning.

"She never wants to go anywhere. She doesn't even have a social life. Part of the problem is that she works so hard—her company has been downsizing, and she's been picking up the slack. I told her she was going to burn out if she didn't take a break. But she still wasn't crazy about leaving. She's such a good girl—out of my three children, Molly is the one who stays close to home and keeps an eye on me and Ed. I mean, she *kept* an eye on me and Ed," she amends, and her eyes are filled with a fresh flood of tears.

"Yet she decided to go on a cruise by herself, and she bought the ticket with money you gave her for Christmas," LaJuanda reminds her, to keep her on track.

"Yes, because she finally realized she needed a break from her job, and that she'd better start living her life, instead of waiting around to find a husband to do things with. I kept reminding her what a good time she was going to have, and how proud I was of her, going off on such an adventurous vacation all alone." The woman's voice breaks. "Why would someone else be wearing her clothes? Where is she?"

Nancy has repeatedly asked that last question of LaJuanda since their first telephone conversation.

It had taken her a few days, she said then, for her to realize that her daughter was missing.

Back at home in Ohio, Molly rents an apartment just a few blocks from her mother and they speak every day, but . . .

"I was trying to give her some space," she told LaJuanda. "We lost my husband a few months ago, and she'd already bought her cruise ticket. She'd been through so much—she was the one who found Ed lying on the floor—and I wanted her to get away and put it behind her. She was worried about leaving me, and I told her I'd be fine while she was gone. I didn't want to bother her with phone calls."

Molly, she said, had been planning to spend the weekend

sightseeing in Miami before flying home to Ohio. Nancy was worried when her daughter didn't call on Friday to let her know she was off the ship, and even more worried when she didn't answer the messages her mother left on her cell phone over the weekend. But her worry became full-blown panic when Molly failed to confirm the plan for Nancy to pick her up at the airport in Cleveland.

"And when she didn't get off that plane," she said, "I knew something awful had happened to her."

The officers who were handling the missing persons report weren't so sure—and neither was LaJuanda when she first took the case.

From the start, she had reminded herself—and the worried mother—that unexpected things can happen when a single woman, no matter how respectable, goes on a decadent vacation for the first time in her life. Molly might have met someone and impulsively decided to run away with him—or *her*—and start a new life. LaJuanda has seen it before here in Miami.

Nancy's reaction to that theory was, of course: "Not my daughter. She'd never just take off and let me worry like this."

That's always the parent's knee-jerk response, whether the missing person in question is a respectable grown woman or a fourteen-year-old runaway suspected of turning tricks on Biscayne Boulevard.

Sadly, though, in Nancy Temple's case, it's probably true. Her daughter wouldn't have just taken off. The more LaJuanda has learned about the missing woman over the past week, the more convinced she's become that Molly fell victim to a predator.

It might have been someone she'd met at sea and agreed to see again in Miami, or—more likely, LaJuanda guessed—someone whose path she'd had the misfortune of randomly crossing after she left the hotel on foot less than an hour after checking in.

If, indeed, she *had* checked in.

Someone certainly did.

LaJuanda reaches out to click the mouse, freezing the image onscreen. She stares at the woman she's had no reason to believe, until this moment, isn't Molly Temple. She's wearing a hat and sunglasses, but that's not unusual in Florida.

Still . . .

LaJuanda rewinds the footage a bit, then lets it play again, checking out the other people in the lobby. Some have sunglasses pushed up on their heads, or dangling from cords around their necks, but none is wearing them.

Was the sun shining at the hour when Molly Temple walked into the hotel?

LaJuanda makes a mental note to check that out as she watches Molly talk to Pamela, the desk clerk who'd checked her in using her ID and credit card. It's not a good angle; she can't get a good look at Molly's face, but she can see that the interaction appears to be routine.

When LaJuanda interviewed Pamela, she said she hadn't noticed anything amiss. She confessed that she barely remembered Molly, though.

"I check hundreds of people in and out of this hotel every day, you know. A lot of them are coming and going on cruises. I'm sorry . . . like I told the police, I just don't remember much about her."

Maybe because she didn't want you to, LaJuanda thinks now, suppressing a shudder. If that's not Molly—what happened to her between the cruise dock and the hotel? Or—was it even sooner?

The surveillance tape is nearing its end. In silence, LaJuanda and Nancy watch Molly emerge from her hotel room shortly after she first entered it, hanging the "Do Not Disturb" sign on the knob. She's carrying one of the bags she brought into the hotel, and it looks fairly heavy, judging by the way she shifts it from shoulder to shoulder while waiting for the elevator.

There's a cut back to the lobby, where she goes from the elevator to the exit. Through the glass, she's visible having a conversation with one of the doormen before she exits the picture, never to be heard from again.

Yesterday morning, LaJuanda spoke to the doorman, a sharp-eyed grad student in his early twenties.

"You mean that woman the cops were here asking about a few weeks ago?" He looked her up and down, taking in her curve-hugging teal dress, four-inch wedge sandals, and dark hair falling in loose waves down her back. "You're not a cop, are you?"

"I'm a detective."

"No kidding."

"I never kid a kid."

"Ouch."

"Sorry. I say that all the time to my son. You remind me of him." She flashed him a smile. "What do you remember about Molly Temple?"

"Just that she didn't need a cab," he told LaJuanda's cleavage, "and then she walked away, heading south, toward downtown."

"You have no idea where she was heading?"

"A lot of tourists go that way. There's a lot to do down there. The park, the Convention Center, Bayside Marketplace, Riverwalk . . . She could have gone anywhere."

Yes—and she must have crossed paths with a predator along the way, LaJuanda thought at the time.

Now, she shifts her thinking: What if the woman who'd left the hotel *was* the predator?

Then she was making her escape, LaJuanda realizes. This changes everything.

The tape over, Nancy Temple turns to her, trembling. "That wasn't Molly. What in the world is going on?"

Good question. Her mind working through various scenarios, LaJuanda clicks the mouse and briskly presses a few keys, pulling up a new file on the computer. "There's footage from the Carousel's security cameras. Can you take a look at that, too?"

Nancy nods mutely, and LaJuanda notes that her eyes are no longer dry. She plucks a tissue from the box and passes it over. Molly's mother takes it with a wan thank-you.

"Hang in there." LaJuanda pats her hand again.

"Believe me, I'm trying."

"I know you are, honey."

"Do you think . . . do you think it's a *good* sign that it's not her?"

Of course it isn't. How can it be? Someone else wearing a missing person's clothing, using her credit cards . . .

All signs point to foul play.

LaJuanda learned long ago that a lie—even one meant to be kind—can be cruel in the long run.

So she tells Nancy Temple, "All you can do is hope for the best. Let's take a look at this other footage."

The Carousel's security cameras show Molly in the public areas of the ship over the course of her week on board: dining in restaurants, browsing in shops, coming and going at ports of call, and disembarking in Miami on the last day.

Nancy weeps openly through most of it as LaJuanda hands her tissues, keeping her own gaze trained on the video looking, once again, for signs that Molly attracted unwanted attention from a stranger.

Not a thing. For the most part, she moves about the ship alone, spending long hours on sea days lying in a chair with a book. At evening meals, she dines with several other women, all of whom were randomly assigned to her table.

No one in Molly's orbit seems to be paying unwarranted attention to her. As far as LaJuanda can tell, the fellow passengers and crew members she encountered had only polite, casual interaction with her.

It takes a couple of hours to work through the footage, even with LaJuanda fast-forwarding through several long stretches of Molly reading in the sun.

Nancy Temple has grown increasingly subdued, her elbow propped on the arm of her chair, chin in hand, fingers splayed across her cheek as she watches the last known evidence of her daughter's existence.

Then, all at once, she sits up straight. "There—see that? It's not her! Can you back it up? There . . . stop it!"

LaJuanda works the mouse, doing just as the woman asked—backing up the video and then freezing on a frame that shows Molly coming up the gangplank at the final port of call in Saint Antony.

"That's not her!" Nancy Temple rakes a hand through her short gray hair. "Look at the way she's walking! That's not her walk!"

Even LaJuanda can see, this time, that something about Molly has changed. She's wearing the same clothes she had on earlier, when she got off the ship, but . . .

Can it be? Is it true?

Incredulous, she realizes that Nancy Temple might be right. And if she is . . .

Something happened to Molly on that island. She got off the ship there, but she never got back on.

Who did?

The patio behind the deserted house next door to the Mac-Kennas is pretty fancy, with a wet bar and an outdoor fireplace. It's easy to imagine it all lit up on a summer Saturday night, filled with furniture and people.

Tonight it's shrouded in darkness beneath a waning crescent moon. As always, the shadows serve Carrie's purpose well. She sits on the low brick wall that borders the patio, watching the house next door through the trees, waiting . . .

Allison and Mack, she knows, aren't home. Earlier, her heart pumping in excited anticipation, Carrie stole across the property line and crept up to the nearest ground floor window. But instead of seeing familiar faces, she saw a teenage girl. She was talking on her cell phone, and her voice floated out through the screen.

Within a few minutes, she'd revealed to an eavesdropping Carrie that she was the babysitter and that Mack and Allison had told her they'd be home by eleven.

Carrie took that cue to return to the house next door. It was shockingly easy to gain entrance through an unlocked basement window. She didn't dare turn on a light as she prowled through the house, scarcely able to believe her good fortune—particularly when she plugged in her laptop and saw the list of wifi networks in the vicinity.

One was called *mackandallie*, and you didn't have to be a genius to know whose it was. Nor did you have to be a genius—even a tech genius—to hack into the network. Thanks to the simple software Carrie had installed on her computer back in Florida, she was able to get right into the MacKennas' electronic world, allowing her access to everything they'd done on their computers next door.

Tempted as she was to browse through their online lives, she didn't want to miss their homecoming, so she headed outside to keep watch from the patio.

It's ten-forty-five. Any minute now . . .

Carrie hears a car coming down the street and sees the arc of headlights pulling into the driveway next door.

Her legs feel a bit wobbly when she stands, and it's not just from almost an hour sitting here on the low wall.

Jittery anticipation courses through her as she steals swiftly over to the hedgerow, bracing herself for her first sighting not just of the man to whom she was married for over a year of her life—but of the woman whose very existence was once Carrie's bitter cross to bear.

Once—and always.

Her mind flashes back to the last time she found Allison.

That was in the fall of 2000, not long after she and Mack had eloped. All through that spring and summer, her budding relationship with Mack had occupied Carrie's waking hours and her dreams, eclipsing any desire to continue searching for Allison Taylor.

But when Mack took up a death vigil at his mother's bedside, she found herself spending her evenings and weekends alone again. The familiar feeling of abandonment triggered memories of her father, and renewed her desire to pick up where she'd left off months ago in her search for Allison.

This time, her effort paid off. She found her through the Internet using the new Google search engine. Just months earlier, there had been nothing on Allison. But the world was leaping into the electronic age, and information availability was changing by the second. One day, Carrie typed in Allison's name and suddenly, there it was: listed on the Web site for *7th Avenue* magazine.

On a brisk fall evening, rather than taking the PATH train across the river to Mack's apartment, where they were then living, Carrie waited for Allison to come out of her midtown office building.

More than a decade had passed since she'd last set eyes on her, and Carrie had been worried she wouldn't recognize her. But there was no mistaking Allison. She was blond now, and all grown up, but Carrie spotted her right away when she stepped out onto the sidewalk. The sight took Carrie's breath away, and a barrage of emotions washed over her. Anger, yes—but also regret. Enough regret so that she didn't even follow Allison, just watched her walk away, thinking about how different things could have been, if only . . .

If only.

It was enough, then, for Carrie just to know where Allison was. No . . . it was almost too much.

She had a new life now, with Mack. She didn't want to live in the past anymore. She didn't want to risk upsetting the fragile balance between a life of normalcy and one of futile longing for what might have been—or violent impulse that could strike at any time.

The only way to keep it in check, she knew, was to focus on the present—and the future.

Mack's mother died soon after that, and he was back at home, where he belonged. He was vulnerable; he needed Carrie. She threw herself into being a wife to him, and when he started talking about having children, she actually believed she could become a mother as well.

Fool.

Pushing the ugly memories from her mind, she watches the car doors open on the driveway across from the dense shrubbery where she's hiding.

Mack steps out first.

She drinks in the sight of him: still tall and handsome, his dark hair graying at the temples now. She was steeling herself to feel some kind of remorse for letting him believe she had died in such a horrific way. But all she feels is a vague sense of indifference tinged with incomprehension that she ever knew this stranger as intimately as she did.

Then the other car door opens.

All at once Allison is there, close enough to touch, if Carrie wanted to. Close enough to . . .

No. She doesn't want to hurt Allison. That's not why she's here.

She just wants to . . .

What? What is it that you want with her, Carrie? What are you hoping to accomplish?

Allison starts to follow Mack up the driveway toward the back door. But suddenly she stops and turns her head, looking directly at the spot where Carrie is standing.

Panic screeches through her, and she stays absolutely still, holding her breath, wondering what she'll do if Allison calls out to her.

It doesn't happen, thank goodness. After what seems like a minute or two—but is really only a couple of seconds—Allison gives a little shrug and heads toward the house.

Carrie watches, her hands clenched into fists.

Allison looks as lovely as ever in a black sleeveless dress and heels.

You always were the pretty one, Carrie thinks darkly.

Even now, even with her hair several shades darker than it was the last time Carrie saw her. It's almost the same color as it had been all those years ago, in childhood.

She hears Mack's voice saying something but she can't make out the words, and then a ripple of laughter reaches her ears. Allison's laughter.

At the sound, something hardens inside Carrie.

Allison is laughing; she's been laughing all these years, all her life. Happy, lucky Allison.

It isn't fair.

She has everything, just like she always did.

And I have nothing.

After looking in on the children, all of whom are sound asleep, Allison changes out of her black dress and throws on a pair of pink summer pajamas. In the master bathroom, she scrubs off her makeup, brushes, flosses, then smiles into the mirror.

Good. No spinach in her teeth now.

Back at dinner, Randi had kicked her under the table and

gestured at Allison's mouth. She'd discreetly pulled out the shiny silver compact the girls had given her for Mother's Day, glad she had tucked it into her bag.

"Is that new?" asked Randi, who didn't miss a trick.

"Yes. It's from the girls. When they gave it to me, Hudson told me I can use it when I put on makeup and that I should carry it with me wherever I go. I think that was a big hint that Mommy's been a little too frumpy lately."

Randi didn't argue with that, just told her about a new shade of lipstick she'd seen that would be perfect with Allison's coloring. Message received, loud and clear.

Back in the bedroom, she climbs into bed, then right back out again. Too soon. She's still wired from the social evening.

She decides to stay up for a while and wait for Mack. He's out driving Sara, the teenage babysitter, home to the wealthy estate area where Randi and Ben live. Sara's family occupies one of the large mansions in their neighborhood, but there's a "For Sale" sign on their front lawn. Her unemployed father lost his Wall Street job two years ago and Sara is saving every penny of her babysitting money for college.

She's been here several times since Randi recommended her last winter. The girls love her because she plays Barbies with them, and she's adept enough at handling J.J. that Allison actually dares to leave the house before he's safely tucked in for the night.

Allison can find only one fault with Sara: every time she babysits, they come home to find that the house is blazing with light in every room.

"Why does she do that?" Mack asked tonight when they pulled into the driveway. "Do you think she's afraid of the dark or something?"

"I think she's afraid of what happened next door."

"But it's not like there's still a killer out there on the loose."

No, it wasn't. Still, as Allison stepped out of the car earlier in their driveway and glanced at the house next door, she couldn't help but notice that a sense of foreboding somehow seemed to hang in the air even now. Maybe Sara felt it, too.

Worried that Sara might become skittish about sitting here, Allison had paid her almost twice her hourly rate.

"This is too much," Sara protested.

"You deserve it." And God knew she needed it—and the MacKennas needed her. "We'll call you again soon— although probably not until after we get back from our vacation."

"Oh, the girls told me you're driving out to your hometown. They're so excited. I didn't know you were from Nebraska, Mrs. MacKenna."

"I am, but . . ." How to explain? "I haven't even been there since I was about your age."

"You must be thrilled to be going back home after all these years."

She agreed that she was, because it was easier than telling Sara the truth; easier than explaining that Nebraska wasn't "home" anymore—that it never had been.

Allison goes back downstairs, turning off lights as she makes her way to the living room. She turns off the television and all but one lamp, then settles on the couch with her laptop.

As Allison waits for the hard drive to boot up, a vague uneasiness steals over her. She finds herself darting repeated glances at the window, almost expecting a face to pop up there. A soft night breeze flutters the wine-colored drapes and tinkles the wind chimes beyond the screen, where crickets keep up a steady chatter. She hears a car down the street, but it can't be Mack's; it's too soon. She wishes he'd hurry.

Why is she so jittery tonight?

For all the healing she's helped the children do over the course of the last seven months, she never once experienced

this residual sense of fear and foreboding. It was enough—
until now, anyway—to know that the Nightwatcher was
dead. He couldn't hurt anyone ever again.

It's the Nebraska trip, she realizes as her desktop icons
begin to pop up onscreen. The prospect of going back there
has set her nerves on edge, and the anxiety, in turn, has
kicked her imagination into high gear.

Psych 101. Who needs Dr. Rogel?

A good night's sleep should help.

She decides to go to bed now after all. When Mack gets
back he'll want to talk—or more, knowing him, once he
sees her in this sheer baby doll pajama top. She has nothing against sex with her husband, but she's not the kind of
person who can roll over and fall right to sleep afterward.
It'll be midnight, at least, by the time she drifts off. Tomorrow is Father's Day. The girls will be up before the sun to
execute their plan to make breakfast in bed for Mack.

They did the same thing for Allison on Mother's Day,
and she spent a good part of that afternoon scrubbing sticky
maple syrup from every surface in the kitchen, including
the narrow space between the stove and cabinets, and trying
to figure out why the garbage disposal was clogged. (Tea
bags—with strings attached—and banana peels.)

Tomorrow morning, she'd better be up bright and early to
help the girls prepare their planned menu for Mack, which
is top secret but probably involves the broiler, since Hudson
wrote "bakin" on the grocery list a few days ago, trying to
disguise her kindergarten handwriting for Allison's.

About to log off the computer after all, she notices that the
mailbox icon on her desktop indicates new mail. Clicking
on the box, she sees that it's from brettandcindylou@gmail.
com. Her brother and sister-in-law share an account, so it
could be from either of them.

She clicks on the message.

Dear Allison, it begins, below a typed dateline, and she

smiles. Cindy-Lou always composes her e-mails like formal letters.

> *How is your weekend going? Fine, I hope. Ours is fine, too.*
>
> *Brett and I are so excited that you will be coming here in July! Which day are you planning to arrive? It's such a long drive from New York and I don't know if you'll feel like getting back into the car after you get here, but we are trying to plan some things to do while you are around. I know you haven't been back to Nebraska since you left, but not all that much has changed—for better or for worse! Since there's nothing much to do close by, check out these links to some of the sights that are within a couple of hours' drive from here and tell me what you think.*

There are several links—to a farm equipment museum, a local arts festival, and of course, the county fair. Beneath them, Cindy has signed off with:

> *Sincerely,*
> *Cindy-Lou Downing*

Downing is Brett's last name—the one their mother grew up with. Allison wonders, not for the first time, whether her own father ever considered adopting him. Maybe she'll ask Brett about it when she sees him.

Or maybe she won't ask him about anything tied to the past. Maybe she doesn't want to know, even now.

Then why are you wondering about it at all?

Who are you kidding?

You're not just going back to Nebraska to see Brett, and you might as well admit it, if only to yourself.

One of the Web site links Cindy-Lou sent is to a doll museum not far from Centerfield. If it had been there when Allison was growing up, no one ever mentioned it or thought to take her there.

She types a quick response to Cindy-Lou.

> *If the drive goes as planned, we'll be getting to the farm on July 3. Thanks for the info. The girls would love the doll museum.*

She hesitates, then deletes the last line.

After a moment, she retypes it.

Then she deletes it again, replacing it with, *How about if we just take it day by day when we get there?*

She hits send before she can change her mind, then closes her laptop and goes up to bed.

*N*ebraska.

Carrie stares at the intercepted e-mail, stunned.

Of all the cosmic signs that have come her way, this is the greatest of all. Greater, even, than Mack's name being Mack.

It can't be pure coincidence that Allison is going back to Nebraska, where it all began—and that Carrie got here in time to follow her out there.

Well, perhaps not *literally* follow her.

Remembering how complicated it was—and how long it took—to make her way north from Florida, Carrie realizes she doesn't have time to do the same thing all the way to the Great Plains. A road trip is out of the question.

But if Allison is going to be in Nebraska by July 3, then . . .
So am I.

She'll have to fly.

That means she'll need a new identity right away. Luckily, she's done her homework—again. She knows just where to go for a fake driver's license and credit card—advertised, on an illicit Web site, as being guaranteed to get her a plane ticket on any airline, and past the TSA at any airport.

Chances are that there are no direct flights to Omaha. That's okay. She'd be better off flying between major cities with crowded airports. Any of the three in metropolitan New York will do, and she'll fly into Denver, maybe, or Minneapolis, Kansas City . . . Anyplace that will land her close, but not too close, to Nebraska.

Yes. It's a good plan.

Of course, there's always a chance that the fake identity won't work with all the new regulations. But this is one time Carrie's willing to take a risk. If she gets caught, they'll find out everything she's done and she'll probably spend the rest of her life in prison.

But if she doesn't . . .

She'll be free at last. Free of the nightmares and the memories; free of the burden of guilt she's been carrying around for years.

Out there by the driveway earlier, seeing Allison again, hearing her easy laughter—that, for Carrie, was the turning point.

Yes, meeting Allison in Nebraska will be an incredibly perfect, full-circle ending to a journey whose purpose didn't become clear until tonight.

Gone is any naïve illusion that the two of them might actually connect on some level, perhaps build a relationship to replace all the ones that had shattered in the past.

No, Allison stole everything that ever mattered to Carrie—including Mack.

He was supposed to have been Carrie's ticket to normalcy. Together, they should have had everything—*could* have had everything. A happy marriage, a beautiful home, children . . .

A life. A happy, normal life . . .

The kind of life he now has with Allison.

It's time she learned that nothing—not even happiness—comes without a price.

Chapter Twelve

Saturday, June 30, 2012

"**A**ll set, Al?"

She turns to see Mack in the doorway of the master bedroom and quickly tosses the last few pillows on the just-made bed. "Yes. Are they still sleeping?"

"Still sleeping."

"Even Hudson?"

"Even Hudson."

Their seven year-old has been more excited than anyone about the road trip to Nebraska—so excited that when Allison tucked her into bed last night, she thought she'd never get to sleep.

Indeed, Hudson was still awake at eleven o'clock when Allison checked on her. She was in bed, but with a flashlight and the map of the United States that she'd marked with a highlighter to trace the cross-country route they're planning to take.

"Are you sure we can't stop in Chicago, Mommy?" she asked. "It's only about thirty miles out of the way."

"Not this trip," Allison told her yet again. "We want to spend as much time as we can with Uncle Brett, and we're already wasting six whole days of Daddy's vacation on the road."

"*Wasting?*"

"Not *wasting*," Allison told her apologetically. "The drive is going to be really fun. You'll see."

Fun . . . but long.

"Get some sleep," she told Hudson, taking away the flashlight and the map.

"You too, Mommy."

Knowing that a last-minute client emergency could have curtailed the whole trip, Allison didn't breathe easily until Mack pulled into the driveway close to midnight, having stayed at the office to tie up loose ends.

"Good to go?" she asked him.

"Unless something somehow goes wrong between now and tomorrow morning."

"What are the odds of that?"

"In this business," he told her, "I learned never to say never."

She went to bed wondering if maybe some part of her had been hoping that a crisis would arise at the office and keep them from leaving.

But the rest of the night passed uneventfully.

Now it's four-thirty A.M., three sleeping kids are strapped into the backseat, and it's actually going to happen. They're actually going to Nebraska.

"Come on, Al," Mack says around a yawn, jangling the car keys. "We've got to get on the road if we're going to beat the holiday weekend traffic over the bridge."

It's the same route they follow every year on the way to the Jersey Shore. But this year, once they've crossed the Hudson River, they'll continue heading west, not south.

Allison takes one last look around.

The next time I walk into this room, it'll be over.

She'll have gone to Nebraska, faced down the past, and survived. Then she'll be able to get on with normal life again, focusing on going forward, not back.

She turns off the bedside lamp, plunging the room into predawn darkness, and follows Mack down the shadowy stairs.

"Oh—wait, did you get the girls' tote bags? They were by the door."

"I got them. What the heck was in them? Rocks?"

"Books. Hudson wants to read the Little House series since we're heading out to the prairie, so I brought that—"

"The whole series?"

"What's wrong with that? They were mine when I was a little girl, just like some of the books in Maddy's bag."

"Allie, it's really sweet that you saved your favorite books for your own little girls and lugged them all the way here from Nebraska—but do we really need to lug them all the way back again?"

"Yes," she says simply, not bothering to explain to him that salvaging all those well-worn books from her childhood bedroom years ago had nothing to do with preserving them for future daughters. Nor was it because her father had bought them for her and read them to her.

She did it for herself, because she thought she might need them someday. Growing up, she'd learned that when the real world became hard to bear, she could always pull a book off the shelf and lose herself in a make-believe one. It was a relief to step into a fictional character's shoes and deal with someone else's problems instead of her own, knowing that things would work out in the end.

Outside, it feels like the middle of the night. The street-lights are still on, crickets are chirping, and the newspaper trucks have yet to toss plastic bags containing the *New York Times* or *Wall Street Journal* onto driveways up and down the street.

Standing beside Mack as he locks the front door, Allison remembers something. "I'll be right back."

"Where are you going?" he asks as she hurries down the steps.

"To check the backyard." It's been raining the past couple of days, and she never found a chance to get outside and make sure the sandbox was covered, the little plastic pool was drained, and everything was put away.

She called Randi last night to give her Brett's name, address, and phone number, so that someone on this end would know where they were headed. Randi promised to drive by and check on the house every couple of days while they're away, but Allison doesn't want her picking up grungy plastic toys from the lawn.

Dewy grass brushes her toes, bare in flat summer sandals, as she makes her way around the side of the house. Through the trees and shrubs that border the edge of the property, she can see the large house looming next door.

A year ago, it was full of life. Phyllis and Bob Lewis were living there. Their two children were home from college for the summer, using the saltwater pool and the sunken patio with its outdoor stone fireplace and wet bar, hosting loud parties most weekends when Phyllis and Bob retreated to their Vermont cottage.

To think Allison and Mack used to complain—if only to each other—about the noise. Now she'd take wee-hour laughter, music, and slamming car doors any day over the eerie silence that's fallen over the vacant house.

Desperate to get away from the horror of what happened here, Phyllis's grieving husband accepted a year-long overseas assignment in February. Their son had graduated from college in May and taken a job on the West Coast, and their daughter, Bob told Allison in a recent phone call, didn't have the heart to return to an empty house for the summer.

"I'm going to see if I can rent it out until I get back," he told her. "I hope you don't mind."

"Not at all, Bob. Let me know what I can do to help."

"Thank you. I will," he said in a hollow voice, and she knew that he, too, was remembering the last time he'd needed her help. As keeper of the Lewises' spare set of keys, Allison was the one who discovered the grisly murder scene after a worried Bob called from a European business trip and asked her to go check on his wife.

Every time she looks at the house, she remembers that night. Remembers Phyllis's bloodied corpse in the master bedroom and remembers, with a shudder, that she'd actually suspected, at one point, that Mack might have had something to do with it.

She's glad the house hasn't been rented yet. She doesn't want to see it come to life again, occupied by strangers. That would feel just as wrong as the "For Rent" sign does, and—

Frowning, Allison stares into the dense foliage that separates her own yard from the Lewises'.

There, amid the branches, she could have sworn she just saw a human shadow . . .

Just like that night a few weeks ago.

She blinks, and it's gone.

Unnerved, she gives the backyard a cursory glance, making sure there are no stray toys on the lawn. As she hurries back around front, she takes a long last look at the property line.

Nothing. It must have been her imagination again, playing tricks on her as it had a few weeks ago. It makes sense. She's anxious about leaving, not to mention deliriously tired.

Mack certainly is. He yawns deeply as they head to the car.

"Did you sleep at all?" Allison asks him.

"I must have. Last thing I remember, the clock said three forty-five."

The alarm, she knows too well, had gone off at four.

"You only got fifteen minutes. I got almost four hours. I'll drive the first leg."

Predictably, Mack argues with that.

But Allison is behind the wheel when they pull out of the driveway a minute later, her husband sleeping as soundly as the three kids by the time she merges onto the Saw Mill River Parkway, heading southbound toward the George Washington Bridge.

Traffic is already starting to build. The Fourth of July falls on Wednesday this year, and a lot of people are taking the whole week off, or at least a five-day weekend.

That's the thing about living where they do. When you're competing for space with the millions of others who occupy the metropolitan area, even the simplest endeavor demands a serious head start and considerable advance planning.

It's going to be nice, Allison tells herself, approaching the bridge at last, to have some breathing room for a change. Out on the wide open plains of Nebraska, she recalls, it's possible to drive for miles without seeing another car. At least, that used to be the case. She wonders if it still is.

Noticing that the sun is coming up out to the east, behind the city, she reminds herself that in just a few days, she'll see it rise over a grassy horizon for the first time in years.

She told the girls all about that just the other day—about how you can see all the way across a great, flat expanse to where the earth meets the sky.

"You've never seen anything like it around here," she told her daughters.

"That's how it is down the shore," Hudson reminded her.

"Only there, it's water meeting the sky. Does Nebraska look like that? But green instead of blue?"

"Not exactly. The ocean only stretches in one direction. You can stand in the middle of a field in Nebraska, and it spreads out all around you, so that there's nothing but grass and sky no matter which way you turn. And when the sun sets at night, it looks like it's lying right on the grassy edge of the earth."

"That sounds like the card I made you for Mother's Day!" Maddy exclaimed. "See, Hudson? I told you it was okay to put the sun on the grass."

"There's no edge to the earth," Hudson replied, to both of them. "It's round."

"But it looks flat in Nebraska," Allison told her. "All the way to the sky, there's nothing. Not a house, not a tree, not a person."

"It sounds peaceful."

A wide-eyed Madison disagreed with her sister. "I think it sounds scary. What if you needed help? Or what if you needed to hide?"

"You wouldn't need help, and you wouldn't need to hide," Hudson told her before Allison could respond, "because Mommy said there's not a person around. So there wouldn't be any reason to hide."

Those words—and the haunted look on Madison's face—sent a pang of sorrow through Allison. Her poor girls had been through so much at the hands of a depraved human being. Thank goodness they weren't going back to the shore anytime soon. Thank goodness they were headed far, far away.

Now, Manhattan's skyline falls into the rearview mirror as they head west. Dawn is breaking, its rainbow sherbet palette tinting the glittering steel and glass facade of the new Freedom Tower rising above the scarred ground that once held the burning ruins of the World Trade Center.

For a fleeting, foolish moment, Allison considers waking Mack to show him the spectacular sight. She quickly thinks better of it, not just because he's exhausted.

Even now, over a decade later, still riddled with guilt over what happened to his first wife, he balks at reminders of that fateful day.

Even so, he recently mentioned that last year around the tenth anniversary, he'd actually considered looking into Carrie's past. He'd thought it might be time to uncover her true identity: who she'd been before her family vanished into the witness protection program. He never got around to doing it, and when he mentioned it to Allison, she was glad.

She still remembered what her brother had said to her years ago, when she briefly toyed with the idea of searching for the father who had walked out on her.

"Why would you want to go dredging that up again after all these years? Why can't you leave well enough alone?"

She'd have said the same thing to Mack, had he told her he was going to delve into Carrie's roots.

That situation was entirely different from her own.

Carrie was dead. Mack wasn't looking for her. He was looking for truth; perhaps, even after all these years, for closure.

Can Allison blame him?

Isn't that what I'm doing right now? she wonders as she drives west through New Jersey.

Nothing but highway stretches behind her now in the rearview mirror, but again she thinks of the Freedom Tower.

She visited the site only once, when there was nothing to see other than steel girders, blue scaffolding, and a large sign that read "Never Forget."

Built to symbolize rebirth and strength, the soaring structure now casts its long shadow over the gaping footprint where the twin towers once stood, and the bronze memorial etched with the names of the victims who died on that spot.

Carrie Robinson MacKenna, of course, is among them.

"Do you want to go see it?" Allison had asked Mack last fall, when the memorial opened and the victims' families were invited to be among the first to visit.

His reply was the same as it had been a few years earlier, when he was invited to join other bereaved spouses at ground zero on the 9/11 anniversary to ceremoniously read from the long list of victims' names: a flat, predictable no.

Allison hadn't pressed the issue then, and she didn't now.

What if her father's name were etched in stone somewhere? Would she be drawn to the spot, or fiercely determined to avoid it?

It's different, she reminds herself again, focusing on the road ahead.

Carrie Robinson wasn't the name Mack's first wife had been born with. And Allen Taylor . . .

For years, Allison has refused to allow herself to think about what her brother had once told her: that her father had, most likely, been living under an assumed name.

Now, the thought barges into her mind again.

She can't seem to push it back out.

Why live a lie?

What was he hiding?

Maybe it wasn't a dark secret, as she had assumed. Maybe it was a noble one. Maybe there was some redeeming aspect to the situation; some self-sacrificing reason that he'd left his family. Maybe her father had been a hero after all. Or a victim.

Was he, like Carrie Robinson, in the witness protection program?

Ha. What were the odds of that?

Only a fool believes in coincidences, Detective Rocky

Manzillo told Allison last fall, after the Nightwatcher case was resolved.

Yes. And only a fool would believe that a man who'd turned his back on his own child could have been anything but a miserable scoundrel.

She isn't going back to Nebraska in search of answers. She's going to visit her only living relatives. Period.

The only relatives who matter, anyway.

The man she had known as Allen Taylor might not be dead and buried, but he might as well be.

"**E**xcuse me, ma'am?"

Carrie looks up from the airline magazine she's been pretending to read as the other passengers board the plane. She can't focus on it, but she doesn't want to make eye contact with anyone.

Now, however, she's forced to, looking up to see a gray-haired woman standing in the aisle.

"Would you mind switching seats with me, ma'am? I'm in this row, too, but I'm on the aisle and I'd rather have the window." She lets go of the handle of her rolling carry-on suitcase to gesture at Carrie's seat with a wrinkled, blue-veined hand.

"Sorry," Carrie mutters, shaking her head. "I can't."

"Ma'am, please . . ." The woman shifts her weight, and her smile grows forced. "I have back and leg problems, so I need to lean against the window whenever I fly, but my travel agent made a mistake and got me an aisle seat."

Travel agent? In this day and age?

Even Carrie, who hadn't flown in well over a decade, had figured out how to book her flight online.

Naturally, she had carefully studied the airline's online seat map before selecting hers. She had learned the back of the plane boarded first and that the overhead bins filled very quickly in this era of checked baggage fees. Checking her luggage—and risking the chance that it could go astray and ultimately fall into the wrong hands—was out of the question.

She settled on a window seat in the rear of the plane with an as-yet unfilled middle seat beside it, hoping it would stay vacant. She chose one on the left-hand side because she wanted the best view of Manhattan upon takeoff.

Of course, there were still no guarantees she'd be able to glimpse the skyline from the air even if the weather turned out to be perfectly clear—which it is this afternoon—but she conducted considerable online research into flight patterns to give herself the best chance. And there's no way in hell that she's about to give it up for this clueless stranger who didn't even board twenty minutes ago when their row was called.

"We all have our problems," she says curtly. "Please don't expect me to make yours into mine."

The woman's jaw drops.

Carrie turns away, going back to pretending to read her magazine.

She hears the woman asking a harried flight attendant to find her a window seat.

"I'm sorry, ma'am, they're all full."

"I have a medical condition. I can't sit on the aisle."

"What is the condition?"

"My back, and my hip—I'll be crippled with pain by the time we land if I can't lean against the window, and"—she lowers her voice to a stage whisper—"that woman sitting there in my row was very rude when I asked her to change with me."

"I'm sorry, ma'am. I'll see what I can do after takeoff, but for now I just need you to take your assigned seat because we can't close the cabin doors until you do."

"But my back—"

"Ma'am, please, if you don't take your seat right now, we'll lose our takeoff slot, and this is a very busy airport. You'll be inconveniencing an entire plane full of passengers."

"What about *my* inconvenience? What about my health and well-being?"

"Ma'am, please. Stow your bag and be seated."

Out of the corner of her eye, Carrie watches the flight attendant retreat to the galley as the woman huffily opens the overhead bin above their row. Of course it's full, as is the one across the aisle. And the two behind them, and in front of them . . .

"Stewardess! I can't find a place for my bag."

What did you expect? Carrie wonders, and clenches her jaw.

"I'm going to have to check it. I'll take it up front and—"

"I can't check it. I can't afford it, for one thing—"

"There's no charge for gate-checking items that won't fit."

"But my prescriptions are in there, and my other glasses, and—"

"Ma'am, please take those items out if you need them, but you'll need to do it quickly because we really do have to close the cabin door."

With what seems like deliberate sluggishness, the woman begins removing items from her bag and placing them on the middle seat. Seething, Carrie sneaks a peek at one of the orange prescription bottles.

It's from a pharmacy in Mankato. The woman's name is clearly typed on the label: *Imogene Peters.*

Carrie files it away for future reference.

At last, Imogene allows the flight attendant to take her bag and settles into her aisle seat with a loud moan to ensure that everyone around her knows that she's in extreme physical pain.

Five minutes later, the captain comes on the loudspeaker

and apologetically announces that they've lost their slot for takeoff and will be delayed for at least forty-five minutes, bringing a collective groan from the passengers.

Carrie sticks the magazine back into the seatback pocket and gazes out the window, eyes narrowed, fists clenched.

This is all Imogene Peters's fault, she thinks, when—an hour later—the plane finally creeps out to take its place in the endless lineup of planes waiting to take off. Someone should teach that woman a lesson. Someone should . . .

Maybe someone will, Carrie tells herself, *but it's not going to be you. No matter how much you want to see that she gets what she has coming to her . . .*

You can't.

It's all about self-control.

Self-control—she's had to dig deep to find that ever since she took up residence a few weeks ago in the house next door to the MacKennas. Spying on Allison in the yard with her children, it was all she could do not to push through the shrubbery and confront her on the spot.

But it wasn't time for that yet. It was going to happen back in Nebraska.

In the meantime, all Carrie could do was watch.

A couple of times, Allison glanced idly in the direction of the Lewises' deserted house. Once—early this morning, when Carrie snuck out for one last look at the MacKennas before they drove away—Allison even seemed to look right at the spot where she was standing.

Carrie swiftly and silently stepped back, grateful for the cover of trees and shrubs . . .

So different from the landscape where they were headed. On the wide-open plains, she knew only too well, there would be no place to hide.

That was okay. When the time was right, she would be all too willing to step out of the shadows at last.

The pilot's voice comes on the intercom again. "Ladies and gentlemen, we're next for takeoff. Flight attendants, please be seated."

With a great rumbling rattle, the plane hurtles down the runway. Carrie smiles as it lifts off the ground, and presses her forehead against the window.

Her online research paid off. The aircraft banks sharply as it begins its steep climb, allowing her to glimpse Manhattan's skyline off to the left.

She thinks of the passengers on the doomed flights that crashed into the twin towers on September 11. This was one of the last things they ever saw on this earth—albeit with the World Trade Center still intact on the lower tip of the island.

As the historic events unfolded on that fateful day, Carrie had been in full-on carpe diem mode, making the most of the opportune situation for her own benefit. Only when she was safely out of the country did she allow herself to reflect. For her, hindsight brought mostly relief—and self-serving glee.

Now, catching her first glimpse of the island without its familiar anchor, a new structure rising where the twin towers once stood, she's caught off guard by a stirring of emotion deep inside her.

Regret. That's what it is.

She remembers what it was like to belong there, in an office high above the bustling city streets. She remembers her choreographed commute through a network of corridors and elevators and tunnels that no longer exist. She remembers the night she deviated from that daily routine and met a man named Mack because she listened to her gut as Daddy had taught her. She remembers the dream catcher, and believing in dreams, and a sense of loss trickles in like contaminated groundwater seeping through fissures in a stone foundation.

Things could have turned out differently if she hadn't given up and let go.

Things could have turned out differently if Allison hadn't stepped in to take what should have belonged to Carrie.

Regret gives way to rage, just as it has in the past.

I was so mad . . .

Rage, undiluted, leads to loss of self-control.

The plane has begun to level off as they head west. Far below, she knows, the MacKenna family is moving in the same direction.

In a few days, their path and Carrie's will converge at last. She and Allison will come face-to-face again—right back where it all began.

Of course, Allison might not even recognize her. Just as before, in New York.

But don't worry, Carrie tells her silently. *This time, I'll be sure to tell you exactly who I am.*

In the meantime, she needs to do something about the turbulent emotions that are now bubbling inside her. If she doesn't find a way to let off some steam, she's going to explode.

She sneaks a sideways glance at Imogene Peters just as a two-bell signal dings through the cabin, followed by the click of an intercom.

"Ladies and gentlemen," the flight attendant says, "we have now reached a cruising altitude and it is safe to use approved portable electronic devices. Wifi service is available."

Internet on an airplane? Incredible. Carrie reaches under the seat in front of her and takes out her laptop. She opens it and angles the screen toward the window, just in case Imogene is as nosy as she is obnoxious.

A few moments later, Carrie is online looking at a Minnesota road map.

She'd already plotted her course from the airport across the state to her first stop, in South Dakota. But that doesn't mean a detour can't be arranged. The MacKennas won't even be in Nebraska until Tuesday.

There will be plenty of time to visit Mankato.

Plenty of time to expel this brewing rage from her system.

"**C**an we go sightseeing after dinner?" Hudson skips a little as they cross the hotel parking lot, her *Child's First Atlas* in hand.

"*Sightseeing?*"

Allison and Mack echo their daughter's ludicrous question in perfect unison, exchanging a weary, but amused, glance.

It's been a long day—one that started five hundred miles ago, at four A.M.—and Allison suspects it might be an even longer night. J.J. dozed all morning in the car, woke infuriated to find himself strapped in a car seat, and fussed against the restraints for the next several hours until he exhausted himself into unconsciousness again. Allison was so relieved not to have to ride backward in the front seat, trying to entertain him so that Mack did the driving, that she let him sleep through most of the afternoon.

She actually had to wake him when they reached the hotel just off the interstate in Ohio. As his glassy-eyed parents and sisters dragged themselves out of the car, J.J. was refreshed, wanting to play. At this point, his schedule is so thrown off that she's certain they're looking at a restless night—all five of them crammed into a small hotel room.

Allison and Mack would have been content to go straight to bed after they checked in, but the girls got a second wind and are hungry. Allison is hoping she can muster enough energy to make it through a meal without her head falling into her salad bowl.

But *sightseeing*?

"Sweetie, we can't," she tells Hudson as she straps a loudly protesting J.J. back into his car seat.

"The Rock and Roll Hall of Fame is around here someplace. I want to see it, and the zoo, too. There's a lot to do here."

"I know, but it's really much too late for that."

"It's still sunny out!"

"I know," Allison says again, summoning every ounce of patience, "but look at the time."

Hudson, who never goes anywhere without her watch, glances at her wrist, and her green eyes widen.

"What time is it?" Madison wants to know, buckling her seat belt.

"Almost nine o'clock," her sister tells her, and it's Maddy's turn to look surprised.

"We're so far west that the sun doesn't set until after nine at this time of year," Mack explains, climbing into the front seat beside Allison. "Any idea where we're going to eat?"

"There were a bunch of restaurants back by the exit where we got off the road."

"Did you notice which ones? I'm already sick of fast food."

"So am I."

The girls, naturally, are not. Much to their delight, they'd eaten breakfast at McDonald's and lunch at Arby's, something they get to do maybe once or twice a year back home in the land of healthy snacks and organic everything.

Allison pulls out her iPhone and taps on a search engine app. "I'll see what's around here."

"There's a children's museum around here," Hudson tells her, consulting her atlas.

"I meant restaurants."

"I know! I mean for after dinner, Mommy."

"After dinner we're all going to bed," Mack informs her.

"But I wanted to go sightseeing!"

"Stop whining, Hudson!"

"Don't snap at her, Mack!" Allison immediately regrets contradicting him in front of the kids, something they both try never to do. But her nerves are fraying fast—and so are everyone else's.

To his credit, Mack apologizes. "I know you're just excited to be here, right, Huddy?"

She nods vigorously.

"We'll have to make sure we come back another time."

"Promise, Daddy?"

"Promise."

"You mean we'll come back to Cleveland?" Hudson sounds like an attorney repeating a witness's testimony for the court record.

"Sure." He looks at Allison. "Right, Mommy?"

"Sure, Daddy." She rolls her eyes. "Why not? Another fourteen-hour drive to Cleveland will be a breeze."

"Hudson told me it wasn't supposed to take fourteen hours," Madison speaks up, and her sister nods vigorously.

"My atlas said it was s'posed to be less than nine."

"That's not allowing for stops," Allison points out. They'd made quite a few—several for the bathroom, a couple for more coffee to keep the drivers alert, and of course, breaks for breakfast and lunch.

"It's not allowing for holiday weekend traffic, either," Mack puts in, braking and flipping on the left signal and waiting to make what looks like an impossible turn onto the highway.

Traffic, traffic, and more traffic—even here.

They thought they'd seen the worst of it this morning near the junction with Interstate 81, which branched off south toward Hershey. But they hit another massive crunch near the outlet malls of Grove City. Then they were stuck for over two hours behind a pileup involving a jackknifed tractor-trailer just north of Youngstown.

So much for her theory that the Midwest would be un-crowded. It isn't here in suburban Cleveland, anyway. Prob-ably farther west.

Mack finally makes a right turn, then a U-turn at the next light—an illegal one, but Allison bites her tongue. She gazes out the window as reminders of her old life fly past. A field of corn, a parking lot carnival, grocery and retail store chains you don't see in the Northeast: Kroger's, Von Maur, Cracker Barrel . . .

"Crackers! I love crackers!" Hudson shouts, seeing the sign. "Can we go there?"

Allison's mind tumbles back to her own childhood. Her friend Tammy Connolly's mom was a waitress at the local Cracker Barrel restaurant. Once in a while, Allison and Tammy visited her there, and she would buy them old-fashioned candy buttons from the country store at the front of the restaurant.

"Might as well. What do you think, Allie?"

"Hmm?" She gives Mack a blank look.

"Cracker Barrel. Should we eat there?"

She nods, toying with the iPhone in her hand, wondering what ever happened to Tammy.

"Too bad it's on the left-hand side of the road." Shaking his head, Mack brakes and puts on the turn signal in the face of an endless stream of oncoming traffic.

Maybe I should look up Tammy, Allison thinks. She wouldn't want to actually *see* her, of course—they'd have nothing in common after all these years. She's just curious, now that the memories are trickling in, about where life has taken her old friend.

Before she can change her mind, she types "Tammy Con-nolly, Nebraska," into the phone's open search engine.

The query comes back with thousands of results, as she'd expected. But the top one seems to fit. There's a Tamara

Connolly Pratt, age thirty-five, living in Ashland, a small town between Omaha and Lincoln.

Of course, they'll be driving right past there tomorrow and have a reservation to spend the night nearby, at the famous Cornhusker Hotel in Lincoln.

Tamara Pratt has a Facebook page. Allison, who does not, is blocked from viewing her photo or any information about her.

She changes her search engine query to "Tamara Connolly Pratt, Ashland, Nebraska," and is routed to several other sites. One lists an e-mail address.

"Mommy!"

Allison blinks, realizes Mack is pulling into a parking space at the restaurant, and Madison is waiting for her reply to a question she didn't hear.

"What, Maddy?"

"I said, do they have anything besides crackers here?"

"Oh . . . sure they do. They have chicken and French fries and all kinds of things you like."

"Do they have spaghetti?" she asks, as her little brother grabs a fistful of her long blond hair.

"I don't think so, but—"

"Ouch!" Poor Madison, always so patient, is trying to disentangle her hair from J.J.'s fingers.

"J.J., no!" Allison says sharply.

"Mommy, I really feel like spaghetti." Madison sounds as though she's going to burst into tears.

"You know what they definitely have?" Allison says quickly. "They have candy. All kinds of candy."

"How do you know?"

"Because I used to go to Cracker Barrel when I was a little girl. My friend Tammy's mom worked there."

"*Here?*" Hudson asks, with interest, as they climb out of the car.

"No, it's a chain. There was one in my hometown."

Predictably, Allison's firstborn is full of questions about that. "Does her mom still work there? Does she get free candy? Can we go see her in your hometown?"

"She's not there anymore. She moved away and we lost touch, but . . . I just found out she's still in Nebraska."

As she leans into the backseat to get J.J., Allison sees Mack glance at her in surprise.

"I looked her up," she tells him simply, and puts her son into her husband's outstretched hands.

"I thought you didn't want to do that."

"I changed my mind."

"Are we going to go see Tammy when we get to Nebraska, Mommy?" Hudson persists.

"No."

"Why not?"

"Here, hold my hand. You too, Maddy. This parking lot is crazy. I bet there's going to be a long wait for a table even at this hour."

As they make their way toward the entrance, with its trademark rows of wooden rocking chairs—most filled with customers waiting for tables—Allison's thoughts drift back to Tammy, her daughter's question echoing in her ears.

Why not?

LaJuanda's Cuban heritage is rooted in this part of the world, but she's been to the Caribbean only twice in her life. The first time was on her Jamaican honeymoon, when she and Rene toasted their marriage and promised each other they'd return annually. The next—and last—visit was the following year on her anniversary.

"I feel like we belong here," she told her husband as they sat holding hands on the beach in Negril, watching a bright pink sun sink into the turquoise sea. "There's something about this place that speaks to me."

"That's because it's in your blood."

"I'm Cuban, not Jamaican."

"Cuba is only a hundred miles away from here. I think your subconscious is sensing that you're close to home."

"Home is Miami. That's the only place I've ever lived."

"Yes, but you're Caribbean at heart," Rene pointed out. "You're free-spirited and resilient and full of passion and you live in the moment."

That was entirely true back then. Still is, on some levels. But life got in the way of her plans to reconnect with her island roots and spend every anniversary barefoot on those sugary sands. Rene decided to go to law school, she made detective, he passed the bar, they wound up with a mortgage and a couple of kids . . .

Now here she is, all alone on a tropical island very much like the one where they'd honeymooned twenty years ago. Rene is back in Coral Gables with the kids, attempting to hold down the fort at home in the midst of trying a grueling case.

"When will you be back?" their oldest son, Ricky, asked when he dropped her off at the airport this afternoon.

"I'm not sure. Maybe tomorrow. Maybe even tonight."

"*Tonight?*"

Of course not tonight. Even if the island proved to be a dead end, there were no flights back to Miami until tomorrow afternoon.

But with Rene absorbed in his trial, LaJuanda doesn't want her teenagers tempted to take advantage of her absence with a free-for-all. Let them think she might show up at any minute.

"It all depends on how long it takes for me to find out what I need to know," she told her son, and kissed him good-bye.

Thunderstorms were moving into Miami as they took off, and most of the flight over open water was turbulent.

LaJuanda barely noticed. She was absorbed in rereading

everything she'd learned about what had happened on Saint Antony after the Carousel, with Molly Temple on board, dropped anchor.

Namely: the explosion that very evening at Jimmy's Big Iguana, a bar not far from the harbor. Eight people were killed, including Jimmy Bolt, the owner. According to published accounts, the local police had confirmed foul play but had no suspects. It seemed that for every local who adored the famously charismatic Jimmy, there was another who despised him—perhaps enough to want him dead.

Apparently, one of his enemies had planted a bomb in a storage room off the bar's kitchen. Had it gone off just an hour earlier, a police officer was quoted as saying, there might have been dozens, perhaps hundreds, of casualties. Jimmy's Big Iguana was popular with cruise ship passengers.

"Luckily, it happened after they were all back on their ships," the officer told the press.

According to the initial publications, it appeared that the dead included six men and two women, though the remains were badly burned.

She wondered right away about the women, especially when she read that the bodies were too charred to be identified right away. It took a few days for their names to be published in the local papers. When they were, LaJuanda put aside her notion that Molly could have been among them, because all were confirmed as locals. One of the two female victims had stopped at the bar after work with her husband, who'd also been killed; the other was a bartender at the Big Iguana.

LaJuanda couldn't help but think that there was something fishy about the timing of the explosion. What if there had been another body and the investigators had missed it? Or covered it up? The small island police force wasn't entirely corrupt, but it had endured its share of well-publicized scandals in recent years. That would be good reason, LaJuanda decided as the plane landed, to keep a low profile for the time being, rather than approach the local authorities with her suspicion, which is . . .

What, exactly?

All she knows for certain is that Molly Temple got off the Carousel on that island, and she didn't get back on. Someone else did—and shortly after it sailed, there was an explosion on shore.

It might have been a coincidence.

Something told her that it wasn't.

By the time she had cleared customs and stepped into the bedlam outside the airport terminal—which resembled a Quonset hut—LaJuanda was itching to roll up her sleeves and get to work. But first, she had to check into her hotel, a moderately priced resort on the opposite end of the island. She waited in a long line to get a cab, and after a misleadingly breakneck start along the relatively new highway from the airport, the ride slowed to a creep and crawl when they reached a traffic rotary. The driver took a spur that led through the main harbor town, where several anchored cruise ships dwarfed the cluster of low buildings near the pier.

Armed with a map, LaJuanda looked longingly at the turnoff she knew led to the site of the Big Iguana. But it would have to wait. She couldn't conduct an investigation while dragging luggage along with her.

The car bumped along through dusty streets crowded with cars, the occasional dog or chicken, and people who reflected the island's African, British, and Spanish cultural melting pot. At last, they left the town behind and began the climb up a steep coastal road with hairpin curves that made LaJuanda regret having asked the driver to please hurry.

She needn't have bothered. When they reached the hotel, a long line of waiting guests—many of them Americans

LaJuanda recognized from her packed flight—snaked through the open-air lobby. Official check-in wasn't until four, and when it got under way—well after that—the line moved at a *torturous* pace.

"Guess we're on island time now," the man in front of LaJuanda commented.

"Guess so."

"Are you here for the pharmaceutical sales conference?"

"Yes," she said, without missing a beat. "You too?"

He nodded. "Guess I'll catch you at the mixer later. Can I buy you a drink? You look like a red wine kind of girl. Or maybe one of those frozen drinks. Do you like rum?"

"Can't stand the stuff." The lies were just falling off her tongue today, LaJuanda thought with amusement, pushing her hair back with her left hand, making sure he saw her wedding band.

She wasn't above letting a stranger attempt to hit on her when it might lead to information, but she wouldn't waste her time on an out-of-town pharmaceutical salesman who couldn't shed any light on her case.

At last, she was able to get into her room, where she quickly changed her clothes, unpacked her camera, and made it back down here to the harbor before sunset.

Well—if there had been sun, it would be setting. This is the rainy season, and the sky above the turquoise water is a charcoal-tinged blue that borders on purple at the horizon, where thunder is beginning to rumble.

It's quiet down here at this hour. The tourist trade in this waterfront district revolves around the cruise ships, and the ones that were docked here earlier are mere specks out on the water now. LaJuanda walks up and down the pier, snapping photos, retracing Molly's likely steps when she disembarked.

A couple of lingering vendors approach her, selling everything from painted seashells to marijuana. She speaks to them in Spanish, showing them photos of Molly; also shows the pictures to a couple of fishermen. Predictably, no one has ever seen the missing woman before.

She'll need to come back down here on Monday, when the ships come in and it's busy again. Until then, she decides to focus on the Big Iguana.

The bar—rather, what's left of it—is a three-minute walk along the sandy street that leads away from the dock. Chickens strut and cluck alongside LaJuanda as she makes her way past low, shuttered buildings painted in shades of yellow, aqua, and coral. Barefoot children dog her heels, clamoring for money. The moment she hands them some spare change, other waifs come out of the woodwork. She finds some coins for them, too.

There but for the grace of God, she thinks as she watches them scamper away.

Her mother's entire family is still back in Cuba; LaJuanda has first cousins whose children are possibly, like these urchins, barefoot and hungry. LaJuanda frequently tells her own son and daughter what their lives might have been like had their grandmother not bravely migrated to the United States when she was just their age.

"If she hadn't done that, we wouldn't even be here, Mom," is Raquel's usual response, "because you wouldn't have met Dad."

True enough. Rene's family, like LaJuanda's father's, had come to Florida long before Castro's regime took hold. LaJuanda herself feels as all-American as her husband and children are.

But somehow, being here, she feels the same stirring in her blood that she experienced on her Caribbean honeymoon all those years ago: that same innate sense of connection with this place and these people.

She thinks of Molly, wondering, once again, if her disappearance was intentional. Particularly now that she knows that Molly vanished here, and not in Miami.

Plenty of people come to the Caribbean to start a new life—often under a new identity. This balmy paradise would be appealing to anyone looking for a reprieve from harsh Great Lakes winters, and the laid-back, transient nature of the island would make it fairly easy for an outsider to fly under the radar.

Her mother had said that Molly was burned out on her job, had no social life, and had no romantic prospects. Really, she had nothing but her parents to tie her to Cleveland—and her father had just died. Maybe she had decided to make a fresh start here on the island . . .

And sent a doppelganger back to the States to throw everyone off her trail? But how would she even have arranged such a thing? There had been nothing in her phone records or computer files to indicate unusual correspondence in the months after she'd bought the cruise ticket.

And what about Nancy Temple? Would the daughter she'd described really have gone to such lengths to break her newly widowed mother's heart?

It just doesn't make sense.

Reaching the old-fashioned wooden crossroads signpost she'd seen earlier from the cab, LaJuanda reaches into her bag for the small flashlight she always carries. The arrow bearing the name "Big Iguana" points to a well-worn path through a grove of lush fronds.

It's dusk now, and the air is heavy with the imminent threat of rain. Insects buzz noisily and she can hear creatures rustling, slithering, and scampering in the undergrowth just off the path.

I'll take a quick look, LaJuanda decides, slapping at a mosquito that buzzes around the sweat-dampened hair at her forehead, *and then I'll head back to the hotel.*

A hot shower and room service are sounding awfully good right about now. First, of course, she'll have to call Nancy. She's gone back to Ohio to attend her granddaughter's high school graduation tomorrow, but will be waiting by the phone to hear from LaJuanda.

She gingerly picks her way along the uneven ground, glad she changed into long pants when she got off the plane, but wishing she'd thought to swap her sandals for closed-toed shoes. She's never been a delicate girly-girl, but living in Florida has made her all too aware of what's lurking in the dark along the overgrown path.

Rene wouldn't like this one bit. After two decades of marriage, he's accustomed to the danger that goes along with her career as a private investigator, but that doesn't mean he doesn't worry about her—especially when she ventures this far from home.

"You're too fearless for your own good," he likes to say.

"And you're too old-fashioned for yours."

LaJuanda can smell the Big Iguana before she sees the remains looming in the flashlight's murky beam; a faint hint of smoke and burnt rubber mingling with the scent of jungle blooms and sea air.

Back in the States, the site would have been taped off, fenced in, or tarped to discourage trespassers—human and otherwise. Here, there's nothing but a hand-scrawled "Keep Out" sign to deter looters and scavengers from wandering right up to the site.

People—and animals—have clearly done just that. Amid scattered piles of charred boards, tangled wires, and melted plastic, rotting kitchen garbage is strewn about. Bouquets of flowers lie at a makeshift memorial to the victims, and a flickering votive candle indicates that there has been at least one other recent visitor.

Thanks to photographs she studied on the Big Iguana's Web site, LaJuanda can picture the place as it used to be. The thatched roof and walls are long gone, but she spots the concrete slab that marked the main entrance, the remains of several stools and paddle fans poking from the rubble beyond it, and, around back, dented appliances and part of a metal stairway. The building, she recalls, was two stories tall, with an apartment on the second floor. Its tenant was the female bartender identified among the dead.

Hearing movement behind her, LaJuanda whirls around to see a man standing there.

For all the times she assured her husband that she's just fine without a big, strong man around to protect her, she desperately wishes Rene himself—and not this stranger—had popped up behind her.

His dark skin and dreadlocks tell her he's a local even before she hears his lilting patois. "What are you looking for, *mon*?"

"Not what—whom." She notes that his eyes, while wary, are not menacing. "My friend was here, I think, right before this place burned down."

"It did not burn down." He imitates the sound of something detonating and throws his hands to indicate an explosion.

"Yes. I know. Who did it?"

He shrugs.

She transfers her flashlight to her left hand and holds out her right. "I'm LaJuanda Estrada. From Miami. And you are . . . ?"

"Crispin."

"Do you have a last name?"

"Just Crispin."

"Got it." She nods to show him that she's not going to probe. "Can I show you my friend's picture, Crispin?"

He doesn't say yes or no, just stands there as if waiting for her to do it. She takes a step closer and holds up a photo, shining the flashlight's beam on it.

He starts to say something, then stops himself.

"What? What is it?"

He doesn't reply. LaJuanda holds her breath as he leans in to look closer.

Thunder rumbles in the distance, not as far away as before.

"No," he says after a long moment. "I do not know her."

"Are you sure about that?"

He nods.

She's tempted to shine the light directly on his face, not certain she believes him.

"But you were going to say something," she points out, "when you first looked."

"I thought I recognized someone I know."

"Who?"

"It is not her." He shrugs as if to say that it doesn't matter.

But it does. It matters a lot, to LaJuanda, who can't help but wonder if she just found her doppelganger.

A warm raindrop falls on her bare arm; another on her nose.

Seeing Crispin hold his hand out, palm upward, and glance at the sky, she asks hurriedly, "What's her name? Your friend?"

"Not a friend. No."

Trying to keep the urgency out of her voice, she rephrases the question: "What is the name of the person you thought you recognized?"

"Jane. But . . ." Crispin shrugs. "That is not her. She just looks like her, you know . . . at first glance."

LaJuanda's heart is racing.

"Who is Jane? Where is she? Can I talk to her?"

"You can talk to her, *mon*," Crispin says, "but she cannot answer. She was killed when the bomb went off."

When she got home from the airport earlier, Imogene Peters found her apartment sweltering. It's on the second floor of a duplex, right beneath the flat roof, and the old wiring in this place makes her too nervous to seriously consider getting a window air-conditioning unit.

For the most part, the cool Minnesota summer evenings and a nice cross breeze keep her comfortable. Not tonight, though. The temperature outdoors is still in the high eighties, and it's taking a long time to cool the place down since the windows have been closed and locked for a week. She wouldn't dare leave them open even a crack while she was gone; anyone could climb up onto the side porch roof and crawl right into her bedroom, which overlooks it.

The neighborhood isn't what it used to be, and Imogene lives alone now that her late husband, Ned, is gone and their only son has moved away. She's used to it, but you can't be too careful.

She wipes the sweat from her forehead as she walks across the living room in her summer bathrobe, a fancy white waffle-patterned one her son Paul gave her for Mother's Day. It's stamped with the Ritz Carlton emblem, which made her ask him if he'd stolen it.

"No, I didn't steal it! Mother! I bought it from the gift shop when I went to the Ritz spa on Easter."

"Well, I don't know how you can afford to give me expensive gifts and stay at the Ritz." Paul is a struggling actor living in Manhattan, supplementing his income with a telemarketing job.

"My friend Bartholomew paid."

"That's some friend," Imogene said—but of course, it turned out Bartholomew isn't just a friend. He's Paul's roommate, and a very nice young man. Handsome, too. The girls must go crazy for him—but, like Paul, he doesn't have a girlfriend right now. He says he's too busy with auditions—acting being something else he and Paul have in common.

Imogene settles her aching hips heavily into the easy chair in front of the television set.

"Ouch," she says aloud, and once again curses that horrid woman from the airplane. If she hadn't so rudely refused to give up her seat, Imogene wouldn't be hurting like this.

It's just shocking what people's manners have come to in this day and age.

Or is it just people in New York, as she suspected long before she flew there to spend this week with her son?

How could Paul possibly choose to live in that city?

Her husband must be rolling over in his grave. Years ago, back in '93 when the terrorists first bombed the World Trade Center, Ned had said, "They'll be back. Anyone with a brain in his head would get the hell out of New York. Who in his right mind would want to live there in the first place?"

Our own son. That's who. Where did we go wrong, Ned?

When Paul first broke the news to Imogene that he was moving to Manhattan last summer, right after he graduated from Minnesota State, it didn't even occur to her that he meant New York. She was thinking Manhattan, Kansas—which was bad enough, being five hundred miles away from Mankato.

"Why would I move to Kansas with a degree in musical theater?" Paul had rolled his big blue eyes just like Ned, God rest his soul, used to do.

"Why would *anyone* move to Manhattan after September 11? The terrorists are going to attack again. It's only a matter of time. Your father always said they'd keep on coming back until they destroyed the whole city."

Paul dismissed her with a wave of his wrist. So she went ahead and listed all the reasons he shouldn't live there, beginning with the fact that it was dangerous . . .

"Bad things can happen anywhere, Mother. Even Mankato. You could be struck by lightning sitting in your own house."

. . . and ending with the fact that New Yorkers are unfriendly.

"How do you know that, Mother?"

"Everyone knows that."

"Have you ever been there? No. So why don't you wait until you can see for yourself?"

Well, now Imogene *had* seen for herself.

She'd spent a whole week sleeping on the lumpy pullout couch in Paul's tiny apartment, which didn't help her spinal, neck, and hip issues—all the more reason that woman should have switched seats with her. She could stand a lesson in manners from Bartholomew, who hadn't even complained about giving up the couch, where he normally slept.

To thank him, Imogene invited him to come along with her and Paul to dinner last night, and let the two of them choose the restaurant—Ellen's Stardust Diner, where the waiters took turns singing show tunes.

"I hope you didn't mind squeezing into Paul's room for an entire week," she told Bartholomew. "There couldn't have been much room for a big guy like you in half of a double bed."

"Queen," he said, and Paul, who was in the midst of sipping his soda, started choking on it.

"He . . . means . . . the . . . bed," he sputtered, as Imogene patted him on the back. "It's a queen. The bed in my room."

"She knows that, *Paul*," Bartholomew said so pointedly that Imogene wondered if they were sharing some kind of inside joke.

They were quite a silly pair, her son and his friend.

But Imogene liked Bartholomew. She liked the restaurant, too. It reminded her of the diner where she and Ned used to go to when they were dating.

"I told you we wouldn't go anyplace fancy. We thought you'd feel right at home here," Paul told her, and she did—until the bill came. She couldn't believe how expensive it was. Still, she'd said she was treating and she did. She even left a fifteen percent tip for the waiter, who had a beautiful voice and was friendly, too.

Really, the only unpleasant person she met throughout her stay in New York had been that woman on the plane home, the one who wouldn't trade seats. It was people like her who gave New York City a bad name.

Oh well. At least one thing is certain: Imogene will never have to cross paths with her again.

Settled into her chair, she picks up the remote control and begins to channel surf, still thinking about New York City.

She's glad Paul is happy there. Really, she is. It's just lonely here without him, and Ned.

Maybe she really should get a dog, as Paul suggested. Or a cat. Cats are quieter. The neighbors who live on the first floor of this duplex have a terrier that's always barking at something. In fact, Imogene can hear it yapping its head off right now.

She knows better than to bother going downstairs to complain. The first floor was dark when she got home from the airport. The neighbors always go out on Saturday nights, and they don't come home until late.

Aggravated by the racket, Imogene shouts, "Shut up, you stupid mutt!"

The dog goes right on barking, and she raises the volume on the television, trying to lose herself in a *Golden Girls* rerun.

After a minute or so, the canine frenzy downstairs is curtailed so abruptly that Imogene wonders if the owners suddenly showed up and muzzled the dog. She picks up the remote and mutes the television, listening for footsteps below, but hears nothing.

Noticing that Betty White has come back onscreen, she raises the volume, puts the remote aside again, and turns her attention back to the television.

Too bad they don't make funny sitcoms like this anymore. Imagine if they did, and if Paul could get himself a starring role on one! She would be so—

Amid the laughter coming from the television, a new sound reaches Imogene's ears.

Footsteps . . . but they're not coming from downstairs. A sudden chill seems to permeate the overheated apartment as she realizes it sounded like it came from the next room.

As she turns to reach for the remote, she catches sight of a figure standing in her bedroom doorway.

A scream lodges in her throat.

She makes a futile attempt to rise and flee, but she's far too stiff and slow. The intruder is upon her before she can even lift her aching hips from the chair, and she collapses back into it when she sees the knife.

Fixated on the blade held steady in a black-gloved hand, she tries to swallow, her mouth flooded with the sour taste of fear.

Bad things can happen anywhere, Mother. Even Mankato . . .

"No," Imogene whispers, as the knife slashes toward her.

Oh, Paul. You were so right . . .

And I was so wrong, she realizes, catching sight of her attacker's face in the split second before her throat is sliced wide open.

She'd been so certain she'd never cross paths again with the woman from the plane . . .

But those icy blue eyes are the last thing Imogene sees on this earth.

Chapter Thirteen

Monday, July 2

The MacKennas spent the entire weekend driving west, following what is essentially a horizontal line Hudson traced across her own map of the United States.

New York, New Jersey, Pennsylvania, Ohio, Indiana . . .

Now it's Monday morning, and Allison and Mack are squeezed into a tiny hotel bathroom just outside Gary; Mack standing over her shaving as she brushes her teeth.

They were hoping to make it all the way into Illinois last night, but massive thunderstorms slowed them down.

All afternoon, as they drove into and out of violent weather, Allison instinctively kept an eye on the sky for funnel clouds and listened for warning sirens, something she would never think to do back home. But she was back in tornado country now, and this, she remembered, was the height of the season.

Once again crossing those wide expanses of farmland beneath blue-black skies, she could almost taste the trepidation she used to feel on summer afternoons when storms rolled in from the west.

Her father had taught her how to tell, even before the sirens went off, if atmospheric conditions were ripe for twisters. It wasn't just a matter of high winds, rain, and hail, he told her. Tornadoes often weren't prefaced by precipitation, and they didn't always strike in the afternoon or early evening.

"You have to look out there for dark, heavy, low-hanging clouds, Allie," he said, pointing to the western horizon, "when the air is warm and humid and still."

She nodded and pretended to be as fascinated as he was, just as she always did when he got into one of his long, involved explanations involving scientific facts—or historical or mathematical or political or literary facts, as the case might be.

She tried to pay attention even to the boring parts because her kindergarten teacher, Mrs. Barnes, once said it was good to know a little bit about everything.

"It's better to know everything about everything," her father said with a hint of disdain when she told him that. He added that he'd always wanted to be a teacher, but his parents couldn't afford to send him to college.

"At least I get to teach my kids about how the world works," he said. "You're going to be a smart girl when you grow up, Allie, if you just listen to me and remember everything I tell you."

For a long time, she earnestly tried to do just that.

After he left, she switched gears, doing her best to erase every memory of him, good, bad—all of them.

But yesterday, gazing out the windshield at the layered storm clouds hanging low where the grassland met the murky sky, she could hear her father's voice so clearly that it was as if he were right there beside her again.

"Before a tornado, the air becomes electrically charged, so if you walk outside and your hair gets all staticky and starts standing up on your arms—look out! Get into the storm cellar as fast as you can, do you hear me?"

"Yes, Daddy."

"I want you to be real careful and look for those signs whenever you're home alone and the weather starts to turn, okay?"

"Okay, Daddy."

She might have long since tried to block out his voice and his face, but the advice stayed with her, especially in later years, when she was so frequently home alone—or might as well have been.

Technically—*legally*—her young life was in her mother's hands, but most of the time, the harsh reality was just the opposite. Brenda was often passed out cold by afternoon, or too high to take heed of even the wailing sirens. Allison can remember literally dragging her unconscious mother down to the storm cellar, then weeping softly as she waited for the storm to pass.

But that was after her mother developed her full-blown drug habit; after her father left. Things were different in the old days. Back when he was home, Allison was never particularly anxious about impending bad weather.

"Come on, Allie," his voice echoed back over the years, "help me gather up flashlights and candles and make sure the crank radio is wound and ready."

How she loved to crank that radio; loved the game her father made of guessing how high they'd be able to count between thunder booms and lightning bolts.

If the power went out—which it often did—they made shadow puppets on the walls in the flashlight's beam, and her father dished up gigantic bowls of ice cream, telling her they had to eat it all before it made a melted mess.

Funny—Allison had anticipated that as she made her way

back to Nebraska, memories might come at her fast and furious, as harshly unwelcome as April sleet.

But that hasn't been the case so far. The memories have been coming, yes—triggered by everything from license plates on passing cars to the smell of summer rain mingling with warm asphalt and wildflowers.

But they haven't all been bad, not by any means.

A roadside Dairy Queen reminded Allison of how her mother once took her out for a hot fudge sundae on the last day of school to celebrate her good report card.

"You only got a good report card one time, Mommy?" Madison asked when she shared the memory with the girls.

"I always got a good report card. But my mom took me out for a sundae one time to celebrate."

"Just once?"

"Just once."

"Maybe you forgot the other times," Hudson said.

"Maybe I did," Allison agreed, though she knew it wasn't true. Once, her mother was so proud of her that she took her out to Dairy Queen. Once, in her whole childhood.

Memories . . .

At a rest stop, two little girls skipping rope reminded Allison not just of her own daughters but of her old friend Tammy Connolly, who taught her to jump to the rhyme about Lizzie Borden taking an axe and giving her mother forty whacks.

"Why did she do that? Why did she kill her parents?" Allison interrupted her counting to ask breathlessly as they jumped.

"I don't know. Because they were mean to her, I guess."

"So she *killed* them?"

"You're making me lose count, Allison! Start over! One . . . two . . . three . . ."

Memories . . .

A sign advertising Runza sandwiches—pockets of dough

filled with seasoned meat, a Nebraska specialty that now seems to have spread east beyond the state line—reminded her of her father. On the rare occasions they went out to dinner, he always ordered a Runza if it was on the menu.

"Here, try it, Allison. It's really good."

"No, thank you. I don't like it."

"How do you know that if you don't try it?"

"I just know."

"That's a stupid thing for a smart girl to say. You should try it."

"Maybe I will—someday."

She never did. But maybe she still will someday.

Maybe even tomorrow.

Memories . . .

A child's bike attached to the back of a camper reminded her of when Brett taught her how to ride a two-wheeler, running alongside her, promising he wouldn't let go of the sissy bar on the back of her banana seat. She glanced over her shoulder to see him far behind her and instantaneously went from infuriated to exhilarated as she realized that while he'd broken his promise, she hadn't fallen down.

"I'm doing it, Brett! I'm doing it all by myself!"

"Good job, Allison, but don't look back. Just keep looking forward!"

Yet all day yesterday, as she gazed through the windshield at the road ahead, she kept looking back—though not, for a change, with regret. She remembered the good times, even when the thunderstorms came rolling in.

After a few hours mostly spent crawling along in blinding rain, clinging to the taillights of the car in front of them, they were forced to call it a night, still a hundred miles short of their destination. That will make for a longer day today, driving all the way across both Illinois and Iowa and into Nebraska at last.

Last night, they ate again at Cracker Barrel—the girls'

new "most favoritest restaurant in the whole wide world!" thanks to the old-fashioned store in the front. The candy counter is just as Allison remembered it, stocked with retro treats—caramel bull's-eyes, horehound drops, Necco Wafers, Clove gum . . .

She bought candy buttons for her daughters and told them how she and her friend Tammy used to tear them into strips and trade with each other.

"What was your favorite color, Mommy?"

"Blue," she told Madison. "Tammy always said to me, 'You just like blue because your eyes are blue,' and I'd tell her that she should like green, in that case."

"Blue's my favorite, too, Mommy. What was Tammy's favorite color?"

"Pink," she answered readily, surprised that she remembered.

"I like yellow best, because it's the happiest color," Hudson decided. "Are you going to see Tammy when we get to Nebraska?"

Allison's smile faded. "No. We don't have time."

"We can make time," Mack said, "if you really want to."

"I don't really want to."

Back at the hotel after dinner last night, even Mack fell right to sleep when they collapsed into bed, but not for long. It turned out to be another rough night with J.J. Having once again dozed away the day in the car, he wanted to play all night.

Allison and Mack took turns holding him, trying to shush him so that the girls could sleep. Finally, their son drifted off about an hour and a half before their six-thirty A.M. wakeup call came.

"We can always stop sooner tonight." Mack's razor scrapes a path through foamy white shaving cream on his cheek.

"I told Brett we'd be getting there by tomorrow at around noon," Allison says around her toothbrush.

"It's not like we have to punch a clock, though."

"No . . . but I've always wanted to stay at the Cornhusker. And I booked a suite when I made the reservation, remember? I figured we might need an extra-good night's sleep before we start the last leg of the trip."

"You figured right. Okay, so we'll go to Lincoln."

"Okay." Allison spits into the sink, then steps back so that Mack can rinse his face.

"I'll go get the kids up and moving while you take a shower," he tells her. "We should get on the road within the next twenty minutes or so if we're going to go all the way to Lincoln. Are you sure you want to do that?"

"Positive."

When she was growing up, the Cornhusker was the fanciest hotel in Nebraska—still is, as far as she knows. Some of the girls she knew from school once spent a long weekend there with their mothers, but of course Allison wasn't invited.

She and Tammy spent that weekend listening to the latest New Kids on the Block album, indulging their mutual infatuation with the band members: Allison was going to marry Donnie and Tammy was going to marry Jordan. They'd be musicians' wives together, they said, traveling around the country on the tour bus. For her birthday that year, Tammy even made her a framed collage of New Kids photos torn from her precious fan magazine collection.

The collage hung on her wall long after her New Kids obsession faded; long after Tammy left town. But Allison herself tossed it into the Dumpster when she and Brett cleaned out everything after their mother died.

At the time, feeling utterly alone in the world—and resenting it—she never imagined that she'd ever want to see Tammy again, even if she knew where she was.

Now, she knows . . . and now, she's not so sure.

As she gets into the shower, she thinks about Tammy yet again, wondering whether Tamara Connolly Pratt is indeed the Tammy in question.

There's only one way to find out.

When she sat holding J.J. on her lap in the middle of the night, remembering all the good times that had come back to her over the weekend, she imagined a happy reunion like the ones Randi had with her high school friends.

You never know, Allison. It might be a healing experience.

Maybe Randi was right after all. Maybe it would be a healing experience to reconnect. Not with all the mean girls from her hometown, but with Tammy.

She's afraid to mention it again to Mack, though, until she makes up her mind.

She lathers her hair with cheap hotel shampoo, going through various scenarios.

What if Mack tries to talk her into it?

Or out of it?

He's as anxious as the kids are to reach their final destination, if only to get out of the car at last. But the closer Allison gets to seeing her brother again, the more inclined she feels to stall.

What if that particular reunion *isn't* healing? For all these years, she could at least hang on to the remote possibility that she might one day have a relationship with the one person in this world who shares her blood—besides her father, anyway.

There's no way she'd even bother to plug his fake name into a search engine again.

No, there's just her brother. And until she comes face-to-face with Brett, she can still cling to that shred of hope. Once she crosses the threshold into his house, that precious hope will either wither and die, or bloom into a happy ending, at last, to her family's tragic story.

She's had plenty of time to prepare for this—more than half a lifetime, really—yet she's still feeling too vulnerable to deal with it just yet.

I need a little more time.

Time to steel her bruised heart for yet another loss in this final chapter, or open it to letting someone new breach the walls and enter her fiercely guarded private world.

Either way, she'll have to tap into a well of strength she's no longer sure she possesses, regardless of what Dr. Rogel told her that day in his office.

She wonders what he would say about her impulse to get in touch with Tammy.

That she might just be delaying one possibly unhappy ending only to replace it with another?

She shakes her head as she towels off and throws on the clothes she took off last night and hung on the hook on the back of the bathroom door. Might as well be rumpled for one more long day in the car.

"Okay—who's ready to hit the road?" she asks, coming out of the bathroom to find the girls jumping from one bed to the other as J.J. crawls around on the floor between them. Mack is sitting in the room's lone chair, tapping away on his BlackBerry keyboard.

"Mack! What are you doing?" Allison snatches J.J. off the carpet, not the cleanest in the world. It reeks of cigarettes, despite the "No Smoking" sign on the door.

"Everyone smokes around here," Hudson observed just last night, in the restaurant parking lot. "Even kids. Some-one should tell them it's bad for them."

"That someone shouldn't be you," Allison said quickly, seeing her daughter take a step in the direction of a group of skateboard-toting teenage boys puffing away.

"You should tell them, then, Mommy. Or Daddy should."

Allison quickly changed the subject, wondering what her daughter would say if she knew that both Mommy and

Daddy used to smoke. Back then, when they were in their early twenties and thirties, the habit was much more prevalent, even in New York. Back then, when they thought they were immortal . . .

Yeah. That notion changed pretty abruptly, didn't it?

Struggling to keep her hold on a wriggly J.J., she looks at Mack, still focused on his BlackBerry. "I thought you were going to get the kids ready."

Still thumb-typing intently, he says, "Girls. Go brush your teeth. Mommy's out of the bathroom."

"We're jumping across the Mississippi River!"

"No, the Missouri River," Hudson corrects her sister. "That's what we're going to cross when we get to Nebraska tonight, remember?"

"Yes! The Missouri River! One more jump!"

"One more," Mack tells them, not looking up from his BlackBerry, "and then brush your teeth."

"I'm named after a river!" Hudson announces, getting ready to jump. "Right, Daddy?"

"There's a Hudson River. Right. But you were named after the street."

"Is there a Missouri Street in Nebraska, Daddy?"

"Hmm?"

"Do most rivers have streets that are named after them, too?"

"I don't know," Mack murmurs.

"How many rivers are there in America, Daddy?"

"That's a good question."

"I know. I always ask good questions. Are you going to answer it?" Hudson bounces on the bed.

"Yes, just as soon as I finish this, I'll look it up."

"Have you seen the diaper bag?" Allison asks him, balancing J.J. on her hip as she rummages through the bags cluttering the floor by the door.

No answer. The girls are squealing, still jumping.

"Girls, go brush your teeth!"

"Two more jumps!"

"Hudson, now! Both of you!" she says so harshly that they scramble for the bathroom. "Mack!"

"I already brushed."

"The diaper bag. Where is it?"

"Probably still in the car. Didn't you bring it when we went to dinner last night?"

"Probably. Here, hold J.J. and keep him off the floor while I go out and look."

"I'll go look," he offers, and before she can thank him, he adds, already halfway to the door, "I have to go outside to call the office anyway—the kids are way too loud in here."

There are so many things wrong with that statement that she doesn't know where to begin.

"Mack . . . you're on vacation! Why would you do that?"

"There's some stuff going on with one of the clients . . ."

Of course there is.

Allison clenches her jaw as Mack reaches for the door-knob, still talking.

"Kathy comes in at eight"—she's his assistant—"and I need her to take care of a couple of things for me because as soon as—"

"It's barely seven now," Allison cuts in, no longer able to hold her tongue, "and you said you wanted to get on the road."

"It's eight in New York, and it'll only take two minutes."

It doesn't, of course.

It takes twenty-five.

By the time he returns to the room with the diaper bag, J.J. stinks to high heaven, the girls are bickering, and Allison is at her wit's end.

"Daddy! How many rivers are there? You never answered my good question!"

"Sorry about that," Mack says mildly, handing the bag to Allison.

"About not answering her question, or about disappearing for half an hour?"

"Both."

Determined not to argue about it, Allison wrestles J.J. onto the bed and unsnaps his pajamas. "It's okay. I'll just change him really fast and we'll go."

"Take your time. I have to wait for Kathy to call the agency and they don't open until nine."

"*What?*"

"She has to call them and call me back. If I call, I'll get sucked in and you don't want that to happen, do you?"

"What I want to happen," she says evenly, "is for us to get on the road. I'll drive the first leg so you can answer your phone and talk to Kathy when she calls back."

"No, the cell signal is too sketchy when we're out driving in the middle of nowhere."

"Mack—"

"You're the one who said it yourself!"

"Well, if you miss the call, you can get back to her when we stop for gas or breakfast. The kids are going to need to eat in—"

Mack's BlackBerry rings, and she watches him check the screen.

"Is it Kathy?"

"No. The client. I'll be right back."

He steps out of the room again.

Shaking her head, Allison methodically changes J.J.'s diaper, telling herself not to be angry with Mack. He's just trying to do his job, and it's a demanding one. If she were in his shoes, supporting the family in a demanding job in this struggling economy, she'd be doing the same thing.

It's just been such a long time since she was actually in his shoes; such a long time since she's done much of anything other than take care of her family and negotiate a suburban lifestyle that suits her just fine—most of the time.

Only now does she realize that she's starting to experience hints of the same sense of unfulfilled restlessness she was feeling last fall, before disaster struck. In its wake, she was so thankful to have emerged with her family intact that the little things, the day-to-day mundane aspects of motherhood and marriage, were more than enough.

Now, she looks at her life—at the woman she's become—and she wonders if she's simply chosen the path of least resistance.

Not marrying Mack, because she loves him with all her heart. The children, too, of course.

But she had let go of her career so easily—the fashion industry career she'd worked so hard to achieve. Maybe too easily, leaving it behind just as she had old friends and family and everything else that complicated matters along the way. Better to avoid conflict and tough decisions than to face them head-on, right?

The thought is so troubling that she pushes it away.

Tries, anyway.

What about Tammy? a nagging voice persists as she sets J.J. back on his feet and steps into the bathroom to wash her hands.

Why can't you even put yourself out there enough to send an e-mail to say hello after all these years?

What are you so afraid of?

"Mommy?"

She looks up to see Hudson standing in the doorway.

"Are we leaving soon? I want to cross the Missouri River!"

"So do I," Allison tells her, surprised to find that she means it. "We just have to wait for Daddy to finish his phone call, and I have to send a quick e-mail."

Before Crispin vanished into the stormy shadows Saturday night as the sky opened in a violent downpour, LaJuanda had convinced him to give her the contact information for a more knowledgeable source named Jonas.

"First or last name?" she asked Crispin, who shrugged. Either he didn't know, or he'd decided it was none of her business.

Unfortunately, the number she dialed wasn't a home or cell phone.

"Office hours are Monday through Saturday from nine A.M. until six P.M.," announced a locally accented voice, without bothering to indicate what kind of office it even was. "Please leave a message and someone will get back to you."

Even if this Jonas person worked at the office in question, what could LaJuanda possibly have said into a voice mailbox?

You don't know me, and I can't tell you why I'm calling, but please call me back . . .

Or: *I'm calling for information about a dead female bartender who happens to bear a resemblance to a missing woman from Ohio . . .*

No. No way. She wasn't even sure it was a legitimate number. The voice on the outgoing message was female, and she'd gotten the impression that Jonas is a man.

When she went online and searched further for him, she found that Jonas is a popular last name on the island. There was no way to tell which one she wanted.

LaJuanda hung up without leaving a message, knowing she would have to wait to talk to Jonas in person.

Just as she'll wait to approach the authorities, either here on the island or back in the States.

What would she tell them? That a mysterious man had stepped out of the shadows and momentarily mistaken a photograph of Molly Temple for Jane Deere?

Who supposedly *died*, LaJuanda reminds herself as she sips a cup of strong black coffee on the small balcony of her hotel room. The sun has been up for an hour, but it's still too early to make phone calls.

Just as well. She needs to sharpen her senses before she gets down to business today, and that's going to take more than one cup of coffee. She barely slept last night, nagged by a growing hunch that Jane Deere might have had something to do with Molly's disappearance.

LaJuanda had plugged the name "Jane Deere" into various search engines, too, hoping to find a photograph or some information about her background.

But there was nothing at all, other than the woman's name listed among the victims in published reports about the explosion at Jimmy's Big Iguana.

That in itself is interesting.

In this day and age, just about everyone LaJuanda investigates has left some kind of electronic trail—unless they were trying to avoid it. You have to work pretty hard to do that, though, even on a tropical island. Some people even go the opposite route to throw off the authorities, going to great lengths to create a fake online presence.

Was Jane Deere deliberately flying under the radar? Is that why there's no information about her on the Web, not even a photograph?

LaJuanda spent hours online studying pictures that had been snapped at Jimmy's Big Iguana, both on the bar's bare-bones Web site—which has yet to be updated to reflect the tragedy—and posted on Saint Antony travel forums by tourists.

It was slow going, though. Even the Internet here is on island time. The pictures loaded with painstaking slowness, and in the few shots she found that showed the bar in the background, the bartenders' faces weren't clearly visible.

Frustrated, LaJuanda can only take a stranger's word for her resemblance to Molly Temple. No, not even that; he wasn't willing to say much. All she has, really, is Crispin's initial reaction to the photo of Molly. Crispin, who had refused to give her his own phone number or address.

When she did an Internet search for the name "Crispin" along with "Saint Antony," she had far better luck than she had with "Jane Deere" or "Jonas."

Crispin Bishop is a local dealer with a long history of drug arrests, and the online photos clearly depict the man LaJuanda met prowling the ruins of the bar.

A shady character, to be sure, but he hadn't harmed her on Saturday night. She's willing to take her chances with him. Hoping to run into him again, she revisited the spot yesterday morning, and again at around sunset. He wasn't there.

She wandered around the pier and the streets, hoping to find someone she could ask about Crispin, and about Jane, again to no avail. Most of Saint Antony's residents are devoutly Catholic, and everything grinds to a halt on Sundays. The harbor area becomes a ghost town, with all the tourist action confined to the beach resorts that rim the coast. Aside from a couple of skulking young men who were only interested in selling her drugs—and clammed up as soon as she mentioned the name of their fellow dealer Crispin—LaJuanda couldn't find a soul, not even the child beggars.

Everything would have to wait until Monday, she realized then—and Monday is finally here. Keeping an eye on her watch, she pours herself a second cup of coffee and calls home. The kids are still sleeping, but Rene is on his way out the door to the courthouse.

She asks him about his case; he asks her about hers. As always, they give each other brief, barebones feedback, to protect each other as well as themselves. Rene, a criminal attorney defending a pedophile accused of murder, knows how she feels about his client. And the less Rene knows about what she's doing down here, the better.

"What are the kids doing?"

"They're both still asleep. Ricky doesn't go to work until

noon"—their son is a summer lifeguard at a day camp—
"and Raquel is babysitting tonight. They miss you. So do I."

She smiles. "I figured you were too busy to miss me."

"I'm not. Are you?"

"No, unfortunately. I'm sitting here twiddling my thumbs
until nine." She wishes Rene luck in the courtroom before
hanging up, then goes back to sipping coffee and watching
the clock for another hour.

She forces herself to wait until ten after nine. Then she
steps through the glass sliders into the room, not willing
to risk being overheard, and at long last dials the number
Crispin gave her.

A woman answers on the first ring. "Dockside Tours."

She hesitates only slightly, hoping this is the right number.
"I'm looking for Jonas."

"One moment." There's a click, and after a few moments,
a man comes on the line. "Yes?"

"Mr. Jonas, my name is LaJuanda Estrada and I'm here
from Miami, looking for a friend."

"Yes."

"Crispin said you might be able to help me."

"Yes," he says once again, and she can tell by his tone that
Crispin told him to expect her call.

"Can we meet and discuss this?"

"Later. I am doing shore excursions today. I will be busy
until after the ships go out."

She arranges to meet him at six o'clock at the Clucking
Parrot, a local restaurant near the pier.

Between now and then, she decides, she'll head into town
and see if she can talk to the locals who work around the
pier when the cruise ships are in port. With luck, someone
will remember seeing Molly Temple or be able to tell her
something more about the enigmatic—perhaps deliberately
so—Jane Deere.

The hot Dakota wind stirs the tall prairie grasses, tickling Carrie's bare legs as she walks the vast, flat acreage, looking for the well.

It's around here someplace, she's sure . . . but *around here* isn't good enough.

She wants to see the exact site. Now. *Needs* to see it. Needs to make sure everything is as it should be, needs to prepare for tonight—and she doesn't have much time.

She tried once before to find it, right before she moved to New York. But the section of land—her father's land, officially listed as abandoned property after failing to sell years ago at a foreclosure auction—was blanketed in a foot of December snow that day and more was falling: an inch an hour, probably more. Bitter gusts enveloped Carrie in swirling white so that she couldn't see more than a few feet ahead of her.

Shades of things to come: smoke and dust from fallen towers . . .

Funny how the pattern seems destined to repeat itself in her life.

Nine years ago this week, the surrounding prairie was changed forever in an eerie echo of what had happened in New York on September 11. Here, the destruction also— quite literally—dropped out of the clear blue sky on a warm summer Tuesday, when a record sixty-seven twisters touched down in this part of the state.

A little ways down Highway 14, an entire town, Manchester, was wiped off the map, never to be rebuilt.

Just like this farm . . . and good riddance to it.

No lives were lost here on the Great Plains on Tornado Tuesday, as the press called it, but all things relative, the physical toll seems as apocalyptic as what had happened in Manhattan.

When Carrie later read about it from her far-flung tropical island, her initial reaction—aside from a general sense of detachment—was to welcome the news as she had the fallen towers: yet another cosmic coincidence. It was almost as though some higher power were determined to help her erase every trace of her existence in both South Dakota and New York.

Then, with growing uneasiness, she remembered the level of destruction a powerful tornado could wreak out here on the Great Plains: flattening homes, uprooting trees, even disturbing the earth. An F4 or F5 storm like the one that had passed over this acreage was capable of scouring the ground a few feet deep, possibly unearthing . . .

But surely she'd have heard about it if *that* had happened.

How? It's not as though anyone around here would have any idea whatever happened to her after she left. For all they know, she's as dead as her parents are.

So, no, they wouldn't come looking for her if something had been unearthed on the farm. The media would have jumped on it, though—wouldn't they?

Just to be sure, she did a search on her laptop last night, plugging in every possible word and phrase she could think of. Plenty of hits concerning dinosaur bones that had been found in South Dakota—but nothing about human remains.

That was good news enough to allow Carrie to come out here today as planned. If she honestly believed anything had been found here, she'd never have dared to set foot on the property—or even in this part of the state—again now. She'd have convinced herself that it was best to leave well enough alone.

You never seem to do that though, do you? an inner voice scolds. *You're always compelled to go looking for trouble, aren't you?*

Not really. Not today. Today, she's just making sure that trouble stays buried in the past where it belongs. As for yesterday . . .

She thinks of Imogene Peters. For someone who had been

such a pushy big mouth on the plane just hours earlier, she had basically gone down without a fight.

Just like Mrs. Ogden had all those summers ago back in her fourth floor apartment on Hudson Street—the one Carrie and Mack would soon be able to rent, because its elderly tenant had fallen and hit her head . . .

With a little help, Carrie remembers with a smile.

But Mrs. Ogden had never known what hit her. Getting rid of her had been a basic necessity. Carrie had simply slipped into her apartment through a fire escape window on the first warm May night, given the old bat a hard shove, and watched her head hit the bathroom tile. It didn't crack open, as she'd hoped—just hit hard, and when Carrie felt for a pulse a minute or two later, there was none.

It was much more gratifying to see all that blood gushing over Imogene Peters's white bathrobe with its fancy hotel emblem. Even so, Carrie slipped out of her apartment late Saturday night still feeling vaguely dissatisfied.

Too many years have passed since she's allowed herself to vent her pent-up frustration. She doesn't regret for one second having taken out some of it on Imogene Peters. But it hadn't been nearly enough.

She has to stay strong. She's come too far to lose control now and throw it all away.

Oh, really? Then what about Nebraska? And Allison? If you're not going there to stir things up, then what are you planning to do? Give her a hug and wish her well?

The disapproving voice in her head sounds very much like Daddy's, and Carrie instinctively walks more quickly through the prairie grass, wanting to outrun it.

The sun is high overhead, its scorching heat penetrating her scalp.

She wishes it were raining, as it had been yesterday, throughout the entire midsection of the country.

When she was growing up here, she'd watch the western

horizon for funnel clouds, the way Daddy had taught her. She never spotted one, but Arthur, the kindly farmhand, did on occasion. Then he'd hustle Carrie and her mother to the storm cellar.

The summer after Arthur died, the summer she was sixteen, she stopped watching the sky. She didn't care if a tornado came along. In fact, she wished it would happen— wished a big black funnel cloud would sweep across the prairie and kill her, along with the child she was carrying.

It belonged to the man her father hired to keep an eye on things after Arthur was gone. He had greasy graying hair and a pock-marked face and he smelled like sweat.

He didn't stick around for very long—just a few weeks. But that was long enough for him to rape Carrie.

Telling her mother was out of the question. They didn't really talk much. Carrie had always been a daddy's girl— even though Daddy was hardly ever around anymore.

If he had been, Carrie thought, the hired man would never have raped her.

Summer turned to fall, and Carrie waited for her father to come home. Her waistline grew thicker and she knew why, but it was too horrific to admit, even to herself. When her father came home, she'd tell him, and he'd help her get rid of it.

October turned to November and he didn't come home; he didn't even call. He was on the road, same as always, her mother said.

"Are you getting a divorce?" Carrie asked her, and her mother denied it.

It was just the two of them, day after day, all alone. The sky was always bleak and the wind blew rain and snow. Carrie was convinced that her father was staying away because he didn't want to see her mother, and Carrie hated her for it.

If he didn't come soon, it was going to be too late to get rid of the pregnancy. She was growing bigger every day, so big that one day, her mother noticed.

"You're pregnant!" she shrieked. "You're pregnant and it's *his*. Oh my God, I should have known. I should have known . . ."

Carrie didn't understand, at first, what she was saying; what she was thinking. Then it hit her: her mother thought Daddy—her own father—had gotten her pregnant.

White-hot anger swept over her. How could anyone believe that her father was capable of such an ugly thing? How could her mother accuse him—accuse *her*—

Even now, rage slips in when she remembers what happened that day. She wipes sweat from her forehead and tells herself that her mother had deserved what had happened to her.

Carrie walks on, wishing she'd thought to wear a hat and sunglasses. If only there was a shady spot somewhere in the six hundred and forty acres she has to comb until she finds the well. Squinting into the harsh glare, she searches the empty landscape for some kind of landmark; something that might help her identify the spot.

There is none. The vortex that roared through the property on that Tuesday morning almost a decade ago destroyed everything in its path, just the way she'd imagined, just the way she'd longed for, when she was sixteen. It's all gone now: the house, the shed, the century-old stand of cottonwood trees . . .

Even the long road that led from the highway to the house, which had never been more than parallel dirt ruts, has vanished, overgrown and filled in. This landscape she once knew so well, having spent the first eighteen years of her life here, has been reduced to nothing but swaying grasses in shades of green and gold, dotted with purple and yellow wildflowers, stretching clear out to the blue horizon in every direction.

It was so different on that frigid afternoon when she last visited here, in the final days of the last millennium, and her old life.

There were landmarks then—the road, the trees. Even the house was still standing, albeit long abandoned, much too far off the beaten path for anyone to care or notice.

She had come on impulse that December day, needing one last look before she left the heartland forever—or so she had promised herself. She hadn't been back since she was just sixteen, having fled to Minnesota and then Chicago, losing herself in the bustle of big cities where anonymity wrapped around her like a warm blanket.

She had tried for almost fourteen years to forget what had happened. When she finally realized that she never would, she looked for Allison and managed to trace her as far as New York City.

And so it began: the homework. Planning and preparation. She liked that. She still does.

When she was finally ready to move east, she rented a car and drove hundreds of miles west across the frozen prairie.

Alone in a blizzard on this desolate rural landscape, well aware that her life was hanging in the balance, she had searched for hours.

What would you have done that day if you'd found what you were looking for? Fallen to your knees and kissed the snowy ground? Left something behind to mark the spot?

Ultimately, she gave up, though not because she was afraid, or discouraged. Not, either, because she was cold and hungry. It was because a fresh start lay before her, full of promise. On the cusp of a new millennium, the whole world seemed to be tying up loose ends, looking ahead not just with trepidation but with anticipation, ready to begin anew.

What had happened years earlier on this barren spot might eventually come to matter even less, Carrie hoped, when she found her way to New York . . .

To Allison.

Even then, she didn't know what she would do when she found her. *If* she found her. She only knew that she had to try. On that stormy day, the prospect of her upcoming mission snuffed out her desire to see this one through.

Now New York lies behind her—for the second time in thirteen years. Now she knows exactly where to find Allison—when she's ready.

This time, when we come face-to-face, she's going to know exactly who I am. At the very least, she's going to apologize for taking what should have been mine. At the very, very least.

Chances are, though, that it will go much further. Chances are that Carrie will have the pleasure of hearing Allison begging for her life.

But I won't listen to her. Why should I? She wouldn't listen to me when I tried to tell her—

Whoa—is that it?

Carrie halts and stares. Right there, just a few feet away from her left shoe, is a slightly sunken, sparse patch of grass. She steps closer, pushes the grass aside, and sees a sliver of the weathered wooden plank lid of the old well.

She smiles.

So. It's still covered, after all these years; after countless storms, including the tornado that had torn apart the buildings and trees surrounding it.

She backtracks patiently to the rental car to get the shovel she bought—using cash, of course—at a big chain hardware store somewhere between Mankato and the South Dakota state line. Her other purchases—rope, duct tape, and a small wheelbarrow—are in the trunk. For now. The shovel wouldn't fit, so she laid it across the backseat.

Back at the well site, the sun beats down on her as she digs away chunks of grass and sod. Finally, the entire square of wood is exposed. She pokes at the edge, wedging the tip of the shovel farther and farther beneath the rim until it lifts from the crumbly earth. Pushing the wooden handle like a lever, she pries the lid off at last, flipping it over onto the grass beside the gaping hole.

The first time she'd lifted the cover on her own, without Daddy, she'd braced herself for the black widow spiders who lived beneath it to come crawling out. She'd quickly dumped her cargo, hearing it land with a thud in the soil eight feet below, remembering what her father had told her about filling it in. There was a law now about old wells in South Dakota—they had to be properly sealed.

The next—and last—time she'd lifted the lid was just a few days after the first; on that occasion, she encountered not the dreaded spiders, but the horrible stench of rotting flesh. When she closed the lid again that day, she never expected to come back here and open it again.

But this has to be done. Only then will it be over at last. Only then will she be free.

This time, as she leans over the hole, Carrie smells nothing but damp dirt, sees nothing but shadows. But that doesn't mean they aren't there—nocturnal creatures, down in that dank hole, lurking, waiting . . .

Waiting.

"Don't worry . . ." Her whisper is all but lost on the hot prairie breeze rustling the tall grass around her. "I'll be back tonight—and she'll be with me."

Chapter Fourteen

"**M**ommy, are we in Nebraska yet?" Madison asks—yet again—from the backseat of the SUV.

She's been repeating that question for hours, ever since they stopped for lunch just over the Iowa border. Allison gives her the same answer every time.

"Almost, sweetie."

This time, though, she actually means it. According to the dashboard GPS, Iowa is about to fall behind them, and Nebraska lies just a few miles ahead.

"How many more hours, Mommy?"

"Not hours now. Just minutes. About ten. Maybe fifteen with this traffic."

"But when we cross into Nebraska, we'll still have almost four hundred miles to go," Hudson pipes up. "Right, Mommy?"

"Noooo!" Madison wails.

Allison sighs. She'll just have to remind her middle child, once again, that they're having fun. Maybe if she says it often enough, she'll believe it, too.

It hasn't really been a horrible drive today, though. Not like yesterday, with all that rain. Today was just long, and the scenery has been a monotonous stretch of farmland, with very few landmarks and not even a cloud in the blue sky to conjure those old memories that had livened up yesterday's trip.

"Noooo! Mommy!"

Allison realizes, when she turns to reprimand Maddy for whining, that J.J. has a fistful of her long hair.

"He's hurting me!"

"It's your own fault." Hudson doesn't even look up from her Atlas. "You should keep your head out of reach, like I do."

"I *can't* keep it out of reach. My neck is too short and his arms are too long!"

Under other circumstances, that remark might have struck Mack, at least, as amusing. But he's been grumpy behind the wheel the last few hours, and barks, "Guys, please be quiet! This is a car, not a carnival!"

"But he's hurting me! J.J.! Ouch! No!"

"Noooooo!" J.J. shouts gleefully, and holds tighter.

Mack clenches the wheel. "Shh! I'm trying to drive, here."

"J.J., stop that!" Allison hisses, trying to reach his little fists.

Mack darts a glance into the rearview mirror, then the driver's-side mirror, and the rearview again. "Allie, can I get over? I need to get over."

She turns her head and sees a tractor-trailer alongside them. "No!"

"No!" J.J. echoes again. "No, no, no, nooooo!"

Mack swerves back into the right lane. "Dammit!"

"Mack! Watch the language! All we need is a cursing baby."

"All we need is to miss the turn," he shoots back, "and end up in South Dakota. I need to merge into that lane. Why the heck is there so much traffic?"

"It's rush hour!"

"It's Council Bluffs!"

"Rush hour happens everywhere," Hudson comments, adjusting her map. "Um, you're supposed to be way over there, Daddy!"

"I know that!"

"He knows that!"

"That's where the Missouri River is. We can't cross it if we don't go that way. Do you think someday we can cross all the rivers in America?"

Neither Mack nor Allison answers her.

"There are a quarter of a million rivers," she goes on, courtesy of the fact Mack finally looked up for her this morning. "How long would it take to cross them all?"

Stifling a sigh, Allison consults the GPS, checking to see where they'll end up if Mack misses the exit. Not in South Dakota. Not yet, anyway—it's almost a hundred miles from here.

"Mommy! Help!" Madison whimpers, and J.J. tightens his grip on her hair, babbling happily.

"Hold still, Maddy, you're making it worse by trying to pull away." Keeping an eye on the traffic, Allison reaches back again to disentangle her son's sticky fingers from her daughter's hair.

This time, she frees the strands. "Okay, sweetie, go ahead, move over."

"What? Now?" Mack starts to pull into the left lane.

A horn blasts and he swerves again with a curse, narrowly missing a passing car.

"What are you doing?" Allison asks, shaken.

"You told me to move!"

"I told *Maddy* to move."

"I thought you were talking to me."

"I said sweetie!"

"You call me sweetie sometimes!"

"Since when?"

Not since this morning, that's for sure. She's been too pre-occupied, most of the day, to do much talking at all.

Mack asked her, after they stopped for breakfast, why she'd been so quiet. "Are you still mad because I had to call the office?"

"What? No. I'm just . . . tired."

He bought that. Who wasn't tired at this point?

But the truth was, she was wondering whether Tamara Connolly Pratt had yet seen the e-mail she spontaneously sent this morning before they left the hotel.

She kept it straightforward.

> *I'm looking for an old friend, Tammy Connolly, who lived in Centerfield, Nebraska, in the 1980s. If you're her, I'll be staying at the Cornhusker in Lincoln tonight, and I know it's short notice, but I'd love to catch up.*

She provided her cell phone number and signed it simply *Allison Taylor MacKenna*. She was about to reread it, thinking she might want to edit it—or delete it—when Mack came back into the room, putting his BlackBerry back into his pocket.

"I'm glad that's over. Ready to go?"

"Yes." The e-mail zinged into cyberspace.

Her first thought after she impulsively hit send was that she might regret it. But so far, she hasn't. In fact, she's been hoping for a response. So far, there's been nothing. Her iPhone is set to vibrate whenever an e-mail comes in, but maybe she missed something. The signal has been fading in and out as they made their way across Iowa, and she hasn't looked in a while. Now that they're in a city, she should—

"Daddy, you have to move over *now*! This is your last

chance!" Hudson shouts from the backseat, checking the signage and her map.

With a curse, Mack looks into the rearview mirror and turns his head briefly to check behind them. He jerks the wheel, pulling into the left lane and cutting off a pickup truck whose driver honks loudly.

"Great job, Daddy!" Hudson shouts.

"Yeah, great job, Daddy." Shaking her head, Allison presses her hand against her pounding heart. "I think it's my turn to drive again."

"You did enough driving today. Just relax."

"I'll try." She pulls her iPhone out of her pocket and presses the button to light up the screen. Sure enough, there's a new e-mail waiting for her. It must have come in while they were between cell tower coverage in rural Iowa.

"Look! Look at the sign!" Hudson bounces excitedly.

Allison glances up to see a smattering of tall buildings just ahead. Omaha.

"I didn't know Nebraska was the home of Arbor Day!" Hudson exclaims, reading the big green welcome sign that begins: "NEBRASKA . . . THE GOOD LIFE." "I didn't even know there were any trees here. Mommy said there weren't any."

"I said there weren't *many*," Allison corrects her.

"I see some right there. And over there, too. How many trees do you think there are? Can you look it up, Mommy?"

"Sure . . . in a minute." Allison opens her mailbox.

Hi, Allison! Yep, it's me, Tammy Connolly. I can't believe you found me after all these years! I would love to catch up when you get to Lincoln, just the two of us. My cell phone number is 605–555–3424. Text me when you get to town and I'll give you directions to my house. I work until 9 so I hope that's not too late.

Allison bites her lip nervously, then gives a decisive nod.

It's not too late at all, she types, and means it with all her heart.

At ten minutes to six, LaJuanda makes her way along a rutted, overgrown lane adjacent to the pier. A patch of white sand and turquoise sea lies at the far end, the proverbial light at the end of the tunnel, marking the spot where she'll meet Jonas at the Clucking Parrot.

An afternoon spent trying to find someone who might have either known Jane Deere or seen Molly Temple had yielded nothing at all. The locals were far too busy tending to the crowds of cruise passengers to bother with her. LaJuanda finally gave up and spent some time back in her room, futilely checking the Internet for a glimmer or glance of the elusive female bartender.

Now, as the lush greenery falls away, she steps into a beachfront clearing marked by a crudely painted plywood sign that reads "Clucking Parrot."

The locals-frequented restaurant—described on a travel Web site as "great food, if you can get past the no-frills atmosphere"—appears to be little more than an open-air hut beside a cluster of picnic tables on the sand, set off by bare bulbs strung between palm trees. No-frills is an understatement. Beneath the hut's tin roof, a hefty island woman with thick coils of braids wreathing her round dark face stirs a bubbling cast-iron pot over an open flame. A couple of children squat near her bare feet, peeling huge shrimp and tossing them into a dented metal pail.

The woman greets LaJuanda with a wave and an unintelligible but cheerful phrase that was most likely an invitation to seat herself. She does, settling on the bench closest to the water, with her back to the sea so that she can keep an eye on the path, waiting for Jonas.

A bottled beer seems the safest beverage choice, and she orders one from the oldest child, who, in lieu of handing her a menu, gestures at a handwritten whiteboard propped against the trunk of a coconut palm.

She's keeping one eye on the path while reading through the choices—most of which consist of fresh fish and jerked meat—when a shadow falls across her table. Turning, she sees a tall man whose head is completely shaved, with skin the color of undiluted coffee.

"Are you Jonas?" she asks, wondering how he managed to come up behind her when the crescent of beach is secluded by dense jungle and rock formations. Then she sees the small boat anchored just off the shore.

He doesn't answer her query, just sits across from her. Immediately, the boy who brought LaJuanda's beer materializes with a plastic cup filled with ice and amber liquid. He hands it silently to the man, who nods, sips, and motions for the boy to go away.

Opting not to pull out her pad and pen, LaJuanda gets right down to business. "What can you tell me about Jane Deere?"

"Why do you want to know?"

She weighs the wisdom of telling him about her suspicions, and decides she has nothing to lose. "I'm investigating a murder, and I think she was involved."

Jonas doesn't so much as raise an eyebrow. "And so you know that is not her real name."

"Jane Deere?" Of course she'd figured as much. "What was her real name?"

He shrugs, and she realizes she'll have to try another tactic. She's prepared to offer to pay him for information—the Temples have set up a fairly modest fund to be used toward her efforts—but something tells her that might not be necessary if she takes the right approach. The fact that he's here at all makes her think he might have his own reasons for wanting to see this so-called Jane Deere dragged out of the shadows.

"Do you *know* her real name?" LaJuanda asks.

"I know many things about her. Much more than *you* know."

Yeah—no kidding.

Then he adds, "Much more than she wanted anyone to know."

Now we're getting somewhere, LaJuanda thinks. "When did you meet her, Mr. Jonas?"

"Before she even arrived on Saint Antony. I was the one who brought her here."

Startled, she can't keep the questions from flying out. "What? How? From where?"

"Florida. By boat."

There are countless other questions she wants to ask in response to that bit of information. Seeing the wariness in his black eyes, she settles on the one that seems least likely to shutter them. "Why did she come here?"

"Why do most people come here? To get away from it all." He is clearly parodying the trite phrase used on so many of the island's resort brochures.

"She wanted to hide here. Okay. When was this?"

"September 15, 2001."

LaJuanda *does* raise an eyebrow. "You know the exact date?"

"Of course."

She angles her head, and then it hits her. September 2001. Just a few days after . . .

"Was she involved in terrorism?" LaJuanda asks, wondering if she just stumbled across something that had global implications.

"No. Not at all. Not that."

"Are you sure? How do you know? What do you know about her?"

"I know that she worked in the World Trade Center and that she made it out. I know that she left New York that day and came to Florida."

New York. September 2001. LaJuanda's thoughts are spinning. "She told you all that?"

"She told me lies. I found the truth later."

"How?"

"I saw her picture in the newspaper. Hundreds of pictures . . . thousands. Almost three thousand."

Almost three thousand people had died on September 11 in New York.

"All those faces. I looked for hers because I guessed it would be there, and sure enough, it was."

"Do you mean . . ." LaJuanda clears her throat. "Was she listed as one of the victims in the World Trade Center attack?"

Jonas nods.

"Why didn't she tell anyone she'd lived?"

"Because she didn't want anyone to know."

"What was her real name?"

It's precisely the same question she asked him just minutes ago.

Only this time, he answers it.

"Carrie Robinson MacKenna."

The Cornhusker Hotel is every bit as elegant as Allison imagined when she was a girl, and the king-sized bed in the suite couldn't be more inviting—even with the girls jumping on it in their summer pajamas.

"Hey, guys, you're sleeping on the pullout couch, remember?" Mack catches Maddy in mid-bounce and she giggles.

He sets her on the floor, does the same with her sister, and turns to Allison with outstretched arms. "I'll take him so you can go get ready."

"It's okay." She rests her cheek against J.J.'s silky head. "I don't have to leave for at least another hour."

"I wish you weren't going out alone so late."

"Nine o'clock isn't late, Mack."

"In a strange city—"

"It's Lincoln, Nebraska!"

"It's still a strange city, and you're a woman out there all alone at night. I don't like it."

"Should I not go?" she asks, almost hoping he'll say that she shouldn't. If he does, she'll agree, and when nine o'clock rolls around, she'll be sound asleep beside him in that big soft bed instead of making stilted small talk with a friend she hasn't seen in twenty years.

"Are you kidding? You should definitely go."

"Are you sure?"

"Don't you want to?"

"I don't know. Maybe. Maybe not."

"Look, you should go. If nothing else, it'll be a good warm-up for seeing Brett tomorrow, right?"

"I guess." But if this doesn't go well, how is she ever going to deal with *that*?

"Don't worry, Al. It'll be fun. You'll see."

"I hope so. I just wish she'd hurry up and send me her address so that I at least know where I'm going." Allison had sent Tammy a text, as requested, as soon as they'd checked into the hotel, but so far, she hadn't heard back.

"You said she's at work until nine, right? Maybe she's busy. What does she do?"

"I have no idea. I probably should have asked."

"Well, you'll have plenty of time to catch up when you see her. Here, hand over J.J. so that I can change him, and you go take a nice long bubble bath and relax."

"I love you, Mack." The last shred of this morning's lingering irritation at her husband melts away and she smiles at him, then leans down to kiss their son good night. J.J. jerks in her arms, head-butting her so hard she instantly tastes salty blood in her mouth.

Hearing her cry out, the girls are beside her instantly.

"J.J.! You hurt Mommy!" Hudson scolds. "She's bleeding!"

"It's okay, he didn't mean it." Allison gently sets him down on the bed and sees Maddy watching with big, scared eyes as Mack hands over a white washcloth he'd hurriedly grabbed from the bathroom.

"You're going to have a nice big fat lip when you meet your friend if you don't get some ice on that right away," he tells her, reaching for the bucket sitting on a polished desktop. "I'll go down the hall and grab some."

Left alone with her children, Allison blots the blood from her mouth, creating scarlet blotches on the plush white terrycloth.

"I bet the hotel is going to be mad that you stained their nice washcloth, Mommy."

"Hudson! Don't say that to Mommy. They can just wash it!"

"It's blood. Bloodstains don't come out. Do they, Mommy?"

"Sometimes they do, sometimes they don't, but either way, it's all right. I just hope . . ."

"What? What do you just hope?" Hudson presses when she trails off, never one to let something go.

"I just hope they have stain remover in the hotel laundry room," Allison tells her daughters with a forced smile.

And I hope this isn't some kind of ominous warning about the kind of night I have in store.

In one quick motion, Rocky Manzillo strikes a match and tosses it into the bed of lighter-fluid-laced charcoal.

"Now we're cooking," he says with a grin as it goes up in flames.

"Now *you're* cooking," his oldest and dearest friend Vic

Shattuck amends, standing beside him holding two open beers. "I'm just the audience—and a skeptical audience at that."

"What, you don't believe I can barbecue a couple of steaks?"

"I'll believe it when I see it with my own eyes."

"Well, you're about to. But not until this grill is good and hot, because with steak, you have to sear it really good, and then—"

"I don't need your recipes, Rock. I've got plenty of my own."

"Since when?"

"Shut up and drink your beer." Vic hands one of the bottles to Rocky and lifts his own in a toast. "*Salute.*"

"*Salute.*" As they clink their bottles together, Rocky asks, "What are we drinking to? The Fourth of July?"

"That's not until the day after tomorrow. How about to the miracle that you're cooking dinner?"

"I do this every night. How about that our wives are letting us eat red meat tonight?"

"Let's just drink to retirement."

"We drank to that last night."

"We should drink to it every night, Rock. Feels good, doesn't it?" Vic settles into a webbed lawn chair on the small patch of grass behind the house Rocky and Ange have shared for over thirty-five years, in the same Bronx neighborhood where they all grew up, the three of them: Rocky, Ange, and Vic.

"You're the one who didn't even want to retire in the first place," Rocky points out.

"No choice there." An FBI profiler, Vic had grudgingly accepted his mandatory retirement a few years ago, taking up golf, joining the lecture circuit, and becoming a bestselling author.

By contrast, Rocky had been glad to leave the NYPD

Homicide Squad just months ago, though he, too, loved his work. He could have retired a decade ago with full benefits, but he'd planned to stay on as long as he was physically able.

He changed his mind about that after Ange suffered a debilitating brain aneurysm last August. Almost losing the love of his life was enough to make him change his mind about everything: how long he would continue to work a demanding career, what he ate for breakfast, whether he exercised—*everything*. Except, of course, his love for Ange. That's one thing that will never change.

His wife of thirty-nine years has been on a long, painstaking road back from the brink of death. She went from comatose to blinking to grunting to single words to full sentences; from twitching her toes to making several halting steps using a walker. One day soon, the nurses at the rehabilitation hospital promised Rocky, she'll be up and around again. For now, she's in a wheelchair.

She was released from the rehab hospital just in time for a Memorial Day visit from all three of their sons, including their youngest, Donny, with his girlfriend Kellie and their three-month-old daughter, Angelina. Rocky had been hoping Donny and Kellie would be married by now—or at least engaged—but this is a different world from the one he and Ange inhabited at that age.

He tried to talk some sense into his son. Tried to tell him that if you love someone enough to have a child with her, then you should be willing to stay by her side for richer and for poorer, in sickness and in health . . .

Those were the vows Rocky and Ange had taken thirty-nine years ago.

For better and for worse . . .

Now it's time for better.

Ange returned to a newly retired husband and a house that's been newly fitted with a wheelchair ramp, a stair lift, and bathtub bars. When she's up to cooking again—and she assures Rocky that she will be—he's going to install new lower countertops and accessible appliances.

But for now, he does all the cooking. Mostly on the grill. Mostly chicken and fish. After all those years of Ange nagging him about his unhealthy diet, he's lost thirty pounds and is shooting for ten more. On the cusp of his sixty-first birthday, he feels better than he has in twenty, maybe thirty years.

Watching Ange fight her way back to life has been all the inspiration he needs. If she's that determined to stick around, then so is he. Growing old together with Ange is the only thing he ever really expected out of life, and he never thought it would come so close to being an elusive dream.

Today, with Vic and his wife, Kitty, visiting from their home in Vermont, Rocky skipped his daily thirty minutes on the treadmill. And he's planning to indulge heartily in porterhouse, Budweiser, and Carvel—with a flag-bedecked ice cream cake stashed in the freezer.

Life is good, Rocky thinks, sipping cold beer and slapping mosquitoes beside his best friend as the orange sun sinks below the roofline. There's still no hint of the massive storms that are supposed to roll in from the west later tonight. Charcoal smoke from his grill mingles with the pungent scent of sizzling meat wafting from neighbors' yards. Up and down the block, illegal firecrackers snap and whistle, kids cool off in open hydrants, a car alarm chirps and wails—and somewhere nearby, beyond a screened window, a telephone rings.

Moments later, Ange rolls over to the back door in her wheelchair. "Rocco! You got a call!"

"Who is it?"

"I don't know."

"Well, did you ask?"

She doesn't reply, having rolled back into the kitchen again.

"What does it matter?" Vic asks him as he stands up,

grumbling. "As long as it's not the desk sergeant with a case."

"You got that right." Rocky sets his beer on the step and goes in to answer the call.

Ange hands over the phone. As she rolls back over to the table where she and Kitty are shucking fresh corn, she asks, "How long before the steaks go on?"

"The grill should be good and hot now. I'll be off the phone in a minute and then I'll throw them on."

But a minute later, the steaks are the last thing on his mind.

Carrie Robinson MacKenna.

It's been a long time since Rocky's heard that name. Now a private detective—a female one, with a slight Hispanic accent—is calling him from an airport in the Caribbean, about to board a flight to New York, where she wants to meet with Rocky.

Her flight lands at JFK just before midnight. "I can take a cab from there to meet you. Just tell me where you'll be."

Where will he be at midnight? Right here at home, in bed with his wife, with a stomach full of steak and ice cream and beer and the permanent peace of mind that had come with retirement from the homicide force.

That's what he wants to tell LaJuanda Estrada.

Instead, he hears himself agree to meet her at an all-night diner in Manhattan to discuss a woman who supposedly died over a decade ago in the World Trade Center. A woman whose supposedly widowed husband had been wrongly accused of murder just last fall, in one of the final cases of Rocky's career.

"That's how I found you," LaJuanda tells Rocky, her voice hurried as a boarding announcement is audible in the background. "Your name was in the press about that case and the first round of murders that Allison MacKenna witnessed right after September 11."

The Nightwatcher—that was what the New York tabloids dubbed the serial killer who preyed on lower Manhattan in the days just after the terrorist attacks reduced the twin towers to burning rubble.

Startled, Rocky asks, "Do you think Carrie had something to do with those murders, too?"

"No. From what I can tell, they happened after she'd left New York, heading to Florida. But I think she's responsible for at least half a dozen deaths here on Saint Antony, and it looks like she might be back in the States already. She's dangerous, Detective Manzillo, and—"

"I'm retired," he cuts in. "A retired detective. I'm not on the force anymore."

"Neither am I. That means there are a hell of a lot less rules for us to follow when we go after this woman, right?"

Before Rocky can agree—or disagree—she goes on hurriedly, above the crackling of another intercom announcement on her end, "That's my final boarding call. Give me your e-mail address, and I'll send you a link to an article about the explosion at the bar and another one about Molly Temple. Just please don't tell anyone about this until I get there. On second thought . . . are you still in touch with James MacKenna and his wife, Allison, by any chance?"

"Why?"

"Their number is unlisted, but I guessed you might have it. Am I right?"

"Yeah, you are."

"That's why I'm a great detective," she returns, and he can't help but like her, even if he is still wondering whether she's some batshit crazy prankster. "Listen, you need to call and tell them that Carrie is still alive. And I need to hang up now. See you in a few hours."

A few minutes later, with Vic outside dutifully manning the grill, Rocky heads upstairs to what had once been his youngest son's bedroom. Now it serves as both his home office and gym, with a treadmill wedged into one corner and a desk in another.

Still reeling from what this strange woman told him, he sits down, boots up his computer, and checks his e-mail. The articles she mentioned haven't come through yet.

He'll look again in a minute. For now, he Googles the name "LaJuanda Estrada."

Okay. So there really is a Miami-based private detective by that name—if that was really her on the phone just now.

Rocky clicks through a series of case files, looking for information he collected on the MacKenna case. Somewhere in those folders, he's certain he has their phone number.

But is he really going to call and tell James MacKenna that not only is his long-dead wife still alive, but that she might have killed a woman—and faked her own death for the second time?

What if this is some kind of prank?

Rocky shakes his head, checking again for the e-mail LaJuanda said she'd send.

This time, it's there, generated by the same e-mail address that was listed on her private detective agency Web site.

He clicks on the links and scans the articles. Then—just in case she faked them—he rechecks the facts in a search engine. That search yields plenty of information confirming that Molly Temple did, indeed, go missing from a cruise on the very day she disembarked on Saint Antony, where an explosion claimed a number of lives, including that of the mysterious bartender Jane Deere.

Only DNA testing can confirm that it was really Molly Temple, as LaJuanda suspects—and that's going to take some time.

"Rocky?" Ange calls from downstairs. "Vic said he just heard thunder. Do you want him to put the steaks on the grill?"

"No! *I'm* cooking! I'll be down in a minute!"

Frowning, he goes back into his own case file, searching for a photo of Carrie Robinson MacKenna. After a moment, he locates the picture—a head-and-shoulders close-up—her grieving husband used on the missing posters that were hung all over the shell-shocked, smoldering city, alongside photos of Rocky's fallen colleagues and friends. So many innocent lives lost on that terrible day.

Rocky had always seen MacKenna's wife as yet another tragic victim.

Now, staring at her face, he wonders if LaJuanda's claim could possibly be true.

There have always been theories and rumors, in the press and on the street and even among the cops on the force, that the official number of September 11 victims very likely includes one or more troubled, opportunistic New Yorkers who seized the catastrophic events as the means to disappear and be presumed dead.

Is Carrie Robinson MacKenna among them?

Is she . . .

Wait a minute.

Frowning, Rocky leans closer to the computer screen, then grabs the mouse and clicks on the magnification button several times, zooming in on the lower left corner of the photograph.

It probably doesn't mean anything, but . . .

But it might. And that's enough to send Rocky back into the files, searching for the MacKenna family's home telephone number up in Westchester. He dials it quickly and listens to it ring once . . . twice . . . three times . . . voice mail.

Dammit. He hangs up, not wanting to leave a message. He needs to talk to them in person.

Certain he has James MacKenna and his wife Allison's cell phone numbers somewhere in the file, he begins clicking through document after document, looking for the numbers, all the while thinking about the green carnation pinned to Carrie's lapel in the missing poster photograph . . .

A green carnation that's eerily similar to the calling card left by the elusive Leprechaun Killer who killed a woman named Janice Kaminsky back in March 2000, before apparently falling off the face of the earth . . .

Something Carrie Robinson MacKenna seems to specialize in.

They'd lifted a couple of prints from the flower, but they never led to a match. That didn't mean that the perp didn't have a previous record; it only meant that the prints hadn't belonged to anyone whose information was in the databases available to Rocky at that time.

Technology has come a long way in twelve years. Databases become more standardized every day; systems that were previously incompatible with each other are now linked. It might be worth running those prints again, Rocky decides.

That's something that would have taken an inordinate amount of time even when he was still on the force, let alone now that he's retired.

But Rocky happens to have a secret weapon on his side— one who might also be retired, but not from the NYPD. From the FBI, with its Integrated Automated Fingerprint Identification System. Vic is still well connected and might be willing, in exchange for a juicy seared steak and another cold beer, to call in a couple of favors.

The dashboard clock reads nine o'clock as the sun disappears over the flat horizon, and Carrie smiles. Perfect timing. Her plan can unfold under cover of darkness, the way she's always imagined.

Yes. Because I'm a nocturnal creature too, just like the black widows Daddy told me about all those years ago. And my venom is just as deadly.

Despite the heat wave that settled over the region today, she has the air-conditioning turned off and the windows rolled down. It's uncomfortably warm in the car, but that's okay. She has to listen for the sound of a car coming down the road behind her.

She'll let Allison drive past her. Carrie doubts she'll even notice the parked car at the side of the road. She'll most likely be searching for the mailbox bearing the address in the text message she received less than an hour ago.

Cutting it so close isn't Carrie's style. She prefers to take her time planning things. But she'd only intercepted that e-mail this morning, and answered it on a whim. Before that, she wasn't sure how or where she was going to get to Allison.

But this was perfect. Allison was going to come straight to her. She just had to figure out where. And before she could do that, she had to find the well, so that it would be ready, and then she had to make the long drive down from South Dakota, and find this house, the perfect house: a deserted one-story ranch with an above-ground pool out back and fake brick along the chimney and foundation. It's the kind of house the owners won't bother to worry much about if they left town.

Driving by as she cruised the outskirts of Lincoln a little while ago, Carrie spotted a thick Sunday newspaper still sitting in its bag on the front steps. She boldly pulled into the driveway and knocked on the door.

Had someone answered, she'd have asked for directions.

No one did. She walked around the side of the house. The lights were off in every room, drapes drawn and windows closed with the exception of a couple that held portable air conditioners. They were definitely not running even though the windows were closed and the temperature was still in the high eighties.

In the backyard, the swimming pool was covered—not

casually, as it might be overnight, but tightly, and heavily weighted all the way around. Yesterday's rain pooled where the blue plastic cover dipped low in the center.

Today had been so scorchingly hot that you'd expect anyone living here to have gone for a dip.

Carrie noted that the pool pump was on, but attached to an automatic timer set to go on every night at seven. There was another timer on the nearby garden sprinkler, aimed at a patch of nearly drowned tomato plants. Clearly, the patch had been watered relentlessly by the sprinklers despite the weekend deluge.

To Carrie, it all added up to absolute certainty that the house was vacant.

That doesn't mean its occupants won't return any second now, but given the looming midweek holiday, she's betting against it. Anyway, it doesn't matter. As long as they don't show up in the next ten or fifteen minutes or so, she'll be fine.

Headlights appear in her rearview mirror, sending anticipation through Carrie, but the car that passes is an old pickup truck.

Patience. Allison will be here soon.

She leans back against the headrest, wishing she'd had time to take a nap after the long drive to Lincoln from South Dakota. It had taken her over four hours, plus another hour to find the house. She'd texted Allison immediately with the address. Moments later, the cell phone Carrie had bought just this morning using stolen ID had buzzed with a cheerful return text: *Great, see you there at 9:15!*

After all these years, she's about to meet Allison . . . again.

The first time doesn't really count, but the second—

Carrie closes her eyes, remembering the day she and Mack had stepped out the door of their fourth floor apartment on Hudson Street and run into Allison.

The moment had been inevitable from the time they'd

signed a lease to rent the apartment directly across the hall from her. Carrie had considered what she would say when it happened; how she might react if she was alone and Allison didn't recognize her; what she might do if she was with Mack and Allison *did* recognize her . . .

Neither of those things happened.

Carrie was with Mack—and Allison didn't have a clue that this wasn't the first time they had ever seen each other.

Mack spoke first. "Do you live there?"

Under any other circumstances, Carrie might have said, "That's a stupid thing for a smart guy to say."

After all, Allison had a set of keys in her hand, had just unlocked the door, and was about to step over the threshold. Even if Carrie hadn't known exactly where she lived—and who she was—long before they'd moved in, she'd have assumed the apartment belonged to Allison.

Carrie could only guess that Mack was so flustered by their neighbor's striking blond beauty that his brain had momentarily gone numb. But she wasn't jealous.

You can only be jealous of someone who has something you want for yourself, and that wasn't the case back then. Carrie had Mack, and she had the hope that despite what the doctors had told her, she might be able to get pregnant after all.

And now?

Are you jealous of Allison now that she's Mack's wife and you're not? Because she bore Mack's children and you couldn't? Is that what this is about?

Or is it about the other thing she stole from you years ago, the moment she was born?

She pushes the questions aside, forcing her mind back to that summer day in the dimly lit hallway between the two fourth floor apartments.

She remembers how Allison smiled and told Mack that she did, indeed, live behind the door she'd just unlocked, and then she asked an equally stupid question: "Are you guys my new neighbors?"

On some level, Carrie decides, she and Mack deserve each other. Idiots.

"We moved in a few weeks ago," Mack told her, and introduced himself and Carrie.

"I'm Allison Taylor. Nice to meet you." She shook Mack's hand, then reached for Carrie's.

Carrie remembers recoiling mentally, but not allowing herself to do so physically; remembers trying to relax as her fingers clasped Allison's; remembers glancing into her eyes to see whether the touch might have triggered something, some primeval awareness, perhaps . . .

But there was nothing.

After all of it—every tear Carrie had shed over her, every moment she had wasted searching for her, wondering about her, worrying; after all of it, everything, there was . . .

Nothing.

And that's exactly what I feel for you now, she tells Allison silently.

As if in answer to that realization, the sound of tires rolling along the road behind her reaches her ears. Opening her eyes, she sees in the rearview mirror that a pair of headlights are approaching, too high above the road to belong to a car.

Is it another pickup truck?

No, an SUV. A Lexus, Carrie realizes.

Allison is here.

Chapter Fifteen

The flight to New York took off right on time, and it looks like they might even land early enough to beat the wall of thunderstorms firing up in the Northeast.

LaJuanda was as happy to hear that as she was to discover that the plane is equipped with wifi, enabling her to get online and continue her research into Carrie Robinson MacKenna.

Unfortunately, her laptop isn't fully charged. She hadn't anticipated that she'd be scrambling to leave the island so soon. But after meeting with Jonas, she'd known she had to go straight to New York. She booked the flight over the phone and dashed to her hotel to collect her things.

When she's safely back on American soil, she'll call the missing persons bureau back in Miami and tell them that she has reason to believe that one of the female victims of the explosion on Saint Antony had been incorrectly identified and that the remains most likely belonged to Molly Temple. They'll order DNA testing.

For now, she's racing against time—or at least, against the draining battery—to find out everything she can about the woman who lived as Jane Deere.

There isn't much information online about Carrie Robinson MacKenna, despite her high-profile "death" in the World Trade Center.

Perhaps most intriguing of all is that there is no record of this particular Carrie Robinson's existence before she began working at Cantor Fitzgerald in early 2000. By contrast, there was plenty of information about her husband, James MacKenna, and his second wife, Allison Taylor MacKenna.

"Rum punch, ma'am?"

"No, thank you," LaJuanda tells the flight attendant, barely looking up from the e-mail she's typing rapidly. Under other circumstances, she'd have gladly accepted, and thought to acknowledge how nice it is to be flying on a foreign airline that not only hands out free alcoholic beverages, but will be serving a full meal, has wifi, takes off on time, and lands early.

The only thing missing is an electrical outlet beneath LaJuanda's seat, and without one, she's going to lose touch momentarily.

After sending yet another e-mail to Rocco Manzillo—this one asking whether he managed to get in touch with the MacKennas and warn them—she realizes she'd better send one to Rene, telling him that she's headed from Saint Antony to New York to follow a lead.

A warning flashes on the computer screen telling her that the battery is dangerously low and the computer will shut down if she doesn't connect to a power source.

She hastily hits send, then checks to make sure the e-mail to Rene went through. It did—and she has a new one from Rocco Manzillo. Opening it, she sees that it's short, just a couple of lines.

The cell phone numbers I had for the MacKennas were disconnected, but I'm trying to track them down. Meanwhile, I have more information about our friend. I'm sure you won't be surprised to learn that Carrie Robinson wasn't her real name, either. I ran some old prints on a hunch and came back with a match.

Already? That's impossible, LaJuanda thinks. Well, not physically impossible—you can get a hit from the FBI's IAFIS database in a matter of minutes. But unless you're some kind of powerful government agent—or have friends in high places—running prints can take a notoriously long time. If Rocky's telling the truth, then LaJuanda has new-found respect for the man.

She goes on reading,

She was arrested a few times for solicitation, begin-ning back in 1987 in Minneapolis, and her real name is—

The computer screen flickers and goes black before she can finish.

Allison double-checks the address on the mailbox as she pulls past it, into the driveway, noticing that the house is dark.

That's the right number on the mailbox, though—unless she got it wrong in the text?

She puts the car into park and reaches for her straw tote on the passenger's seat, feeling around inside for her phone. It's not easy to find. The bag is crammed with road trip clutter:

everything from antibacterial hand wipes to J.J.'s teething ring to a packet of oyster crackers that have been reduced to powder.

As she feels around inside, something drops out, bounces off her foot, and lands near the brake.

Was it her phone?

She leans over and runs her left hand over the floor.

No—it was the silver compact the girls got her for Mother's Day.

"Mommy! You look so pretty!" Maddy had exclaimed when Allison emerged from the bathroom back at the hotel.

"You're wearing makeup!" Hudson noticed. "Make sure you bring your compact with you!"

Not wanting to risk losing the precious gift now, Allison shoves it into the deep side pocket of the cotton skirt she's wearing, making a mental note to zip it into her cosmetics bag when she gets back to the hotel.

She just hopes she hasn't lost her cell phone. She knows she had it when she left the room, because Mack asked her, twice, if she did.

"Do you have enough battery power to last all night?" he asked when she held it up.

"I have three bars. But don't worry. I'll only be gone two hours at the most. I'm exhausted, and we have to be up early to drive the rest of the way. I shouldn't even be going out."

"Yes, you should. And you should have fun. I'm sure it'll be good to see your old friend."

It might be, Allison thinks now, digging for her cell phone, *if I can ever connect with her.*

Her fingers close around it just as headlights swing into the driveway behind her, reflecting off the rearview mirror and momentarily blinding her.

It must be Tammy, finally coming home from work. Relieved, Allison turns off her own car engine and climbs out of the Lexus, keys and phone in hand. She leaves the tote bag on the seat, not wanting to lug it inside.

The night air is warm and still after the chilly hum of the SUV's air-conditioning.

She walks toward the small car parked behind hers, still running. Despite the glare of the headlights she can see a female driver silhouetted behind the wheel.

A hand pops out the open window, waving her over. "Hi, Allison! Is that you?"

"It's me! Is that you?" she returns, trying to sound cheerful and casual.

"It's me! Sorry I'm late!"

"It's okay. I just got here." Allison approaches the car, wishing it weren't so dark out—and inside the car—to get a good look at her old friend. Why isn't Tammy getting out? She'll feel better if she can just see her familiar face—except it's probably not going to be all that familiar after all these years.

"Do you mind hopping into the car for a few minutes, Allison? I have to run a quick errand."

"What?" She halts a few feet away, confused.

"I was planning to swing by the store to pick up some wine and cheese and crackers on my way home," Tammy explains, "but I got out late and I figured if I took even more time to stop, you might give up on me and leave."

"Oh—that's okay. You don't have to go to the store just for me. I can't drink wine because I have to drive back, and anyway, it's so warm out tonight I'm fine just with ice water. Really."

"Great, then we'll buy a bag of ice, too," Tammy says with a laugh. "I swear, I'm out of everything. Guess that's what happens when you live alone."

So she isn't married with children? For some reason, Allison finds that surprising. When they were kids, they always talked about what life would be like when they became wives and mothers. Granted, they were going to marry a boy band, but still . . .

"Come on, we can start catching up on the way to the store. It's just down the road."

"You really don't have to buy anything for me. That's sweet of you, but—"

"Trust me, it's not that sweet of me." Tammy laughs again. "I'm dying of thirst, and I haven't eaten since breakfast. I really want that cheese and crackers. Maybe some chocolate, too." She waves Allison around to the passenger's side.

Okay, fine. She might as well ride along to the store. It's better than waiting here alone in the driveway again. Anyway, it'll probably be easier to launch their initial conversation in the dark, both of them facing forward, looking out into the night rather than at each other. Allison turns back to her own car to get her bag.

"Wait, where are you going, Allison?" The urgency in Tammy's voice stops her in her tracks.

This is strange, isn't it? The way Tammy showed up after she did and still hasn't even gotten out of the car to say hello. The way she wants to rush right back out again, taking Allison with her . . .

She always was impulsive, though.

She was frequently late, too, Allison remembers. For school, and everything else. And a little scatterbrained. It would have been just like her to invite someone over without making sure she was equipped to play hostess.

Allison's misgivings subside and she tells Tammy, "I was just going to grab my wallet."

"You don't need a wallet. Everything is on me. You're my guest!"

"Are you sure?"

"Positive."

"Okay—thanks." Allison aims the key remote at the Lexus. She hears the locks click into place as she presses the button, and the horn gives two sharp chirps.

"Come on," Tammy calls again, then adds apologetically, "I don't mean to rush you, but they're going to close any minute now."

Climbing into the passenger's seat of Tammy's little car, she notices that the air-conditioning is off, and that the overhead light didn't go on when she opened the door. She glances over, curious, still trying to get a good look at her old friend. Does she look the same? She doesn't sound the same—but then, Allison wouldn't expect her to. There's definitely something familiar about her voice, yet she could swear that the girl she remembers had more of a Midwestern twang, and a higher-pitched voice . . .

Of course she did. Because she was a young girl, remember? I bet I don't look or sound anything like she was expecting, either.

"Are you thirsty?" Tammy asks, holding out a bottle of Pepsi. "I bought it in the vending machine at work, but I meant to get Diet Pepsi and this is regular. I'm diabetic, so I can't drink it."

"I never knew you were diabetic."

"I never knew it either back then. I found out a few years ago. Go ahead—you can have that. I only took one sip."

Realizing she *is* thirsty—who isn't in this heat?—Allison accepts it and takes a long sip.

Tammy puts the car into reverse. "Ready?"

"Ready." Allison sets the Pepsi in the cup holder and pulls on her seat belt.

Tammy backs up quickly, then shifts into drive with an abrupt jerk. Startled by the recklessness of the move, Allison glances over at her.

It's too dark to see much of anything in the low light of the dashboard.

Suddenly, Allison is uneasy again. As they speed off down the street, the hot night air blowing in the open window on the driver's side, she presses a button on her phone, illuminating the rectangle of screen.

"What are you doing, Allison?"

"I was just going to text my husband and tell him we connected. He's a little worried about me, and I promised I'd let him know when I got to your house."

"Here—let me see it."

"What?" She looks down at Tammy's outstretched hand, bewildered.

"Your phone. Can I see it for a second?"

Not wanting to hand it over—foremost, because they're careening along and Tammy shouldn't be distracted behind the wheel—Allison shakes her head.

"Just give it to me for a second. Come on—don't be silly. I just want to show you something."

Is she being silly? Feeling like a middle school girl who thinks she just did something embarrassing, Allison puts the phone into Tammy's hand—then watches, stunned, as, in one swift motion, she tosses it out the open window.

"What are you *doing*?"

Tammy laughs, a strange sound, mirthless and hard.

Oh, God. Allison's stomach turns, and she thinks about Mack. Mack, back at the hotel, so worried about her going out into the night alone.

She reaches out, finding the door handle.

"It's locked," Tammy tells her. "And I disabled the unlock switch on that side. But even if I hadn't done that, you wouldn't dare jump out of a moving car at seventy miles an hour, Allison, would you? You're not stupid. You know you'd be killed."

Panicky, Allison turns to look behind her, into the backseat, wondering if those doors are locked, too.

Her heart stops when she sees what's lying across the backseat.

A shovel.

Dear God.

She turns back to Tammy, trying to keep her voice calm. "What are you doing? Where are we going?"

"We're going someplace quiet where we can talk. It's been such a long time, hasn't it?"

The truth dawns on her. "You're not Tammy."

"I'm not? Do you recognize me, then?"

"Who are you?"

"Do you recognize me?" Holding the wheel with one hand, the woman reaches up and flips the dome switch with the other. She gives Allison a long, hard look.

Allison gasps. "Oh my God."

It can't be. It can't be.

She's *dead*.

But . . .

"So you do know me." With a satisfied smile, she flips off the light. "I thought you would."

This is impossible. Mack's wife—his first wife, Carrie—died over ten years ago.

Except, she's sitting right here, driving and talking, both at breakneck speed. "It's been a long time, hasn't it? More than twenty-five years since that night. But I always thought you must remember me, deep down. Daddy always said that human beings are wired with far more knowledge and capability than most people ever tap into."

"What . . . what are you talking about?"

Allison's thoughts are whirling. Twenty-five years ago, she was just a little girl. She didn't meet Carrie until ten, no, eleven years ago. Eleven years ago this month.

Carrie . . . No. Carrie's dead.

But she's not.

"You remember that night, don't you, Allison? You know . . . the night I came into your room. You were sleeping, but I woke you up, and I explained who I was. Don't you remember? Remember how I introduced myself to you? Remember my name?"

"What . . . what is it?" she asks in a whisper.

"You mean, what *was* it?" She laughs. "Go ahead. Ask me. Ask me what it *was*."

Allison can't find her voice.

"ASK ME!"

She manages to choke out, "What is—what was your name?"

The answer isn't the one she's expecting.

The answer isn't Carrie.

It's . . .

"Winona."

The ringing telephone startles Mack awake. He rolls over on the king-sized bed and fumbles for his BlackBerry on the nightstand. He notices the unfamiliar surroundings as he answers it, remembering that he's in a hotel suite in Lincoln and Allison is . . .

Out. Allison is out. Determined to stay awake until she got back, Mack had been lying, fully clothed, on the bed watching *SportsCenter* on ESPN, trying to catch the highlights on the Yankees game back home. He must have dozed off.

"Hello?"

The phone is still ringing; it's not his BlackBerry, it's the hotel room phone.

In the portable crib beside the bed, J.J. stirs. One of the girls calls, "Daddy?" from the sofa bed in the next room.

Mack snatches up the receiver. *"Hello?"*

"Hi . . . is this . . . I'm looking for Allison Taylor," a female voice says. "I mean, Allison MacKenna."

"This is her husband."

"Oh! Hi! My name is Tammy Pratt, and I'm sorry to call so late, but I just got an e-mail from Allison about getting together while she's in Lincoln. Is she there?"

The words slam into Mack, knocking the wind out of him.

"Isn't . . . isn't she with you?"

"With me? No, I'm in Florida on vacation with my family. I can't believe I'm going to miss seeing—"

"Didn't you send Allison an e-mail telling her to meet you at your house tonight?"

"What? No!"

Stunned, Mack clutches the phone hard against his ear, heart racing.

If Tammy didn't send it . . . then who did?

And where the hell is Allison?

"**D**addy, can you drive me over to Carly's house?" Lexi asks, appearing in the doorway of the master bedroom.

How is it, Randi wonders, that the whole family walked in the door less than five minutes ago, yet her daughter has already changed her clothes? Fifteen-year-old Lexi has traded a tasteful black dress for a tank top and a pair of short shorts that bare too much tanned skin, while Ben hasn't even finished loosening his tie and Randi, sitting on the edge of the bed, has only taken off one black dress shoe.

"You want him to drive you to Carly's right now when he just drove for three and a half hours?"

"I was asking Daddy, Mom. Not you."

"I just drove for three and a half hours, Lex." Ben opens the door to his walk-in closet.

"Most of it wasn't actual driving," Lexi argues. "Most of it was sitting in traffic."

"Believe me, that's worse."

Randi couldn't agree more. She can think of only one thing more horrendous than the endless trip home from Long Island just now with Lexi and her ten-year-old brother, Josh, bickering in the backseat, and that would be the endless trip out there this morning for Great-Aunt Rhoda's funeral.

They had beach traffic and rush hour traffic all the way out, and Randi had been hoping to avoid it by heading home early. But after the service, the slow parade out to the cemetery, and the ceremonial tossing of dirt on the coffin, her cousin Mindy insisted that everyone come back to her house for, as she put it, "a little nosh." That turned out to be a catered affair populated by every annoying relative in Randi's family tree, with the exception of Great-Aunt Rhoda, now sadly mourned by a roomful of people who couldn't stand her.

Oy. Randi sinks backward onto the bed, staring at the ceiling.

"Daddy . . . come on. I really want to see my friends."

"Lexi, stop begging."

"Please, Daddy?"

"Why do you only call me Daddy when you want something?"

"Please, Dad?"

"That's still begging."

Ben is softening, though. Randi can hear it in his voice.

"It's *polite* begging. You should be proud of me. All Mom's crazy old relatives told me that I have nice manners."

"They also all told you that you look exactly like me," Randi points out, "and you made a face every time."

"I did not."

"You sure did."

The telephone rings before Lexi can reply—most likely with another *I did not*.

"That's Carly, wondering where I am." She reaches for

the receiver on the bedside table. "I'll tell her I'll be there in five minutes."

"Lexi—"

"Mom, come on. Admit it. You guys don't want to hang out with me tonight any more than I want to hang out with you. We've all had too much togetherness." She grabs the phone. "Hello?"

"Charming," Randi mutters, shaking her head.

Ben grins at her. "I'll run her over to Carly's and then—"

"Phone's for you." Lexi thrusts the receiver at Randi and heads for the door, her long black hair swaying behind her. "I'll call Carly from my cell."

With a sigh, Randi lifts the phone to her ear. "Hello?"

"Mrs. Weber? This is Rocco Manzillo—we met last fall. I was the detective who—"

"I remember." She sits up quickly.

"I'm trying to reach the MacKennas. Do you know where they are?"

"They're . . . away." She was about to tell him they're in Nebraska, but thought better of it. How does she know this is really Detective Manzillo? It might be some kind of crazy stalker. He wouldn't be the first to come after Allison and Mack.

"Can you put me in touch with them?"

"I can call them on their cell phones and tell them to—"

"I tried their cells. The numbers are disconnected."

That's right. Both Allison and Mack changed them in the midst of all the media commotion last November. Randi has the new numbers, of course, along with contact information for Allison's brother, Brett. But she's not going to share that part with Detective Manzillo just yet.

"I'll get in touch with them for you," she tells him. "What do you want me to say?"

He hesitates. "Tell them that they might be in danger, and they need to call me right away."

"I told you . . . I don't know the address of the house! Whoever sent it texted it to my wife's phone, and she took her phone with her when she left, and now she's not answering!" Mack runs a frustrated hand over his dark hair.

"I understand that, sir. I'm just trying to make sure I have all the details straight here. Why don't you just take a deep breath while I write this down . . ."

Mack doesn't want to take a deep breath. Locked in the bathroom of the suite, clutching his cell phone against his ear, he's just about had it with this conversation with a Nebraska cop whose patience, under any other scenario, would be exemplary. Right now, Mack wishes he could throw the guy up against a wall. Slow and steady don't always win the race. Not when your wife's life might be at stake.

Somehow, someone posing as Allison's old friend Tammy intercepted the e-mail she'd sent and lured her . . . God only knows where.

If only Mack hadn't been too caught up in his BlackBerry, when that text came through, to ask her exactly where she was going. If only he'd gone with her . . .

But of course, he couldn't have done that. Not with three sleeping children on his hands.

Forced to call the police instead of racing down there in person, he doesn't want the kids to overhear him freaking out, because then they'll freak out, and maybe—just maybe—there's no reason for panic.

Mack's phone beeps, indicating that another call is coming in.

"Officer, hang on!" he shouts, seeing that the call is coming from a private number. He puts the police on hold and answers with a breathless hello.

"Mr. MacKenna? This is Rocco Manzillo. Do you remember me?"

Of course he does. Detective Manzillo. Finally, someone who knows how to get something done.

Blindly willing to accept the call as providence, rather than pausing to wonder how the detective knew to call now, Mack blurts, "Allison's missing! Please—you have to help us."

"Missing?" There's a pause on the other end of the line. "Okay, just tell me what happened . . ."

Mack does, in a rush, pacing the bathroom like a caged animal, trying to remember as many details as he can. Unlike the Nebraska cop holding on the other line, Detective Manzillo doesn't keep stopping him and making him back up.

He just listens until Mack runs out of story with a helpless " . . . and then I called the cops."

"So you have no idea who this woman might have been?" Manzillo asks. "The one who sent the e-mail and the text?"

"No. I just know that it wasn't Allison's friend Tammy, because she's in Florida. At least, that's what she says."

Mack sinks down onto the edge of the tub in despair, not sure what—or whom—to believe.

The seat of his shorts is instantly dampened by water Allison splashed over the edge when she took her bath before going out. The bathroom still smells like her perfume, and the shorts and T-shirt she'd worn for the last couple of days are tossed in a corner.

She'd been wearing a pretty blue and white print skirt when she left, a navy sleeveless top, and sandals that were black or dark blue leather. He'd described the outfit to the Nebraska cop, who had asked.

Rocky Manzillo has not.

Why, Mack suddenly wonders, is he calling? *How* is he calling? This is a new number.

"How did you get this number?" he asks abruptly, thinking of Allison's phone, wondering if she might have tried to call Manzillo for help—

But that doesn't make sense, because if Allison needed help, she'd call Mack.

And if Allison, alone and desperate, needed help—that kind of help—that phone would be a lifeline she wouldn't let go.

No. I can't even think about it.

"I got the number from Randi Weber. I called her because I couldn't reach you at home. I don't know how to tell you this, Mr. MacKenna . . ."

"Tell me what?"

"You might want to sit down."

"I am. I'm sitting." Mack closes his eyes and he's back at his desk in New York on a sunny Tuesday morning in September, and the phone is ringing, and the world is burning.

Mack gulps, his blood running as cold as the sweat on his forehead. "Please don't tell me . . . she's not . . ."

"It's not about your wife," Manzillo says quickly, adding cryptically, "not Allison, anyway."

"What—"

"This is going to come as a shock. I wish I could tell you in person instead of over the phone, but—"

"What? What the hell is it?"

"Your wife—your first wife—is alive. Carrie. She's alive."

Driving through the night, heading north on the lonely highway toward South Dakota, Carrie casts another sideways glance at Allison.

Sound asleep in the passenger's seat, she hasn't stirred in a while now. Good. The fuel tank is running low, and as long as Allison is out cold, she can stop to fill it.

Carrie had been worried when Allison only took a few sips of the Pepsi, but the sedative she'd slipped into it is powerful stuff. Good thing she brought it along when she left the island. Illegal but readily available on Saint Antony, the powder is probably much harder to come by in the States.

Oh well. After this, Carrie won't have any use for it anymore. After this, she's going to turn over a new leaf. She'll hitchhike out to the Pacific Northwest, where summers are cool and cloudy.

Maybe that's what she should have done twelve years ago, instead of heading for New York, chasing after Allison.

But she couldn't even think straight back then. Her life was a mess. Her parents were dead, and she was all alone in the world, living in Minneapolis, earning a living by selling the only thing she had: her body.

What did it matter? It wasn't like she was a virgin, saving herself for marriage to some mythical Prince Charming. And it wasn't like she could get pregnant—though she didn't know that for sure at the time.

She suspected, of course. You didn't go through a self-induced late-term coat hanger abortion without butchering your reproductive organs.

Only years later, when she was married to Mack and trying to start a family, was the ugly truth confirmed by her obstetrician. The infection that had set in after she terminated the pregnancy had scarred her fallopian tubes, making it difficult—if not impossible—for her to conceive. Assuring her that her husband wouldn't have to know what had caused the infection, he referred Carrie to Dr. Hammond, an infertility specialist at the Riverview Clinic. Dr. Hammond told her there was hope, and for a while there, she clung to it, stubbornly . . . foolishly.

But she wasn't meant to be a mother.

Nor was she meant to be a wife, or . . .

Or a big sister.

But that's why you went to New York to find her, isn't it?

Because you got lonely, right? Because you realized that Allison was the last link to Daddy; the only other person in the world who has Daddy's blood running through her veins . . .

She thinks back to the day she realized that her father had another daughter.

It was around Thanksgiving, a week or so after Carrie's mother had accused her of being pregnant with her own father's child. A week after she'd hacked her mother to death with a kitchen knife and dumped her body into the well.

When she heard a vehicle splashing up from the highway, she thought it was going to be the police. She had long since scrubbed every drop of blood away, and sealed the well up good and tight, and she hadn't seen another living soul since it had happened. Still, she worried that somehow, someone had found out what she had done.

But it wasn't the police on that rainy November day.

It was her father.

Beside herself with excitement and relief, she let him into the house.

"Where's your mother?" he asked, draping his damp jacket over a kitchen chair the way he always did, and looking around. She followed his gaze, making sure she hadn't missed any bloodstains. Nope, all clean.

"I have no idea."

"What do you mean?"

"She left, Daddy."

"How many times have I told you—you should call me Dad now. Daddy is for little girls. And how could she have left? The car is parked right outside."

She thought quickly. "Someone picked her up."

That upset him. She could see it in his eyes. He was suspicious. Jealous, maybe. Wondering if her mother had another man.

"Who was it? Who picked her up?"

"I don't know. I didn't see. All I know is that she left, and she hasn't come back."

He asked a lot of other questions, and a terrible thought occurred to her. What if he decided to call the police?

She couldn't let that happen.

"We had a fight before Mom left," she said belatedly. "Maybe she took off because she was mad at me."

Yes. That made sense. But then, just as she was trying to find the right words to tell him about the baby she was carrying, he abruptly said he had to leave.

"But—what about me?"

"What *about* you?"

"You have to take me with you."

"I can't do that. I have to work."

"But . . . I can't stay here by myself."

"Sure you can. You're almost seventeen, Winona. You're not a little girl anymore. You stay here, and I'm sure your mother will show up in a day or two. And if she doesn't, well, I'll be back next weekend."

Next weekend?

Something snapped inside her.

Her father went into the bathroom, the way he always did before he left. The moment the door closed behind him, she went into the pocket of his jacket and found his wallet.

She had no idea how much an abortion cost, but she knew it had to be a lot. Looking for cash, she found something else instead: his driver's license.

No—not *his* license.

A license, from Nebraska, with his picture on it. But it bore the name Allen Taylor, and an address on Third Street in a town called Centerfield.

Shaken, she heard him coming out of the bathroom. She shoved the license back into his wallet, and the wallet back into his pocket.

He came out and picked up the jacket.

"Please . . . please don't leave me."

"Are you crying? You're too old for tears, Winona. Pull yourself together."

"I can't . . . I'm afraid . . . Daddy, please."

Again, he told her to stop calling him that. Again, she begged him not to leave. Back and forth they went, until he said, in disgust, "I can't do this anymore. I'm sorry. Goodbye."

She waited until the sound of his truck faded into the distance. Then she opened a drawer and she took out the knife she'd used to kill her mother. She put it into her pocket and she got into the car and she started heading south, in the opposite direction on the very road she's driving on right now.

What was she thinking as she drove? What was she planning?

She doesn't remember anything about that drive, other than the fact that the weather was miserable that day. The road was slippery, and she didn't even have her license yet; had never even driven on a highway. Yet somehow, she drove all the way into Nebraska, stopping twice to ask for directions until darkness fell and she found herself in Centerfield.

It was a tiny town, just a cluster of gabled houses and squared-off nineteenth-century storefronts rising off the plain. The highway became Main Street, crossing First Street, Second Street . . . Third Street.

From the intersection, she could see her father's truck parked halfway down the block, in front of a small gray house. She drove another block, rounded the corner, and left the car on Fourth Street, parked in the lot behind an elementary school that was deserted for the night.

The pavement was shiny in the yellow glow from a single light pole, pooled with icy rain that was still falling. She slipped through the muddy schoolyard, and she saw the back of the gray house. Lights were on. Looking through a window, she saw her father. He was sitting on a bed in a little girl's bedroom . . .

Dazed, she saw that it was purple and white, just like her own room back at home. There was a painted shelf filled with books, the same books she'd once had in her own room, and a hanger draped with a fancy dress that looked just like her own long-ago favorite dress, the one her father said he'd accidentally tossed into the Goodwill bag, and on the bed was a doll . . .

Papoose.

Carrie stared, wide-eyed, at her own doll, the one that had disappeared years earlier. In that instant, she understood that her father had taken it, and the dress, too, and he had given them to someone else. To the girl who sat beside him on the bed, a girl with long dark hair and blue eyes and a nice smile, a girl who was listening as he read to her from a book on his lap.

Allison.

Heedless of the freezing rain, Carrie stood watching for a long time, until she saw her father put the book back on the shelf and tuck the girl into the purple and white bed. He turned out the light and left the room. She snuck over to another window, and watched him as he sat on the couch and talked to a woman who was drinking a glass filled with whiskey; a woman who looked so much like the girl that anyone could see they were mother and daughter.

How, Carrie wondered, did her father fit into this picture?

Of course, she already knew, deep down.

"Always listen to your gut," Daddy used to tell her. "If you tune in to your intuition, you'll find that you know much more than you think you do."

She snuck into the house after all the lights were turned off. After her father had climbed into bed with a woman who wasn't her mother—although, what did it matter? Her mother was dead. She had killed her, and now she was pregnant and all alone and her father was here with another family.

What am I going to do? she wondered, prowling through the house, looking through papers until she found a folder filled with documents that proclaimed the truth she sought.

A man named Allen Taylor lived here with his wife, Brenda; and their daughter, Allison, had been born just over nine years ago, during the summer of 1977.

Allen Taylor. That was what her father was calling himself, or maybe that was who he really had been all along.

She found her way to the girl's bedroom and she stood for a long time, watching her sleep.

How many times have I told you—you should call me Dad now. Daddy is for little girls.

Now it all made sense. This little girl wasn't too old to call him Daddy. She wasn't too old for dolls, or picture books.

Tears rolled down Carrie's cheeks. She sniffled and reached over to pluck a tissue from the box on the painted white nightstand.

The child stirred and opened her eyes sleepily.

"Who are you?"

"I'm your sister," she whispered. "My name is Winona."

"Okay." Allison's eyes fluttered closed again.

She left the room, made her way back down the hall, heading for the back door, feeling her way through the dark. Her legs were wobbly and she felt sick, light-headed. She tripped, bumping into a chair.

"What's that?" her father's voice called from the next room. "Allison?"

She didn't answer, just stood there for a moment shaking in fury.

Then, hearing footsteps, she slipped out the door, into the rainy night.

She was halfway across the muddy backyard when she heard his voice.

"Winona?" He sounded so incredulous that she stopped short. "What the hell are you doing here?"

Trembling, she waited for him to catch up to her. Then she whirled to face him. "What am *I* doing here? What the hell are *you* doing here, Daddy?"

She doesn't remember what he said—or tried to say—before she stabbed him the first time. Doesn't remember dragging him through the dark yard to the deserted parking lot and dumping him into the trunk of the car . . .

What she does remember is that he was moaning as she closed it, and she realized he was alive.

Just as she was about to drive away, she realized something else.

The rain would wash away the blood in the yard, but that woman—Brenda, his wife—was bound to report him missing. What if the police managed to track him to South Dakota? What if they found her? What if they wanted to know where her mother was? What if . . .

She hurried back to the house. There, she wrote a quick, terse note, doing her best to imitate her father's jagged handwriting.

Can't do this anymore. I'm sorry. Good-bye.

Those were his own words, after all.

She left the note in the kitchen and then she drove all the way home, numb, trying to make it under cover of darkness.

The first streaks of light were just appearing on the flat eastern horizon when she pried the cover off the well. The stench hit her: her mother's body, decaying in the depths.

She hoisted her father out of the trunk and into the rusted old wheelbarrow, the one he used to use to work in the yard; the one he let her climb into so that he could give her a ride.

"Your turn, Daddy," she said, and pushed it over to the yawning hole in the ground. Just as she heaved the weight forward, he opened his eyes and looked up at her.

"Winona," he said. "I—"

Too late. She gave the wooden handles a mighty shove, and he toppled into the well.

She would never know what he was about to say. That bothered her later.

Was it *I told you to stop calling me Daddy?*

Was it *I'm sorry?*

Or *I love you?*

It doesn't matter, really, does it?

It certainly didn't matter that night, as Carrie took a coat hanger out of the closet, went into the bathroom with it; it didn't matter as, with her pelvis cramping painfully, she scrubbed bloodstains from the floor for the second time in a week—this time, her own.

And it doesn't matter tonight, as Carrie covers the same stretch of highway she did on that cold November night in 1986.

All that matters now is that Allison is finally going to see her father again after all these years . . . right up close and personal.

What's left of him, anyway, Carrie thinks as she makes the final turn on the road toward home.

"Well? How did he take it?" Vic asks, as Rocky hangs up the telephone.

"How would *you* take it if your wife just came back from the dead?"

"Don't even say that."

"Sorry." Rocky leans his head back momentarily against the chair's faux leather padding, grasping a certain note of irony here. His own wife, Ange, had been all but dead, and now . . .

Ange's survival was a blessing.

This is not.

The woman James MacKenna had known—and married—as Carrie Robinson MacKenna is up to no good. Rocky suspected it before he called Mack with the news that she's alive; now he's certain of it.

"Allison MacKenna is missing," Rocky says flatly, and Vic curses under his breath.

"She got to her before we could."

"Looks that way."

Rocky quickly explains the situation to Vic.

"Are you going to let Randi Weber know?"

"I'd better." He scrolls through the redial numbers on the phone, looking for the Glenhaven Park exchange he'd dialed earlier. Randi had given him both Mack's and Allison's phone numbers as soon as Rocky told her they might be in danger.

It's hard to believe that was just a matter of minutes ago.

At that point, Rocky had considered that this woman, Carrie—whose real name, or at least the name under which she'd been arrested, was Winona Carroll—might eventually pose some kind of vague threat to the MacKennas. Never in a million years did it occur to him that she'd follow them all the way to Nebraska.

But then, she was no stranger to that part of the country.

Like Allison MacKenna, Winona Carroll had grown up on the rural Great Plains. She was raised in east-central South Dakota, an only child who had been homeschooled, according to the records Vic had quickly unearthed.

Winona was an old Sioux name, and she had a bit of Native American blood in her veins, courtesy of her father. Born in Iowa on December 7, 1941—Pearl Harbor day—he'd been given an unusual first name that had also come from the Sioux: Macawi. But—incredibly—he was known as Mac.

"Her father was Mac," Vic pointed out, "and she married a Mack? That's a hell of a coincidence."

"There are no coincidences. Maybe she had some kind of Daddy complex, and that's why she married a guy who had the same name," Rocky suggested. "Where's the father now?"

"Good question."

As Rocky made his phone calls trying to track down the MacKennas, Vic had been looking for Winona Carroll's parents.

There's no trace of them after 1987—the same year their daughter was arrested for solicitation—one more "hell of a coincidence," as Vic put it.

Mac Carroll was a long-haul trucker who apparently lived—when he wasn't on the road, which was probably much of the time—on a section of land inherited from his own parents, and now listed as abandoned. A self-employed independent contractor, he filed tax returns until twenty-five years ago, and regularly paid his property taxes, too.

Winona's mother, Robin, was a decade younger than her husband and had been raised in Iowa foster homes in the fifties and sixties. She'd married right out of high school— not uncommon in that era or that part of the country—and Winona was born seven months later.

The Carrolls appear to have largely kept to themselves: no memberships in local organizations, no church affiliation, no volunteer work . . .

Perhaps no one to miss them when they vanished, Rocky thinks grimly as he tells Vic what MacKenna just told him—that Carrie claimed to have grown up in the witness protection program.

"And he bought that?"

Rocky shrugs. "When you love someone, your tendency is to believe what they tell you."

The Webers' telephone starts to ring on the other end of the line.

Randi answers immediately. "Did you get ahold of Allison? Because I just tried, and she didn't pick up. I was about to call Mack—"

"Don't. Allison is missing."

"Oh God. Oh no. What happened?"

He tells her—and this time, he includes what he learned about Mack's first wife.

"I never liked her," Randi says, "not from day one. Ben didn't, either. I knew right away that what she'd said about the witness protection program was bullshit. She wasn't even Mack's type. But when he met her he'd just broken up with someone and he was trying to date women who were the opposite of her."

"And what was she like?"

"Shallow gold digger. Her name was Chelsea. I didn't like her either, but—"

"Chelsea?"

"Right."

"Do you remember her last name, by any chance?"

"No. Maybe Ben does. He just left to drive our daughter someplace, but when he gets back I can—"

"Was it Kamm?"

"Kamm. Yes. I think that was it. Why?"

Because I just found the motive in the Leprechaun case.

Rocky shakes his head grimly, remembering what had been done to the lovely blond Chelsea Kamm.

Chapter Sixteen

"Oh, Al-lison!" The voice is singsong. "Time to wake uh-up!"

She's trying, but her eyelids are like boulders, and the voice is coming from so far away, down a dark tunnel . . .

"Allison!"

It's not Mack talking to her.

It's not a man's voice.

It's a female . . .

The girls?

No. They call her Mommy.

Mommy . . .

Her children . . .

Mack . . .

"Allison!"

She forces her eyes to open, and a flash of bright light instantly closes them again.

"You're awake! I saw you! Open your eyes. Here, I'll turn off the flashlight. I was just making sure you weren't dead. Yet."

The voice laughs.

Terror takes hold in Allison's gut, the kind of terror she's known before in her life; terror that can paralyze you if you let it take over.

Don't let it take over.

The only way out of this is to stay focused.

"Allison!"

She opens her eyes again. This time, to darkness. As her vision adjusts she can see a figure standing over her, silhouetted against a starlit sky.

"He was awake when I did this, and I wanted to make sure you were, too. Like father, like daughter."

"What . . . who . . . ?"

"Daddy! Our father! Did you forget again?"

"Forget?"

The shadow sighs and says, with exaggerated patience, "I'm Winona, your sister. We had the same father. And the same husband. Both named Mack. We're just alike, see? Like the song." She clears her throat and sings off key, something about a pair of matching bookends being different as night and day.

"I'm night," she tells Allison. "That's what Mack told me once, years ago, when we were dating."

Mack . . . she was dating Mack. Yes, because she's Carrie. Carrie is alive.

"Mack said I was night and he was day, and that was a good thing. He said we balanced each other out. Just like me and you. I'm night, and you're day."

Allison feels herself being jerked violently. She's moving. But she isn't in the car. She's outside, in the open air, being bumped over the ground. The movement jars her head and her cheek hits a hard surface. She's in some kind of metal cart, or a wheelbarrow.

The voice, Carrie's voice, continues its bizarre soliloquy.

"I like the way it all fits together, don't you? I like it when things fall neatly into place. I'm night, and you're day. I've never been a day person, Allison. I've always liked the night so much better. The dark—it hides things, you know? Messy things that are just out there in the daylight. How about you? Do you like the dark? I really hope so."

Another harsh laugh.

The bumping continues.

"Are you ready? We're almost there. No, never mind, don't tell me. I don't care if you're ready. I don't want to hear anything from you. I'll do all the talking. I know just what to say, too, when we get there. The perfect last words for you to hear."

Last words. Oh no. Oh please . . .

"They're not original—the words. I know you've heard them before. Or at least, you've read them."

She's going to kill me. I'm going to die. I'm never going to see Mack again, or my girls, or my baby, J.J. . . .

"You really thought he left you, didn't you? You thought he just took off one night and didn't come back."

Dragging her frantic thoughts away from her own family, Allison comprehends that she's talking . . .

About my father. About . . .

Our father?

"That must have been painful for you, Allison. In fact, I know it was. Because that's what he did to me. He left, and he didn't come back. Well—not for a long time. That's probably what would have happened to you, too, if he'd stayed alive. He probably would have started spending more and more time on the road, and he would have told you to stop calling him Daddy and he would have taken your doll and your dress and your books away and given them to some new little girl, some little sister you didn't even know you had."

She's huffing and puffing now as she talks.

"But I didn't give him the chance to do that again. You

should thank me. I took Daddy away from you before he left you himself. It's easier that way. Trust me. Okay, here we are."

The movement has stopped.

"Here they are, Allison. Are you listening? Here are the last words." Carrie—Winona—whoever she is—takes a deep breath. Then she says, "I can't do this anymore. I'm sorry. Good-bye."

The cart is tilting beneath Allison. She's falling forward. She reaches wildly, trying to grab on to something, but there's nothing, and she's falling through the air, falling into endless darkness, blacker than the night sky.

Mack stares bleakly out the window of his hotel room at the few lights that are still on at this hour in the unfamiliar city.

Allison is out there somewhere.

They're looking for her.

Not just here in Lincoln, Detective Manzillo told her when he called again a few minutes ago, but in Centerfield, too, and in South Dakota. That's where Carrie grew up, he said.

She wasn't in the witness protection program. That was a lie.

The whole thing was a lie. Her life—her death.

"Daddy?"

He turns to see Hudson standing behind him in her summer pajamas. She gestures at the wristwatch she wears everywhere, even to bed. "It's two-fourteen A.M."

"Is it?" he asks dully.

"What are you doing?"

"I'm just . . . looking out the window."

"Where's Mommy?"

Good question, Hudson. You always ask good questions. But this time, I don't have an answer for you.

Carrie slams the trunk of the car, locking the wheelbarrow inside, angry with herself.

It's done—but she made a mistake.

She doesn't make mistakes.

Yes, Allison is as good as dead and buried, deep down in the well, with the black widow spiders and the bones of their father and Winona's mother.

But now Carrie has to trek all the way back out there—a good mile from where the car is parked along the highway.

She reaches into the backseat, grabs the shovel she'd forgotten, and sets out to hoist the cover back over the well, and bury it forever.

LaJuanda hangs up the phone and looks at Rocky Manzillo and Vic Shattuck, seated across from her at the Formica-topped table in the small kitchen.

"They're going to order the DNA testing on those remains," she tells them. "It's going to take some time, and we already know what we're going to find out, but . . ."

"At least it'll bring some closure to Molly's family," Rocky says. "That's important."

She nods and reaches for the still-steaming coffee he'd poured for her after she arrived at his Bronx doorstep, courtesy of a yellow cab from JFK, half an hour ago.

Her flight hadn't beaten the thunderstorms to New York after all, thanks to air traffic. When she finally landed and called Rocky, she was stunned to hear what had transpired as she circled for several hours high over New York City. The air was turbulent at times, and for the first time in her life, LaJuanda was afraid on an airplane.

She couldn't help thinking of all the people who had been on the planes flown into the World Trade Center.

How dare she? LaJuanda kept thinking. How dare Carrie

take such a tragedy and use it to cover her tracks? What kind of person does that?

By the time LaJuanda was on the ground, she was convinced the woman was pure evil.

Then she called Rocky, and found out she was absolutely right about that.

Now, she shakes her head at him and Vic. "I just pray that Allison's family has a happier ending than just 'closure.'"

"So do I." Rocky looks at his watch, and LaJuanda knows what he's thinking. Vic, too.

They've all worked in law enforcement. They know the missing persons statistics only too well.

With every minute that ticks by, the odds of finding Allison alive are diminishing.

The pain in Allison's ribs and legs is excruciating, yet she forces herself to stay on her feet, to keep trying to claw her way out of the hole. When she's standing on her tiptoes, her fingertips just graze the ground around the edge of it. Not enough to get any kind of hold on it and pull herself up.

But the moment she allows herself to sink into the depths of the hole is the moment she faces her own death, and she's not about to do that.

Mack . . .

Hudson . . .

Maddy . . .

J.J. . . .

Her family needs her. And she's going to find her way back to them, one way or another. She's going home.

Home.

What she wouldn't give to be back in their house in Glenhaven Park right this very moment, back in the Happy House she'd been so tempted to leave behind after what had happened last fall.

That made about as much sense as . . .

As wanting to leave Nebraska behind forever?

She'd wasted all those years, over half a lifetime, trying to avoid coming back here, because she thought it meant coming back to the ugly past.

She was wrong.

The ugly past can follow you wherever you go if you let it.

I'm Winona, your sister. We had the same father.

I took Daddy away from you before he left you himself.

I can't do this anymore. I'm sorry. Good-bye.

Those were the words from the note her father left that day. But he didn't write it. She understands that now. Winona did. She wrote the note.

And her father—he didn't leave.

When Allison landed in the hole, she felt around in the dirt for something to stand on. Her fingers found . . .

Bones.

Even in the dark, she knew they were bones.

And she knew whose they were.

Oh, Daddy . . .

Hearing movement above her—footsteps—Allison goes absolutely still. Her instinct is to cry out for help, but she quells it. If it's her again—Winona—it's better to play dead.

The beam of a flashlight bounces across the top of the hole. Allison sees a fat, shiny black spider just inches from her outstretched left hand resting against the dirt wall. It's crawling toward her fingers. She fights the urge to flinch.

A shadow falls across the hole.

She sees the tip of Winona's shoe, right at the end.

She feels the spider crawling on her skin in the instant before she moves her hand. As she lunges upward to grab the shoe, a stinging pain pierces her ring finger.

Her hands, both of them, close around Winona's foot. She pulls as hard as she can, and she hears Winona scream.

"**A**re you sure?" Vic asks, pacing with the phone.

Sitting beside LaJuanda at the kitchen table, Rocky exchanges a glance with her.

"Okay, keep me posted," Vic says, and hangs up.

"What's going on?" Rocky asks.

"A woman fitting Carrie's description stopped for gas a few hours ago just off Interstate 29 in Elk Point, South Dakota. The security camera footage shows a female companion slumped in the front seat. It looked like she was asleep."

"I hope to God that's the case." LaJuanda crosses herself.

"If it's Allison, then she was taken across state lines. The FBI is involved now."

"I'll call Mack and tell him." Rocky reaches for his own phone.

"He already knows. He's on his way to South Dakota."

"**N**ooooooooo!"

She's falling.

Falling into the well.

Just like in the frightening visions that used to wake her up in the night all those years ago, when she was a little girl.

Winona's last thought, before she slams into the shadows and her spinal cord snaps, is that Daddy was wrong.

The dream catcher couldn't keep away the nightmares after all.

"**H**ow are you doing, Mr. MacKenna? Hanging in there?"

Mack shifts his gaze from the barren flatland and the milky morning sky beyond the window of the SUV to the dark-suited man behind the wheel.

His name is Agent DiCaprio.

"Like the actor," he told Mack when he introduced himself, adding, "but no relation."

"What?"

"To the actor. Leonardo DiCaprio. You know . . ."

Yeah, Mack knew. He and Allison had seen one of his movies, *Gangs of New York*, on their first date.

"I love everything Leonardo DiCaprio does," she sighed when it was over, and Mack found himself wishing she felt the same way about him. What would it be like, he wondered, to have Allison fall head over heels for him?

Soon enough, he knew.

And now . . .

Now that the FBI is involved in the search for his wife, Mack should probably feel better, but the news only made him grasp—as if he hadn't already—just how dire the circumstances are.

He thinks of their children, his and Allison's, probably waking up now back at the hotel. The agents who showed up at his door assured him that they'd be in good hands. Still, the decision was agonizing for Mack: stay with his kids, or go look for his wife?

"Mr. MacKenna?"

Mack blinks. "Sorry. Yes. I'm hanging in there. And you can call me Mack."

"Okay. Mack."

"How much further?"

They're headed to the land once owned by Carrie's father, Macawi Carroll.

He, too, was called Mac.

He wasn't in the mob, as Mack always suspected. He was a truck driver.

Just like Allison's father.

So many coincidences . . .

Too many.

"Just a few more miles," Agent DiCaprio tells him.

Mack nods and goes back to staring out the window.

A faint buzzing sound reaches Allison's ears.

Opening her eyes, she sees a bright light at the end of the long tunnel.

I'm dying, she thinks. *Just like they did.*

Winona's body is cold now, slumped beneath Allison, providing a layer of protection above the bones.

For a long time, she tried to stay on her feet. But the pain in her legs and her rib cage was gradually eclipsed by an agonizing sting in her left hand where the spider had bitten her. It got so bad that she finally did what she'd sworn she wouldn't do: she allowed herself to sink to the ground.

The last thing she remembers is feeling for Winona's pulse with her right hand, and finding none.

Now . . .

I'm dying.

The buzzing grows louder, and she blinks.

The bright light, she realizes, is the sun; the tunnel is the hole.

Daylight lies beyond it. As she gazes at it with longing, something crosses the patch of blue sky overhead.

An airplane, a small one, flying low.

That's Mack, looking for me.

It's a crazy thought. Mack wouldn't have the first idea where to find her.

Yet, he would try. If he knew she was lost, he would do whatever he could to find her.

"Mack," she whispers. "I'm here."

She manages to get to her feet, stretching, reaching up toward the light. It illuminates her left hand and she sees that it's bright red and horribly swollen, as though her wedding ring is trying to burn its way through her skin.

The plane is passing her by, and Allison is buried alive in this hole, with no way to let anyone know that she's here. They'll never see her.

"Help!" she cries hoarsely. "Help! Help! I'm down here!"

But of course, they'll never hear her, either. The plane is too far away, the roar of its engines drowning her weak, small voice.

If only Winona's flashlight had fallen into the hole with her, so that Allison could signal—

Wait a minute.

She lowers her right hand and reaches into her pocket.

No. It isn't there. It must have fallen—

No. She remembers now: she picked it up with her left hand after she dropped it on the floor of the car near the brake; probably put it into her left pocket.

Now her left hand is useless. Twisting, she strains to reach her right hand deep enough into the left pocket. Her fingertips graze something round and hard.

Trembling, triumphant, Allison pulls out the compact her girls had given her for Mother's Day.

She fumbles with it, one-handed. It snaps open at last and she thrusts it up, high over her head, tilting the mirror into the sunlight that lies just beyond her fingertips.

Back and forth, back and forth . . .

"**Y**eah, I hear you," Agent DiCaprio says into his mouthpiece. "Give me the coordinates."

"What is it? What's going on?"

Agent Fink, the woman who joined them at the end of the dirt road where they parked the SUV, motions for Mack to be quiet.

Ignoring her, he asks DiCaprio, "Did they find something?"

" . . . and latitude 44.369. Okay, got it." DiCaprio finishes writing on the small pad in his hand and looks up to meet Mack's questioning gaze. "I don't know."

"You don't know . . . what?"

"The flyover pilot thought he saw something."

It's getting harder to breathe now.

Tremors wrack Allison's body; every muscle is clenched with intense pain.

Lying in the bottom of the hole on top of Winona's corpse, she drifts in and out of consciousness, waking every time to the same tunnel of light—grateful every time to see that it's still just sunlight at the top of the hole.

She may be dying, but she isn't dead yet.

And the sun . . .

It's there. That's what counts, right? That's what she told herself months ago, when Maddy made that Mother's Day card for her.

You weather the inevitable storms, and you take the sunshine wherever you can get it—even if it's lying in the grass.

It seems so long ago, but it was just weeks, really. A few days, only, since they were back home. And just hours since she last saw them all.

Mack . . .

Hudson . . .

Maddy . . .

J.J. . . .

Home. I want to go home.

She thinks of her brother. Brett. She was so close to seeing him again, so close to apologizing for the distance she'd put between them, so close to forgiving him for what he'd said to her all those years ago, when she tried to find her father.

He's not Allen Taylor . . . that couldn't have been his real name.

He didn't want us to know his real name, or where he was born, or when.

All this time, Allison realizes now, some part of her had resented Brett for that. Some part of her had wanted to believe that it was a lie; that her father was who she always thought he was, despite what he'd done, despite the way he'd left.

Now she knows Brett was telling the truth—but she knows something else.

Her father hadn't left her by choice. His love had been real. Maybe he was capable of terrible things—maybe he'd done terrible things to Winona, and to Mom, and to Allison herself—but he hadn't walked out on her in the middle of the night without looking back.

For some reason, despite the horror of it all, everything that had happened—that makes a difference.

Why do people lie?

To protect themselves, or someone else . . .

And because they have something to hide. Something dark, or damaging, or ugly.

Another life.

Another wife.

Another daughter.

Now her broken body cradles Allison's as she struggles to draw another breath. Just one more.

Please.

I don't want to die.

I don't want to leave them.

Please . . .

What will they do without me? My girls . . . they need me.

But they'll go on, of course. Just as Allison did when she lost her own mother.

Your daughters are survivors, Mrs. MacKenna, Dr. Rogel's voice echoes in her head.

Then she hears another voice.

Faint, but real.

The sound of Mack's voice, calling her name.

"Allison!"

She fights for another breath, fights to find her voice.

She's so weak . . .

But you can do it.

It comes back to her now: the other thing Dr. Rogel said that day, about the girls.

They're blessed with extraordinary strength—as is their mother.

Yes. You're strong.

Your strength is strength, remember?

Mustering every bit of it, she drags air into her lungs, finds her voice at last. "Mack!"

She hears a shout.

Running footsteps.

Then, incredibly, she sees her husband's face, haloed in golden sunlight.

Epilogue

"**H**appy birthday to you . . . Happy birthday, to you . . . Happy birthday, dear . . ."

The chorus of voices, singing in unison until now, diverge.

Some sang "Allison," some sang "Mommy," some sang "Aunt Allison," and one—J.J., on her lap—just babbles.

It's all music to her ears.

" . . . Happy birthday to you!"

Smiling, she leans forward to blow out the thirty-six candles on the triple-layer chocolate cake her sister-in-law made for her.

"But Mommy's only turning thirty-five, Aunt Cindy," eagle-eyed Hudson protested as they lit the candles.

"I know, but we always put one candle for every year, and an extra one for good luck."

"I'll take all the extra luck I can get," Allison told her.

"I think you're the luckiest person I've ever known," her brother said, sitting next to her at the big redwood picnic table he'd built with his own hands. "But you better watch out, because tomorrow is Friday the thirteenth."

Thinking of Randi and the big party she's throwing tomorrow, Allison grinned. Her friend has called her every day for the past week and a half, just making sure she's okay.

"She must really love you," Cindy-Lou said after the latest call.

Allison smiled. "She really does."

A lot of people do.

"Make a wish, Mommy."

She closes her eyes, makes a wish, and blows out the candles in one big breath.

"What was the wish?" Maddy asks, as everyone claps.

"She can't tell you," Hudson says, "or it won't come true."

"Guess what? It already did," Allison informs her daughters.

Gazing at the people gathered around the table, with Mack's arm resting on her shoulders, she really does feel like the luckiest person in the world.

True to the promise she made to herself years ago, when she was in her early twenties and thinking about what she wanted out of life, she's never taken her husband and daughters and son for granted. Back then, she swore that if she were ever fortunate enough to have a family, *I'll be there for them, and I'll hold on tight, no matter what, because nothing in this world is more precious.*

What she failed to realize at the time was that *all* family ties are precious.

But she figured it out the moment her big brother Brett walked into her hospital room in Sioux Falls, where she'd been taken to recuperate from her injuries and the poisonous spider bite.

The hefty blond man in the doorway didn't look anything like the boy who once ran along behind her bike, and let go.

But he was her big brother. She knew it the moment she saw the relief in his eyes. He cared about her. And so did the pleasantly plump woman who came up behind him, holding a vaseful of bright yellow blooms she'd cut from her garden.

Sunflowers. They couldn't have been more fitting.

There are more in a red tin milk pitcher sitting on the blue and white checked tablecloth, along with the remains of a decadent, deep-fried dinner doused in creamy country gravy.

The table is perched not on a deck or a fancy flagstone or brick patio, like the outdoor dining furniture tends to be back home, but on the wide stretch of lawn behind the big white farmhouse. The warm air is sweetly scented with freshly mown grass, fireflies are flitting about, cicadas have taken up a steady chatter in the fields, and a pale slice of waning moon has appeared in the wide open purple-blue sky.

"Samantha," Cindy-Lou says, "will you please run into the kitchen and get the ice cream I made to go along with the cake?"

"I'll help!" Hudson is on her feet immediately.

"Me too!" Maddy follows suit, and the girls trail their pretty teenage cousin into the house. They've been doing that from the moment they met her, and good-natured Samantha seems amused by it.

The screen door squeaks and bangs, a homey sound that made Allison jump every time she heard it for the first few days. She's used to it now. She likes it.

"You made homemade ice cream, Mom?" Jeff, a quiet boy with his father's gentle disposition, lights up.

"Remember, we have company, so you can't eat it all yourself like last time," Brett tells his son, and Jeff reddens.

Allison smiles, bouncing J.J. on her lap and imagining a

time when he'll tower over her the way Jeff does over Cindy-Lou.

She feels Mack's arm tighten around her shoulders and she looks up to see him smiling. He might be thinking the same thing. Or he might still be marveling at how very lucky Allison is.

It's been more than a week now since the ordeal she survived at the hands of Winona, the half sister she'd never known existed—the wife Mack had thought was dead. With the help of Rocky Manzillo back East, they had pieced together the tragic details of her life, and the path she'd followed into Mack's life—and Allison's.

Strangely, despite all the evidence that her father was a selfish scoundrel living a double life, Allison feels more capable of forgiving him now than she ever did before.

"It's because you have closure," Brett told her when she mentioned it one day, as they went walking over his property at sunset. "You were such a daddy's girl when you were a kid. He took good care of you when he was around. I know why it broke your heart when he left."

Daddy really hadn't left Allison, though. Not by choice.

But he *had* left Winona. Had the emotional pain she'd endured turned her into a monster? Or was she just wired differently than most people—capable, as she was, of unthinkable, rage-driven acts?

It's going to take some getting used to—this new version of an already troubled family history.

But Allison is willing to work on accepting what is, and letting go of what can never be. She's ready to lay the ghosts to rest and start looking ahead from now on.

Tomorrow morning, she and Mack and the kids will bid farewell to this peaceful farm where they've spent more than a week of vacation that was, if not entirely restful, then at least healing.

Allison is sorry to say good-bye, but they've already made

plans to visit again next summer. Anyway, it's time to set out for home.

To think she was feeling unfulfilled, just weeks ago, with her life there. Questioning her choices, bored and restless, what-if-ing her days away.

The screen door squeaks opens again and bangs shut.

I'm going to miss that sound.

"Mommy! Aunt Cindy-Lou made ice cream!" Hudson announces.

"And cones, too!" Maddy puts in.

"You are really quite something, Aunt Cindy-Lou," Allison tells her sister-in-law.

"Can we make ice cream when we go back home?" Hudson asks.

"And cones?"

"Sure," Allison tells her girls.

"Promise?"

"Promise."

Mack looks at her. "Better not make promises you can't keep."

"I never do."

From where she sits, looking at the summer days ahead, she can't think of anything better than licking homemade ice cream cones in the bright sunshine with her children.

Mack leans closer to her as Cindy-Lou and Samantha dish up dessert for everyone. "Are you ready to go home, Allie?"

"Definitely."

"We've got a long road ahead of us."

"Not as long as the one we took to get here."

Resting her cheek on her husband's shoulder, Allison smiles contentedly, watching the fireflies dance like stars across the night sky.

And now a sneak peek at

THE GOOD SISTER,

the first in Wendy Corsi Staub's

chilling new series

Coming in 2013

from HarperCollins Publishers

That it had all been a lie shouldn't come as any surprise, really.

And yet, the truth—a terrible, indisputable truth that unfolds line by blue ballpoint line, filling the pages of the black marble notebook—is somehow astonishing.

How did you never suspect it back then?

Or, at least, in the years since?

Looking back at the childhood decade spent in this house—an ornate, faded Second Empire Victorian mansion in one of the oldest neighborhoods in the city—it's so easy to see how it might have happened this way.

How it *did* happen this way.

There is no mistaking the evidence. No mistaking the distinct handwriting: a cramped, backhand scrawl so drastically different from the loopy, oversized penmanship so typical of other girls that age.

Different . . .

Of course it was different.

She was different from the other girls; tragically, dangerously different.

I remember so well.

I remember her, remember so many things about her: both how she lived and how she—

Footsteps approach, tapping up the wooden stairway to this cupola perched high above the third story mansard roofline, topped by wrought-iron cresting that prongs the sky like a king's squared-off crown.

"*Hellooo-oo.* Are you still up there?" calls Sandra Lutz, the Realtor.

"Yes." *Where else would I be? Do you think I jumped out the window while you were gone?*

Sandra had excused herself ten minutes ago, finally answering her cell phone. It had buzzed incessantly with incoming calls and texts as their footsteps echoed in one empty room after another on this final walk-through before the listing goes up tomorrow.

The entire contents of the house are now in storage—with the exception of the rocking chair where Mother had passed away and gone undiscovered for weeks.

"I don't think that chair is something you'd want to keep," Sandra said in one of their many long-distance telephone conversations when the storage arrangements were being made.

Of course not. The corpse would have been crawling with maggots and oozing bodily fluids, staining the brocade upholstery and permeating it with the terrible stench of death.

Presumably, someone—surely not the lovely Sandra—tossed the desecrated rocking chair into a Dumpster, while everything else was transported to the storage facility somewhere in the suburbs.

As for Mother herself . . .

I'd just as soon have had someone toss her into a Dumpster, too.

But of course, the proper thing to do was arrange, also long distance, for a cremation.

"We have a number of packages," the mortician said over the phone, "depending on how you want to set up visitation hours and—"

"No visitation. I live almost five hundred miles away, and I can't get up there just yet, and . . . there's no one else."

Pause. "There are no other family and friends here in the Buffalo area who might want to—?"

"*No one else.*"

"All right, then." He went over the details, mentioning that there would be an additional seventy-five-dollar charge for shipment of the ashes.

"Can you just hold on to—" *It? Her?* What was the proper terminology, aside from the profane terms so often used to refer to Mother—though never to her face—back when she was alive?

"The remains?" the undertaker supplied delicately.

"Yes . . . can you hold on to the remains until I can be there in person?"

"When would that be?"

"Sometime this summer. I'm selling the house, so I'll be coming up there to make the final arrangements for that."

The undertaker dutifully provided instructions on how to go about retrieving what was left of the dearly departed when the time came.

The time is now here, but of course there will be no trip to the mortuary. Mother's ashes can sit on a dusty shelf there for all eternity.

As for the contents of this old house . . .

"I'm sure you won't want to go through it all just yet," Sandra Lutz said earlier, handing over the rental agreement and a set of keys to the storage unit. "Not when the loss is so fresh. But empty houses are much more appealing to buyers, and this way, at least, we can get the home on the market."

Yes. The sooner this old place is sold, the better. As for the padlocked compartment filled with a lifetime of family furniture and mementos . . .

Good riddance to all of it.

Well . . . not quite *all*.

Right before she answered her phone, Sandra had taken the Ziploc bag from her leather Dooney & Bourke purse.

"These are some odds and ends I found after the moving company and cleaning service had finished in here. I didn't want to just throw anything away, so . . . here you go."

The bag contained just a few small items. A stray key that had been hanging on a nail just inside the basement door, most likely fitting the lock on a long-gone trunk or tool chest. A dusty Mass card from a forgotten cousin's funeral, found tucked behind a cast-iron radiator in the front parlor. A tarnished, bent silver fork that had been wedged in the space behind the silverware drawer.

And then there was . . .

This.

The notebook, with a string of black rosary beads wrapped around it twice, as if to seal it closed.

According to Sandra Lutz, the notebook, unlike the other contents of the bag, hadn't been accidentally overlooked. It was deliberately hidden in one of the old home's many concealed nooks.

"I stumbled across it last night when I stopped by to double-check the square footage of the master bedroom," she reported. "I noticed that there was a discrepancy between the measurements I took a few weeks ago and the old listing from the last time the house sold, back in the late seventies."

"What kind of discrepancy?"

"The room was two feet longer back then. Sure enough, that's exactly the depth of the secret compartment I found behind a false wall by the bay window. I was wondering whether you even knew it was there, because—"

"The house is full of secret compartments. My father said that it was probably used to hide slaves on the Underground Railroad."

"That's the rumor about a lot of houses in this neighborhood because we're just a stone's throw from the Canadian border, and there was Underground Railroad activity in western New York. But I don't think this would have been an actual safe house."

"Why not?"

"Because historical documentation shows that there just weren't very many of them in Buffalo. Slavery was abolished in New York State years before the Civil War started, so escaped slaves who made it into the city either stayed and lived openly, or they were taken from rural safe houses into the city and directly across the border crossing at Squaw Island."

She added quickly, as if to soothe any hard feelings from her bombshell that the home hadn't served some noble historic cause, "I've always admired this house though, and wondered what it looked like inside. Did I mention that this is my old stomping grounds? I grew up just a few blocks over, and I just moved back to the neighborhood."

Yes, Sandra had mentioned that over the phone several times, and in e-mail, too. She has no qualms about sharing that she's a recent divorcee living alone for the first time in her life.

"I bought a fabulous Arts and Crafts home on Wayside Avenue, just down the street from Sacred Sisters High School," she prattled on, as if she were revealing the information for the first time, but quickly added, "Not that I went to Sisters, even though it was right in the neighborhood; I went to Nardin instead."

Ah, Nardin Academy: the most upscale all-girls Catholic high school in western New York. No surprise there.

"Anyway, when I saw that house on Wayside come on the market, I snatched it up. Of course, it isn't nearly as big or as old as this one, and it doesn't have any secret compartments, but it does have all the original—"

"The notebook—what were you saying about finding the notebook?"

"Oh. Sorry. I guess I tend to ramble."

No kidding.

If there's anything I can't stand, it's a motormouth.

Sandra shrugged. "I was just going to point out that the secret compartment where I found it was different."

"Different how?"

That was when Sandra's phone rang. She checked the caller ID, said, "Excuse me, but I have to take this one," and disappeared down the steps.

Now she's back.

And now that I've seen what's in that notebook, I really need to know what she meant about "different."

"Sorry about that," Sandra says. "I thought that call was only going to take a minute, but I had to go check some paperwork I left in the car. Oh, it's warm up here, isn't it?"

"Yes."

The windows are open, but there's not a breath of cross breeze to diminish the greenhouse effect created by four walls of glass on a ninety-degree July afternoon.

Sandra fans herself with a manila folder, though she doesn't appear the least bit flushed or winded from the climb.

A perfumed, expertly made-up fortysomething blonde wearing a trim black suit, hose, and high-heeled pumps, she's probably never broken a sweat outside the gym or had a bad hair day in her life.

When she introduced herself, she pronounced her first name as if it rhymed with Rhonda. Most locals would say it Say-and-ra, the western New York accent stretching it out to three syllables with a couple of distinct flat *a*'s.

"I'm *Sahndra*," she said as she stepped out of her silver Mercedes in the driveway to shake hands. Heat shimmered off the blacktop, yet her bony fingers were icy, with a firm, businesslike grip. "It's so nice to finally meet you in person. How was the drive in last night?"

"The drive?" *Oh, so we're doing the small talk thing. Let's get it over with.* "It was fine."

"Did you come alone or bring your family?"

Is she fishing for information or did I tell her I have a family?

Sandra had asked so many questions through their two months of long distance phone calls and e-mails, it was difficult to keep track of what she'd been told—truth, and lies.

"I came alone."

"It's about nine hours, isn't it, from Huntington Station?"

Huntington Station. Not Long Island, not Nassau County, not even just Huntington, but Huntington Station. So damned specific.

"I went to college in the Bronx, at Fordham," she mentioned, "and my boyfriend back then was from Levittown. A nice Irish boy—Patrick Donnelly . . . ?"

She actually paused, as if to ask, *Do you know him?*

Question met with a cursory head shake, she went on, "Well, anyway, I know exactly where you live."

She has the address, of course. She's been FedExing paperwork for a couple of months now.

Sandra went on to inquire about the suburban Buffalo hotel she had recommended for this weekend stay, referring to it not as the hotel or the Marriott, but the Marriott Courtyard Inn.

After being assured that the room was satisfactory, she said, "Be sure and tell the front desk manager, if you see her, that I referred you. Her name is Lena."

"Is she a friend of yours?"

"Oh, I've never met her, but she's a dear friend of a sister of a client."

And so it became clear early on that Sandra Lutz is the kind of woman who not only tends to ramble on and make dreary small talk, but she also remembers the most mundane details. That characteristic probably serves her very well when it comes to her line of work, but otherwise . . .

Someone really should warn her that sometimes it's not a good idea to pay so much attention to other people's lives.

Sometimes, people like—people *need*—to maintain more of a sense of privacy.

"I always try not to take cell phone calls when I'm with a client," Sandra says breezily now, pocketing her cell phone, "but that was an accepted offer for a house that's only been on the market for a week. I thought it would be a hard sell, but it looks like this is my client's lucky day. And mine, too. Let's hope all this good fortune rubs off on you. Now that we're finished looking the place over, we can—"

"Wait. When you said the compartment was different, what, exactly, did you mean?"

Sandra's bright blue eyes seem startled at, then confused by, the abrupt question. "Pardon?"

"When you found the *notebook* behind the *wall*"— *Careful, now. Calm down. Don't let her see how important this is to you*—"you said the compartment was different."

"Oh, that's right. I meant that it wasn't original to the house. Here, let's go downstairs and I'll show you what I mean."

She leads the way down the steep flight to a noticeably cooler, narrow corridor lined with plain whitewashed walls and closed doors. Behind them are a bathroom with ancient fixtures, a couple of small bedrooms that once housed nineteenth-century servants, and some large storage closets that are nearly the same size as the bedrooms, all tucked above the eaves with pairs of tall, arched dormers poking through the slate mansard roof.

The third floor hasn't been used in decades, perhaps not even when the previous owners, a childless couple, lived here. The first two floors of the house were plenty large enough for two; large enough even for four.

And then there were three . . .

No. Don't think about that.

Just find out where the notebook was hidden, and how much Sandra Lutz knows about what's written in it.

Down they go, descending another steep flight to the second floor.

Here, the hallway is much wider than the one above, with high ceilings, crown moldings, and broad windowed nooks on either end. A dark green floral runner stretches along the hardwood floor and the wallpapered walls are studded with elaborate sconces that were, like most light fixtures throughout the house, converted from gas to electricity after the turn of the last century.

"The same thing was probably done in my house," Sandra comments as they walk along the hall, "but I'd love to go back to gaslights. Of course, the inspector who looked at it before I got the mortgage approval nearly had a heart attack when I mentioned that. He said the place is a firetrap as it is. Old wiring, you know—the whole thing needs to be upgraded. It's the same in this house, I'm sure."

"I'm sure."

The mid-segment of the hall opens up with an elaborately carved wooden railing along one side. This is the balcony of the grand staircase—that's what Sandra likes to call it, anyway—that leads down to the entrance hall. Or foyer, pronounced *foy-yay* by Sandra.

Realtors, apparently, like to embellish.

The master bedroom at the far end of the hallway isn't large by today's standards. And it isn't a suite by any stretch of the imagination, lacking a private bath, dressing room, or walk-in closet.

But that, of course, is what Sandra Lutz calls it as she opens the door for the second time today: *the master suite.*

The room does look bigger and brighter than it did years ago, when it was filled with a suite of dark, heavy furniture and long draperies shielding the windows. Now bright summer sunlight floods the room, dappled by the leafy branches of a towering maple in the front yard.

"Here." Sandra walks over to the far end of the room and

indicates decorative paneling on the lower wall adjacent to the bay window. "This is what I was talking about. See how this wainscot doesn't match the rest of the house? Everywhere else, it's more formal, with raised panels, curved moldings, beaded scrolls. But this is a recessed panel—Mission style, not Victorian. Much more modern. The wood is thinner."

She's right. It is.

"And this"—she knocks on the maroon brocade wallpaper above it, exactly the same pattern but noticeably less faded than it is elsewhere in the room—"isn't plaster like the other walls in the house. It's drywall. Did you know that?"

"No."

There wasn't even wainscoting on that end of the room twenty years ago. Obviously, someone—Father?—rebuilt the wall and added the wainscoting, then repapered it, undoubtedly using one of the matching rolls stored years ago on a shelf in the dirt-floored basement.

"There's a spot along here . . ." Sandra reaches toward the panels, running her fingertips along the molding of the one in the middle. She presses down, and it swings open. "There. There it is. See?"

Dust particles from the gaping dark hole behind the panel dance like glitter into sunbeams falling through the bay windows.

"Like I said, it's about two feet deep. I wish I had a flashlight so that I could show you, but . . . see the floor in there? It's refinished, exactly like this."

She points to the hardwoods beneath their feet. "In the rest of the house, the hidden compartments have rough, unfinished wood. So obviously, this cubby space was added in recent years—it must have been while your family owned the house, because as I said, the room was two feet longer when it was listed by the previous owner."

"When you opened the panel, was there . . . was this all that was inside?"

"The notebook?" Sandra nods. "That was it. It was just sitting on the floor in there, wrapped in the rosary. I gave it to you just the way I found it. I figured it might be some kind of diary or maybe a prayer journal . . . ?"

The question hangs like the dust particles in the air between them and then falls away unanswered.

Predictably, Sandra waits only a few seconds before filling the awkward pause. "I just love old houses. So much character. So many secrets."

Sandra, you have no idea. Absolutely no idea.

"Is there anything else you wanted to ask about this or . . . anything?"

"No. Thank you for showing me."

"You're welcome. Should I . . . ?" She gestures at the wainscot panel.

"Please."

Sandra pushes the panel back into place, and the hidden compartment is obscured—but not forgotten, by any means.

Does the fact that the Realtor speculated whether the notebook is a diary or prayer journal mean she really didn't remove the rosary beads and read it when she found it?

Or is she trying to cover up the fact that she did?

Either way . . .

I can't take any chances. Sorry, Sandra. You know where I live . . . now it's my turn to find out where you live.

That shouldn't be hard.

An online search of recent real estate transactions on Wayside Avenue should be sufficient.

How ironic that Sandra Lutz had brought up Sacred Sisters' proximity to her new house before the contents of the notebook had been revealed. In that moment, the mention of Sacred Sisters had elicited nothing more than a vaguely unpleasant memory of an imposing neighborhood landmark.

Now, however . . .

Now that I know what happened there . . .

The mere thought of the old school brings a shudder, clenched fists, and a resolve for vengeance. That Sandra Lutz lives nearby seems to make her, by some twisted logic, an accessory to a crime that must not go unpunished any longer.

They descend the so-called grand staircase to the first floor.

"Shall we go out the front door or the back?"

"Front."

It's closer, and the need to get out of this old house, with its dark, unsettling secrets and lies, is growing more urgent.

"I thought you might like to take a last look around before—"

"No, thank you."

"All right, front door it is. I never really use it at my own house," Sandra confides as she turns a key sticking out of the double-cylinder deadbolt and opens one of the glass-windowed double doors. "I have a detached garage and the back door is closer to it, so that's how I come and go."

Oh, for God's sake, who cares?

"You know, your mother just had these locks installed about a year ago. She was afraid to be alone at night after your father passed away."

Mother? Afraid to be alone?

Mother, afraid of anything at all—other than the wrath of God or Satan?

I don't think so.

"What makes you assume that?"

"Not an assumption," Sandra says defensively, stepping out onto the stoop and holding the door open. "Bob Witkowski told me that's what she said."

"*Who?*"

"Bob Witkowski. You know Al Witkowski, the mover?

He lives right around the corner now, on Redbud Street, in an apartment above the dry cleaner's. His wife just left him. Anyway, Bob is his brother. He's a locksmith. I had him install these same double-cylinder deadbolts in my house when I first moved in, because I have windows in my front door, too. You can't be too careful when you're a woman living alone—I'm sure your mother knew that."

"Yes." The wheels are turning, turning, turning . . .

Stomach churning, churning, churning at the memory of Mother.

Mother, who constantly quoted the Ten Commandments, then broke the eighth with a lie so mighty that surely she'd lived out the rest of her days terrified by the prospect of burning in hell for all eternity.

"A lock like this is ideal for an old house with original glass-paned doors, because the only way to open it, even from the inside, is with a key," Sandra is saying as she closes the door behind them and inserts the same key into the outside lock. "No one can just break the window on the door and reach inside to open it. Some people leave the key right in the lock so they can get out quickly in an emergency, but that defeats the purpose, don't you think? I keep my own keys right up above my doors, sitting on the little ledges of molding. It would only take me an extra second to grab the key and get out if there was a fire."

"Mmm hmm."

"Of course, now that it's summer, I keep my windows open anyway, so I guess that fancy lock doesn't do much for me, does it? I really should at least fix the broken screen in the mudroom. Anyone could push through it and hop in."

It's practically an invitation.

Stupid, stupid woman.

Sandra gives a little chuckle. "Good thing this is still such a safe neighborhood, right?"

"Absolutely."

Yes, and thanks to Sandra's incessant babble, a plan has taken shape.

A plan that, if one were inclined to fret about breaking the Ten Commandments—*which I most certainly am not*—blatantly violates the fifth.

Thou Shalt Not Kill.

Oh, but I shall.

It won't be the first time.

And it definitely won't be the last.

If you missed

Wendy Corsi Staub's

first two books in this thrilling series,

take a look at

NIGHTWATCHER

and

SLEEPWALKER

On sale now!

An Excerpt from

Nightwatcher

Case closed.

Vic Shattuck clicks the mouse, and the Southside Strangler file—the one that forced him to spend the better part of August in the rainy Midwest, tracking a serial killer—disappears from the screen.

If only it were that easy to make it all go away in real life.

"If you let it, this stuff will eat you up inside like cancer," Vic's FBI colleague Dave Gudlaug told him early in his career, and he was right.

Now Dave, who a few years ago reached the bureau's mandatory retirement age, spends his time traveling with his wife. He claims he doesn't miss the work.

"Believe me, you'll be ready to put it all behind you, too, when the time comes," he promised Vic.

Maybe, but with his own retirement seven years away, Vic is in no hurry to move on. Sure, it might be nice to spend uninterrupted days and nights with Kitty, but somehow, he suspects that he'll never be truly free of the cases he's handled—not even those that are solved. For now, as a profiler with the Behavioral Science Unit, he can at least do his part to rid the world of violent offenders.

"You're still here, Shattuck?"

He looks up to see Special Agent Annabelle Wyatt. With her long legs, almond-shaped dark eyes, and flawless ebony skin, she looks like a supermodel—and acts like one of the guys.

Not in a let's-hang-out-and-have-a-few-laughs way; in a let's-cut-the-bullshit-and-get-down-to-business way.

She briskly hands Vic a folder. "Take a look at this and let me know what you think."

"Now?"

She clears her throat. "It's not urgent, but . . ."

Yeah, right. With Annabelle, everything is urgent.

"Unless you were leaving . . ." She pauses, obviously waiting for him to tell her that he'll take care of it before he goes.

"I was."

Without even glancing at the file, Vic puts it on top of his in-box. The day's been long enough and he's more than ready to head home.

Kitty is out at her book club tonight, but that's okay with him. She called earlier to say she was leaving a macaroni and cheese casserole in the oven. The homemade kind, with melted cheddar and buttery breadcrumb topping.

Better yet, both his favorite hometown teams—the New York Yankees and the New York Giants—are playing tonight. Vic can hardly wait to hit the couch with a fork in one hand and the TV remote control in the other.

"All right, then." Annabelle turns to leave, then turns back. "Oh, I heard about Chicago. Nice work. You got him."

"You mean *her*."

Annabelle shrugs. "How about *it*?"

"*It*. Yeah, that works."

Over the course of Vic's career, he hasn't seen many true

cases of MPD—multiple personality disorder—but this was one of them.

The elusive Southside Strangler turned out to be a woman named Edie . . . who happened to live inside a suburban single dad named Calvin Granger.

Last June, Granger had helplessly watched his young daughter drown in a fierce Lake Michigan undertow. Unable to swim, he was incapable of saving her.

Weeks later, mired in frustration and anguish and the brunt of his grieving ex-wife's fury, he picked up a hooker. That was not unusual behavior for him. What happened after that *was*.

The woman's nude, mutilated body was found just after dawn in Washington Park, electrical cable wrapped around her neck. A few days later, another corpse turned up in the park. And then a third.

Streetwalking and violent crime go hand in hand; the Southside's slain hookers were, sadly, business as usual for the jaded cops assigned to that particular case.

For urban reporters, as well. Chicago was in the midst of a series of flash floods this summer; the historic weather eclipsed the coverage of the Southside Strangler in the local press. That, in retrospect, was probably a very good thing. The media spotlight tends to feed a killer's ego—and his bloodlust.

Only when the Strangler claimed a fourth victim—an upper-middle-class mother of three living a respectable lifestyle—did the case become front-page news. That was when the cops called in the FBI.

For Vic, every lost life carries equal weight. His heart went out to the distraught parents he met in Chicago, parents who lost their daughters twice: first to drugs and the streets, and ultimately to the monster who murdered them.

The monster, like most killers, had once been a victim himself.

It was a textbook case: Granger had been severely abused—essentially tortured—as a child. The MPD was, in essence, a coping mechanism. As an adult, he suffered occasional, inexplicable episodes of amnesia, particularly during times of overwhelming stress.

He genuinely seemed to have no memory of anything "he" had said or done while Edie or one of the other, nonviolent alters—alternative personalities—were in control of him.

"By the way," Annabelle cuts into Vic's thoughts, "I hear birthday wishes are in order."

Surprised, he tells her, "Actually, it was last month— while I was in Chicago."

"Ah, so your party was belated, then."

His party. This past Saturday night, Kitty surprised him by assembling over two dozen guests—family, friends, colleagues—at his favorite restaurant near Dupont Circle.

Feeling a little guilty that Annabelle wasn't invited, he informs her, "I wouldn't call it a *party*. It was more like . . . it was just dinner, really. My wife planned it."

But then, even if Vic himself had been in charge of the guest list, Supervisory Special Agent Wyatt would not have been on it.

Some of his colleagues are also personal friends. She isn't one of them.

It's not that he has anything against no-nonsense women. Hell, he married one.

And he respects Annabelle just as much as—or maybe even more than—just about anyone else here. He just doesn't necessarily *like* her much—and he suspects the feeling is mutual.

"I hear that it was an enjoyable evening," she tells him with a crisp nod, and he wonders if she's wistful. She doesn't sound it—or look it. But for the first time, it occurs to Vic that her apparent social isolation might not always be by choice.

He shifts his weight in his chair. "It's my wife's thing, really. Kitty's big on celebrations. She'll go all out for any occasion. Years ago, she threw a party when she potty trained the twins."

As soon as the words are out of his mouth, he wants to take them back—and not just because mere seconds ago he was insisting that Saturday night was *not* a party. Annabelle isn't the kind of person with whom you discuss children, much less potty training them. She doesn't have a family, but if she did, Vic is certain she'd keep the details—particularly the bathroom details—to herself.

Well, too bad. I'm a family man.

After Annabelle bids him a stiff good night and disappears down the corridor, Vic shifts his gaze to the framed photos on his desk. One is of him and Kitty on their twenty-fifth wedding anniversary last year; the other, more recent, shows Vic with all four of the kids at the high school graduation last June of his twin daughters.

The girls left for college a few weeks ago. He and Kitty are empty-nesters now—well, Kitty pretty much rules the roost, as she likes to say, since Vic is gone so often.

"So which is it—a nest or a roost?" he asked her the other day, to which she dryly replied, "Neither. It's a coop, and you've been trying to fly it for years, but you just keep right on finding your way back, don't you."

She was teasing, of course. No one supports Vic's career as wholeheartedly as Kitty does, no matter how many nights it's taken him away from home over the years. It was her idea in the first place that he put aside his planned career as a psychiatrist in favor of the FBI.

All because of a series of murders that terrorized New York thirty years ago, and captivated a young local college psych major.

"Back when I first met him, Vic was obsessed with un-solved murders," Kitty announced on Saturday night when she stood up to toast him at his birthday dinner, "and since then, he's done an incredible job solving hundreds of them."

True—with one notable exception.

Years ago, the New York killings stopped abruptly. Vic would like to think it's because the person who committed them is no longer on this earth.

If by chance he is, then he's almost certainly been sidelined by illness or incarceration for some unrelated crime.

After all, while there are exceptions to every rule, most serial killers don't just stop. Everything Vic has learned over the years about their habits indicates that once something triggers a person to cross the fine line that divides disturbed human beings from cunning predators, he's compelled to keep feeding his dark fantasies until, God willing, something—or someone—stops him.

In a perfect world, Vic is that someone.

But then, a perfect world wouldn't be full of disturbed people who are, at any given moment, teetering on the brink of reality.

Typically, all it takes is a single life stressor to push one over the edge. It can be any devastating event, really—a car accident, job loss, bankruptcy, a terminal diagnosis, a child's drowning . . .

Stressors like those can create considerable challenges for a mentally healthy person. But when fate inflicts that kind of pressure on someone who's already dangerously unbalanced . . . well, that's how killers are born.

Though Vic has encountered more than one homicidal maniac whose spree began with a wife's infidelity, the triggering crisis doesn't necessarily have to hit close to home. Even a natural disaster can be prime breeding ground.

A few years ago in Los Angeles, a seemingly ordinary man—a fine, upstanding Boy Scout leader—went off the deep end after the Northridge earthquake leveled his apartment building. Voices in his head told him to kill three strangers in the aftermath, telling him they each, in turn, were responsible for the destruction of his home.

Seemingly ordinary. Ah, you just never know. That's what makes murderers—particularly serial murderers—so hard to catch. They aren't always troubled loners; sometimes they're hiding in plain sight: regular people, married with children, holding steady jobs . . .

And sometimes, they're suffering from a mental disorder that plenty of people—including some in the mental health profession—don't believe actually exists.

Before Vic left Chicago, as he was conducting a jailhouse interview with Calvin Granger, Edie took over Calvin's body.

The transition occurred without warning, right before Vic's incredulous eyes. Everything about the man changed— not just his demeanor, but his physical appearance and his voice. A doctor was called in, and attested that even biological characteristics like heart rate and vision had been altered. Calvin could see twenty-twenty. Edie was terribly nearsighted. Stunning.

It wasn't that Calvin *believed* he was an entirely different person, a woman named Edie—he *was* Edie. Calvin had disappeared into some netherworld, and when he returned, he had no inkling of what had just happened, or even that time had gone by.

The experience would have convinced even a die-hard skeptic, and it chilled Vic to the bone.

Case closed, yes—but this one is going to give him nightmares for a long time to come.

Vic tidies his desk and finds himself thinking fondly of the old days at the bureau—and a colleague who was Annabelle Wyatt's polar opposite.

John O'Neill became an agent around the same time Vic did. Their career paths, however, took them in different directions: Vic settled in with the BSU, while O'Neill went from Quantico to Chicago and back, then on to New York, where he eventually became chief of the counterterrorism unit. Unfortunately, his career with the bureau ended abruptly a few weeks ago amid a cloud of controversy following the theft—on his watch—of a briefcase containing sensitive documents.

When it happened, Vic was away. Feeling the sudden urge to reconnect, he searches through his desk for his friend's new phone number, finds it, dials it. A secretary and then an assistant field the call, and finally, John comes on the line.

"Hey, O'Neill," Vic says, "I just got back from Chicago and I've been thinking about you."

"Shattuck! How the hell are you? Happy birthday. Sorry I couldn't make it Saturday night."

"Yeah, well . . . I'm sure you have a good excuse."

"Valerie dragged me to another wedding. You know how that goes."

"Yeah, yeah . . . how's the new job?"

"Cushy," quips O'Neill, now chief of security at the World Trade Center in New York City. "How's the big 5–0?"

"Not cushy. You'll find out soon enough, won't you?"

"February. Don't remind me."

Vic shakes his head, well aware that turning fifty, after everything O'Neill has dealt with in recent months, will be a mere blip.

They chat for a few minutes, catching up, before O'Neill says, "Listen, I've got to get going. Someone's waiting for me."

"Business or pleasure?"

"My business is always a pleasure, Vic. Don't you know that by now?"

"Where are you off to tonight?"

"I'm having drinks with Bob Tucker at Windows on the World to talk about security for this place, and it's a Monday night, so . . ."

"Elaine's." Vic is well aware of his friend's long-standing tradition.

"Right. How about you?"

"It's a Monday night, so—"

"Football."

"Yeah. I've got a date with the couch and remote. Giants are opening their season—and the Yankees are playing the Red Sox, too. Clemens is pitching. Looks like I'll be channel surfing."

"I wouldn't get too excited about that baseball game if I were you, Vic. It's like a monsoon here."

A rained-out Yankees-Red Sox game on one of Vic's rare nights at home in front of the TV would be a damned shame. Especially since he made a friendly little wager with Rocky Manzillo, his lifelong friend, who had made the trip down from New York this weekend for Vic's birthday dinner.

Always a guy who liked to rock the boat, Rocky is also a lifelong Red Sox fan, despite having grown up in Yankees territory. He still lives there, too—he's a detective with the NYPD.

In the grand scheme of Vic Shattuck's life, old pals and baseball rivalries and homemade macaroni casseroles probably matter more than they should. He's rarely around to enjoy simple pleasures. When he is, they help him forget that somewhere out there, a looming stressor is going to catapult yet another predator from the shadows to wreak violent havoc on innocent lives.

September 10, 2001
New York City
6:40 P.M.

"**H**ey, watch where you're going!"

Unfazed by the disgruntled young punk, Jamie continues shoving through the sea of pedestrians, baby carriages, and umbrellas, trying to make it to the corner before the light changes.

Around the slow-moving elderly couple, the dog on a leash, a couple of puddle-splashing kids in bright yellow slickers and rubber boots . . .

Failing to make the light, Jamie silently curses them all. Or maybe not silently, because a prim-looking woman flashes a disapproving look. Hand coiled into a fist, Jamie stands waiting in the rain, watching endless traffic zip past.

The subway would have been the best way to go, but there were track delays. And God knows you can't get a stinking cab in Manhattan in weather like this.

Why does everything have to be such a struggle here?

Everything, every day.

A few feet away, a passing SUV blasts its deafening horn.

Noise . . .

Traffic . . .

People . . .

How much more can I take?

Jamie rakes a hand through drenched hair and fights the reckless urge to cross against the light.

That's what it's been about lately. Reckless urges. Day in, day out.

For so long, I've been restrained by others; now that I'm free, I have to constantly restrain myself? It's so unfair.

Why can't I just cross the damned street and go where I need to go?

Why can't I just do whatever the hell I feel like doing? I've earned it, haven't I?

Jamie steps off the curb and hears someone call, "Hey, look out!" just before a monstrous double city bus blows past, within arm's reach.

"Geez, close call."

Jamie doesn't acknowledge the bystander's voice; doesn't move, just stands staring into the streaming gutter.

It would be running red with blood if you got hit.

Or if someone else did.

It would be so easy to turn around, pick out some random stranger, and with a quick, hard shove, end that person's life. Jamie could do that. It would happen so unexpectedly no one would be able to stop it.

Jamie can feel all those strangers standing there, close enough to touch.

Which of them would you choose?

The prune-faced, disapproving biddy?

One of the splashing kids?

The elderly woman, or her husband?

Just imagine the victim, the chosen one, crying out in surprise, helplessly falling, getting slammed by several tons of speeding steel and dying right there in the gutter.

Yes, blood in the gutter.

Eyes closed, Jamie can see it clearly—so much blood at first, thick and red right here where the accident will happen. But then the gutter water will sweep it along, thin it out as it merges with wide, deep puddles and with falling rain, spread it in rivulets that will reach like fingers down alleys and streets . . .

Imagine all the horror-struck onlookers, the traumatized driver of the death car, the useless medics who will rush to the scene and find that there's nothing they can do . . .

Nothing anyone can do.

And somewhere, later, phones will ring as family members and friends get the dreaded call.

Just think of all the people who will be touched—tainted—by the blood in the street, by that one simple act.

I can do that.

I can choose someone to die.

I've done it before—twice.

Ah, but not really. Technically, Jamie didn't do the choosing. Both victims—the first ten years ago, the second, maybe ten days ago—had done the choosing; they'd chosen to commit the heinous acts that had sealed their own fates. Jamie merely saw that they got what they deserved.

This time, though, it would have to be different. It would have to be a stranger.

Would it be as satisfying to snuff out a life that has no real meaning in your own?

Would it be even better?

Would it—

Someone jostles Jamie from behind.

The throng is pressing forward. The traffic has stopped moving past; the light has changed.

Jamie crosses the street, hand still clenched into an angry fist.

An Excerpt from

Sleepwalker

Her husband has suffered from insomnia all his life, but tonight, Allison MacKenna is the one who can't sleep.

Lying on her side of the king-sized bed in their master bedroom, she listens to the quiet rhythm of her own breathing, the summery chatter of crickets and night birds beyond the window screen, and the faint hum of the television in the living room downstairs.

Mack is down there, stretched out on the couch. When she stuck her head in about an hour ago to tell him she was going to bed, he was watching *Animal House* on cable.

"What happened to the Jets game?" she asked.

"They were down fourteen at the half so I turned the channel. Want to watch the movie? It's just starting."

"Seen it," she said dryly. As in, *Who hasn't?*

"Yeah? Is it any good?" he returned, just as dryly.

"As a former fraternity boy, you'll love it, I'm sure." She hesitated, wondering if she should tell him.

Might as well: "And you might want to revisit that Jets game."

"Really? Why's that?"

"They're in the middle of a historic comeback. I just read about it online. You should watch."

"I'm not in the mood. The Giants are my team, not the Jets."

Determined to make light of it, she said, "Um, excuse me, aren't you the man who asked my OB-GYN to preschedule a C-section last winter because you were worried I might go into labor while the Jets were playing?"

"That was for the AFC Championship!"

She just shook her head and bent to kiss him in the spot where his dark hair, cut almost buzz-short, has begun the inevitable retreat from his forehead.

When she met Mack, he was in his mid-thirties and looked a decade younger, her own age. Now he owns his forty-four years, with a sprinkling of gray at his temples and wrinkles that frond the corners of his green eyes. His is the rare Irish complexion that tans, rather than burns, thanks to a rumored splash of Mediterranean blood somewhere in his genetic pool. But this summer, his skin has been white as January, and the pallor adds to the overall aura of world-weariness.

Tonight, neither of them was willing to discuss why Mack, a die-hard sports fan, preferred an old movie he'd seen a hundred times to an exciting football game on opening day of the NFL season—which also happens to coincide with the milestone tenth anniversary of the September 11 attacks.

The networks and most of the cable channels have provided a barrage of special programming all weekend. You couldn't escape it, not even with football.

Allison had seen her husband abruptly switch off the Giants game this afternoon right before the kickoff, as the National Anthem played and an enormous flag was unfurled on the field by people who had lost loved ones ten years ago today.

It's been a long day. It might be a long night, too.

She opens her eyes abruptly, hearing a car slowing on the

street out front. Reflected headlights arc across the ceiling of the master bedroom, filtering in through the sheer curtains. Moments later, the engine turns off, car doors slam, faint voices and laughter float up to the screened windows: the neighbors returning from their weekend house in Vermont.

Every Friday, the Lewises drive away from the four-thousand-square-foot Colonial next door that has a home gym over the three-car garage, saltwater swimming pool, and sunken patio with a massive outdoor stone fireplace, hot tub, and wet bar. Allison, who takes in their mail and feeds Marnie, the world's most lovable black cat, while they're gone, is well aware that the inside of their house is as spectacular as the outside.

She always assumed that their country home must be pretty grand for them to leave all that behind every weekend, particularly since Bob Lewis spends a few nights every week away on business travel as it is.

But then a few months ago, when she and Phyllis were having a neighborly chat, Phyllis mentioned that it's an old lakeside home that's been in Bob's family for a hundred years.

Allison pictured a rambling waterfront mansion. "It sounds beautiful."

"Well, I don't know about *beautiful*," Phyllis told her with a laugh. "It's just a farmhouse, with claw-foot bathtubs instead of showers, holes in the screens, bats in the attic . . ."

"Really?"

"Really. And it's in the middle of nowhere. That's why we love it. It's completely relaxing. Living around here—it's more and more like a pressure cooker. Sometimes you just need to get away from it all. You know?"

Yeah. Allison knows.

Every Fourth of July, the MacKennas spend a week at the Jersey Shore, staying with Mack's divorced sister, Lynn, and her three kids at their Salt Breeze Pointe beach house.

This year, Mack drove down with the family for the holiday weekend. Early Tuesday morning, he hastily packed his bag to go—no, to *flee*—back to the city, claiming something had come up at the office.

Not necessarily a far-fetched excuse.

Last January, the same week Allison had given birth to their third child (on a Wednesday, and not by scheduled C-section), Mack was promoted to vice president of television advertising sales. Now he works longer hours than ever before. Even when he's physically present with Allison and the kids, he's often attached—reluctantly, even grudgingly, but nevertheless inseparably—to his BlackBerry.

"I can't believe I've become one of those men," he told her once in bed, belatedly contrite after he'd rolled over—and off her—to intercept a buzzing message.

She knew which men he was talking about. And she, in turn, seems to have become one of *those* women: the well-off suburban housewives whose husbands ride commuter trains in shirtsleeves and ties at dawn and dusk, caught up in city business, squeezing in fleeting family time on weekends and holidays and vacations . . .

If then.

So, no, his having to rush back to the city at dawn on July 5 wasn't necessarily a far-fetched excuse. But it was, Allison was certain—given the circumstances—an excuse.

After a whirlwind courtship, his sister, Lynn, had recently remarried Daryl, a widower with three daughters. Like dozens of other people in Middleton, the town where he and Lynn live, Daryl had lost his spouse on September 11.

"He and Mack have so much in common," Lynn had told Allison the first morning they all arrived at the beach house. "I'm so glad they'll finally get to spend some time together. I was hoping they'd have gotten to know each other better by now, but Mack has been so busy lately . . ."

He *was* busy. Too busy, apparently, to stick around the beach house with a man who understood what it was like to have lost his wife in the twin towers.

There were other things, though, that Daryl couldn't possibly understand. Things Mack didn't want to talk about, ever—not even with Allison.

At his insistence, she and the kids stayed at the beach with Lynn and Daryl and their newly blended family while Mack went home to work. She tried to make the best of it, but it wasn't the same.

She wondered then—and continues to wonder now—if anything ever will be the same again.

Earlier, before heading up the stairs, Allison had rested a hand on Mack's shoulder. "Don't stay up too late, okay?"

"I'm off tomorrow, remember?"

Yes. She remembered. He'd dropped the news of his impromptu mini stay-cation when he came home from work late Friday night.

"Guess what? I'm taking some vacation days."

She lit up. "Really? When?"

"Now."

"*Now?*"

"This coming week. Monday, Tuesday, maybe Wednesday, too."

"Maybe you should wait," she suggested, "so that we can actually plan something. Our anniversary's coming up next month. You can take time off then instead, and we can get away for a few days. Phyllis is always talking about how beautiful Vermont is at that time of—"

"Things will be too busy at the office by then," he cut in. "It's quiet now, and I want to get the sunroom painted while the weather is still nice enough to keep the windows open. I checked and it's finally going to be dry and sunny for a few days."

That was true, she knew—she, too, had checked the forecast. Last week had been a washout, and she was hoping to get the kids outside a bit in the days ahead.

But Mack's true motive, she suspects, is a bit more complicated than perfect painting weather.

Just as grieving families and images of burning skyscrapers are the last thing Mack wanted to see on TV today, the streets of Manhattan are the last place he wants to be tomorrow, invaded as they are by a barrage of curiosity seekers, survivors, reporters and camera crews, makeshift memorials and the ubiquitous protesters—not to mention all that extra security due to the latest terror threat.

Allison doesn't blame her husband for avoiding reminders. For him, September 11 wasn't just a horrific day of historic infamy; it marked a devastating personal loss. Nearly three thousand New Yorkers died in the attack.

Mack's first wife was among them.

When it happened, he and Carrie were Allison's across-the-hall neighbors. Their paths occasionally crossed hers in the elevator or laundry room or on the front stoop of the Hudson Street building, but she rarely gave them a second thought until tragedy struck.

In the immediate aftermath of the attacks, when she found out Carrie was missing at the World Trade Center, Allison reached out to Mack. Their friendship didn't blossom into romance for over a year, and yet . . .

The guilt is always there.

Especially on this milestone night.

Allison tosses and turns in bed, wrestling the reminder that her own happily-ever-after was born in tragedy; that she wouldn't be where she is now if Carrie hadn't talked Mack into moving from Washington Heights to Hudson Street, so much closer to her job as an executive assistant at Cantor Fitzgerald; if Carrie hadn't been killed ten years ago today.

In the most literal sense, she wouldn't be where she is now—the money Mack received from various relief funds and insurance policies after Carrie's death paid for this house, as well as college investment funds for their children.

Yes, there are daily stresses, but it's a good life Allison is living. Too good to be true, she sometimes thinks even now: three healthy children, a comfortable suburban home, a BMW and a Lexus SUV in the driveway, the luxury of being a stay-at-home-mom . . .

The knowledge that Carrie wasn't able to conceive the child Mack longed for is just one more reason for Allison to feel sorry for her—for what she lost, and Allison gained.

But it's not as though I don't deserve happiness. I'm thirty-four years old. And my life was certainly no picnic before Mack came along.

Her father walked out on her childhood when she was nine and never looked back; her mother died of an overdose before she graduated high school. She put herself through the Art Institute of Pittsburgh, moved alone to New York with a degree in fashion, and worked her ass off to establish her career at *7th Avenue* magazine.

On September 11, the attack on the World Trade Center turned her life upside down, but what happened the next day almost destroyed it.

Kristina Haines, the young woman who lived upstairs from her, was brutally murdered by Jerry Thompson, the building's handyman.

Allison was the sole witness who could place him at the scene of the crime. By the time he was apprehended, he had killed three more people—and Allison had narrowly escaped becoming another of his victims.

Whenever she remembers that incident, how a figure lurched at her from the shadows of her own bedroom . . .

You don't just put something like that behind you.

And so, on this night of bitter memories, Jerry Thompson is part of the reason she's having trouble sleeping.

It was ten years ago tonight that he crept into Kristina's open bedroom window.

Ten years ago that he stabbed her to death in her own bed, callously robbing the burning, devastated city of one more innocent life.

He's been in prison ever since.

Allison's testimony at his trial was the final nail in the coffin—that was how the prosecuting attorney put it, a phrase that was oft-quoted in the press.

"I just hope it wasn't my own," she recalls telling Mack afterward.

"Your own what?" he asked, and she knew he was feigning confusion.

"Coffin."

"Don't be ridiculous."

But it *wasn't* ridiculous.

She remembers feeling Jerry's eyes on her as she told the court that he had been at the murder scene that night. Describing how she'd seen him coming out of a stairwell and slipping into the alleyway, she wondered what would happen if the defense won the case and Jerry somehow wound up back out on the street.

Would he come after her?

Would he do to her what he had done to the others?

Sometimes—like tonight—Allison still thinks about that. It isn't likely. He's serving a life sentence. But still . . .

Things happen. Parole hearings. Prison breaks.

What if . . . ?

No. Stop thinking that way. Close your eyes and go to sleep. The kids will be up early, as usual.

She closes her eyes, but she can't stop imagining what it would be like to open them and find Jerry Thompson standing over her with a knife, like her friend Kristina did.

Sullivan Correctional Facility
Fallsburg, New York

One hour of television.

That's it. That's all Jerry is allowed per day, and he has to share it with a roomful of other inmates, so he never gets to choose what he wants to watch. Not that he even knows what that might be, because it's been ten years since he held a remote control.

Back then—when he was living in the Hell's Kitchen apartment that was a palace compared to his prison cell—he liked the show *Cops*. He always sang along with the catchy opening song, *Bad boys, bad boys . . . whatcha gonna do when they come for you?*

It was so exciting to watch the cops turn on the sirens and chase down the bad guys and arrest them. Then one night, they came—in real life, the cops did—and they arrested Jerry because Mama was dead in the bedroom and they thought *he* was a bad boy. They thought he had killed her, and two other ladies, too.

"Admit it, Jerry!" they kept saying. "Admit it! Tell us what happened!" They said it over and over again, for hours and hours, until he started crying. Finally, when he just couldn't take it anymore, he did exactly what they were telling him to do: he admitted it. He said that he had killed his mother and Kristina Haines and Marianne Apostolos, and then he signed the papers they gave him.

He did that because you have to do what the police tell you to do, and also because maybe he really had killed the women. Maybe he just didn't remember.

He doesn't remember a lot of things, because his brain hasn't been right for years, not since the accident.

Well, it wasn't really an *accident*.

Someone doesn't *accidentally* bash a person's head in with a cast-iron skillet. But that's what Mama always called it, an accident, and that's what Jerry always thought it was, because the truth about his injury was, of course, just one more thing he didn't remember.

Ten years ago, right before he was arrested, he finally found out what had really happened to him on that long-ago day when his head was bashed in.

His twin sister, Jamie, had attacked him.

Once he knew the terrible truth, he tried to forget it, because it was too horrible. For years, he couldn't even remember anything about that night. Now, bits and pieces come back to him, though most of the time, when his mind tries to think about it, he can push it away.

Sometimes, though, usually late at night, when he's lying awake in his cell, the terrible truth sneaks back into his head, and he can't get rid of it.

It's the same with Doobie Jones, the big, mean inmate who lives in the cell next to Jerry's. He talks to Jerry in the night sometimes, and Jerry can never seem to shut out his voice. Even when he pulls the thin prison pillow over his head and presses it against his ears, Doobie's voice still seems to be there, on the inside, saying all kinds of things Jerry doesn't want to hear.

Sometimes, Jerry wonders if Doobie is even real.

Jamie wasn't.

That's what the cops told him, and so did his lawyer, and the nice doctor who came to talk to Jerry a lot back when he was first arrested.

Everyone said that Jamie had died years ago, and now only lived in Jerry's head.

It was hard to believe, because Jamie seemed so real, walking and talking, and bringing Jerry cake . . .

"That was you, Jerry. You said and did those things," the cops said on the awful day when Jerry found Mama dead in the bedroom, and Jamie ran away just before the police came to the apartment . . .

That was what he thought had happened, anyway. But when he told the policemen that the bloody dress and the bloody knife belonged to Jamie, they didn't believe him.

"Jamie only exists up here." Detective Manzillo tapped his head. "Do you understand, Jerry?"

He didn't at the time.

Even now, when he thinks about it, he's not quite sure he understands how someone who only lives in your imagination can go around killing people.

Maybe that, too, is because Jerry's brain is damaged.

Anyway, it's not his fault that he is the way he is.

You can't help it.

That's what Jerry's lawyer told him, and that's what she told the judge, too, and the jury, and everyone else in the courtroom during the trial. She said Jerry shouldn't worry, even though he had admitted to killing people and signed the papers, too.

"You were not responsible for your actions, Jerry," his lawyer would say, and she would pat Jerry's hand with fingers that were cold and bony, the fingernails bitten all the way down so that they bled on the notebook paper she was always scribbling on.

"You're going to be found not guilty by reason of insanity," she said. "You're not going to go to prison. Don't worry."

"I won't," Jerry said, and he didn't.

But then came the day when the judge asked the lady in charge of the jury—the tall, skinny lady with the mean-looking face—"Have you reached your verdict?"

The lady said, "We have, Your Honor."

The verdict was guilty.

The courtroom exploded with noise. Some people were cheering, others crying. Jerry's lawyer put her forehead down on the table for a long time.

Jerry was confused. "What happened? What does that mean? Is it over? Can I go home now?"

No one would answer his questions. Not even his lawyer. When she finally looked up, her eyes were sad—and mad, too—and she said only, "I'm so sorry, Jerry," before the judge banged his gavel and called for order.

Jerry soon found out why she was sorry. It was because she had lied. Jerry *did* go to prison.

And he's never going to get out. That's one of the things Doobie says to him, late at night.

He scares Jerry. He scares everyone. His tattooed neck is almost as thick as his head, and he's missing a couple of teeth so that the ones he has remind Jerry of fangs.

He's in charge of the cell block. Well, the guards are really supposed to be in charge, but Doobie is the one who runs things around here. He decides what everyone else gets to say, and do, and watch on TV.

Tonight, though, the same thing is on every channel as Doobie flips from one to the next: a special news report about the tenth anniversary of the September 11 attacks.

After shouting a string of curses at the television, Doobie throws the remote control at the wall. When it hits the floor, the batteries fall out. One rolls all the way over to Jerry's feet. He looks down.

"Touch that, and you're a dead man," Doobie warns.

Jerry doesn't touch it.

He's sure—pretty sure, anyway—that he doesn't want to be a dead man, no matter what Doobie says.

Doobie is always telling him that he'd be better off dead than in here. He tells Jerry all the things he'd be able to do in heaven that he can't do here, or even back at home in New York. He says there's cake in heaven—as much cake as you want, every day and every night.

He knows Jerry's favorite thing in the whole world is cake. He knows a lot of things about Jerry, because there's not much else to do here besides talk, and there aren't many people to talk to.

"Just think, Jerry," Doobie says, late at night, when the lights are out. "If you were in heaven right now, you would be eating cake and sleeping on a big, soft bed with piles of quilts, and if you wanted to, you could get up and walk right outside and look at the stars."

Stars—Jerry hasn't seen them in years. He misses them, but not as much as he misses seeing the lights that *look* like stars. A million of them, twinkling all around him in the sky . . .

Home. New York City at night.

The thought of it makes him want to cry.

But the New York City they're showing on television right now doesn't bring back good memories at all.

He remembers that day, the terrible day when the bad guys drove the planes into the towers and knocked them down. He remembers the fire and the people falling and jumping from the top floors, and the big, dusty, burning pile after the buildings fell, one right after the other.

"*Sheee-it*," Rollins, one of the inmates, says as he stares at the footage of people running for their lives up Broadway, chased by the fire-breathing cloud of dust.

"I was there."

All of them, even Doobie, even Jerry, who had the exact same thought in his head, turn to look at B.S., who uttered it aloud.

B.S. is small and dark and antsy, with a twitch in his eye that makes him look like he's winking—like he's kidding around. But he's not. He told Jerry that he always means what he says, even when everyone else claims he's lying.

"I don't care what they say, because I know I'm telling the truth," he told Jerry one night after lights-out. "You do, too, don't you?"

"I do what?"

"You know I'm telling the truth, right, Slow Boy?"

That's what they call him. Slow Boy. It's just a nickname, like B.S. and Doobie.

Doobie says nicknames are fun. Jerry doesn't think they are, but of course, he doesn't ever want to tell Doobie that.

As nicknames go, that's not the worst Jerry has had. Back in New York, a lot of people called him Retard. And in the courtroom, during his trial, everyone called him The Defendant.

"That's a big ol' pile of bull," Doobie tells B.S. now. "Just like your name."

"No!" B.S. protests. "I was. I was there. I was a fireman."

"You wasn't no fireman in New York City," Rollins tells him. "*Sheee-it.* You from Delaware. Everyone know dat."

B.S. is shaking his head so rapidly Jerry thinks his brains must be rattling around in his head. "I climbed up miles of stairs dragging my fire hose, and—"

"Your fire hose was *miles* long?"

"Yeah, yeah, it was long, like miles long, and I got to the top floor right before the building collapsed—"

"If you were up there," one of the other inmates cuts in, "then how the hell are you sitting here right now? How'd you get out alive, you lying mother—?"

"I jumped. That's how. I jumped, yeah, and the other firemen, they caught me in one of those big nets."

Jerry regards him with interest as the others shake their heads and roll their eyes because they're thinking B.S. makes things up all the time.

Jerry usually doesn't know if B.S. is telling the truth or not, and he doesn't really care. He talks all the time, especially at night, and Jerry usually has no choice but to listen. Like Doobie, B.S. lives in the cell next to Jerry's, but on the opposite side.

But this time, for a change, he's interested in what B.S. is saying.

"I was there, too," Jerry says, and they all turn to him. "When the terrorist attack happened."

"Yeah? Did you jump out the window too, Slow Boy?" someone asks.

"I wasn't in the building. But I was near it. I saw it burning. I saw . . ." Jerry's voice breaks and he swallows hard.

He squeezes his eyes closed and there are the red-orange flames shooting out of white buildings, gray smoke reaching into a deep blue sky, black specks with flailing limbs, falling, falling, falling . . .

There are some terrible things that, despite his brain injury, he has no problem remembering.

September 11 is one of them.

That was the day before he killed Kristina Haines, the other lawyer, the one who didn't like Jerry, said at the trial.

"On the morning of September eleventh, The Defendant was teetering on the edge . . ."

At first, Jerry thought the lawyer was confused. He tried to speak up and tell everyone that he wasn't in the towers on that morning. A lot of people were teetering on the edge up there, but he wasn't one of them.

But he found out that you aren't allowed to just talk in the middle of a trial, even if you're The Defendant and what they're saying about you is wrong.

Anyway, Jerry soon discovered that the lawyer wasn't talking about teetering on the edge of a building.

Sanity: that's the word he kept saying. Teetering on the edge of sanity.

"When those towers fell," he told the courtroom, "a lot of people lost their already tenuous grip on sanity. Jerry Thompson was one of them."

He told everyone that Jerry stabbed Kristina Haines to death in her own bed because he was angry with her for turning him down when he asked her out.

The lawyer was right about that.

Jerry *did* ask Kristina to go eat cake with him.

He *was* angry with her when she said no, especially because she gave him the finger as she walked away, and—

"Tell us more, Slow Boy."

Doobie's voice shoves the memory of Kristina from Jerry's mind. "What?"

"Tell us what happened in New York that day."

He doesn't want to look at Doobie, or at anyone else, either. He can feel their eyes on him, burning into him, and he turns away, toward the television. He stares at the pictures of the mess the bad guys made when they flew the planes into the buildings. He takes a deep breath and his nose is full of the smell of burning rubber and smoke and death.

Jerry shakes his head. "I don't know why they did that."

"Why who did what?"

"Why the bad guys made that mess. Why they killed all those people. They even killed themselves. Why would they do that?"

"Because they knew the secret, Slow Boy," Doobie says, leaning closer so that the only way Jerry won't be able to look at him is to close his eyes. He doesn't do that, though, because he thinks it might make Doobie mad.

"What secret?"

"The one I told you. Remember?"

"No." Jerry doesn't remember Doobie telling him any secrets.

Doobie's face is close to Jerry's, and his black eyes are blacker than black. "The bad guys knew that heaven is the best place to be. They wanted to go there. They chose to go there. It's better than anywhere on earth. A hell of a lot better than here. Hell . . . Heaven . . . get it?"

He grins, and Jerry can see that his teeth are black in the back.

"So . . ." Doobie shrugs and pulls back. "You should go. That's all I'm saying."

"Go where?"

"Heaven."

"Heaven?" Rollins echoes. "Ain't none of us goin' to heaven, brother. We all goin' straight to—"

"Not Slow Boy," Doobie cuts in, turning to look at Rollins.

Jerry can't see his face, but it must be a dirty look because Rollins quickly shuts his mouth and turns away.

"You . . . you're going straight to Heaven," Doobie whispers, turning back to Jerry. "You can go now, if you want to."

"Why would I want to do that?"

"I told you. It's better than being stuck here for another fifty years, or longer. You can have cake there."

Jerry's mouth waters at the thought of it.

He hasn't had cake in years. Ten years.

"But I . . . I can't fly a plane into a—"

"You don't have to." Doobie's voice is low. So low only Jerry can hear it. "There are other ways to get there, you know? There are easy ways to get yourself out of here, Jerry."

Jerry.

Not Slow Boy.

"I could help you," Doobie says. "I'm your friend. You know that, don't you?"

Jerry swallows hard, suddenly feeling like he wants to cry. A friend—he hasn't had a friend in a long time.

He thinks of Jamie . . .

No. Jamie wasn't your friend. Jamie was your sister, and she died when you were kids. She didn't come back to you all those years later, like you thought. That wasn't real.

"Jerry," Doobie is saying, and Jerry blinks and looks up at him.

"What?"

"We'll talk about this later, okay? After the lights go out. I'll help you. Okay?"

Jerry doesn't even remember what they were talking about, but he doesn't want to tell Doobie that, so he says, "Okay."